FRANK MOO
DEATH FROM
ROOM. HE H
TIMES IN HIS TWENTY-ODD YEARS AS A POLICEMAN, BUT HE NEVER GOT USED TO IT. IT WAS A SICKLY SWEET SMELL ...

Heavy scarlet puddles had congealed on the carpet, the bedding and all across the dressing table. Splashes of blood intermingled with pieces of human flesh had dried on the walls, and everywhere there were feathers; curled pieces of down covered the room and stuck to the pools of blood in a scene reminiscent of a poultry slaughterhouse. For nearly a minute Frank forgot to breathe as he took in the horrors which the small room contained ...

ABOUT THE AUTHOR

Sean Martin Blain was born the youngest of six children in Dublin in 1947. At thirteen he joined the FCA, the Irish equivalent of the Territorial Army, and in 1962 he ran away from home with a stolen birth certificate to join the British Army in Belfast. There followed a nationwide search and, once found, he was discharged from the FCA, complete with the rank of Corporal in the Military Police for being under age. Nevertheless, he joined the British Army at the age of seventeen with his parents' blessing and then went on to serve in Germany, Kenya, Libya, Canada, Scotland and Hong Kong.

In 1970 Sean married a Danish national, and seven years later they had a son. He was discharged from the army at his own request and moved to Denmark a year afterwards to be with his wife and child. He spent his time working in a slaughterhouse and in a dairy, attending a five-month course to learn Danish and eventually owning and running a pub and disco. However, these ventures were not successful, and he returned to England to seek employment. He was divorced in 1988 and then began writing in earnest. *Java Man*, his first novel, was published in 1995, and he is now working on two further novels.

SEAN MARTIN BLAIN

THE JAVA MAN

A SIGNET BOOK

SIGNET

Published by the Penguin Group
Penguin Books Ltd, 27 Wrights Lane, London W8 5TZ, England
Penguin Books USA Inc., 375 Hudson Street, New York, New York 10014, USA
Penguin Books Australia Ltd, Ringwood, Victoria, Australia
Penguin Books Canada Ltd, 10 Alcorn Avenue, Toronto, Ontario, Canada M4V 3B2
Penguin Books (NZ) Ltd, 182–190 Wairau Road, Auckland 10, New Zealand

Penguin Books Ltd, Registered Offices: Harmondsworth, Middlesex, England

First published by Michael Joseph 1995
Published in Signet 1995
1 3 5 7 9 10 8 6 4 2

Printed in England by Clays Ltd, St Ives plc

For my son Nils Sean

Acknowledgements

I would like to thank Robert Kirby of Sheil Land and Luigi Bonomi of Signet for their help and their belief in me, and Andrew Crofts for his help in pulling the whole lot together.

Chapter One

THE CITY WAS LIKE a restless sleeper, not quite awake, yet not fully unconscious. Nightlife moved in and out of the shadows among the dark streets. Shattering glass broke the silence and a voice screamed its frustration at the world. The occasional late-night car, mostly taxis hunting that one last fare before going home, moved past anonymously, headlights picking out details and as quickly abandoning them to the darkness again. Litter stirred in the alleyways and the mating howls of cats could be heard.

A cloud, slowly drifting across the night skies, extinguished the moonlight; the door to a small Portakabin on a building site on the north side of the city opened. No light appeared as a shadowy figure emerged from within, pausing momentarily to fit a new padlock to the door. Checking the street for cars or late-night pedestrians the figure swiftly crossed the road, disappearing into the darker shadows of a narrow lane between the terraced houses.

The man's eyes were used to the darkness; he had waited three hours in the cabin before making his move. He slid cautiously along the lane, avoiding the litter and stopping by a worm-eaten wooden gate set into the eight-foot high garden wall of one of the houses. A black-gloved hand dipped into a leather jacket pocket and produced a small can of penetrating oil. Liberally lubricating the twin hinges of the gate he waited for the oil to seep in. With bated breath he undid the simple catch on the gate and pushed gently with his shoulder. It opened noiselessly.

Pausing only to return the oilcan to his pocket he entered the garden and made his way silently along the narrow cement path that led to the back door.

Once again the gloved hand dipped into a pocket, this time producing a small suction cup and a wooden-handled glasscutter. The suction cup had once been fitted to a toy arrow, long discarded in a rubbish bin in the centre of the city. Holding the cup close to the mouthpiece of his black ski-mask he gave it a quick lick, then pressed it gently against one of the panes in the kitchen door. With the cutter in his right hand he etched an uneven circle in the glass, near to where the lock was situated and large enough for his gloved hand to go through. Holding the suction cup steady with his left hand, using the wooden end of the glass cutter as a hammer, he tapped the pane just once. The circle of glass separated out and he was holding it in his left hand.

He paused to see if the slight noise had attracted any attention, but no light appeared. Once again a hand entered a pocket, emerging this time with a small padded envelope large enough to contain the circle of glass. With the glass inside, the envelope was returned to his pocket, along with the suction cup, and the zipper drawn shut.

Easing his left arm through the hole he found the simple Yale lock. He twisted gently. It turned, and with a slight shove the door opened. Setting the lock on its catch he closed the door behind him.

The kitchen was black, the venetian blinds closed from earlier that evening. The only sound was the hum of the electric clock on the wall and the thumping of his own frightened heart. Taking several deep breaths he tried to relax. He was experiencing a mixture of fear and elation. His fear stemmed from the possibility of being caught; the elation at having got this far. But the adrenalin surging through his body made him ready to go through with it. From his left sleeve he withdrew a wicked looking fishing knife, stainless steel and razor sharp. It flashed momentarily as a sliver of moonlight slid into the kitchen, reflecting on the blade. Forcing himself to breathe slowly he quietly opened the kitchen door and entered the hallway.

Directly in front of him, at the other end of the hallway, was the main door. Moonlight streamed in from the crescent-shaped translucent window above the door. To his left was the staircase, the underneath part panelled-in to form a small cupboard. To his right were two doors. Ignoring the cupboard he listened at both doors before opening them in turn. The first room was a dining-room, the other a living-room, both containing a minimum of cheap furniture. There was nothing to interest him in either. Closing the doors behind him he moved to the staircase.

Testing each step before committing his weight to it, he made his way up towards the bedrooms, the knife now held in his right hand, blade uppermost, ready for an upward thrust if necessary. Although he had never visited this particular house before, its design was common to thousands of others, so he knew what to expect on the first floor. Three bedroom doors faced the stairs. To the right was the bathroom. Stepping on to the landing he noticed that the bathroom door was ajar, but the room was in darkness. Taking no chances he gently eased the door fully open. Nothing out of the ordinary.

Mantis-like, he approached the first of the bedrooms. Dropping to one knee he brought his ear close to the door panel. Raising his ski-mask above his nose he sniffed at the door join. A slight odour of cheap perfume tickled his senses. It must be the main bedroom. He didn't need to get close to the second door to smell the stale male sweat emanating from the room. Moving finally to the smallest bedroom – always described in estate agents' brochures as such although little more than six feet square – he was surprised to find the door fitted with a padlock. He guessed that the contents of this room would be the most interesting to him. A standard Yale lock on the back door, but a secure padlock fitted here!

Returning to the main bedroom door he hesitated. Could he go through with it? This was the point of no return. Once he entered the room he was committed. He could leave now and all they would know was that an intruder had called. There was nothing that could be traced to him. But once he stepped inside that bedroom . . . Very gently he turned the handle, eased the door open and slid inside.

He could make out two single beds to his right, one close to the door, the other at the wall by the window. The scent, the shape and the breathing told him that Maura was in the nearer bed. Dropping to his knees beside her sleeping form he reached out with both hands. Crossing them he placed his left hand over her mouth, digging into her cheeks with his gloved fingers, and with the right he pressed the blunt edge of the knife to her throat. She woke immediately but his hold prevented her from rising.

'Make a sound Maura and I'll rip your throat out. Nod if you understand.' His menacing tone told the woman that the threat was not an idle one. With eyes bulging from their sockets she nodded her head. She tried to swallow, but almost choked from the pressure of the knife.

'Now, I'm going to take the hand over your mouth away, but don't make me use the other one. OK?' He pressed deeper into her throat with the blade but she managed to nod her head. 'You're going to sit up when I say, and do it very very slowly. I'm very nervous Maura. Don't do anything to make me jump. OK, sit up, nice and slow.'

His left hand lifted from her mouth. She drew a deep breath – and almost choked again as the pressure on the knife increased. 'Maura!' he admonished, releasing the pressure on the knife.

'Sweet Jesus, I was just trying to breathe,' she whispered, 'I swear it.'

He nodded.'OK, take a few breaths. Nice and easy, that's it. Now pull yourself up in the bed.' She did as ordered, aware that the nylon nightie she wore was semi-transparent. For the first time in a long while she was conscious of her female form.

'I want you to put your feet on to the floor – towards your husband. We're going to wake him nice and quietly also. Move slowly because I'm going to get on the bed behind you. One sudden move, one word of warning, and I'll cut your head clean off with this thing, and he'll be dead before he even wakes. So do it nice and slowly.'

She did as instructed, feeling his weight on the bed behind her. 'I want you to go down on to your knees and move across to him. Wait until I get down beside you. Right. Now move.'

Maura felt that she would have laughed at the pair of them, and the way they moved the short distance between the beds, had it not been for the fact that she was scared to death. She stopped at the edge of her husband's bed.

'Wake him,' the man in black whispered into her ear. 'Do it gently and tell him not to move a muscle. He has to understand the situation immediately, or you are both dead. Go ahead. Wake him.'

Trembling, she reached out and shook the sleeping man as gently as she could. 'Michael,' she whispered. 'Michael. For Christ's sake Michael wake up. Michael.' She shook him a little harder and the man stirred.

'Huh? . . . What? . . .' Bleary eyed he started to sit up.

'No,' she hissed. 'Don't move, Michael. There's a man holding a knife to my throat. He'll kill me if you don't do exactly as he says. Just lie still . . . please.'

The terror in his wife's voice kept Michael frozen in his sleeping position. Slowly moving his head he made out the dark silhouette beside Maura.

'Good man, Michael,' the menacing whisper told him. 'Just lie there and do everything you're told. Now Maura, we're going to put on the bedside light. *Wait* . . . not yet. Put your finger on the switch but don't press it until I tell you.' Maura's unsteady hand reached out and her finger rested on the lamp's switch. 'I want both of you to screw your eyes up tight, and keep them that way until I tell you to open them. Do it. Okay Maura, press the switch.'

It was a conventional bedside lamp designed to light only a small area of the room, just sufficient for a person to read in bed. He half closed his eyes, allowing them to get used to the sudden brightness. When he opened them fully Maura and Michael still had theirs closed tight. They both looked so pathetic that he had to remind himself who they were – and why he had come.

'Michael, keep yours shut. Maura, you can open yours and stand up.' He moved away from her as he spoke and rose to his feet. Maura moved as slowly as she could, supporting herself with one hand on her husband's bed. She blinked several times, then looked at the intruder.

He was covered from head to foot in black; black ski-mask, black leather jacket and gloves, black jeans and black trainers. Even his eyes, which watched her every move, appeared to be black. If there was an Angel of Death, she thought, then this is what he must look like.

'Now Maura, we are going to tie Michael up. Michael, keep your eyes closed and turn over on to your belly, with your hands behind your back.'

Michael seemed reluctant to move. Instantly the knife was at Maura's throat, the blade digging into the flesh.

'Do it,' Maura hissed, and Michael obeyed.

With his left hand the intruder pulled the bedclothes down off Michael, leaving him lying face down on the bed in his striped pyjamas. 'Hands behind your back, grip each wrist, and keep them like that.' This time there was no hesitation. Michael did as he was ordered.

'You must have some tights round here somewhere. Where?' She pointed to one of the drawers in the built-in units on the wall facing the beds. 'Get them.'

His body moved with her as she walked the few paces to the drawers. When she had opened the drawer the point of the blade dug deep into her throat and she froze. His eyes stared into hers as his free hand reached into the drawer and searched. It contained nothing but tights. He grabbed a bundle of them and indicated with his head that she should return to the bedside.

'Now tie him up tight. I'll check the knots, so don't do anything stupid.'

Wrapping several pairs of tights round her husband's arms and wrists she pulled them as tight as she could, then knotted them, mindful of the eyes watching her every move. When she was done he checked her handiwork.

'Now do his feet, and also just below the knees. Do it.'

Once more she complied and watched as he checked. Noticing the wicker linen basket by the window he flicked the top off, reached inside, and retrieved what turned out to be a pair of grubby socks.

'Open wide Michael.' The socks were roughly stuffed into the open mouth. Michael gurgled, almost choking. 'Easy, easy Michael. Breathe gently through your nose and you'll be all right. Maura – wrap a pair of tights round the gag.' That done he gave all the knots one final check.

'Now for the boy.'

'Oh, dear God, not the boy.' Maura was close to hysteria. 'Please leave him. There's money in the house. A lot more than you'd think. I'll show you where it is. Take it all. Take . . . take . . .' she gulped, trying to make saliva in her dry mouth. 'Take me as well if you want. Fuck me as much as you want. I'll be quiet. I swear I'll be quiet. We won't wake the boy. He's a sound sleeper.'

For a moment she thought he was considering her offer. It was his silence that misled her. Is that what she thought he was? A rapist? A thief? Slowly he drew his breath, calming himself before he spoke.

'Don't insult me or flatter yourself Maura. We are going to get the boy and bring him in here and you're going to tie him up just like you did Michael there. Do like I tell you, and continue to do so, and nobody will get hurt. Now move.'

She realized that it was pointless to argue with him. Silently they went to the room next door. She repeated the waking procedure just as she had done to Michael. The boy, acne-faced and stocky, made as if to leap out of his bed until stopped by his mother. 'Don't Sean. Just do as he tells you. Just do it.' Her voice hardened slightly as she spoke, trying to put across the urgent necessity for him to do exactly as he was told if they were to live.

Obeying her, he eased himself out of the bed and stood

up. Naked but for a pair of boxer shorts he clasped his hands behind his neck as ordered and preceded them back to his parents' bedroom. Here he was instructed to lie face down on his mother's bed, where she proceeded to tie and gag him, just like his father.

'Now it's your turn, Maura. Sit in the chair.' Maura sat in the wicker chair by her dressing table. Her arms were bound to the arms of the chair and her legs to its legs. Finally a pair of her own soiled panties were shoved into her mouth and bound with yet another pair of tights. From inside his jacket he produced a roll of plastic masking tape which he used to reinforce the bindings of his prisoners.

'You all stay nice and quiet until I come back. Don't try and get out of these. It's pointless – and you'll only upset me if you try, so don't. Maura, if, when I come back, I find any of you have tried, or if I hear the slightest noise from this room – the boy gets it first. Do I make myself clear? Just nod your head that you understand.' Glaring at him, her eyes now filled with hatred more than fear, she nodded.

At the door he turned back to look at them. He could almost hear the silence in the room. Then, leaving the door ajar the man went downstairs to the kitchen.

'Jesus, Jesus, Jesus,' he gasped, lowering himself on to his haunches, his masked face between his knees trying to avoid a fainting spell. His breathing was coming in gasps. He stood up and ripped off the face mask. His face was sore and damp with sweat. He ordered himself to stand still and breathe in deeply through his nose, exhaling through his mouth and in a few moments he regained control.

'I did it,' he whispered. 'I bloody well did it.' He leaned

back against the wall, wiping sweat from his face with his gloved hands.

'God I need something to drink.' His mouth was parched but it was not alcohol he needed. Coffee. Hot, sweet coffee. In the darkness he set about making himself one. Finding the electric kettle he pressed the stud and immediately heard the hissing sound as it began to heat up. Mugs hung on hooks on the wall above the kettle. Taking one he spooned in four large sugars and two heaped spoons of coffee and some milk from a bottle in the fridge. He savoured the hot sweet taste, his body greedily absorbing the caffeine into his bloodstream, relaxing him. He replaced the milk and stood by the sink wondering what his next move was.

Everything he had done up to now had been a test for himself. First the small tests: the research, getting the address, returning to Dublin, staking the place out, buying the clothing, the glasscutter, the sucker, the oil, even the fisherman's knife. Then came the first big one: breaking in. He had passed them all. He was here, he was in charge and he could do as he pleased. Leave . . . or go on. The major test was yet to come. He drained the last dregs of the coffee.

It was only as he was putting his glove back on that he realized he had actually taken it off. 'Shit!' he exclaimed into the darkness. Pulling it on tight he commenced cleaning up after him. He rinsed the mug and the spoon and dried them both with a tea-towel. Using the same cloth he wiped the coffee jar, the handle of the fridge, the surfaces and the doors of the cabinets. Satisfied with his cleaning up, and feeling more relaxed and in control of himself, he made his way back up the stairs to the main bedroom.

Neither Maura nor Michael had attempted to move, but

the boy, Sean, had. He was half hanging over the side of the bed. Gripping him by the hair, he hauled him back on to the bed and cuffed him across the back of the head. The boy grunted in pain but the man didn't speak. It wasn't necessary. Leaving the boy he walked across and stood in front of Maura.

'If he moves again I'll kill him.' As before his voice was only just above a whisper. 'Now to business, Maura. Where are the keys to the padlock for the other door?' As he moved to extract her gag her eyes betrayed her with a glance towards the bedside cabinet. Leaving the gag he went to the cabinet where he found a bunch of keys. He went to the locked bedroom.

Unlocking the padlock and leaving it hanging, he opened the door gently. Pitch blackness met him, blacker than the darkness of the hall. Reaching inside the door he found the switch. With a 'click', the room was bathed in light.

A heavy drape hung over the window preventing any light being seen from outside. To his left was a metal writing desk and padded chair. A reading lamp was fitted to the edge of the desk. The room was too small for anything else.

The flat desk top was bare so he tried the drawers. The centre drawer contained nothing more than a few pens, a ruler, some stamps and writing paper. The three drawers on the right hand side of the desk contained handbills and leaflets, but the deep filing drawer on the left was locked. Going through the bunch of keys he tried two without success. On the third the drawer opened. It contained a large, locked, security box. He lifted it on to the desk, grunting at its weight. For the third time he went to the bunch of keys and found the correct one. Opening the lid he stared at the contents. Maura had not lied to him about there being a lot of money in the house.

Bundle after bundle of banknotes stared up at him. There were American and Australian dollars, Deutschmarks, Dutch guilders, and British and Irish notes. He had no idea how much it all came to – but it must be tens of thousands. It was as he lifted the bundles out that he found what really interested him: an address book, a diary and a gun. The revolver was fitted with a .22 barrel and lay beside a small box of ammunition. Leaving the two books to one side he checked the weapon. Sliding the spring-loaded catch that held the cylinder he flicked it open. It was fully loaded and one of the rounds slid out on to the desk. He tilted the gun down to prevent more rounds falling out. As he was sliding the round back into the cylinder he noticed that the end was slightly flattened. He slowly turned it in his fingers. Not only had it been flattened, other work had been carried out on it too.

A .22 was not the kind of weapon that could be totally relied upon to kill, especially a handgun, unless it was in the hands of an expert, so the ammunition had been treated. He emptied the remaining five rounds from the gun and checked them. All were the same. The pointed end of each had been cut off and he guessed a small hole had been drilled in the remaining parts of the lead and filled with a few drops of mercury. The top and been slightly flattened with a small hammer then soldered back on to the round. What he was holding was a lethal round of ammunition known as a Dum-dum, designed to explode on entry sending droplets of mercury in all directions at a velocity of hundreds of feet per second. A hit anywhere in the torso with one of these would mean certain death. This was a professional assassin's gun. Small calibre rounds – but completely lethal. He reloaded the revolver and laid it to one side to check the ammunition in the box. It was all the same. Any doubts about what he had to do next vanished.

Leaving what was obviously Maura's 'office' he went to the boy's room and checked the built-in wardrobe. He found what he was looking for, a leatherette, designer sports bag. Emptying it, he returned to the office and filled the bag with the cash. He extracted a British fifty-pound note from one bundle and left it in the security box. He dropped the knife and the diary into the bag. The address book had coded entries, so neither the names nor the addresses made any sense to him. Maura would provide the key to the code. His earlier indecisiveness was gone. Leaving the bag on the desk he took the address book and the revolver back to the master bedroom.

Chapter Two

THE SCREAM OF THE SIREN faded to a whine and then died as the unmarked police car drew to a halt. Three men got out, looked at the crowd of sightseers round the house and moved towards the garden gate. Television news cameras turned over and cameras flashed. There were some shouted questions from the journalists, which the men ignored. The uniformed garda at the gate saluted.

'Afternoon sir. The Sarge is in the house.' He swung the gate open for them.

Acknowledging the salute, Detective Inspector Frank Mooney of the Irish CIB (the Criminal Investigation Branch of the Garda Síochána), led his team to the front door of the house. As they approached, the hall door opened and a uniformed sergeant stepped forward.

'Hello Frank; lads. Not a pretty sight I'm afraid inside. When I got here I placed a man at the back to seal off the lane and I don't think anything's been touched there. The dead woman's sister found the bodies. Her screaming brought the next door neighbour and a couple of my lads. They didn't know what they were going to find so they may have touched a few things . . .' The sergeant shrugged his shoulders apologetically on behalf of his men.

Mooney stopped him with a wave of his hand, accepting the apology. 'It's OK George, it happens. What about this lot?' He gestured at the crowd in the street.

'The usual collection for a scene like this, Frank. At least they've all been kept out.'

Both men knew that in the past vital pieces of evidence

had been trampled, broken or even stolen as grisly souvenirs by some who arrived at times like this. Mooney nodded, accepting the assurance.

'So what have we George? Domestic, is it?'

'Not this one Frank. This is the O'Grady household, *the* O'Gradys . . . as in the political wing of the Popular Front. She never was a pretty woman, and she sure as hell ain't a pretty sight now.'

'OK, we'll go in. Can you get a call to the Castle and get forensic over here. If the meat wagon arrives keep them out until I say so. You say you've got a man at the back. Is there a back entrance?' The sergeant nodded and Mooney turned to the man standing by his side. 'Bob, get round there and see if you can find anything interesting. Cowboy, you come with me.'

Detective Constable Christopher 'Cowboy' Johnson was the youngest of the trio. 'Bob' was Detective Sergeant Brian O'Brien, called Bob because of his initials.

As Bob turned away, heading for the back of the house, the uniformed sergeant spoke in a loud whisper. 'There is one other, eh, problem, Frank. I've got the local parish priest in the living-room. I don't know who called him, but he arrived shortly after I got here. I've managed to keep him confined to the downstairs room, but he's wanting to go upstairs to view the bodies and do his stuff. You know what they're like, Frank . . .' Once again he shrugged his shoulders in apology.

Mooney shook his head. 'Who will rid me of this turbulent priest?' he sighed, looking mischievously at Cowboy.

'Henry the Second said that I think, Chief.'

'It's not a quote, Cowboy, it's an order – and for Christ's sake stop calling me "Chief" – you make me feel like a bleedin' Indian. Go in there and use your charm on the man. Engage him in some fascinating conversation and keep the bugger out of my hair until I'm ready to allow him up.' Turning to the sergeant he added, 'Lay on, Macduff.' Without looking back he called over his shoulder. 'Now that, Cowboy, is a quote.'

As the other two started up the stairs Cowboy knocked politely on the sitting room door and entered.

'Careful of the puke on the landing, Frank,' the sergeant advised. 'One of my lads, he's new on the job, and even I . . . well, you'll see what I mean when you go in.'

Frank Mooney could smell death from outside the room. He had smelt it many times in his twenty-odd years as a policeman, but he never got used to it. It was a sickly sweet smell and was one of the reasons he seldom ate sweet things. Watching where he trod he bypassed the vomit on the landing and stepped into the master bedroom.

Heavy scarlet puddles had congealed on the carpet, the bedding and all across the dressing table. Splashes of blood intermingled with pieces of human flesh had dried on the walls, and everywhere there were feathers; curled pieces of down covered the room and stuck to the pools of blood in a scene reminiscent of a poultry slaughterhouse. For nearly a minute Frank forgot to breathe as he took in the horrors which the small room contained.

On the bed nearer the door lay the headless corpse of a young man. On the other bed lay an older but equally male body. Both bodies had their hands and legs bound. Tied to the wicker chair by the dressing-table was the third headless body, female this time.

'Jesus wept,' Frank expelled the pent up air from his lungs. He turned back from the room and leaned over the banister. '*Cowboy?*' he called. He felt the squelch under his feet as he stepped into the vomit. 'Fuck it,' he exclaimed, wiping the sole of his shoe on a clean patch of carpet.

Downstairs a door opened and the voice of Cowboy could be heard reassuring the priest. '. . . Won't be long, Father.' Cowboy climbed the stairs two by two, stopping at the bend, looking up at his boss.

'Watch your shoes as you come up,' Mooney gruffly reminded him, pointing to the mess beside his feet. Cowboy gingerly moved to a clean spot on the landing carpet.

'Listen son, I hate to do this to you, but it had to happen sooner or later I suppose.' Cowboy saw a flash of pain in the older man's eyes and wondered what he was in for. 'Go inside lad,' he was instructed gently, 'and take a glimpse of man's inhumanity to man.'

He wasn't in the room above ten seconds before he emerged with his hand over his mouth and ran to the bathroom. Kneeling on the floor with his head over the toilet bowl he regurgitated his lunch. Even when his stomach was empty he continued to retch, as if wanting to throw up everything he had ever eaten.

'Oh my God,' he moaned into the toilet bowl. He was disappointed in his own reaction to this test. As his stomach settled he rose to his feet, took a mouthful of water, and spat it back into the sink trying to get rid of the sour taste in his mouth. Wiping his hands and face on his handkerchief he took his time before going back to the landing to confront Mooney.

Frank felt sorry for the boy. He remembered his own first time at the scene of violent death. No policeman ever forgets his first, no matter how many he witnesses in his career. 'I'm sorry, Cowboy. This is the worst I've ever seen and I've seen a few. You OK?' Cowboy nodded his head, blowing his nose to clear it. 'You'd best go down and bring up the priest. He can do his mumbo-jumbo from the doorway. If he wants to do anything further with them he'll have to wait until they're at the morgue.'

'Do you think . . . I mean . . . is it a good idea for the priest to see . . . that?' He indicated the bedroom with a nod of his head.

Mooney nodded. 'Yes, but warn him that it's bad.' While Cowboy went downstairs to get the priest Mooney turned his attention back to the sergeant.

'If that is Maura O'Grady in there – I suppose the older one is the husband. Any ideas about the third one?'

The sergeant nodded. 'Yep. They had a son, about sixteen or seventeen. A penny'll get you a pound that's him. Whoever did it wiped out the entire family.'

'She was a right nasty bitch in life, but I can't find it in me really to think she – they – deserved this kind of death.' He turned round as he heard the priest approach. 'Evening Father. Did young Johnson tell you what to expect in there? It's not a pretty sight I'm afraid.'

The priest held up his left hand; two fingers and a chunk of his palm were missing and the skin was puckered. 'Whatever is behind that door Inspector, I've seen worse. That I can guarantee you – and some of them were still alive. At least these are gone from this suffering world. Ten years in El Salvador taught me a lot about what men can do to other men – and even worse to women and children. But thank you for the warning, Inspector. I won't disturb anything that might hinder your investigation. I just wish to bless them.'

'You know who they are?' Mooney asked.

'Oh yes, I know who they are – and what they were,

Inspector. I would never condone the violence they were involved in – however remote they were from it – but neither could I ever refuse them a blessing. Most especially now. God bless you in your work Inspector, Sergeant.' With that he turned to the doorway of the murder scene. His whispered words were carried through the still, silent house.

'In nomine Patris, et Fili, et Spiritus Sancti, Amen.'

Another car arrived outside and a young garda called up the stairs. The 'Clever Dicks', the team from the forensic laboratory came into the hall. Frank signalled to them to wait until the priest was finished.

'You've got five minutes, Father – and before you leave see the fingerprint guy. Just to eliminate yours, you understand.' Without waiting for any reply he went downstairs to give his instructions to the newly arrived investigators. Cowboy and the uniformed sergeant followed.

While Mooney gave instructions and made a brief statement to the journalists, the sergeant went to help clear away the still-gathered spectators, Cowboy stood by the door inhaling the cool, fresh, evening air. A chilly twilight was falling over the city and the lack of any action helped the uniformed men to clear most of the voyeurs. A young boy was tugging at the antenna on one of the police cars.

'You want a lift to the hospital?' a young garda asked him.

'What for?' The ten-year old's interest was caught.

'To remove my boot from your arse! Get away from the car!'

'Fuck off, ya big gob shite,' the boy shouted back. 'Me da'll kick the shite outa the likes of you if you touch me.'

Cowboy smiled, remembering a joke Bob had told in the pub at lunchtime. Two kids having an argument and one says to the other 'My da can lick your da, but it's unhygienic'. Jesus, he thought, wasn't life sweet? Here he was, standing outside on a beautiful crisp, cool evening, with just a touch of frost in the air. He had a beautiful home, a truly beautiful woman in his life whom he loved and who loved him in return, and as much money as he was ever likely to need. Yes, it sure was good to be alive on an evening like this – standing beside death in its most horrible form. Although he didn't smoke, he wished he had a cigarette.

It was midnight when Frank, Cowboy and Bob met up again back at their office in Dublin Castle. For hundreds of years this ancient castle, in the very heart of the modern city, had been the seat of English rule over the Irish. The Record Tower dated back to the twelfth and thirteenth centuries. Within the confines of the castle proper were the Irish State Apartments, the Heraldic Museum, and, never far from the Irish, a church; the Church of the Most Holy Trinity. Apart from these historic buildings the castle also housed the very modern facilities and laboratories of the Criminal Investigation Branch of the Gardai.

The forensic scientists had started work on the house in Ballymun with their hi-tech, fine-tooth combs. Preliminary analysis would begin on items taken from the house first thing in the morning. The bodies had been photographed from every conceivable angle and then taken to the city morgue. Autopsies would be carried out despite the very obvious causes of death to see if the bodies themselves could provide clues. The house was completely sealed off on Mooney's orders. Every person who needed access would be required to log their entry and exit with the garda on duty outside. The three detectives themselves had also gone through the house, including a visit to the attic by Cowboy, looking for anything that might assist them. On their return to the Castle, Frank Mooney had gone to see Commander Edwards, head of the CIB, to make an interim report.

The newspaper journalists were going home via their favourite pubs, having written their stories. Only the bare facts were ready for the morning editions, but later editions would bear the fruit of more in-depth research into the backgrounds of the victims.

Cowboy placed three plastic beakers on Mooney's heavily stained and paper-cluttered desk. 'Those two are teas, he indicated with his head, 'and mine's the coffee.'

'Thanks,' responded Bob, taking one of the teas. Mooney picked up the other cup without looking and plonked it in front of him. Tea splashed over the edge and yet another stain was born. He raised his head.

'You better now, Cowboy?' he asked, a hint of paternal concern in his voice.

Cowboy nodded. 'Sorry about my reaction Chief, but when I walked in and saw . . .' his voice trailed off.

'Don't let it worry you. You did nothing to be ashamed of. We all go through it at some stage, eh Bob?'

Bob nodded. 'I can still remember my first one, Cowboy. It's like sex. No matter what happens later in life, you never forget your first time. I've thrown up a few lunches since then as well. We all have. You've nothing to apologize about. You *would* have though, had you done it over me.'

Cowboy smiled. They were trying to put him at his ease and make him feel like one of them. Both the older men could see that the events of the late afternoon had affected him. His first murder case. A 'baptism of fire' Mooney had called it. A baptism of blood was more like it Cowboy thought. He'd been with the CIB for just over a year now and this was the first really grotesque scene he had witnessed. He had seen a few gunshot wounds before and had been at a few bloody accidents when still in uniform . . . But this!

'OK,' said Mooney, clapping his hands together, as if to pray. 'Initial discussion time, then home to bed. But first the bad news. The Boss says that, apart from as many uniforms as we can rustle up, we are on our own; we get no more detectives. We will, however, get "assistance" – and I put that in inverted commas – from Irish Military Intelligence. That means they will want to know everything we have whilst giving us as little as possible in return. I think the Boss believes this is a hopeless one and we're only going through the motions. It *is* going to be a right bastard, but let's see if we can prove him wrong, eh?'

As he spoke Mooney opened a drawer in his desk and extracted a half-full bottle of Paddy whiskey, splashing a liberal portion into each beaker. Leaving the bottle out he swept aside the clutter on the desk and pulled a large black Guinness ashtray into the centre.

'Lend us a fag Bob. I'll buy a pack tomorrow.'

Bob sighed and threw his pack on to the desk. He had as much chance of Mooney buying a pack tomorrow, the next day, or even next week as they had of the murderer walking in the door, and shouting 'I did it. I did it.' Mooney had promised his wife five years ago to stop smoking. He never smoked at home, nor in her company, but as far as everybody else was concerned he had simply changed his brand to 'OP's' – Other People's. Whenever he was working late he haunted the corridors looking for yet another unsuspecting source of nicotine. Regular uniformed members at the Castle were known to disappear on seeing him coming, leaving the new guys, or visitors, to be his prey.

'Why the hell don't you tell her you're smoking again Frank. You're a grown man, for God's sake.'

'So are you. Would *you* tell her?'

Bob thought of Frank's wife, Marjorie. Everybody who knew them knew that even after thirty-odd years together they were still very much in love; but as for telling that mild-mannered, small-statured woman that her man was back on the fags . . .

'Point taken.'

Mooney opened the pack and slid one into his mouth, lighting it with Bob's lighter, and drew the smoke into his lungs. 'Right then. Knowing who the victims are gives us at least several hundred suspects in one go.' He held his right hand up and began ticking off fingers. 'There's the IRA, the PIRA, the Popular Front, any of the Loyalist paramilitary groups, or even the SAS. How's that for starters?'

The other two nodded their heads in agreement. Cowboy seemed to be about to speak, then changed his mind.

'Got something to add, Cowboy?' Mooney asked. 'Don't be afraid. Speak whatever's on your mind. Even Mickey Mouse is a suspect in this one. What were you going to say?'

'Remember the cash box we found? In the office? That's a hell of a large box to be holding a solitary fifty-pound note.'

'So what's your point?'

'I'm not too sure there is a point, but I think the money was a message.'

'To whom?' queried Bob.

'To us. I think there was a lot of money in that box. Let's face it, that was Maura's job. Collecting "contributions" for the Front. The money's gone, but our killer – or killers – didn't want us thinking it was just for the money. They were there to do what they did – kill Maura.'

'Then why not leave all the money? Why look for it in the first place?'

'I understand what you're saying Bob – but I don't think they *were* looking for the money. They found it, yes – would you leave it lying around if it were you? I doubt it. I'd certainly take it. It wasn't going to do Maura any good, was it? Neither was it going to go to those it was destined for, the Popular Front. Why leave it for us?

'As far as we know only one room was searched. That office. Whoever it was was after information. The kind you'd keep in an office. While searching for information they came across the money. Even if I was a professional hitman, I'd take it. Why turn your nose up at additional expense money? The fifty pounds was left deliberately.'

'You could be right there, Cowboy,' agreed Mooney, 'though I can't for the life of me see why the killer should want to leave us a note. But I think you're right about the money not being the motive. Nobody kills like that just for money. They were executed. And that's the bleedin' problem. Have we got anything on the husband or son, Bob? I mean we are assuming the main target was Maura. Do we have any reason to think one of the others might have been the main victim?'

'There is one other possibility,' Bob replied, flicking his notebook open, 'and one that could make the money a prime reason for going there . . . assuming there was a lot of it that is. Drugs. I spoke with the Drug Squad, just to cover any other angle, and they tell me that young Sean

O'Grady was getting himself a bit of a reputation as a pusher. If he was getting too big that might have upset Godfather Duggan. He has the city tied up and I doubt he'd accept any competition without a struggle, even if it was from one of the Republican groups. He wouldn't take kindly to a snotty nosed kid pushing in on his turf. That would make him go for a wipeout, as an example to others. And the money *would* be a prime objective.

'The only thing that puts me off the idea is that it would mean Maura was also involved in the drugs. The cash box was in her office – let's face it, she wore the pants in that family. The Drug Squad have the impression that young Sean was not acting with his mother's full co-operation. In fact she wanted him to stop dealing. She believed it endangered her political activities, making them all vulnerable to the law. But I'll check it out anyway.'

'OK,' said Frank. 'Let's call it a day and go home. Tomorrow Bob you ask the Drug Squad for everything they have on Sean, and get some more uniforms knocking on doors. Somebody must have heard something, for fuck's sake. Cowboy, I want you over at the Mather. The sister, the one who found them, was admitted there. Go over first thing and speak with her. Be nice to her, tell her how terribly we are all taking this, etcetera, etcetera. Make us sympathetic. Use your famous masculine charm on her. I shall try *my* charm with Military Intelligence. I have to call their top man tomorrow and arrange a meet. Edwards has already got the go-ahead for it. Right. Piss off the pair of you. I just want to sort out some of this crap' – he indicated the paperwork still remaining on his desk – 'and pass it on to one of the other teams to finish. From tomorrow all we concentrate on is this one.'

Bob and Cowboy left together and headed for their cars.

Cowboy drove his black Porsche out of the Castle and down on to the Liffey quayside, then stopped. With the engine still purring he debated what to do. He didn't want to go back to his apartment at Ballbridge. He didn't want to be alone with this mental picture of the room in the house in Ballymun. He needed company. Comfort. He needed to know that it was good to be alive, to be loved. He reached for the carphone and dialled the number which was so familiar to him. It rang only twice before a sleepy voice answered. 'Hi. I knew you'd call. Where are you?'

'Hello kitten. How did you know it was me?' Just hearing Marlane's voice created a knot of excitement in his stomach, making him feel alive.

She yawned down the phone, like a sleepy child. 'I saw you on the news. I thought you might need me. I wanted you to call and I just knew it was you. What time is it?'

'Almost 1.30. I'm sorry I woke you.'

'Don't be.' She yawned again. 'Now put that bloody phone down and get over here. I'll have a nice hot bath ready for you and a nice warm bed to slip into.'

'Best offer I've had all day.'

'It had better be, or you're in trouble.' With that warning she hung up.

He put the car into gear and roared off across the city towards Phibsborough, and Marlane's tiny apartment above a grocer's shop at Doyles Corner. He smiled at her warning. Without any doubt the best thing that had ever happened to him was meeting Marlane Davis. Recently voted the Face of Ireland, her beauty went much further than skin deep. He had had his fair share of beautiful women – more than most he had to admit – but since the day he first saw her he'd wanted no one else. It was only later that he found out she felt the same about him, but was wary of his reputation.

It seemed as if everybody in the city knew Cowboy Johnson. The only son of a wealthy property dealer with a law degree, good looks and charm, he seemed to have everything. His father had been looking forward to his entering the family firm on the legal side – but Cowboy had had other ideas. All he ever wanted to be was a policeman. His father had died the week after he received his degree and Cowboy appointed a board of directors to run the company, with his Uncle Ron as managing director. Only Ron, his father's best friend, had known of Cowboy's ambition to join the CIB. Under Ron's direction, the company went from strength to strength. Cowboy had no need to work, but despite his wealth he had always been accepted on merit by his colleagues. Everybody liked 'The Cowboy'. He had carried out the same duties as everyone else and he had earned his transfer to the CIB the hard way.

The name 'Cowboy' had been given to him by Ron. Almost the only game he enjoyed playing as a child had been Cowboys and Indians. Despite his preference for Indians, Ron nicknamed him 'Cowboy' and it stuck. As he grew older his interest in early American history grew, particularly in the lives of the Indian nations. His small library was filled with books on the subject. He possessed a small but valuable collection of authentic Indian dolls. Framed prints of Charles Russell, his favourite western painter, and Remington lined the walls of his apartment.

His first beat had been the Coombe, a rough area of the city. From the word go he made his mark. He took an interest in the community, and helped wherever he could. Within a short space of time he had gained the respect which other policemen took years to win. He helped start youth clubs in an effort to give the kids somewhere to go. He was more interested in playing football with them on the streets, than in arresting them for it. They got to know and trust him, and when he suggested to a potential thug that he visit one of the clubs and use the ring for his fighting, the suggestion was usually complied with.

The one thing he would not tolerate in any way was violence. In some cases he turned his back on petty crimes – but never if violence was involved. The families of some of those he helped to put away weren't forgotten, particularly around Christmastime when a few extra pounds to buy presents for the kids was important.

He built up a small but effective list of street contacts. It was through one of these that he had come to the attention of Frank Mooney. After one particularly violent raid on a sub-post office it was one of Cowboy's contacts who had come up with the information that led to the gang's arrest – and that had led to a transfer to the CIB and on to the team led by Detective Inspector Frank Mooney.

Marlane Davis – Lane to her friends – had known all about Cowboy before she met him. After winning a beauty contest that a friend had entered her for she had been approached by a model agency and was soon earning good money.

Lane knew she was very attractive, but she was looking for respect. She was quite prepared to wash a man's socks and shirts – but only because she wanted to, not because it was expected of her. Several tried to break her – and all failed . . . until she met Cowboy. Each recognized that they had met their equal. They had gone out together for six months before she invited him to her bed and it was a further four months before she surrendered her virginity to him (her Catholic background had always stopped her going 'all the way'). Other men had always made the mistake of trying to pressure her into surrendering, some by bullying, some by begging. Cowboy was the first one to make no demands at all, saying that they would both know when the right moment had arrived.

On the night they had first made love he had been as gentle with her as she had always dreamed her first lover would be. Now what she adored most in the world was snuggling up close in his arms after they had made love, falling asleep on his chest, the rhythm of his heartbeat acting like a lullaby from childhood.

For the past eighteen months they had been an item. Marriage was anticipated in the social columns, but their relationship was not always easy. Cowboy spent most of his waking hours on the job, and Lane was not yet sure she could accept the difficulties of being a policeman's woman for ever. Both believed they would marry one day, but until then it was separate apartments, although each had a key to the other's.

Marlane ran to open the door when she heard his footsteps on the stairs. As he approached she opened her dressing gown and wrapped his head in her arms, holding him close to her breasts. His face was cold from the night air on her hot skin. She ran her fingers through his thick dark brown hair, kissing the top of his head as she whispered to him, 'Tonight you're the baby, *my* baby, and I'm going to take real good care of you.'

His arms went round her, his hands encircling her buttocks. Lifting her up, he carried her back into the apartment and their mouths met in a lovers' kiss. She held the sides of his face as her tongue slipped between his teeth, probing his mouth, the wet tip gliding across his gums.

'God, but you feel good,' he murmured into her long dark hair.

'And you've been drinking,' she replied as she kissed and licked at the corner of his mouth. 'Come on, your bath is ready for you.'

Five minutes later he was stretched out in her tub, the water up to his chin. He sighed as he felt the tension leave his body, luxuriating in the hot water, the smell of her bath essence tickling his nose. She entered through the open doorway, a steaming mug in her hand.

'What is it your Cowboys called this stuff?' she asked, placing the mug on the end of the bath, sliding her dressing-gown down her body and kneeling beside him on the floor.

'Java. They called it Java after one of the first brands of coffee available to them. But I must say I don't think they ever had it made for them by a beautiful young cowgirl wearing nothing but a pair of bikini panties.'

'Knickers,' she replied.

'No. Panties. Knickers were the big navy blue things my sisters used to wear, with pockets in them,' he smiled up at her.

'I mean knickers to you and your cowgirls. I'll bet you've had a few "cows" bring you coffee in your bath.'

He leaned up out of the water and kissed her mouth. 'But none as beautiful as you, my wonderful, beautiful, delicious darling.'

'Hmmm. Thousands wouldn't believe you, but I would. Now be careful, it's hot.' She picked up the coffee mug and brought it to his mouth, holding it while he sipped awkwardly at it. He tasted the liberal portion of brandy she had dosed it with. Taking the mug from his mouth she licked the tiny rivulet of coffee and brandy that ran down his chin.

'Stay there and I'll wash your back for you.'

'If I say I love you, will you wash me all over?' He gave her an innocent looking smile, but there was a glint in his eyes.

'I'll wash up as far as possible and down as far as possible – but you wash "possible", OK?' She stuck her tongue out at him as she reached for the flannel.

Having washed him (all over despite her protests), she wrapped him in a large towel and led him to the bedroom. Turning her kingsize duvet back she ordered him to lie on the bed while she dried him. He enjoyed the way she fussed over him and lay obediently where he was while she roughly rubbed the towel all over his body.

'There now, you big baby. Move up into the bed. I'll be back in a moment.'

Leaving him snuggling under the quilt she went to the bathroom to empty the bath and brush her teeth. She returned to the bedroom to find him fast asleep and stared down at him, happy that he was with her for the night. Washing and drying him, moving her hands over his body, had begun to excite her and she had wanted to make love. But looking at his sleeping form, knowing the kind of day it had been for him, she didn't have the heart to wake him. Sliding in under the duvet she turned him over on to his back and sneaked under his arm, resting her head on his chest. He mumbled some incoherent words to her and remained asleep. Throwing her right leg across his thighs, her hand resting on his stomach, she closed her eyes contentedly.

*

In the centre of the city a man sat in an unlit room. He had drawn up a chair to gaze out of the grimy window over the darkened scene. Beside him, on a small table, lay an overflowing ashtray. Another cigarette burned between his fingers, the ash growing long and the hot tip creeping dangerously close to his skin. He seemed completely unaware of it. Occasionally his eyes blinked as he stared through his own reflection in the glass at some point in the distance, way beyond the rooftops, beyond the unseen sea to another land, to another time and place. Tears oozed from his eyes and his mind filled with memories of a woman in a restaurant, lifting her head and smiling at something he said. He watched her walking on a hard-packed beach in the middle of winter, turning and calling to him to join her from the warmth of the car where he sat. He saw her lying naked on a bed, her eyes watching him as he approached her. That look, that very special look in her eyes. He remembered driving through the night with her beside him, both of them silent, listening to a favourite tape, and feeling the occasional weight of her warm hand on his thigh.

He snapped out of his daze when the heat of the cigarette reached him. Blinking his eyes he looked down at it. Seeing the long ash, he gently brought his hand across his body and stubbed the cigarette out in the ashtray to join all the others he had smoked that night. Forcing the chair back from the window with a loud screech he stood and stretched, twisting his neck to ease the cramped muscles.

The darkness gave the interior of the small, second-floor flat a certain dignity denied it in the daylight. It had been furnished in the sparse style which only city centre landlords can manage, all the furniture bought as cheaply as possible at one of the many auction rooms in the city.

The only new items the flat contained were those he had bought himself; the bedsheets and the coffee machine whose single red eye stared at him from the open door to the tiny kitchen. He walked to the machine and filled the mug that stood beside it. The empty milk bottle on the draining board reminded him to buy some later on, when the shops were open. For now he would have to drink it black. Spooning in two sugars he idly stirred the coffee. He walked back to the living-room and the cigarette packet resting on the low coffee table. Lighting yet another he inhaled deeply.

Behind him was the small bedroom and the bed that beckoned him. He was tired, but dared not go to sleep. Sleep brought images he did not wish to see, although he had seen them a hundred times before. The dream. No, not a dream – a nightmare. He was flying around a crowded railway station and . . . He forced himself to stop thinking about it. It was bad enough having to see repeats of it when he slept without bringing it to mind while awake. Only the dawn brought relief. Somehow it was easier to sleep when the sun shone than at night. He still had the dream even then, but much less frequently. He wiped his eyes and realized that he had been crying. He moved over to the sofa, remembering in time which end to sit on to avoid the broken springs, and laid the coffee mug on the threadbare carpet beside him. From beneath the sofa he withdrew a briefcase. Resting it on the coffee table he fiddled with the tumblers, setting the correct combination, then pressed the brass catches on either side of the carrying handle. He extracted the address book and diary he had taken from the house in Ballymun several nights previously. Laying them on the table beside the case he opened the address book.

*

Researchers at the studios of RTE were busy putting together a programme on Maura O'Grady. Restrictions were placed on them by the Irish government about interviews with all and any terrorist group, but a voice-over on a photographic history of the woman would enable them to get the programme broadcast.

'What's the basic line we are working from, Keven?' Andy O'Connell was the chief researcher for the John Rafferty Show, which covered topical and controversial subjects. Working from a combination of information from other researchers Keven Mallen began to read.

'Born Maura Carmel Keegan. 1 May 1947, in Sligo. Father was Francis Keegan, small fry in the old IRA. Her grandfather, however, was shot by the Free State forces in the Civil War. So, IRA was part of the family. Fluent Gaelic speakers all of them, and from an early age Maura had an inbred hatred of England, the English, and anything associated with them.

'In 'sixty-eight, when the Civil Rights Movement started in the North, Maura got involved with Devlin and the others. However she didn't think they were doing enough. Because of the riots in Derry, and what looked at the time like being an imminent pogrom against the Catholics up there, Maura was instrumental in bringing in the IRA to protect the Catholics. Many of the younger people felt that the IRA had the answer and there was a mass movement of those involved in civil rights across to the IRA.'

He was interrupted as Norah brought in a tray with beakers of tea and coffee for them. He took a sip, and swore.

'Jesus, Andy, can't we get our own bloody kettle and brew kit? This stuff from the machine tastes like monkey's piss.'

'Well stop takin' the piss and get on with the story,' Andy replied with a smile.

'Ha-ha-bloody-ha-ha. Where was I? Oh yeah, the IRA.

'They asked their comrades in the South for arms, but the request was denied. The IRA command in the South maintained that the IRA struggle was classless and non-sectarian, while the struggle in the North *was* sectarian. Therefore no assistance was offered or given. This in turn led to the breakup of the IRA into what we now call the Official IRA and the Provisional IRA. Maura O'Grady linked herself to the PIRA.

'Shortly after this a civil war broke out between the two factions of the IRA. After a number of deaths on both sides the PIRA took control of the North and the Officials, as they were now being referred to, decided to give up the armed struggle with the British and concentrate entirely on a political, but radical, solution to the problem.'

'So what else is new. This is all old hat, Keven.'

'I know, but it's all part of Maura's background. The IRA split was the beginning of all the troubles the Brits have had since. It's when the real violence began. Remember, before the Derry march of the Civil Rights Movement all they ever had in the way of trouble up there was the odd border post getting blown up, or an occasional RUC man or B-Special getting shot. The campaigns of the late forties, early fifties and the odd bit of trouble in the early sixties – they all fell apart after a few months. But this has been going on since 'sixty-eight, and nobody can see an end to it. I think all the background information is relevant to the programme, Andy.'

'OK. We can chop and change once we have a good basic line to begin with. So the PIRA is born and Maura sides with them. What else?'

Without referring to his notes Keven continued. 'Well, funnily enough Maura was actually married to one of the Official IRA guys. A small timer, but involved, if you know what I mean. Michael O'Grady. She married him in 1969 and the son, Sean, was born in 1970. The hubby threw in his lot with her and it was really she who wore the pants in the family.

'A very violent woman was Maura. She was the kind who wanted more and more attacks on the British, and when the Popular Front For the Liberation Of Ireland came into being, under the command of McGuinness, she went over to them. She liked the idea that the Front was going to cause the British as much trouble as possible.

'She formed The Fenian Freedom League as a political side to the Front, with her as the main mouthpiece. And a proper mouth she was too. Organized rallies, fundraising events, even political blackmail and a well-organized protection racket. That bit can't be proved, but she did it all right. We can mention it because now she's dead . . . no libel! She did everything possible to promote the Front and was aided and abetted by Michael – and more recently by Sean. I have a good contact inside the Drug Squad who has promised me some nice little tit-bits on young Sean.

'There is a possibility that the Duggan family may be involved in the deaths, but we can't make any mention of that. They *are* alive. But there could be a link. Our Mr Duggan runs the drugs in the city, and if young Sean was sticking his nose in, then I don't think Duggan would like it – nor care who or what Sean's mother was. If Duggan was losing money because of Sean, then he'd be wanting it, *and* wanting Sean out of the way. But all of that is still only a possibility. It is a better chance that this is IRA, probably the work of Flynn.'

'What do we know about Flynn?'

'Flynn came out of nowhere. Suddenly the PIRA has a new chief-of-staff whom nobody knows. Nobody knows what he looks like, where he appeared from, not even any hints about him. One minute he's not there, and the next he's in charge. He started the recent changes in the PIRA. No more soft targets. No more civilian bombings. Only military targets. A few hard cases in the PIRA disappeared because they wouldn't listen. But when he said don't do it – he meant it.

'He started to take control of all the splinter groups, amalgamating them into the PIRA, and under his control. Anybody who objected disappeared. It's a known fact that at least three of those on the security forces' "top ten" fell out of the charts months ago – it's just that no bodies have been found. The last to hold out is the Popular Front, and along with it Maura's FFL. And now Maura has been . . . if you'll excuse the musical expression . . . "hit with a bullet" . . . literally.

'There's a lot of stuff on her here,' he tapped the folder as he spoke, 'that we can put to good use. At the barricades in Derry, Bloody Sunday, marches in Belfast and here in Dublin. Speeches, the rallies – and a lot of stuff we can't use until some wanker pulls a finger out and lets us get on with our job instead of having our hands tied over what we can and cannot do. It will all make a bloody good story one day.'

'*One* day, Kev, but not today. And it's today we have to worry about. Get together all the stuff that we can use and edit it. I'll get the newsroom boys to keep us fully up to date and get copies of all footage they use over the next few days. But we'll have to be quick. We'll get good ratings with it while it's still in everybody's minds. We can't afford to let it all cool.'

'We'll have it ready Andy, don't worry. Now can I go home? My kids keep asking Joan who the stranger she sleeps with on occasions is.'

'Oh go on, bugger off then. Just leave me here on my own. See if I care about all the work I have to put in, the thanklessness of the job, the ulcers, the wasted life I've spent . . .'

But he was talking to a closing door.

Chapter Three

THE BATTERED GREY VAUXHALL cruised along Wolfe Tone Quay just after 6.30 a.m. Commandant James O'Riley of Irish Military Intelligence was on his way to his office at Collins' Barracks. On the front passenger seat lay copies of the early morning editions of the Irish and British newspapers. MAURA O'GRADY MURDERED screamed the headline on the top of the pile. Just below it, in slightly smaller print, it read BREADMEN TO INVESTIGATE. Several months earlier the name 'Breadmen' had appeared for the first time, just after Detective Constable Johnson had been assigned to the CIB and became a member of Mooney's team. They had received the name because of a well-known bakers called Johnson, Mooney & O'Brien. O'Riley could remember playing with a skipping rope as a boy, singing the skipping rhyme;

Johnson, Mooney and O'Brien
Bought a horse for one and nine
When the horse began to kick
Johnson, Mooney bought a stick
When the stick began to wear
Johnson, Mooney began to swear.

He couldn't remember the rest of it, but it had been on every city kid's skipping rhyme list. It hadn't take any great journalistic talent to make the connection, and the Breadmen were born. The fact that the young copper Johnson was hot news himself only added fuel to it all.

O'Riley's stomach gave an uncomfortable lurch. Over the years that he had commanded the small but highly efficient Intelligence Unit of the Irish Army, O'Riley's stomach had achieved almost mythical status within the Unit. It was regarded as a reliable indicator that something fishy was afoot. He himself encouraged the legend, and only partly in jest. There had been a number of occasions when his stomachache had erupted to inform him not to take whatever it was at face value. On at least one occasion it had, he was sure, saved his life. This morning the telltale twinges were definitely there.

O'Riley drove in through the main gate of the barracks and stopped at the barrier pole. The armed MP who approached the vehicle recognized him, saluted, and indicated for the barrier to be raised. Nodding curtly in return he drove round to the back of the barracks, parking in his allocated space. Tucking his newspapers under his arm he walked briskly to the small, single-storied brick building which contained the offices of HQ and Dublin Section of the Unit. Once again he was stopped by an armed soldier who bade him a polite 'Good morning, sir', and then demanded to see his ID and security classification. O'Riley produced a small leather wallet from the inside pocket of his dark woollen suit, opening it to show both cards. In each photograph he was tight-lipped and unsmiling.

When he had first taken command of the Unit the security had been deplorably lax. His first set of orders were in relation to tightening up security in this particular part of the barracks. All passes were to be thoroughly checked by sentries, irrespective of the rank or the apparent familiarity of the caller. Several of those seconded for sentry duty at the intelligence compound found themselves disciplined in the first few weeks. One two-star corporal reduced to private, a senior sergeant reduced to the rank of two-star corporal, and two privates detained in the guard room. Within a very short space of time he had placed his personal stamp on the section and those odd little leaks to the press had ceased completely. He knew the sentry who checked his passes and the sentry knew him – but also knew better than to merely wave him on.

Passing empty offices along the way O'Riley unlocked the door to his chief clerk's office at the end of the corridor. Turning on all the lights he went straight to the door of his own highly secure inner sanctum, his office within an office. Using the combination known only to himself and his deputy he unlocked the steel-lined door, pressing the alarm-delay switch fitted into the door recess. He was now in what was referred to within the Unit as the Holy of Holies – a steel-lined box. To the best of his knowledge only one other room or office in the entire country was as secure as this one, the prime minister's office – and he wasn't too sure about that one. His own office was totally windowless, containing the bare minimum of furniture. The bulk of the space was taken up by locked steel filing cabinets.

Of average height and in his early forties, O'Riley was significantly unremarkable in appearance. Only the grey coldness of his eyes, and the slightly piercing stare, gave any character to his face, making him look permanently sceptical and suspicious. Living in the grey world of intelligence gathering, he seldom took anything at face value. It was said in jest of him that whereas many considered him to be 'a right bastard' he had himself asked for a second opinion to confirm that his mother was indeed his mother – and even then he retained a doubt.

He was a meticulous man where information was concerned. No detail was ever too small to be retained on somebody's file. His attention to the minutiae of his cases often paid off when some seemingly insignificant item turned out to be the key to resolve a problem. He was of the old school of officers, leading from the front; frequently with his men in the field, seldom if ever interfering with the orders given by local commanders. Those who had served with him for any length of time admired him, and would carry out his orders to the letter, but few of them actually liked him. He never got close to anybody and was not known to have any friends, male or female.

Opening a drawer in his desk he slipped a chalky lozenge into his mouth. It hissed softly on his tongue, slowly mixing with his saliva. Crossing to the filing cabinets he unlocked several and withdrew a number of files, laying them neatly alongside the newspapers he'd already placed on his desk. Each file was a dull grey colour and marked with three large, bright red X's, indicating that there might be material within to which not even members of the government would be privy. In fact, some of the files in the cabinets related to members of Dáil Éireann – a fact that many suspected but which none could verify.

O'Riley settled himself into his chair. The thick alkaline saliva was trickling into his throat, promising some relief to the nagging ache. He opened the first file, folding back the stiff cover and smoothing the edge with his finger. Maura O'Grady. It contained very little that had not been, or would not soon be, documented in the newspapers. This was not particularly remarkable as she had led an unusually 'open' life for someone in her line of business. Odd perhaps, he thought, that she had actually lasted this long. Probably the only information in the file which was not general knowledge was the fact that for just over twelve months Maura, and the house in Ballymun, had been under surveillance by the Unit, and all visitors to the house photographed. In addition her mail had been intercepted, opened and photocopied before delivery. But it soon became apparent that this, and the phone tap, were known to Maura. The bulk of the copies of the letters were kept in another file, but they contained very little information that O'Riley had not already known. Nothing very startling had shown during the surveillance, so when political pressure had been put on him to cease it four months ago it was done without any protest. He had better uses for his men at the time.

Such orders occasionally came, dropping in on him from the ether, sent by some faceless name somewhere in the tangled organization of politicians and civil servants above him. Now, in the light of her death, this order – a simple memorandum on official notepaper that lay before him – became a player in the game. The signature on the memo was that of a fairly senior member of the Dáil, and began: 'Acting on instructions received by myself,' ending with 'Destroy this memorandum on compliance.' Unless he was very much mistaken these 'instructions' – if in fact any had been received – would have been verbal. As for him destroying it after 'compliance' – other careers had been wrecked by less foolish actions. It was too bad for the signatory of the memo if it caused them problems now, or at a later date. O'Riley believed, like that famous Hollywood producer, that verbal contracts weren't worth the paper they were printed on. It was the same with verbal instructions – especially ones such as that about destroying the memo. O'Riley had his 'umbrella'. The possible fate of the signatory was not his concern. O'Riley had a bank security box in England which contained a number of registered envelopes full of instructions which he had received and been ordered to destroy. He sent these 'insurance policies' to his wife, a nursing sister who left him years before and now lived with another man in Liverpool. She deposited the unopened letters under their joint names.

There were many possible reasons for a suspension order such as this one: expenses, anticipation of a leak, personal intervention, a trading of favours with 'unofficial' sources. These were normal occurrences within the world that O'Riley travelled. But in view of the recent events at that address a further possibility crossed his mind. That suspension order might be very important to him, and sooner rather than later. He flicked Maura's file shut and picked up another one. A much thicker one. Its title was just a jumble of coded figures and letters, but to O'Riley it read BRITISH INTELLIGENCE OPERATIONS WITHIN THE REPUBLIC.

Over several years now there had been a number of incidents set in motion by British intelligence officers operating within the borders of the Irish Republic. These were carried out without the sanction of the Irish government, and many of them without even their knowledge. However, those that were known about by senior government officials were given the blind-eye treatment – just as long as they didn't cause problems. If cover were broken a procedure of condemnation was already prepared, ready to be put into immediate action. It was a similar procedure to the one carried out against Israel by Argentina, after the kidnapping of Eichmann. Once he was far enough away, and in the custody of Israel, there was a staged uproar in Argentina. The same thing would happen in the Republic. There would be red faces in Whitehall, backsides would be kicked, the operation in question would be termed as being unofficial, and Irish ministers would rub their hands. But there were some operations known only to O'Riley's unit. Fragments of information collected by several operatives of his were joined, like a jigsaw, to give him, and in most cases *only* him, the overall picture.

Some of these men and women he left alone, let them get on with what they were doing until such time as he might need what they had. Others he put pressure on to pass information to him as well as their British masters in Whitehall. He was quite blunt with them, both in his language and in his threats. They had better not mess with him, or they would be out on their ears at best, or dead. Everything these British undercover agents did was logged in O'Riley's file. The entries were double-checked, cross-checked, and rechecked again. He turned to the back of the file and looked at the photograph collection. Four of the photographs were ringed in red. These were of three men and one woman who were buried so deeply inside both the IRA and the PIRA that two of them were on the 'most wanted' list of the security forces in Ulster. They were inside watching the terrorists, he was on the outside watching all of them, and no doubt somebody was watching – or at least attempting to watch – him. That's what it was all about. The watchers and the watched, with interchangeable roles. The only ones who bothered O'Riley were the great unwatched – such as the man in the third file he reached for.

The creased and grimy cover revealed that he was more than familiar with this file. The name on the cover read MARY THOMAS MCGUINNESS. Mechanically he flicked through the assortment of notes, letters, reports, and photocopies of British security forces reports, and the list of all known associates. He didn't read them. He didn't need to. Although they had never met, O'Riley knew as much about this man as anybody could. And this man had 'disappeared'. That worried O'Riley.

He looked at the photograph of the thin-faced, anaemic looking character who stared back at him from the first page. The face was enough to upset his already grumbling stomach. Thirty-one years of age, reared in the Bogside enclave of Londonderry; father left home shortly before he was born, never to return; mother over-compensated, spoiling the young boy who became a sly, conniving teenager, with no change as he grew to manhood; above-average intelligence, as noted by his Christian Brothers school report; on leaving school he was recommended by them as a junior office-boy to Madigans Accounts in the heart of the city. Initially he tried – or at least seemed to, then £3,000 went missing. A small fortune in those days and equal to about five years' wages to the young McGuinness. It was never recovered and never proved that he took the money, but he was asked to leave. His story about the new furniture bought by his mother was that he had won the money from gambling. The only person who believed the story was his mother. Over the next few years he shifted from job to job, becoming more and more sullen in his attitude. Then, from out of nowhere, he got a sudden dedication to 'the cause'.

Shortly after McGuinness's 'conversion' to the cause, O'Riley started to collect background detail on him. McGuinness's apparent dedication was completely out of character to anything he had done before and caused the acid to churn in O'Riley's stomach. Even then his gut told him that their paths would cross somehow. He was right.

As more and more entries were made in the file the twinges grew in intensity. Now, as he held the file, it felt as if he had been kicked in the belly by a mule.

When the IRA split, McGuinness sided with the PIRA, as did most of those involved in the troubles at the time. It was here that he came into his own. Time and time again he proved his worth, not by any street activity, but by the ingenious ways he invented for laundering PIRA funds. The more expert he became the more apparent it was that he was more interested in the money than in any cause. His lifestyle began to change and this was noted by others within the PIRA. However, as long as he stuck to small amounts and continued to add more to the coffers of the PIRA than he removed, his transgressions were ignored.

By now McGuinness was wanted by the security forces for acts of terrorism. He had been linked to several bombings and other killings over the years, and he was also wanted for questioning by the RUC over yet another matter, the demise of his live-in girlfriend, Brigit O'Riordan. Her body had been found on a city rubbish dump, beaten to death.

It was from a statement made by a disillusioned (and now dead) ex-PIRA member that the accusations of missing funds first came to the notice of the security forces – and via them to O'Riley – in connection with McGuinness. It was beginning to become clear that he was more interested in his own status and wealth than in any desire to see a united Ireland. Soon after that, and before Kevin Flynn became chief-of-staff of the PIRA, McGuinness broke away from the Provos to form his own group – the Popular Front for the Liberation of Ireland. He had decided it was easier to cut out the middle man – the PIRA – and have the funds come direct to him. With Maura O'Grady as the political mouthpiece the two of them were a match well made in hell.

Inside the front cover of the file were cross-references to other files in which McGuinness got a mention, and some of these O'Riley had on his desk. He ignored the one on the organization, structure and aims of the Popular Front – meaningless ramblings meant only to feed those the group sought funds from – and picked up the next file. Flicking it open the face of James Earl McQueedy stared back at him. McGuinness's right-hand man, personal bodyguard and enforcer, and quite possibly the only friend McGuinness had in the entire world.

A starker contrast with the anaemic-looking McGuinness would have been hard to find. Six foot two inches tall, broad-shouldered, thick necked, round faced and with glassy staring eyes, 'McQ,' as he preferred to be called, looked exactly what he was – a psychopathic killer. The file listed incidents in chronological order. The first entry gave an important insight into the relationship of the two men. The incident happened when McQueedy was thirteen and McGuinness eleven and they were at school together. 'Although McQueedy refused to speak,' read the report, 'a pupil in his form stated that Wallace (the assaulted boy) had earlier been involved in an incident with another pupil, Thomas McGuinness. That incident related to teasing over McGuinness's given name of "Mary" – which, in view of the background of all the pupils in the area, was rather an unfortunate decision made by the boy's mother. Apparently McGuinness has a close friendship with, and a great deal of influence over, McQueedy.' The assaulted boy had nearly died, and McQueedy had shown a lack of remorse remarkable in one so young.

At fifteen he served two years in a young offenders' home for an assault similar to the one that got him expelled from the Christian Brothers school. Shortly afterwards he managed to join the British Army as a recruit into the Parachute Regiment. At his court martial, for assault (again) – this time on his platoon sergeant using steel-tipped boots – he was sentenced to nine months at Colchester Corrective Training Centre and given a dishonourable discharge. Owing to his attitude of cold indifference he received no remission on his sentence and it was only because the Army wanted shot of him as quickly as possible that he didn't serve a longer sentence.

Back in Ulster he fell under suspicion over several armed robberies, both in Derry and in Belfast – but he always had good solid alibis. The broken body of the head Christian Brother at his old school was found in the burning building – both the assault and the arson were attributed to him but never proved. Then came his links with the PIRA and his teaming with his old friend – possibly his only friend – McGuinness.

O'Riley's assessment of the man was that he was truly one of nature's genuine sadists. As an ex-member of the British Army, and despite his term at the CCT Unit – possibly *because* of it – McQ had to prove himself to the PIRA. He did this by killing five of his ex-comrades in the Parachute Regiment. As a consequence of this he was accepted as a bona-fide member. His photograph was now widely circulated among the two Parachute Regiments, with an unofficial, 'no questions asked' reward of £10,000 on his head – dead or alive. If he ever fell into their hands he would not survive to stand trial for any crime. He would simply 'disappear' and the word would spread to cease wasting time looking for him.

There then followed a long list of PIRA informants who had been killed or kneecapped. Several who survived secretly confided that McQueedy had performed their punishment, smiling as he fitted his power drill with a Number 8 wood-bore, and set it spinning.

Finally came the names of the three women who had unfortunately and unwittingly attracted McQueedy – and then tried to end the relationships. All three bore disfigured faces in memory of their association with him. O'Riley had long ago promised a good contact in British Military Intelligence, working in Ulster, that if ever McQueedy fell into his hands he would be handed across the border with no court proceedings. O'Riley would be only too pleased to mark the file 'Disappeared'.

The buzzer on his door interrupted his thoughts, and the tiny monitor screen on his desk lit up to show the face of his chief clerk, Sergeant John Kelly. By pressing a button on his desk the electronic bolt on the door was released with a faint thud and Kelly walked in bearing a pot of tea and a mug.

'Morning, sir. Thought you might like a cuppa.'

'Thank you Johnny. That's exactly what I need.' As O'Riley moved the files on his desk to make room for the teapot and mug Kelly noticed which files he was reading.

'Butch Cassidy and the Sundance Kid?' he inquired.

O'Riley nodded. 'I wonder if "butch" is the operative word there Johnny. They certainly make an unattractive pair.' He leaned back in his chair. 'A dangerous combination. And my stomach tells me they are somehow mixed up in this killing in Ballymun. I have been "ordered" to assist the CIB on it. Who knows, there just might be something in it for us. What do you think, Johnny?'

Sergeant Kelly shrugged his shoulders. 'Won't harm to have a listen to them. Depends as well on how much they know – if anything at all – and how much help they want. Now drink your tea before it gets cold. Sir.'

O'Riley watched the retreating back of his sergeant. He and Johnny went back a long way and his first act on getting this job was to find Kelly and have him posted in as his chief clerk. Chief clerks were a dime a dozen he knew. Good ones, ones he could trust, could be counted on the fingers of a one-armed man. Johnny was the only person in the world that he came close to relaxing with. He sipped the tea and picked up the next file, on Abu Nabi.

Abu Nabi – if that was his name, and he had his doubts – was a member of the Libyan People's Bureau – their version of an embassy – in Dublin. It was a somewhat meagre file compared with the others, but what was significant to O'Riley was the fact that on at least three known occasions Messrs McGuinness and Nabi had held lengthy meetings. O'Riley had passed this fact on to the British, just before the Popular Front's bombing campaign on the British mainland had started. Surveillance was maintained on Nabi, but there had been no more meetings for several months now.

Collecting the files together he returned each one to its correct place. Moving to another cabinet he retrieved another file. There was no classification on the cover of this one, and on opening it the face of Detective Inspector Frank Mooney smiled up at him.

'I wonder exactly what sort of a policeman you are, Inspector Frank Mooney?' O'Riley murmured as he scanned Mooney's CIB career with cold eyes.

*

At 7.15 that same morning Cowboy Johnson woke automatically. Lane was wrapped around him, her soft cheek resting on his chest, and he disengaged himself as gently as he could. He smiled at her sleep-mumbled protest as he left her bed. Naked and feeling good, he walked into the small kitchen and prepared coffee in the machine, then went into the bathroom.

For five minutes he stood in the shower, the hot water beating down on his skin. Then he turned the mixer to cold and braced himself for the shock. Thirty seconds was enough for any man in that. He stepped out, wrapping himself in the dressing-gown Lane had bought for him to keep at her flat. Finding a small bottle of Polo he splashed some on his arms and chest, then looked for Lane's Lady Shaver to rub over his face. She complained about him using it – but at least he didn't clog it up with his hair, as she did his.

The aroma of freshly percolated coffee greeted his nostrils as he left the bathroom. It was his second-favourite smell after the sleepy scent of Lane first thing in the morning. He often told her of his wish to bottle it, so he could carry it with him all day: a mixture of her own body aroma and the scent she wore – usually Chanel, which she knew he loved. Filling a mug with coffee he wandered back and sat on the bed looking at her as she slept, his pillow hugged tightly to her, her delicate face resting on it so that she, in turn, could inhale him. He never tired of this vision and each time he saw it, it hit him like a physical blow in his heart. He hoped it would never change between them.

As he watched, the scene changed, the room changed, and a different woman lay asleep in the bed. He almost dropped his coffee mug with shock. This woman was older, not by much, but at least in her mid to late twenties. Her hair was black and shorter than Lane's, and she appeared to be wearing a nightdress. He could see the thin straps on her shoulders. The vision was so vivid he even felt that he himself was somebody else. But the same feeling of deep love was there, for this sleeping woman.

He shook his head, wiping his hand across his eyes, feeling the sudden chill of fear run through him. The vision disappeared and once more he was looking at a sleeping Lane. He didn't understand what had happened – but at the back of his mind a small, faint voice of remembrance was whispering to him that this had happened to him before.

He stood up, shaking his head to rid himself of these hazy images, and returned to the kitchen. He was delighted to find that Lane had had time to do some shopping; there was actually some fresh food in the fridge, including bacon. Toasted, crispy bacon sandwiches for breakfast was his favourite. He set about preparing breakfast for both of them. Glasses of orange juice and bacon toasties. One thing Lane never had to watch was her eating habits. She could, and frequently did, eat like a horse, but never put on an ounce.

'Hi,' she whispered from the doorway. Looking round at her he smiled. She was rubbing her hand through her tumbled hair, yawning at the same time. She wore only a pair of bikini panties and her small breasts pointed their hard nipples at him. He smiled, remembering the first time he had seen her like that. Wrapping her in his arms, and pulling his dressing-gown round the pair of them, he had asked if it was the wonderful, macho sight of him, on opening her eyes, that had caused the passion in her that had swollen her nipples.

'No,' she had replied, yawning into his chest, 'I'm bloody freezing.' He had burst out laughing and it had become a private joke between them. In company, if she ever wanted him to know that she wanted him, that she was wet with desire, she would look him straight in the eye and tell him, out loud, that she was 'freezing' . . . even if it was the height of summer.

Going to her now he once again wrapped his dressing-gown around her, crushing her to his chest. His hands caressed the soft, elegant lines of her back gently, lowering his mouth to kiss the top of her head.

'What time is it?' she asked, speaking through yet another yawn, rubbing herself up against him, like a purring kitten.

'Almost eight. Did you sleep well?'

She nodded against him. 'Yes, too well. When I got to bed you were fast asleep – you bastard.' She kissed his hairy chest then looked up into his face, her gleaming white teeth flashing at him as he picked her up in his arms and carried her back to the bedroom.

'You cheeky little . . .' he began.

'Oh goody. Are you going to rape me?' She opened her eyes wide in mock horror.

He laughed so much at the innocent, eager look on her face, that he dropped her on the bed, falling over her.

'No, I am *not* going to rape you . . .'

'Are you sure?' She teased running her hand down his chest across his stomach to the junction of his legs, groping for his swollen member.

'You leave me alone, you little witch. My mother should have warned me about women like you. Now if you'll kindly let go of my cock I'll bring you your breakfast – and then I'm off to work.'

'Oh *yummy*. Food! Even better than sex.' Rolling her eyes again in wide-eyed innocence she sat up in the bed and clasped her hands together.

'Oh my God,' he groaned, making his way to the kitchen, trying to think of anything other than her, to get his erection to go down. In the kitchen he placed the glasses and toasted sandwiches on a tray then returned to the bedroom. Both of them drained their juice in one go and smiled at each other as they ate the toast and bacon. She began to feel randy once more and she teased him with her eyes and her mouth, her tongue slowly licking the crumbs from her lips. She let the duvet fall from her chest, her exposed nipples hard with her desire for him. He knew she wanted him back in bed, and he desperately wanted to climb in there beside her. But he had a job to do. Calling her a wicked witch he collected the tray and took it to the kitchen, then came back to get dressed.

'Come over here before you do that,' she asked him seductively as he reached for a fresh shirt, socks and underwear from her chest of drawers.

'Don't tease me, Lane. You know I want to crawl back in there with you, but I have to be at the Mather. I have to interview Maura O'Grady's sister.'

'I won't eat you . . . well only for a little while. Come on. A couple of hours – one hour – won't make all that much difference.'

'Please Lane. I can't. I have to go.'

'Always the fuckin' job – or, in this case, no fucking job.' She turned sideways on the bed, her back to him, and pulled the duvet up over her.

Dressed now in his pants and shirt he walked round to her side of the bed and sat on the edge.

'Please let's not have an argument, eh? We've been

through it before. Yes it's my job, Lane. You knew it when you met me and I've tried to explain to you several times, it's not always possible to do what I want, when I want, or to be where I would prefer.'

'Oh no, but you can turn up here in the middle of the night when you need comforting.' She was striking out blindly at him, wanting to hurt him, yet not wanting to hurt him. She felt he was rejecting her. The moment she had said it, she regretted it. Cowboy sighed a sad sigh and got off the bed. He knew she didn't mean what she had just said – but it still hurt. He finished dressing in silence and turned to her just as he was about to leave.

'I love you Lane. I truly do, but I also have a job to do.' She remained silent while he left, gently closing the flat door behind him. As she heard his feet going down the stairs she sprang out of bed and ran to the intercom. She heard the street door open.

'Cowboy,' she called into the handset.

He stopped by the small grille. 'I hear you.'

'I'm sorry darling. Please forgive me. I'm a bitch.'

'Of course I do, and I know you are, that's part of why I love you. Go back to bed, sweetheart. I'll call you later, OK?'

'OK,' she whispered into the handset. 'I love you, you bastard.'

'Yes, darling – but I'm *your* bastard.' He smiled, happy their row was over. He would do his best to get back early that evening.

It was just after 9 a.m. when Cowboy entered the Mather hospital, a few hundred yards from Lane's small apartment. Showing his warrant card at reception he asked which ward Mary O'Sullivan was in, and was directed to the second floor. He reported to the nurse on duty and was asked to wait until the doctor spoke to him.

A junior doctor arrived in answer to his bleeper. 'She was heavily sedated on arrival,' he explained, 'and that kept her under until around three this morning. I gave her a second, milder one then. She's awake, but I'm not too happy with her condition. She's very distressed. Do you have to question her now?'

'I'm afraid so, doctor. The sooner we know what she knows, the quicker we can get on with our business. I promise I'll be gentle and try not to upset her more than I have to.'

'Well,' the young doctor sighed, 'if it's crucial, then it has to be. But please do be gentle with her. She's in Room 18 – just along the corridor, on your right, round the corner. You can't miss it. There's a garda on duty outside her door.' Thanking the doctor, Cowboy made his way as indicated. The guard was more of a precaution against marauding journalists than because of any fear for the woman's life. Mooney did not want any information he had not vetted splashed all over the tabloids. Showing his card to the elderly garda sitting by the door reading, Cowboy tapped gently, waited a few seconds, then entered the room.

The room was larger than he expected it to be – space for at least one more bed he reckoned – though sparsely furnished. The bed was empty but over by the window a middle-aged woman, wearing a hospital-issue dressing-gown, sat in a padded chair. She stared blankly across the room at him and he saw at once the resemblance to the photograph of Maura O'Grady. Without acknowledging him she turned back once more to the window.

'Good morning Mrs O'Sullivan,' he began, 'I'm –'

'– a policeman,' she continued for him, 'and I'd like to ask you a few questions.' She half turned in his direction as he approached her, her face filled with hate. 'I've been waiting for you – or some other bastard like you.'

'Mrs O'Sullivan,' he continued, 'I'm very sorry about what happened to your sister. We –'

'You hypocritical bastard,' she spat. 'You lot have been rubbing your hands together since you heard about her. You don't give a damn so stop pretending. For all I know it was your lot who did it.'

She turned away from him again and stared out on to Berkley Road. Cars and buses sneaked their way to and from the city centre, a mile away. Tears trickled from the woman's eyes.

'Did you see her? Her body.' She gasped between quiet sobs. 'Jesus, Mary and Joseph, that . . . that wasn't necessary . . . the way they did it.'

Cowboy shivered, remembering walking into that room. The feathers and the blood. 'I saw her, Mrs O'Sullivan. Yes, I saw it. And I ran from the horror and threw up all over the bathroom. And I wasn't the only one to be sick either. Despite what you might think of me, or of the police in general Mrs O'Sullivan, we are human. We want to find whoever did this terrible thing – and we need you to help us as much as you can, while it's . . .' he hesitated. Drawing a deep breath he continued 'While it's . . . still in your mind.' He had almost said 'fresh', but the connection between the word and 'meat', and the horror of the death room made him change it.

'I don't know anything. That's the terrible truth, detective. I'd tell you everything I knew if I thought it would help – but I don't know anything. I arrived and found them, that's all.'

Johnson reached out to her shoulders, but she shook him off with a snarl. She continued sobbing for several minutes then wiped her face messily with her hands. She ignored his offer of a fresh handkerchief. Cowboy reached for his notebook and pen.

'You say you know nothing Mrs O'Sullivan, but it might amaze you the help that you can be. Please try and think back to when you arrived at the house. What we need to know are details. You walked along the garden path to the front door. You did go in that way, yes?'

She gave a sigh and was silent for a moment lost in thought. He waited for her to compose herself. Then slowly she nodded her head.

'Anything out of place in the garden?' he asked.

She shook her head. 'No. I opened the door . . .'

'You have a key, or did you ring first?'

'Both. I go round each Wednesday afternoon to do a bit of tidying and cleaning. Maura is not . . . was not . . . the tidiest of people. She had her work. I did the cleaning to try and keep things a bit normal. I had a key, but I always rang first.'

'Was Maura usually in or out on these visits?'

'It varied. I had my own key so it didn't matter. That's all I can tell you. I never asked her where she went or who she saw. You see . . .' She looked up at him, seemingly to seek a degree of intimacy.

'Johnson,' he replied. 'Christy, if you like,' he added awkwardly.

She merely looked at him and continued. 'I tried to stay ignorant about what she did. That way both of us were safe. She need not be afraid of me saying the wrong thing – and I didn't have to be afraid of *saying* the wrong thing. I was never as . . . as "passionate" about it all. I still felt for Ireland, felt we should be totally free, an Eire that covered all thirty-two counties. But I couldn't do the things she did because I didn't feel about it the way she did. If I'm honest with myself it's because I was – am – afraid. Afraid that I might end up like she did. I expected something would happen to her in the end. I don't believe she ever gave it a thought herself. I just never dreamed she'd go the way she did.'

'You say you expected something would happen?'

'Yes I expected it,' she snapped, 'but that doesn't mean I have any ideas. If you play with fire you will eventually get burned. That's what I meant about expecting it to happen. She made many enemies, crossed many people.'

'So. You opened the door and went in. Did you notice anything different on entry? Anything out of place, something like that?'

She was quiet for a moment, thinking. 'There'd been a visitor.'

'How did you know?'

'It might not be anything. They weren't hermits you know. People did visit them.'

'But what made you realize there had been a visitor?'

'There was a mug – on the draining board. Whoever it was had had a coffee. The jar wasn't in its usual place, and there were a few granules on the work surface.'

'Couldn't it have been Maura? Or one of the others?'

Mary shook her head. 'No. None of them drank coffee. Ever. They kept the jar for guests, and for me.'

'OK. What about the mug? What did you do with it?'

'I didn't know if it was clean or not so I rinsed it under the tap and hung it on one of the hooks. On the wall – near the kettle.'

From between his lips Cowboy whispered a quiet 'Shit!'

'Would you be able to show me which mug it was?' he asked. Despite being washed and put away forensic might still be able to pick up something from it, prints, saliva. It was worth a try.

'No need to. I can tell you and you can find it yourself. It's the one with 'I SHOT JR' on it. Maura bought it at some jumble sale. She used to make a joke about changing the "JR" to "Maggie" one day.'

Cowboy scribbled away on his notepad. 'And the coffee jar?'

'It would still be there – where it was left – in the cupboard.'

'You didn't touch it? Put it back in its right place or anything. Did you make yourself a coffee?'

She shook her head. 'No.'

'Anything else you can think of Mrs O'Sullivan?'

Again she was silent for a few moments, then shook her head. 'That's all . . . until I went upstairs.'

'You may not believe it Mrs O'Sullivan, but you have been of great help. It's these small details that help us build up a picture of what happened. Can you tell me anything about the room Maura used as an office. Anything missing from there that you know of?'

She stared up at him. He noticed how ordinary looking she was. Her neck-length hair slightly greasy, nothing interesting or unusual about her in any way, the kind of woman you pass in a crowd every day and never notice. But there was something about her eyes now – something that had flashed when he mentioned the third bedroom – the office.

'I never . . . Maura told me I wasn't to clean in there, just leave it as it was. Anyway, it was always locked.'

'As an office there are certain things I would have

expected to find in it. Files. Records of some sort. Note-books and such. A telephone book with personal numbers in it. An address book. Diary. All that sort of stuff. Even some money. We found none of those things. Did you *never* go in, Mrs O'Sullivan?' He knew that she had. Her look told him so. It was clear that she was considering how best to answer his question.

Chancing the use of her Christian name, he continued in a softer tone. 'Don't misunderstand me Mary. I'm not for a minute suggesting that you took anything from that room, or that you were in it yesterday. I'm just trying to find out if anything is missing from it. That might give us a clue as to the "Why" – and if we find anything from the room . . . well it would help to know it actually came from there. You have been inside that room at some stage, haven't you?'

Slowly she nodded her head. 'Yes. I was in there once. Only once. I was in the house on my own and I found the door unlocked. Maura must have forgotten to lock it. It was the first and last time I found it like that.'

'Do you remember anything of what you saw? Can you describe the room as it was when you went in?'

'She kept the curtains over the window drawn at all times, so it was pitch black, even though it was early afternoon. I switched on the light. There was a desk and a chair, nothing else. There was nothing on the desk. Not even a pen or a piece of paper. I . . . I tried the drawers. Bits and pieces in the top ones . . . but the bottom one, the large one, was locked.'

He swore again, this time mentally. He believed her. She'd been in the office, but there was nothing for her to see.

'What about a diary? Address book? Maura must have

had some kind of book like that. Did you ever see her with one?'

'Yes. She had both. Not one of those . . . what do they call them . . . "fillyfacts" or something. Just an ordinary diary and address book. Leather covered – just like the ones you can buy in Easons. I didn't see them in the office, but I've seen her with both.'

'What about money? Did she keep much in the house?'

'D'ya think she was killed for money? You're barking up the wrong tree if you think that. She wasn't killed for money. She was killed because she was who she was.'

'I tend to agree with you there – but I have to cover all angles. Let's be honest with each other Mary. We both know what Maura's prime job was; collecting money for the Popular Front. There was money in her handbag, and in her husband's wallet, even a savings box in the boy's room, none of that was touched. But we do have reason to believe that there was more money – other money – in the house.'

'Yes, damn you, there would have been money in the house. Hundreds. Thousands. I don't know. All I know is that there would have been quite a lot. Didn't you find any? Maybe one of your "colleagues" took it?' There was a sneer on her face which made her look angry, and more like her sister.

'I can assure you Mrs O'Sullivan that the last thing any of us – and that includes the gardai who arrived first on the scene – were thinking about was money. We saw exactly what you saw . . . and that doesn't exactly make you think of money, does it now?' He was being defensive again.

'Maybe not.'

'OK Mrs O'Sullivan. Just one more question and I'll

leave you in peace. Was there a weapon in the house? A gun of any kind?'

Once again she hesitated before answering. 'Yes. Maura had a gun. Some sort of revolver. Not an automatic; I can remember her saying often that she didn't trust them. Something about them sticking or jamming when you needed them most and she didn't intend that to happen to her. She had a gun and some ammunition. In a box, I think.'

Cowboy put his notebook and pen away and thanked her for her help. He was just at the door when she spoke again.

'Detective Johnson. If you don't know yourself – ask your superiors. Why was the surveillance on Maura and the house stopped? It could be that *you* are being led up the garden path. Maybe the killers are already known. Maybe they are closer to home than you might think. Ask about *that*, Detective.' She turned back to the window, ignoring him as if their conversation had never happened.

As he walked along the corridor towards the stairs he was inwardly digesting her last remark. Who had Maura under surveillance? Was it a team from the Castle? Army spooks? If so – which army? British or Irish? Emerging into the sunlight he was pleased that at least he had obtained some information he could act on. What a bad break that she had washed the mug though. But . . . you never know, he reminded himself. Getting into his car he pulled out on to Berkley Road and turned right, heading towards the scene of the murders.

As he drew up outside the house in Ballymun he could not help but notice all the Gardai activity. There were four patrol cars placed at intervals along the road. Not far from where he parked he could see Bob O'Brien's unmarked Jag. Bob treated it as his own car, growling at anyone else who tried to take it from the pool. It was the one the old hands always told the newcomers to take, leading to some comic relief when Bob found it missing.

A young, fresh-faced garda was stationed at the door and Cowboy timed, dated and signed his entry into the house in the notebook held out to him. Pausing just inside the door he pulled on a pair of surgical gloves.

Remembering his earlier visit, Cowboy felt the hairs on the backs of his hands and neck rise. The house was as silent as a tomb. He moved along the hallway to the kitchen. The venetian blinds on the kitchen window were down and closed, as were all the curtains in the rest of the house; standard police procedure, keeping nosy neighbours from peering in while the house was still being investigated. He parted the blinds and looked out into the back garden. It had been divided into grids by means of white tape. Each grid would have been searched meticulously for clues. Cigarette ends, footprints, and anything else that just might prove important. He found a switch and the fluorescent strip flickered and came on, bathing the kitchen in its harsh white light. He looked immediately to where the kettle was, and above it to the mugs hanging on the wall. There was the JR mug. Taking a roll of plastic food bags from his jacket pocket he snapped one off and with practised care enveloped the mug, sealing the bag with a wire twist and placing it on the worktop. Opening the cupboard doors he located the coffee jar and repeated the process. He hesitated, looking round the room trying to think if there was anything else he should take. He was about to turn his back on the kitchen when he had a blinding flash of inspiration.

Delicately swinging open the fridge door he examined

the contents. Two pints of milk had been inserted into the door recess. Both were unopened. He scanned the room and went to the flip-top waste bin in the corner by the back door. Carefully lifting the lid, he peered inside. A milk bottle with some congealed milk lay at the bottom.

'And who's a clever boy then?' he asked out loud, congratulating himself. 'Come to Papa.' He poked two fingers into the neck of the bottle to remove it. Johnson screamed out loud. An electric shock ripped up his arm. Automatically his hand retracted, dropping the bottle back into the bin. He bent double, taking a deep breath, clasping his right elbow, which seemed to be numb. 'What the fuck . . . ?' And then he remembered.

Two young boys in short pants, nine or ten years of age, running for their daily 'skut' on the back of a delivery van. Every day the van stopped at Hay's Corner Shop, delivering bread and cakes. Every day the two youngsters waited until the van started to move off, deeper into the cul-de-sac, to make house deliveries. The doors were always open as the van only moved a few hundred yards at a time. The two boys would hop on the back step and hang on to the doors to 'skut'. He was one of the kids and Dano, his best friend, the other. But on this particular day the driver decided to teach the pair of them a lesson they wouldn't forget.

Cowboy had reached the moving vehicle first. As he caught hold of the railing just inside the open door he felt an electric shock run up his arm. He had fallen, but as the van had only just started to move he had not hurt himself apart from a bruise on his thigh. But he had had an image in his mind. Dano had managed to get aboard and was laughing at his friend for falling. Cowboy yelled at him to get off, but Dano only laughed more. Suddenly the van gathered speed and began to swerve from side to side. One of the door catches, holding the door in the open position, came loose and the door smacked into Dano's back. Dano fell off the moving van and smashed his head against a lamp post. He died four days later without regaining consciousness – in the very same hospital that Cowboy had just left. He had died just as Cowboy had seen happen in his 'vision', just after the electric shock. Several years later he had refused a lift on the back of another friend's motorbike for a similar reason – and Nickey had crashed, killing himself and his passenger Bango, a mutual friend. Nickey had laughed at him at the time, saying there was nothing wrong with the bike. But Nickey died and Cowboy didn't. It had been hard to live with that guilt too, but he had learnt to repress it, push it to the back of his mind.

Over the years there had been a few more unexplainable things, like the incident that morning in Lane's bedroom, but he had never spoken about them to anyone, afraid he would be laughed at, or worse, that someone would say he was involved with the Devil.

As if guided by unseen hands he knew exactly what he had to do. His back slid down the wall until he was sitting on the floor beside the waste bin. Removing the skin-tight surgical gloves he flexed his fingers, wondering what he would say if anybody should walk in and find him like this. Opening the lid of the bin once more he stared at the empty milk bottle. He knew, with total certainty, that the killer – or one of them – had touched the bottle without the protection of gloves. They must have worn gloves because of the absence of prints anywhere else in the house. It had been completely dusted and all that had been found were the prints of the three dead people, the priest and Mary O'Sullivan.

Cautiously, bracing himself for the shock he knew was to come, he inserted two fingers into the neck of the bottle, spreading them to obtain maximum contact. It started as a slow tingling up his arm, like somebody had tapped him on his funny bone. Slowly and carefully he extracted the bottle from the bin and placed it on the floor between his open legs, maintaining the contact at all times. The tingling intensified, growing stronger and stronger. Just as it became almost unbearable it stopped and in its place came an explosion of light inside his head. Gritting his teeth to stop from groaning out loud his body went rigid. Brilliant whiteness changed to tiny flashing lights of different colours. Then, like thoughts projected on to a screen, came a jumble of images and sounds. Flames. Bright red and amber flames, soundtracked by the most horrible screams he could imagine. From the flames came a white spot. The spot grew into a bird and he could hear the flapping of wings. His own wings. He was a bird, a white pigeon, soaring up into the sky. He looked behind him and saw death and destruction on the ground. Mangled bodies, flames, and the seemingly never-ending screams. He looked upwards. He was speeding like a bullet into the stratosphere, heading for open space. As he gathered speed the screams faded and died and his feathers stretched back tight against his small body, his eyes watering. His breathing became laboured and just as he felt he was going to carry on for ever into the vast emptiness, he turned.

Below him lay the earth, a tiny blue and white ball surrounded by blackness. Then he was speeding back towards it. Faster and faster and faster. Once more he changed shape. He was a hawk, a bird of prey. Down, down, down he sped, approaching the earth at a speed unimaginable. He swelled in size and his feathers grew black. Crashing through a blinding light he raised his ebony wings straight up into the air, slowed, and came to rest. He was standing outside the bedroom door upstairs. He was afraid. Not of what was in the room, but of what he had become. He opened the door and stepped inside. He caught his reflection in the mirror set into the wall with the built-in units. A black figure, from head to foot. It reminded him of that famous scene from *Dracula*, when Christopher Lee, playing the Count, first appears at the top of the stairs. All that was missing was the cloak.

He looked about the room. The woman was tied in the chair staring at him with hate-filled eyes. The boy and the man, each lying face down on the single beds, struggled to look up at him, their arms and legs bound, their mouths gagged. He was an angel. He was *the* Angel: their Angel of Death. As he looked at each in turn, their heads exploded. First the man, then the woman, and finally the boy.

There was a sound in his head, like a bursting valve, and the picture disappeared. He found himself back in the kitchen sitting on the floor, his fingers still stuck in the bottle. He relaxed his fingers then spread them again, touching the glass sides. Nothing. The bottle had discharged all its energy. So had he. He was exhausted, drenched in his own sweat. He felt it dripping from his face and from his armpits. His shirt was glued to his torso. He knew he had just witnessed the deaths of the O'Grady family, and the reason for their executions had nothing to do with internal strife within the Popular Front, nor was it a PIRA or SAS hit. The explanation for their deaths had something to do with the pigeon, the flames and the screams. This was a revenge killing. They could forget all the rest. Somebody suffered a great pain and loss at the hands of . . . O'Grady? No. At the hands of the Popular Front. The piper had played his tune and now he wanted payment. Furthermore this was only the first. There were going to be more deaths. That was why there was no address book, no diary, in the office. The killer came looking for information. Information that could only lead in one direction. To the whereabouts of the leader of the pack – Thomas McGuinness.

He withdrew his fingers from the bottle and reached into his pocket for a clean handkerchief – the same one that he had offered Mary O'Sullivan. Wiping the white cotton across his brow and down his face he took several deep breaths. With some awkwardness he got to his feet, walked to the worktop and rested his hands on it. Spreading his arms and legs, and lowering his head between his outstretched arms he continued to draw air deep into his lungs. Behind his eyes an intense ache began. His jaw felt bruised as though he had gone a few rounds in a boxing ring and hadn't come off too well. He was weakened, totally drained of energy. He willed himself to relax. He inhaled deeply, and slowly exhaled, waiting for his heartbeat to return to normal. He had never explained any of his past experiences from childhood to anyone – how could he begin now? How could he stop Mooney from running round in ever-decreasing circles?

After a few moments of this relaxation technique Cowboy felt better. He straightened, stretched his arms into the air, then bent and touched his toes several times. He rubbed the ache at the base of his head and behind his eyes and was surprised to find it disappearing. Had it really happened? Or had he imagined it all? The lonely milk bottle on the floor told him it had all happened.

He reached for the roll of plastic bags, snapped another

one off, and gently placed the bottle inside. The killer – and he was now positive it was a lone killer they should be looking for – had used the bottle, and what was more important, Cowboy knew there were prints on it.

Collecting the three bagged items he left the house. At the door he noted the time of his departure and signed the garda's notebook, making an entry relating to the items he was taking with him.

'Why don't you love me any more?' she whimpered. It was later that same night and they were lying in Marlane's bed, the bedclothes askew from their bout of lovemaking. 'I hate you,' she added with a sulk, her mouth turned down in an exaggerated pout. Their row of that morning forgotten, looking at her now only made him smile.

He leaned over and stroked her face, his eyes in constant motion, drinking in her hair, her eyes, her cheeks, her mouth. Never had a woman affected him like she did. Was it truly possible that everything he ever wanted or desired in a woman could all be found in this one? Others he had loved had had some of the qualities he yearned for, but Marlane had them all. He kissed the tip of her nose.

'Of course I love you kitten.' He smiled again at her, teasing her. 'Haven't I just proved it?' His eyebrows raised in a question mark. Her small fist banged against his chest as she replied.

'Yes, you dummy, but I want *more*. If you think you're getting away with a . . .' she glanced at the digital bedside radio/clock alarm, '. . . a two-hour quickie, then you're very much mistaken. That was just a warm up. Now I'm ready for the real thing.'

His shoulders shook with laughter as he lowered his face in defeat into her neck. Her arms went round his back, holding him, stroking him as he laughed. She remembered, with a smile on her face, the night they first made love, her first time ever. She had been scared, but knew that the time was right for them both. Her fear had been more that she would fail to please him than of any pain he might inflict while taking her virginity. But he had spent hour after hour stroking her, scratching gently on her skin, his tongue and fingers moving slowly all over her body. Every inch of her was subjected to exquisite pleasure by his feather-like movements. Time after time he brought her to the top of her mountain, then refused to let her fall, keeping her dangling until she could no longer bear it. Eventually she turned into a wildcat, clawing at him, scratching deeply into the skin on his back, biting him with her sharp white teeth wherever she could, screaming for him to enter her. When he did it was all she needed. She fell from her mountain, floating, floating, floating, while shockwaves of pleasure, the like of which she had never known, surged through her body. Even in her wildest romantic dreams she had never imagined that sex could be this good. When she had relaxed that first time, he did it again and again, until he could no longer contain himself and he burst inside her.

She had been scared that he had done himself an injury. His body had gone rigid. His head was thrown backwards, the tendons in his neck almost at bursting point as she felt his warm sperm shooting up inside her. As he came she felt herself once more going into orgasm as her vaginal muscles contracted round his rigid member, squeezing him, holding him inside, milking him. Her body went into convulsions as she thrust herself up against him until he collapsed in her arms, unable to move, sucking in air through his clenched teeth, his heartbeat sounding like the banging of a bass drum. It was so loud she was sure anybody on the darkened street outside could have heard it. They were both drenched with sweat as she held him in her arms, coaxing him back to normal, murmuring small words of love in his ear, stroking his head, kissing and licking his sweat from the parts she could reach. She still felt a tingle go through her body whenever she remembered that night.

Despite their occasional rows – more often than not about his job – what she loved most about their relationship was the teasing element of it all, the fun they had, both in and out of bed. Saying he made her happy was like saying that the Nile was merely a river. He was everything she had ever dreamed her man would be and more, and one thing she was completely certain of was that he was her man – just as she was his woman.

'Well, Mr Lover Boy, if all you can do is laugh, being too weak to know how to treat a woman, then I'm off to the loo.' Pushing him gently so he rolled on to his own side of the bed, she stood up. 'And another thing, buster,' she added, standing naked by the bed, one hand on her hip, the index finger of the other hand wagging at him. 'Tonight I'm sleeping on your side of the bed. You can have the damp patch for a change.' Throwing her head back in mock anger she grabbed her robe and pranced off towards the bathroom.

Still laughing he climbed out of bed, put on his own dressing-gown and followed, heading for the kitchen. Through the open door of the bathroom Marlane stuck her tongue out at him as he passed, from her seated position on the toilet.

In the kitchen he busied himself making them both a mug of hot, thick, drinking chocolate. Adding a dash of cognac to each mug he topped them off with a squirt of cream from the aerosol can she kept in the fridge. Waiting for her to join him his mind returned once more to the morning's incident at the murder scene. What the hell was happening to him, he asked himself, knowing full well what the answer was. 'It' was coming back, stronger than ever before.

'Work?' she queried gently from the kitchen doorway, bringing him out of his trance. She walked the short distance to him, put her arms around his waist, resting her head on his chest.

'Sort of,' he replied. 'But it's something else as well.'

'Wanna talk about it?' she asked, looking up into his face, seeing the tense lines on his forehead. He looked down into her eyes and saw there a mixture of worry and love, and a desire to help in whatever way she could. He lowered his head and kissed her gently on the forehead.

'Let's take these inside.' Taking a mug each they went hand in hand into the living room. Placing her mug on the coffee table she sat cross-legged and sideways on the deep three-seater sofa, and patted her lap. He laid his mug beside hers and stretched out, his head cuddled in the vee of her thighs.

'Do you believe in the supernatural, Lane?' he asked.

'Do you mean devils and witches and the Black Mass and all that bogeyman stuff?' She smiled down at his face, and then realized he was being serious.

'No, not that sort of stuff. I mean a super Nature. People who possess powers others don't seem to have. Like clairvoyants who can see into the future or tell you your past. Mediums who claim they can communicate with the dead. Healers who can heal by just laying their hands on a person, or people – like identical twins – who seem to be able to communicate with each other using telepathy. I mean, even ordinary people who are close to each other – just like you and me – sometimes know in advance what the other wants, like they are on their very own special wavelength. Do you believe in people like that?'

She thought for a few moments before answering. Cowboy reached out for his mug, held his head up while he took a sip, then lay back in her lap, balancing the mug on his stomach. 'I'm not sure,' she answered eventually. 'I mean I've read about people like that. There was a programme on the TV not long ago about some Dutchman who seemed to have special powers. Apparently he has helped police forces in Europe and America – sometimes very successfully, sometimes not. I don't know if I really believe in it or not. I've never actually met someone like that.'

'Well, kitten, I think you might have, now.'

'*You?*' she felt a little shiver of apprehension somewhere deep inside her, and covered it up quickly. 'I think you had better tell me what's on your mind, darling. I can't promise I'll understand – but I'll try. Is it something to do with this case?'

'Yes – and I can't talk to Mooney about it – or anybody else for that matter, except you.'

'Then tell me.' She lowered her mouth and kissed the top of his head and gently rubbed her cheek along his hair.

He described the incident at the murder scene and the sudden memory he had had of his boyhood friend, Dano, and how he had known at the time that something terrible was going to happen. Dano laughing, then Dano dying. 'Other things came back to me also,' he continued, 'things that seemed to crawl up from the deepest recesses of my mind, my memory, as if to prove to me that what had just happened was real and not a figment of my imagination.'

'Such as?'

'Oh just small things really, when compared with what happened this morning, but unusual. Things like knowing what I was going to get for Christmas and my birthday. I'd see wrapped presents and know what was in them. I wasn't always right, but enough times to know even then that it wasn't normal. I even felt it was wrong of me to be knowing. The thing is, I didn't *want* to know what my presents were. I wanted the surprise. Maybe that's part of the reason that it all stopped. I suppose, even then, I suppressed this . . . whatever you want to call it, "gift" maybe, I dunno.

'I remember once telling my mother that my father had just had an accident with the car. I told her quite innocently, like I'd tell her somebody was at the door, whatever. To me it was no big deal. I knew Daddy wasn't injured. My mother was quite angry with me, told me not to go round telling stupid tales like that, trying to upset people. About half an hour later my dad came in and said he had skidded in the car and smashed into a lamp post. He wasn't hurt, but the car was badly damaged. I had forgotten all those things, until this morning – and in that particular incident I remember the way my mother looked at me when Daddy got home and told us about the crash. She was horrified that I had been able to foretell it. Another reason I suppose for my suppression of this gift. There were a few other incidents over the years, but they happened less and less often and I forgot all about them. Until today. Today they all came back with a bang.'

Lane sipped her chocolate thoughtfully. 'So what does this incident this morning mean? Is there some significance in it all?' She was having difficulty accepting all he had told her. What did it mean for him? For her? Or for both of them?

'I'm not sure yet, but somehow or other I have made a connection with the killer. The thing is that Mooney and O'Brien are going on about the killings being IRA or Popular Front connected. Even that perhaps an SAS killing team are operating in the country. But I know all of that is wrong. This is a maverick killer, operating by himself, for his own very personal reasons – but I can't tell the others to stop wasting time with the rest, without having to explain my reasons. And they can hardly change the course of an entire investigation just because I've had a vision.'

'Well, if you do have some special gift, can't it just be a help to you? Maybe it will lead you to finding this killer – then you'll be able to show Frank and Bob how clever my wonderful man really is.' She squeezed him tightly, trying to show that no matter what, she loved him. The one thing he had not mentioned to her was what had happened in her bedroom that morning, when, for a few brief moments, she had become somebody else. He didn't know why he had excluded that bit. He just felt it wasn't the right time to tell her about it. But he also knew that the woman she had become for those brief moments was connected in some way to the killings.

'Come back to bed, darling,' she whispered in his ear, a feeling close to desperation running through her. Was this too, whatever the hell it was, going to be something that would come between them as his job did? She wanted them to be one, to share everything. If they were one, then what he felt, she would feel. She didn't want to be left out.

He looked up at her and smiled. 'I think you are beginning to be able to read minds, kitten – especially mine. Maybe you're gifted too.'

She kissed his nose and pushed him gently off the sofa. 'No,' she replied, taking him by the hand and leading him towards the bedroom. 'I just want to screw you.'

'Be gentle with me,' he pleaded as they left the room.

Chapter Four

DRAWING A COMB THROUGH HIS HAIR with military precision he inspected himself in the patchy full-length mirror set in the door of an ugly nineteen-fifties wardrobe. He had darkened his hair with dye, adding a touch of grey to the sides. It aged him by about ten years. His clothes were anonymous – trainers, blue jeans, shirt and sweater under a blue parka – but still looked good on his slender six-foot frame. He could be anybody, dressed like this. Turning smartly from left to right, then back again, he checked his appearance from every angle. Satisfied with what he saw he was ready to leave.

His morning had started at seven after only a couple of hours' sleep. Thankfully the dream had not returned. Each night it didn't come he accepted as a bonus. He had showered and made a pot of coffee in the tiny kitchen. With his mug filled to the brim he had sat in his dressing-gown in the small living-room to strip and oil the gun. The cleaning kit had been purchased in a sports store, 'for my son's airgun' he had explained to the bored assistant. In another store he had bought a quick-release leather shoulder holster.

It was a month since he had arrived in the city, staying first at a central hotel where he had checked in as Geoffrey Barnes. He had kept to himself as much as possible, avoiding the hotel staff and other guests. He ate mostly in different restaurants in and around the city centre, taking only his breakfast in the hotel room. It had taken him one week to find the apartment. A five-star slum was how he had described it to himself – but it suited his purpose. Right in the centre of the city, up one of the side streets, it was small but compact, consisting of a living-room, bedroom, small kitchen and a toilet with a shower cubicle. It was on the top floor of a three-storied building. Beneath him was a storeroom, and beneath that, on street level, a hardware store. The landlord, one of those elderly men who manage by their dress and manner to appear much less wealthy than they are, seemed uninterested in him apart from the fact that he did not argue over the extortionate rent, and paid the three months' deposit in cash.

It had seemed judicious to have some sort of cover so he had taken on the role of a mildly unsuccessful author out to capture the ambience of Dublin and hoping to do some research and writing. 'Uh huh,' the landlord had replied in response to the information, ignoring the battered portable typewriter on the coffee table, giving all his attention to counting the money. Satisfied that the payment was complete he wished Mr Henderson, as he now was, a successful stay and success with his book – not forgetting to ask for a signed copy once it was published. Business completed, he then returned to the suburbs in his white BMW, leaving four keys on the hinge-leafed kitchen table.

The place suited the man now calling himself Leslie Henderson. There were two entrances. The main one from street level led up past the padlocked door to the stockroom, the other was by way of the metal fire-escape at the back, leading into a high-gated delivery yard. The main staircase was for his sole use, entry to the stockroom being via a stairway directly from the store below. What he liked most was the fact that once the last goods lorry had returned at around 6 p.m, he had the building completely to himself. The rest of the area – old buildings now given over to downmarket financial services offices and various agencies – seemed to empty at around eight o'clock. After that he could come and go as he pleased with very little chance of being observed.

Having oiled the weapon he checked the action on empty chambers. The mechanism had not been tampered with and it took a reasonable exertion by his finger before the hammer clicked and the barrel turned. Fleeting images of the O'Gradys filled his mind as he pulled the trigger several times. But while his mind tormented him with other dreams the killings had not bothered him after the first night. It was no worse than recalling a scene from a horror movie, unreal, distant, as if the killings had been committed by somebody else.

Having serviced the gun he slid it into the holster, laid it on the coffee table and went to wash his hands. As he dressed, the planning and execution that led to the killings and the actual night itself went through his mind. He had been amazed by how easy the preparations had been. Research through old newspapers on the microfiche in the British Library had given him all the information he had needed on the Popular Front. After that it was over to Dublin to reconnoitre the area where Maura had lived. At the time it was still almost a game, something he could back out of at any time. The research, the planning, the purchases, it had all been so easy, even on the night when he set out to *really* start things up. At any stage he could have stopped, could have gone back, tried to forget, tried to get on with his life. Even up to the point where he had sat in Maura's little office, staring at all that money, more than enough to have paid for all his expenses so far, plus interest for his trouble, he could have stopped. It didn't matter that he had broken in, tied them all up. He could still have walked away, taking the money as payment for his trouble. They would never have found him in a million years, or known the reason he had come that night. But something had driven him on. The pigeon. When he had picked up the gun from her desk and headed back towards the bedroom, that was it. He was committed.

Returning to the bedroom he had felt a change in Maura. All three were as he had left them. There had been no attempt to escape – but he could feel the change. She had sensed his uncertainty and with that knowledge her own confidence had returned. She had been afraid of him as a rapist, but not now. She guessed that he didn't intend to kill them, and that, she thought, gave her the upper hand.

He had removed the gag and watched as she sucked in air, her tongue trying to wipe the taste of the soiled pants from her mouth. She stared up at him with hate in her eyes. 'Who are you?' she demanded, 'And what the hell do you want here?'

'I want you to tell me where I can find Thomas McGuinness,' he'd replied.

'Why? What do you want with him?'

When he told her she had spat in his face. He remembered the words she had used, the hatred in her voice matching that in her eyes. On and on she went, her venom striking at him, oozing through the pores of his skin, fuelling the hatred that was burning in his heart. In her own frenzied anger she failed to notice the change that came over him – until he whacked her hard across the side of the head with his fist and replaced the gag. A sudden calmness had come over him and he knew now with total certainty that he had to get on with the job. It was as if he had been injected with pure ice. She seemed to sense her mistake and tried to speak, perhaps to take back some of the things she had said, but he ignored her. Walking to where her husband Michael lay he had covered the back of his head with a folded pillow, pushed the gun deep into it and cocked it while Michael struggled, desperately trying to scream to his wife to give this man what he wanted. He squeezed the trigger once, holding his own body as far back as possible. The sound was only slightly louder than a champagne cork popping. Michael's head exploded, along with the pillow, and a blizzard of feathers swept round the room. The boy on the other bed, watching with staring eyes as his father was killed, fainted with the shock.

'Shall I do him next?' He indicated the boy. 'This,' he said, holding the address book in front of her, 'has some coded entries. I want the code, Maura, and you are going to give it to me.'

Maura was sobbing, all her fury and strength blown away by the destruction of her family. In her own way she had loved her husband. It hadn't been a conventional marriage by any means, but that was because she was driven by a cause. But she did love him, and now he was dead. Now she believed whatever this Angel of Death had to say to her. He removed her gag. He felt calm again and knew he had complete control.

'Sweet Jesus, Mary and Joseph, don't kill the boy,' she snivelled, her nose and eyes both streaming. 'For the love of God, I beg you. Please don't kill him. He's only a lad. I'll tell you whatever you want to know.' And she had.

The code had been simple enough. It was based on the keys of a conventional typewriter. Numbers were always two to the right and letters three to the left. Each line of keys was considered as a circle. He quickly checked the first coded entry against his memory of his portable machine. It made sense.

His next question to her was how he could find McGuinness. She didn't know. As he started in the direction of the boy she had sworn to him she didn't know. All she knew was how to get messages, and especially the money, to him. She told him how the system worked. There was nothing else she could tell him. When he stuffed the gag back into her mouth she knew that they were all going to die. Picking up another pillow he folded it in half and held it to her neck while she struggled. Sean never saw his mother die, nor his own death approach, he was still unconscious on the bed.

Leaving the house by the way he had come he managed to get back to his car, parked a mile away. By this time all his icy self-possession had vanished. Trembling and twitching, his teeth chattering as though he were freezing, he ensured that none of the feathers had stuck to his clothing. He had then sat shaking in the car for fifteen minutes before he could drive off. His luck remained with him. He passed neither car nor pedestrian as he drove away from the scene towards the city centre. He made one stop on his way back to the apartment, on Mobhi Road, by the bridge over the Tolka river, where he got out of the car. He threw the circle of glass from the back door over the bridge on one side of the road, and the small sucker over the other. The glass smashed as it hit a stone jutting out of the shallow flowing river, but the sucker floated further downstream.

Back safely in his apartment he spent the next hour with his head down the toilet bowl, retching. His body and clothing were soaked with perspiration by the time he was through. He stripped and showered, scrubbing himself hard with a nailbrush, trying to wipe out the memories. In his dressing-gown, with a pot of coffee beside him, he spent the remainder of the night looking out over the rooftops. It was the only time he welcomed the image of the pigeon, because this time the pigeon brought justification as a gift for him.

It was time to go. From the holdall he had taken from the O'Grady house he extracted a well-padded envelope. Using his thumb and forefinger like a set of tweezers he withdrew a note, saw it was an American fifty-dollar bill, and replaced it. Running his tongue along the gummed flap he sealed it and proceeded to write the address of a Channel Island bank on the envelope. There were five other such envelopes in the bag and during the rest of the week these would be posted from different post offices around the city and its suburbs. None of them contained British or Irish notes. Some of the British notes would be sent to a private address in England. The remainder would stay here in the apartment along with all the Irish notes as his 'get-the-fuck-outa-here' fund. He smiled at the irony of it as he slid the envelope into his pocket. The Popular Front was providing the funds for its own demise.

From beneath the sofa he withdrew the large attaché case. Setting the code on the tumblers he flicked the locks and the case opened. Inserting his fingers along the inside right-hand side of the case he found the hidden button, pressed, and the false bottom of the case sprang open.

'Hanleys Security Products' read the still new label stuck to the fibre bottom. In the narrow secret compartment lay three British passports and three driving licences. He inspected them, slipping one of each in the same name into his inside pocket, and became Joseph Alexander

Gordon. He pressed firmly on the bottom of the case and it closed. He placed the revolver and holster into the case beside the two small leather-covered books, closed the lid and flicked the numbered tumblers several times, then slid it back under the sofa. By 9.30 that morning Mr Gordon was in the Pearce Street office of the Dan Ryan Car Hire Company.

'There we are Mr Gordon. All checked and ready to go.' The cheery faced young girl smiled openly as she handed over the keys. 'Drive carefully now Mr Gordon. 'Bye.'

He smiled and waved at her as he drove out of the garage and headed through the city in a southerly direction. He fiddled with the radio dial and found some bland music on it; nothing to disturb his thoughts.

He drove along the coast road towards Clontarf and Raheny. It was by no means the shortest route to his destination but he had been in his apartment now for several days and he wanted to savour the drive. The autumn sun managed to warm the window as he looked across the glittering water to a lone fishing boat heading out into the Irish Sea. On the radio Chris De Burgh was singing about a lady in red.

Three miles beyond Raheny he turned towards the military airport at Baldoyle, and the international golf course at Portmarnock. Checking his map again he turned north to Malahide and on to Route 1 and Swords, not far from Dublin International Airport. Although further from the beach than its competitors, Skerries, Rush and Portmarnock, Swords was a popular resort during the summer. Even now there were still a few hardy types under canvas, stocking up the vitamin D for the winter.

Parking the car in the main street, Joseph Gordon got out to stretch his legs. He zipped his jacket against the cold, checking his pocket at the same time for the money-filled envelope, then spent ten minutes casually strolling along both sides of the street. He knew from his map that to the north was the continuation of Route 1, towards the border and into County Armagh, 'bandit country' as it was known to the security forces in the North, where everything needed was brought to their iron forts by helicopter. To those stationed in the forts, fort Apache in the Wild West would have seemed like a soft billet.

To the south lay Dublin, to the east was the Irish Sea, and to the west a minor road leading to Route 2 and the main road to County Monaghan. Somewhere in the surrounding grid square lay Merrion Farm – the name decoded from Maura's little black book, and the place she sent her messages, and funds for onward transmission to Thomas McGuinness.

He backtracked to a general store he had spotted earlier, which doubled as a post office. The sub-postmaster was busy with a customer, weighing a parcel and discussing the summers tourist trade, and while waiting Gordon took the time to look round the cluttered store. As he'd hoped there was a local map on one of the walls. Using the pretext of browsing through some postcards he was able to pinpoint the location of Merrion Farm, a couple of miles west of the village.

'Can I be helping you sir?' inquired the postmaster.

'Yes, thank you. I'd like to send this by registered post.' He handed over the thick envelope with the money and waited until he received his receipt. Paying the required amount he pocketed the change, bade the man good morning and left.

He drove back towards Dublin, this time taking the minor road heading west. Within minutes he was passing the lane that led to Merrion Farm. Just beyond the lane, on the same side of the road, was a five-barred gate leading to a pasture. The grass verge opposite was flattened and obviously used frequently by tractors turning or backing across the road into the pasture. Slipping the car into neutral he allowed it to coast on to the verge. He applied the handbrake, got out, and opened the bonnet. While he fiddled with the accelerator connection under the bonnet his eyes scanned the opening to the lane.

A high hedgerow screened the road on both sides. About 500 yards up the lane he could see a single-storied brick building through the large trees. It had a central doorway, with windows on either side, and what looked like a garage, or probably a barn, set back from the house. There were no immediate neighbours.

Wiping his hands on a handkerchief he closed the bonnet, got back into the car, and revved the engine several times before setting off. A quarter of a mile further on he passed a small layby, just large enough for a single vehicle. It was another mile before he passed the next house. The siting of the farm was obviously very much in the terrorists' favour. It was quiet, away from but accessible to the city, and at least a mile from the nearest neighbour. The siting was also very much in favour of the man using the name Joseph Gordon. Skills which he hadn't used for several years were now returning to him as he drove back to the apartment, planning his assault on Merrion Farm.

While the Breadmen had not been idle during the two days since the discovery of the bodies, Mooney was none too pleased with the progress – or rather lack of it. The search for the piece of glass from the back door and the tools of entry had proved fruitless. Every garden that backed on to the lane had been thoroughly searched three times. Dustbins had been emptied and all the contents sifted and studied. Some broken glass had been found but proved to be too large to be the piece they were searching for. Mooney reluctantly came to the inevitable conclusion that the killer – or killers – had been clever enough to take the glass and tools with them. Most likely they had been disposed of, but where was anybody's guess.

He was becoming more and more convinced that the killings were the work of a professional. Whoever had done it had known exactly what they were doing, and knew what the police would look for. Earth particles found in the bedroom and on the stair carpet proved to have come from the back garden. Every part of the house had been dusted for fingerprints. The only place none was found was on the water tap in the kitchen sink. He had wondered about that until Cowboy arrived with the coffee jar, mug and milk bottle. The fingerprint man had given the toilet handle special attention. He informed Mooney that it was amazing the number of crooks who took a piss while in the process of committing a crime – and forgot all about it. 'Would *you* handle your dick with gloves on?' Apart from the murder victims only Cowboy's prints had been found on the toilet handle.

Bob O'Brien's door-to-door inquiries had produced very little. One neighbour, two doors down from the O'Gradys, *might* have heard shots – but then again it might have been a car backfiring. The only thing the police did discover from the neighbours was that the O'Gradys would not have been voted My Favourite

Neighbours in any poll. Sean had been a malevolent presence in the area for years, and as he approached maturity had simply become more threatening and dangerous. Mooney now knew all about young Sean. His record from Juvenile Crime had been sent to him, plus reports from the Drug Squad. Sean was heading for a life of serious crime, disguised as political activity, when he came to his gruesome end.

There had been one speck of gold – or so Bob had thought – when the foreman of the nearby building site had approached him. 'It might be something, and then again it might be nothing, but some bastard changed the lock on the hut last weekend. We've had them broken into before, but never had the lock replaced!'

Whatever it might have been, it was nothing now. The foreman explained that first of all he had thought that he had the wrong keys with him. It was the same kind of lock as had been on the door on Friday. Rather than go back home to check he had himself cut the lock off with a bolt cutter. Nothing had been stolen, so he hadn't bothered to report it. During the course of Monday he had replaced the lock and forgotten all about it until he heard of the murders, then thought the police might have been interested. Bob swore under his breath. Yes they might have been interested – two days ago. The smart bastard knew that had he just broken the lock off the police would have been on the site the following morning. By replacing the lock he had left some doubt over the key – and now, any clues there might have been in and around the hut were destroyed. O'Brien noted that the hut was an ideal place to watch the lane at the back of the house. He was sure the killer or killers had been there.

Cowboy's milk bottle was the only clue they had. As

well as the prints of Maura and Sean, and those of the garda who had put the two fresh bottles into the fridge, throwing the older one into the waste bin, an unidentified thumb and forefinger print had been lifted from the neck. 'Bingo,' Mooney had exclaimed on receiving the report from forensic. 'What made you look in the bin, Cowboy?' He was smiling with pride at the young detective's work.

'Ah, just a hunch, Chief,' Cowboy had replied. Mooney had been in too good a mood with him to notice the lack of any pride or pleasure in Johnson's tone.

The autopsies carried out on the bodies gave the timing of their deaths as somewhere between Sunday night and early Monday morning – leaning towards the latter. Pieces of the projectiles had been recovered, as were minute traces of mercury. The estimation given was that the gun had a .22 calibre, that the rounds used were dum-dums, and the gun itself was most probably a Smith & Wesson. All of this information pointed towards it being a professional killer – until Cowboy reminded them that the sister claimed that Maura had kept a gun in the house – a small revolver, which was never found. Could that have been the murder weapon – and if so, what professional hitman went on a job, hoping to find the weapon on or with the victims? Mooney and O'Brien were both still of the opinion that behind the killings were either the IRA, the PIRA, an internal dispute within the ranks of the Popular Front, or the SAS. Cowboy disagreed.

'Okay, Cowboy. Why? Know something we don't?'

Cowboy shook his head. 'No, I don't. It's more of a hunch I have.'

'You mean like Quasimodo?' quipped Bob, winking at Mooney.

'Give him a chance, Bob, let him have his say. Go on, Cowboy, we're listening.'

'Well we've jumped to the most obvious conclusions immediately, haven't we? All the terrorist groups and the SAS – even our own Military Intelligence.'

'That last one is a contradiction in terms, Cowboy,' Bob quipped again. They all smiled at the remark, but the others allowed Cowboy to continue.

'And there are grounds for all these suspicions. The kind of people Maura was involved with, there have been internal feuds before with them all. Then there's the British government, pissed off with its people getting blown sky high. The haggling between Dublin and London over extradition and all that shit. So sending in a few professionals to give the terrorists a taste of their own medicine might seem like a good idea. But I honestly don't think they'd do it the way it was done. It *was* very professional – but where did the murder weapon come from? The sister says there was a gun in the house. A revolver. We didn't find one. The killings were done with a revolver. Was it the same one – and if it was, then what did the killer come armed with? How did he know he'd find a weapon there? What about the address book and diary? We know, again from the sister, that they existed – but again we didn't find them.'

Cowboy was warming to his theme. 'Then there's the fingerprints on the milk bottle. If you or I were wearing gloves and wanted to make a cup of tea or coffee we might take the gloves off. A professional wouldn't. This guy made a mistake and tried to rectify it. No prints on the kettle, the coffee jar or the mug. Okay, maybe there were some on the mug, but the sister washed it, so we'll never know. But as this guy, this person, was leaving the kitchen – maybe as he pulled his gloves back on – he remembered. He washed and wiped everything he saw in the kitchen that he'd touched. But he forgot the milk bottle. He took it from the fridge, poured from it, and returned it to the fridge. He didn't see it or remember it as he was leaving, and that's why we found the prints. A professional would not have made that mistake. The bottle remained in the fridge until one of the gardai decided to put the two bottles from the doorstep in. He put the fresh ones in, and threw the other one in the bin.'

Both Frank and Bob watched Cowboy as he spoke. The joking, teasing smile had gone from Bob's face as he realized that what the young detective was saying made sense. Frank too was paying close attention, and noticed how Cowboy was pretty well convinced that the killer was male – he had noticed the interjection of the 'this person' as if to try to show he wasn't certain, but Mooney knew he was. But how? And if he was so sure, why didn't he explain it further? Cowboy was speaking with conviction, even knowledge, and trying to pass it on as deduction. A lot could be arrived at from deduction – but it was more than that, much more. Frank knew that Cowboy moved in worlds both socially and at street level from which he would always be excluded. Was it possible that he had been given some confidential information and wouldn't reveal his sources? He hoped the boy was a better policeman than that. He certainly wasn't going to start accusing him of withholding vital evidence at this stage, but there was something going on with Cowboy which Frank didn't understand, and that made him nervous.

'Why did he make coffee, Cowboy? That's not something I can imagine any killer doing, either before, during, or after the job. Certainly not this kind of killer. I don't think we are dealing with a psycho, with whom the rule-book would go out the window.'

Cowboy spoke slowly, thinking as he went. 'I think the guy came looking for information. Somehow or other he managed to tie them all up and wanted to extract the information from Maura. She was the prime target. Maybe she wouldn't talk, so he had to decide what to do about it. Maybe he took a break and made a coffee while he thought about it. Then he goes back. Something makes him snap, perhaps he gets the information he needs, or perhaps she isn't able to give it to him, and he wastes them all.'

'So who is this guy then Cowboy?' Bob asked.

'Somebody who has good reason to want to exact revenge. And what would cause that? Perhaps we need to put together a list of deaths the Popular Front have caused. If I'm right, then this guy is after McGuinness. These murders are only the beginning. He needed the information from Maura, that was all, and he got that from the diary and address books. Maura was living in the open – she was easy to find, so that's where he started.'

'Shit!' exclaimed Bob.

Mooney sat back in his chair, his fingertips forming a tent across his chest as he stared at Cowboy. Cowboy stared back and there was a silent plea in his eyes to his boss. I can't tell you how I know what I know, but trust me. I'm right. Slowly Mooney nodded his head.

'You might have something there. I'll get on to the Commander and see if we can liaise with Scotland Yard's Anti-Terrorist Squad on this line. But we ain't giving up on the rest.' He looked at his watch before continuing. 'I'm expecting a Commandant O'Riley from Military Intelligence in thirty minutes. He might be of some help. As for you two – hit the streets. Do the rounds, separately, and hit every place and everybody you know. Call in favours – but bring me back something, OK?' The other two nodded. Collecting their coats they left the office with Bob leading.

'Cowboy.' Johnson turned back to face Mooney. 'I want to talk to you later. I want to know everything you know, and I want to know how you know it.'

Cowboy nodded. 'Sure, Chief. Later.' He closed the door behind him and hurried after Bob.

By the time Commandant O'Riley arrived Frank had already spoken to Commander Edwards of the CIB requesting a contact be made with the Anti-Terrorist Squad at New Scotland Yard for some assistance with information regarding all the bombing incidents carried out on the British mainland by the Popular Front. Mooney explained to his boss the reason for the request, giving full credit to Johnson. If he were right, then Cowboy deserved the credit. If he were wrong, little damage would be done and any flak would go no further than Mooney's own desk. It was the way he operated, unlike some of his colleagues and bosses who took all the credit for others' efforts.

O'Riley arrived at the appointed hour and was led to the office by a uniformed garda from the main desk. The two men shook hands and Frank indicated the seat he had placed in front of his desk. O'Riley sat. Neither man spoke. Frank reached into the bottom drawer of his desk and withdrew a bottle of whiskey, an inquiring look on his face as he pointed the bottle at the other man.

'Why not,' O'Riley nodded and smiled, 'just a small one for me.' Tedious though he found it, O'Riley knew only too well how important it was to seem friendly when you wanted to obtain information. He knew that people tend to talk to someone who smiles, even when that smile failed to reach their eyes.

Frank poured the equivalent of two large measures into clean coffee mugs and slid one across the desk to O'Riley. 'Sláinte,' he toasted his guest as each took a sip. 'And thanks for coming, Commandant.' He knew very well what the rules of the game would be with this man. O'Riley might come on with the 'pleased to help you in any way that I can, Frank' act, but he was only there to find out what the police knew. Anything Frank told him O'Riley would pretend he already knew; that way he would always have the upper hand. Anything he told Frank, Frank would owe him for. Men like O'Riley never liked to owe favours.

'I'd been expecting the call. Please call me James. It's Frank, isn't it?' O'Riley was keen to build a professional relationship. Relationships were something he found hard. 'How can I help?'

'Well, James, we're at sixes and sevens at present. We have three dead bodies and about one thousand prime suspects, with nothing to go on.' The information about the fingerprints had been suppressed on his orders and was known only to forensic, his team, and Commander Edwards.

O'Riley nodded, still smiling. 'I could probably add another two thousand to your list.'

The two men were watching each other like a pair of fighting cocks in separate cages. Both were experts at interrogation in their own fields, and both knew the game of talking without actually saying very much. Conversation between them was like a high stakes game of poker.

'This is good . . .' O'Riley indicated his mug.

'Twelve-year old Paddy,' Mooney replied. 'I was weaned

on the stuff by my old man. He liked to drink it with Guinness chasers.' There was another long silence. Frank decided to put one of his cards on the table. 'One of the things we did manage to pick up was that Maura was under surveillance.' He waited for a reply that did not come. Damn! It looked as if he would be forced to put down some more cards. 'It seems that at the very least the house was being watched. Quite possibly the phone tapped and the mail intercepted.'

Still O'Riley was silent, the chilly smile playing at the edge of his mouth as he watched the detective and waited. He was not prepared – at the moment – to give anything away. He knew he had the stronger hand and he wanted to see how much more the other man knew before making any comment.

'Come on James,' Mooney insisted. 'Off the record, OK?'

O'Riley was silent for a few more moments before replying, his eyes boring into Mooney's as he spoke. 'Off the record is for journalists, Frank – who then go and publish it anyway, stating it came from a different source. Nothing is *ever* "off the record".' He took another sip of his whiskey. 'I confirm your source. Yes, Maura was being watched. House, phone, post, movements, everything. But we ceased the operation some time ago.'

'Yes, I know that. And it's one of the little problems I'm having with the case.'

'You want to know why we stopped – and did our pull-out have any connection with her murder? Four months ago Maura O'Grady ceased to be of any concern to me or my department.'

'A coincidence?' Mooney asked sceptically.

O'Riley decided to give away a small amount of information. 'They do happen, Frank, much as I'd like to legislate against them. But no, the answer came from on high and you know how it is with soldiers. Ours not to reason why – just take the money and do as you're told.'

For a second Frank thought he saw signs of a likeable being beneath the icy surface. He found himself believing him, but that still didn't answer his question.

'You know what I'm trying to say, James. I need to know whether or not I'm on a wild goose chase. I need to know whether, if we do seem to be getting somewhere, someone from "on high" will arrive, smack my wrist, and tell me to piss off and mind my own business. You understand?'

'I understand, Frank. Believe me, I know. I've been there myself. All I can tell you is that I pulled my men off Maura four months ago when someone – who, I'm sure you'll understand, has to remain nameless – "advised" me to. But if you want my opinion you *are* looking at one of those unusual coincidences. I think the order to cease surveillance was one of simple economics. She knew she was being watched, and for what we were getting the costs in terms of manpower and equipment were too high. The money could be better used elsewhere. So the plug was pulled. You know yourself you could use twice the men you have at your disposal, twice the equipment, twice the hours in the day. We can only prioritize.'

Frank nodded in agreement. He knew exactly what O'Riley meant. One minute you are on to something that's getting hot, but only because you 'feel' it. No proof. Nothing you can put in black and white – and because you can't the rug gets pulled. 'Yes, I know only too well what you mean, James. Only too well.' He allowed another silence to fall, to see if O'Riley would be willing to give any more insights. It was the right choice to make. O'Riley decided to part with some personal, subjective advice, something he seldom did.

'For what it's worth, Frank, I'd accept the pulling of our surveillance as a coincidence, nothing more. Despite the fact that certain members of the Dáil have a faint smell of cordite about them from way back, and some of them sing "Kevin Barry" in the bath, I don't think that any one of them, let alone a group of them, could organize this kind of thing. It's too risky for them. That course of inquiry is a dead end and will prove to be a waste of your time.'

'What about the British?'

'They could have done it, they're good enough – but they didn't. I'm not saying that my small department is infallible, but I'll stake my reputation that there is no Brit hit team in the country at the moment. They've run a few small items past our noses, but we knew about them. Just kept watch on them, stayed out of the way, let them get on with it. Let them get the assurance they need.' Mooney didn't move a muscle. He'd cracked it. The man was actually opening up to him. It was vital not to frighten him back into his shell. 'They stepped out of line some time back – remember the Littlejohn brothers saga? Bank-robbing on behalf of the PIRA, then claiming they were British agents? As far as we were concerned they stepped over the line and we smacked them for it. They tend to keep their noses clean now. So that's another scratch for you. Only in my own opinion of course.'

This was 22-carat information for Mooney. Half the battle in any investigation was knowing which line *not* to pursue, thus saving time, money, effort and manpower – all of which were in extremely short supply. 'Then I'm back to one of the groups?' He prompted when he was sure O'Riley had finished.

'I think so. Let's face it, McGuinness is the only bugger I know who has managed to anger almost everybody. Not only do the Brits want him, but Flynn wants him. If you want my opinion I'd say that the O'Gradys are only the start. McGuinness is the target . . . unless of course McGuinness himself is behind the killings. It could be an internal struggle for power; I haven't heard any whispers to that effect – but it might just be starting. McGuinness's right-hand man, McQueedy, helps him run a tight ship – and McQueedy is the last bastard alive you want coming after you, believe you me. He, by the way, is more than capable of doing these killings. Next on the list is the mysterious Kevin Flynn, chief-of-staff of the PIRA. Cleaning out the debris to give himself total control over the paramilitaries in the North. I'd bet on Flynn, but there is one other possibility. A thousand to one outsider. Somebody working for themselves for whatever reason.'

'Strange you should mention that one. One of my team just said the same thing this morning. He came up with the suggestion – a bit more than a suggestion really – of a lone killer bent on revenge, and that Maura was the first port of call to get information as to the whereabouts of McGuinness.'

'I want McGuinness and his sidekick McQueedy,' said O'Riley. 'I've promised them as a birthday present to somebody who lives on the other side of the border. I can put out feelers for you to find out if Flynn is behind it. I'll let you know what I find out. As for the possibility of a lone ranger – well that's policework, so I'll leave it to you.'

'Thanks James. I'd appreciate anything you can come up with. I won't forget this.'

Looking at his army-issue wristwatch O'Riley rose to his feet. 'I won't let you.' He extended his hand and briskly shook Frank's, turned and left the room without another word. The inspector looked down at the abandoned mug of whiskey. O'Riley couldn't have had more than a couple of sips, so it wasn't that which had loosened his tongue. Perhaps he genuinely did want to help. Frank drained the second whiskey and went out in search of a cigarette.

Chapter Five

THE SMALL TERRACED COUNCIL house had been built on the Ballyfermot estate in the early fifties as part of the city centre slum clearance scheme. It had immediately been named 'Little Korea' and had become famous for its street fights. It was most certainly not a place to park a Porsche. For that reason Cowboy had checked out one of the cars used for undercover work. Battered and scratched, but with a highly tuned engine, it blended in well with the area.

He had been sitting in the car for the past hour, watching the house, trying to decide if he should go in or not. The house was subtly different from its neighbours. While the paintwork on the metal windowframes was not new, it was not blistered and peeling like most of the others. The garden had well-tended flower beds while the others brimmed over with household rubbish, wet and torn card-board boxes and discarded children's toys. The hedge dividing it from the neighbours was clipped and neat.

The letter was in his inside pocket. A letter he had read and re-read several times since its arrival at the office at the Castle. Addressed to him personally it had been marked, in neat, block-capital print, PRIVATE AND CONFIDENTIAL.

'There ya go, Cowboy, yer first paternity suit,' had been Bob's remark as he handed the letter over. It wasn't, but its contents had given him almost as much of a shock, and now he was trying to work out how he truly felt.

'It's make your mind up time,' he spoke aloud to himself.

Once the decision had been taken he got out of the car, locked it, and walked up the clean concrete path to the front door. After ringing the bell he waited only a few moments before the door opened.

The woman who faced him he estimated to be in her early fifties. About five feet ten, she carried herself extremely well. Still an attractive woman, he found himself thinking. She must have been a real heartbreaker in her youth. Her face still showed ample signs of the beauty she once was although there was now an extra layer of flesh on it and the skin had lost the youthful elasticity it once had. Her hair was immaculately groomed and he guessed that the grey had been covered.

'Mrs Blackmore? Mrs Joan Blackmore?' he inquired.

She smiled an open, friendly smile, showing a full set of perfect, white teeth. 'Yes,' she replied. 'And you are Mr Johnson. I've been expecting you. Come on in.' She stood to one side, allowing him to enter. The house smelt clean and feminine. He felt welcome and immediately relaxed. He was now glad he had come and excited at the prospect of what he might learn. He wondered how she knew his name.

'Your picture has been in the newspapers enough times,' she seemed to have read his thoughts. 'Also, if I'd received the kind of letter I sent you, I'd be very curious, to say the least. I'd want to meet the person who sent it. Go on in. Second door on your left.'

Closing the front door behind her she followed him into the small book-filled room. There were mismatched shelves and bookcases of all sorts and sizes filling every wall, some reaching from floor to ceiling, each filled to capacity. Stacks more books lay on the floor waiting to be found homes.

In the centre of the room was a veneered coffee table with an old and faded sofa to one side and two armchairs on the other. The original open fireplace had been converted to hold a gas fire, which was on, and the room was comfortable, warm and cosy. Cowboy felt very good just being in the room. He felt at peace here without knowing quite why.

'Take your coat off Mr Johnson, please. It's a bit warm in here and you don't want to catch your death of cold when you leave. Would you like a cup of tea? Or coffee perhaps?'

'Coffee would be lovely, thanks. Just black. No sugar.'

She smiled at him again. 'Looking after your health I see. Won't be a sec. The kettle's just boiled. Sit yourself down while I get it.'

Taking his coat off he sat on the sofa, not knowing what to say or do when she returned. He felt easy in her company, yet uneasy about what might lie in store. It was rather like visiting a doctor to hear the results of some important test.

'There we are. One black coffee for you and a cuppa for myself.' She sat down in one of the armchairs facing him.

'I can see that you're a bit uneasy, Mr Johnson. I can understand that, but please . . . Relax. I'm not going to harm you.' She laughed and it was infectious, making him join in. 'Mind you, if I were about thirty years younger it might be different.' She laughed again at her own cheek, this time causing him to feel slightly embarrassed. It was as if she had read his earlier thoughts once again. 'Now. You came to talk about the letter – I expect you want to know how I came to write it. This is your first visit to a medium, isn't it?'

He sipped the coffee then placed his cup and saucer on

the table, opposite hers. 'Yes,' he replied, momentarily lost for anything else to say.

'Well don't let it worry you.'

'I . . .' he hesitated, trying to form the words, hoping they would not sound stupid. 'I don't really know why I came, Mrs Blackmore. I've seen enough crank letters in my work – but . . .'

'But you knew mine wasn't a crank one. And please, call me Joan – and if I may I'll call you Cowboy, perhaps it would make you feel more relaxed, do you think?'

'Please do,' he smiled at her, grateful for her warmth. 'The fact is, I can't remember feeling this relaxed for ages. I felt it as soon as I walked into the room. But then you're not exactly . . .' his words trailed off and he felt embarrassed at what he had been about to say.

'You expected something out of Macbeth, did you?' she laughed. 'A toothless old hag, with long shaggy hair and a boiling cauldron? Don't let it worry you, a lot of people confuse us with witches. Everyone has read things about us, or seen films. And of course the Church has always tried to portray us as mad old hags. Never mind. As for feeling relaxed here, you should do. There are a lot of people in this room right now who care for you very, very much and want to look over you. Some of them you knew when you were a lot younger and they too lived on this earthly plane. Some you have never met, but they know you and watch over you.' She spoke so matter-of-factly that it didn't occur to him to scoff or question her. 'They are your spirit guides. I also feel the presence of your father. The message I sent you came from them, not from me. I am just their instrument. Like a telephone. They talk, if you like, to you through me. I don't even understand the message. It's not necessary for me to understand.

It is only important that you understand the message – at least accept it and listen to it. It is a gift to you.'

'Well, I *think* I understand it. I'm not too sure – which is one of the reasons I came here to see you.'

She sat back in the chair and closed her eyes. Within a few moments she began to breathe deeply, inhaling and exhaling through her nose. Her head fell forward on to her chest and she remained in that position for some time, then sat back, holding her head up high. He watched as she appeared to be having a conversation with some unseen person. Her lips moved, forming words, but her voice was so low he could not catch them. Occasionally she nodded her head in confirmation. She sat like that for several moments then opened her eyes once more.

'You seem to think that the message is a bit garbled. That sometimes happens as communication with the spirit world is not easy – for us or for them. But if I understand it correctly you are mixing up the winged dagger I wrote to you about, with a pigeon. The pigeon means you no harm, and will in fact, at the right time, help you. You have nothing at all to fear from the pigeon, or what it represents. In fact I have the strangest feeling of family connection with this pigeon. A brotherly kind of connection. That is not to say your actual fraternal brother, but yes, yes, I definitely feel that you and this pigeon are related in some way. It's not very clear, but then that's the way it happens sometimes. The winged dagger is a sign of danger for you. You must be very, very careful of this sign when you see it. I feel – but I'm not certain here – that it represents a person. Does that make it any clearer to you?'

'The opposite in fact,' he replied, worry lines appearing on his forehead. 'I know the pigeon *is* a person. A very dangerous person. But the winged dagger bit . . .' He shook his head. 'Means nothing to me I'm afraid.'

'Well remember it, because when the time is right you will understand the message.' They were both silent while Cowboy tried to make sense of the message. She watched him for a few moments, then spoke again. 'This is not the first time you have received messages from the spirit world, is it? You have received others in the past?'

'I'm not too sure what you mean by "spirit world" – but yes, I have received . . . thoughts? . . . warnings? . . . I don't know what to call them. Once, when I was a boy, I got a flash of something that was going to happen. I tried to tell a friend – but he wouldn't listen. He died. I had another flash recently. It was about a pigeon.'

'The pigeon means you no harm.'

He took another drink of his coffee. His mind was a bewildering jumble of thoughts, of questions he wanted to ask, knowledge he wanted to obtain. But where to begin? Where to start?

'For a long time, young man, you have worn a suit of armour around your mind. It has built up over the years. It happens that way with most people. At birth our minds are fully open and alert. We experience many strange happenings as children which at the time we believe in. But adults tell us these things cannot be, that we are merely imagining them. And so, in time, we come to think of these events like the adults do, as the adults we ourselves are becoming. We block them out, refuse to accept them, and the armour starts to build up, slowly at first, but more and more as we grow older. The church, any church, any man-made faith – it doesn't matter which one – they all tell us about devils, God and the saints. Most people then choose not to believe their own personal experiences, and are willing to accept belief in things they have never experienced. We discount our own experiences, because some organization tells us they can't be true. You have many spirit guides, Cowboy. What the Christian religion calls "guardian angels". What's the difference? *Where's* the difference? But, according to the churches, guardian angels exist, but spirit guides do not!

'Your guides have looked after you well and have helped you as much as you have allowed them to. They can help you more, if you will let them. Remove the suit of armour. Open your mind to them and they will come through. You have one special guide – your main one I think – who comes over strongly. He is a Red Indian – a Native American. The North American Indian nations were all spiritualists, believing in one great spirit. They learnt a lot while in the body – living in this world, that is – and many of them are now guides to us who still live in the body. Your guide's name is Blue Water now. It is the name he has chosen to be known by. Since the moment of your conception he has been watching over you, guiding you, helping you as best he can. Through him, and his guidance, you became interested in his people as they lived in the Americas. Although your nickname is Cowboy, it is in fact the Indians you are most interested in.'

To Cowboy, as he sat watching her while she spoke, it all made perfect sense. It was as if he had been searching for something all his life – a belief of some sort, something to show him, to prove to him, that life did in fact exist after death. Now, listening as she spoke he knew he had found it. Something clicked in his mind and the doubts, queries, and answers were all falling into place.

'Blue Water tells me that it was when you first read of him, about his time in the body, that your interest in the

Indian nations began. He was not always a man of peace, as he is now. But when he lived, it was a different time, a different world he lived in from the one we live in now. He was a great war chief. He slew many enemies of his people and counted many coups.' Cowboy knew that the number of coups an Indian counted was a far greater proof of his bravery than the number of enemies he killed. Counting coup consisted of riding towards the enemy, charging right through them, and touching as many of them as possible with the coup stick. 'He tells me that you have many artefacts in your home concerning the Indians, along with a collection of books, many of which contain photographs or drawings of some of the famous chiefs. But you have only one thing of him – his dying words. There are no photos or drawings of him – only the legend of his life.'

It was true, all so true, Cowboy thought. While still at school he had made a frame for some words he found in a book.

LET ME GO MY FRIENDS
YOU HAVE GOT ME HURT ENOUGH

Killed by his own people, Indian police on a reservation, his friends had tried to save his life, but he had whispered the words to them and died soon after in their arms. No known likeness existed of the war chief who had defeated General Custer at the Battle of the Little Big Horn. Chief Sitting Bull had been the politician who had united several warring tribes. His was the vision of one great Indian nation, made up of all the tribes. His 'medicine.' brought them together – but it was the war chief Ta-Sanke Witke, whom the bluecoats called Crazy Horse, who led them in the first – and last – united front against the advance of the white man. The frame Joan Blackmore spoke of, the dying words of Crazy Horse, was one of his proudest possessions and hung on the wall in his apartment, just above his desk.

'You know his name? The name he was known by when he lived in the body?' He nodded slowly. 'He has changed his name now and uses Blue Water to show his advancement since his passing. He is no longer a war chief, but a spirit of peace. He says that as you know the ways of his people you would also understand the changing of his name.'

Again Cowboy nodded. At birth an Indian child was given a name to be known by until manhood. After passing his test and becoming a man, he chose his own name; his child-name was never spoken again. In the course of their manhood test, one of those tests was communication with the great spirit. They would go off to a mountain-top and sit for hour after hour, day after day, not moving, staring at the sun by day, the moon and stars by night, waiting for their spiritual connection. It was from this experience that they chose their new name. Crazy Horse had once again changed his name from the greatest spiritual experience he had known, passing from this world to the next.

'Mrs Blackmore – Joan – I have so many things I want to ask you about . . . so much I want to question, to learn . . . I just don't know where to begin.'

'Start by opening your mind to the influences that are being directed at you from the etheric world. The spirits will help you, and when you have time, and want to come back here, then feel free to do so. You are more than welcome. Just phone – my number is on the letter I sent you – and we can arrange a time to suit us both. And remember the warning they sent you. Be wary of the winged dagger.'

Poossh – bang – silence – grunt. Poossh – bang – silence – grunt. Poossh – bang – silence – grunt. It was beginning to get on his nerves. Thomas McGuinness sat at a dirty kitchen table listening to the sounds of McQ's daily weight-lifting exercises. Normally it didn't bother him, but he had a lot on his mind at present and the grunting and groaning was slowly driving him mad.

'For fuck's sake McQ, will you put those fuckin' things down and give it a rest. I'm trying to think and you're getting on my nerves.'

The bare-chested man in jeans puffed out two lungfuls of air, lowered the weights to the ground and lifted himself menacingly to his feet. Picking up a towel that had not seen washing powder or water for weeks, he wiped it across his brow, his chest, and under his sweating armpits. He said nothing, his eyes fixed on McGuinness's throat as he moved across to the chair where his soiled T-shirt lay. In one violent movement he pulled it over his head. For the last few days, ever since the murders of Maura and her family hit the headlines, McGuinness had been in a bad mood. It unsettled McQueedy to see his friend that way and an unsettled McQueedy was as dangerous as unstable gelignite. They had come a long way together and Tommy had always looked after him. It wasn't right that he should be so worried and McQ wanted to end his misery.

'Stop worrying Tommy,' he said eventually. 'Just because they got Maura doesn't mean they'll get us. Come on. You're too smart to let that happen, eh?' Playfully he punched his friend on the shoulder. The other man was nearly thrown off his chair and winced at the pain.

'The problem is, McQ . . . who the fuck are "they"? Is it that bastard Flynn? Or the Free Staters? The SAS? I'm getting a feeling in my water that it's time we wound up this whole business. Take the money, piss off and retire somewhere.'

McQueedy turned a wooden kitchen chair round and sat facing McGuinness, his arms resting across the back of it. 'And go where?' he asked. The thought of leaving Ireland for some unknown land disorientated him. He felt comfortable in a country where he knew how to survive. Something told him that if they were safely out of Ireland Tommy might not need him any more.

'Any fucking where for Chrissake. We'll get Mullarkey to fly us to Belgium first, pick up the lolly, then just disappear. We could go to Libya for a while. Let things settle down a bit, then pick some place where we won't get kicked out of. We've got enough money to see us right for years. I made some good investments for our old age, so that's no problem. You know what they say . . . "He who fights and runs away lives to fight another day". We've done our bit. Now is the time to enjoy the proceeds.'

'What about the others?' McQueedy inquired, referring to the other members of the Popular Front, several of whom were staying in the same house as them.

'Fuck them, Jimmy. It's gotten to you and me time. Just you and me.'

McQueedy smiled. He liked to hear that. It had always been just the two of them, ever since that first day they met in the schoolyard. It had been Tommy's first day at school. A little runt who looked like he'd piss his pants if you said boo to him, he had stood in the school playground looking round him, searching. When he spotted McQueedy he knew that he was the one, the school bully, and most likely as thick as two short planks. The boy-McGuinness had walked up to the boy-McQueedy and handed him a Mars bar. Not a piece of one but a whole fucking bar. That had really impressed McQueedy. He looked at the skinny runt in front of him and something clicked between them.

He was clever, was Tommy. Even when he did McQueedy's homework for him he never gave him all the correct answers. That would have been suspicious from the word go. No, he had given him just the right amount, building it up slowly. From that time forward McQ had never questioned Tommy on anything he decided for both of them.

They sat in silence for a few moments, McGuinness wondering how they were going to get out of this alive, McQueedy thinking back over the years, confident his friend would come up with the right solution. 'Who else knows where we are, Jimmy?'

McQueedy thought for a few moments before answering. 'The lads here and yer man at the farm. That's it . . . no, wait. There's that snotty bird, the one who brings the parcels from Maura. Or did.'

'That's what I've been thinking too.' Tommy kept his eyes fixed on McQ's face, as if trying to transmit thought waves into his slow, vicious brain. 'Just a handful of us – and that bird. Not even Maura knew about this place – or the other one. Which I think was a fucking good idea, even if I say so myself, in view of what has happened. Maura was due to get another delivery to the farm in the last week or so. Donnelly hasn't been in contact, so maybe she never made it. Or maybe she did hand it over, and that little slut kept it, seeing Maura is no longer with us to tell us about it. Maybe she's done a runner with it. Maybe

Donnelly's done a runner. Maybe the parcel's still with him and he's just keeping stum about it. Tell you what Jimmy. Take a couple of the lads with you and go pay Donnelly a visit. Find out if Maura brought anything. Then find that bird and get rid of her. She's the only weak link in the chain. Bring Donnelly back here with you. That way everybody who knows about this place is here where we can keep an eye on them. Once we get that lot sorted out you and I will decide on the best way to disappear up our own arseholes.'

'Okay Tommy, we'll go today. Eh . . . about the bird. Want me to bring her back here? Entertainment for the troops so to speak?' A sly smile crossed his face as he spoke, and a fleck of foam bubbled up at the corner of his thin lips.

'Nah. Pick her up, have yer fun with her in Dublin, then waste her and get back here. We got enough on our plate without a tart in the back room to distract everyone. Just give her one for me, OK?'

He leaned across the table and slapped the other man on his rock-hard shoulder, smiling a smile that looked more like a rat baring its teeth. Maybe it was time that he and McQ split up for good. The kind of lifestyle he had in mind for himself in the future had no real place for a sadistic bastard like McQueedy. Being together might lead to complications in the future, complications that McGuinness did not need. McQ tended to stick out in the sort of places McGuinness intended to head for. But for the moment he'd make sure that everything remained nice and sweet.

'Sure, Tommy,' McQueedy replied rising from the chair. 'I'll give her one of your specials, eh? Right up her arsehole and blow her fuckin' brains out with my cock.'

He burst out laughing at his own humour, showing a mouthful of jagged teeth.

'Yeah, you do that Jimmy, you do that.' McQueedy was so preoccupied with the pleasures he had coming that he did not notice that his friend did not join in the laughter.

Ireland, and its capital city Dublin in particular, has a reputation for its hospitality and friendliness. Someone once said that the city had been sprinkled with magical 'come-back-quick' dust, and in its hundreds of pubs you were only a stranger for as long as you elected to be.

Doolan's bar, on the quayside of the river Liffey, was no such place. Strangers who dropped in by chance left more quickly than they arrived. Nothing about Doolan's made anybody feel welcome.

The bar, set off to the right as you entered by the main door, was a functional piece of wood, nothing more. The bar top, chipped and stained with numerous spillage rings and cigarette burns, received a periodic wipe from a damp cloth whenever it crossed the mind of the barman to do so. The few scattered tables and chairs were in the same neglected condition. The floor, bare wooden planks, was polished from years of wear, not floor wax.

Doolan's was not the only pub of its kind in the city. There were others with a similar atmosphere of which it was said – and not totally in jest – even the Salvation Army ignored on their collection tours. Doolan's and the others were the meeting places of dedicated men of violence. Men whose hatred was directed towards not only the British Crown, but the government of the Irish Republic also. Drinking hours were seldom if ever adhered to, and should this be brought to the notice of the local gardai, it was ignored. Only one law was enforced in these drinking houses, and that only by a wafer-thin, unspoken agreement of mutual interest among all concerned. No weapons were to be brought into the pubs. While fights in such places were ignored by the uniformed gardai, shots would guarantee the arrival of members of the CIB en masse. The CIB did pay occasional visits, but they were few and far between.

The only group of outsiders treated with any form of respect were members of Irish Military Intelligence, under the command of Commandant James O'Riley. This respect was given out of fear. Any disrespect shown – a fairly frequent occurrence in the initial days of his taking command – resulted in the enforcement of the Special Powers Act. This enabled O'Riley to take into custody every person found on the establishment and to hold them, without recourse to a solicitor, for up to seven days. Every single customer of these drinking houses had at some stage been an overnight guest of the Gardai and thought nothing of it. Being an overnight guest of the Military was something entirely different altogether. Those few who had been held – and always for the full seven days – were loath to repeat the experience.

So it was that on the evening in question, when the solid oak swing doors to Doolan's crashed open to admit O'Riley, accompanied by two others, all conversation in the bar came to a halt. One customer, sitting alone at a table by the side entrance, did attempt to leave. Just as he reached the side door it swung inwards, smacking him full in the face and knocking him to the ground. The two men who entered by the side door picked him up by the armpits and slung him back into his chair. The man said nothing as he sat slumped at the table nursing his bruised face. The unsmiling O'Riley, who had witnessed the episode without speaking, now turned his attention to the burly, unwashed and unshaven barman, Rowan Doolan, grandson of the original owner, and current licensee.

'What the fuck do you want O'Riley?' The hatred in the man's voice was evident. On more than one occasion he had been a 'visitor' to the barracks. A young man sitting with a friend at the far end of the bar sniggered into his half-empty glass.

'Just be thankful it's not yourself I'm after, Rowan my boy.' O'Riley kept his eyes on the barman's face as he answered, but then turned his attention to the two men sitting at the bar. One of them he knew, but the sniggerer was a new face. A youthful face. A ghastly smile lit his face like a searchlight. O'Riley enjoyed the power he had to frighten these people who were frightened of virtually no one else. More than anything he liked to show them the contempt in which he held them. They might be cold-blooded murderers and sadistic torturers, but none of them would ever dare to touch a hair on his head, at least not in front of witnesses.

The men who had accompanied O'Riley into the bar didn't utter a word. They stood, two by two, stone-faced at the two doors, blocking any exit or entrance while O'Riley prowled along the bar to the two drinkers. The remaining customers sat where they were, silently watching and waiting for the outcome they knew was inevitable. The man with the bruised face paid special attention to all of it, watching all the moves O'Riley made. This was the first time he'd met or seen him in the flesh but he'd heard a lot about him. As O'Riley approached the two, the older man moved slowly away from the bar, leaving his youthful companion to face O'Riley alone.

'Well well well, and what have we got here then?' he

asked. 'A new "Top Gun" in town, eh?' His voice was cold as ice, his eyes unblinking, almost dead in their sockets. 'Tell you what, sonny. Why don't you turn out your pockets, nice and slow, and place the contents on the bar.'

He stopped within one foot of the young man. An old bullet wound in his thigh had taught him never to leave too much distance between himself and an adversary. At least two feet was required by a gunman to draw and fire a weapon. Not that he thought for a moment that the man was armed. Young he might be, ignorant of whom he was facing he certainly was, but he would have known better than to bring a gun into Doolan's. But old habits die hard and had kept O'Riley alive to date.

'Gotta fuckin' search warrant, copper?' The accent was from north of the border.

'A visitor to our fair parts, are we then? Well it's obvious, young man, that you and I haven't met before, because if we had, you'd remember. *I* might forget, but you wouldn't. So let me correct you on one, very important, point. I am not, as you surmised, a copper. But if I were . . . I'd still be offended by the tone of your voice. Am I making myself clear to you?'

Too late the young man noticed that everyone else in the bar had frozen, and that all eyes were on him. They all stood or sat where they were, silent and unmoving as statues. He felt a shiver run down his spine. He was beginning to regret his act of bravado in front of the others, older and wiser men as he now knew them to be. Beads of cold, unwelcome perspiration broke out of every pore on his body. He wiped the sweating palms of his hands on his grubby blue jeans and nodded his head.

'Good. So you're getting all this. I'll continue. Now coppers – as you call them – *would* need a search warrant. A nice, crisp piece of paper with lots of pretty writing on it.' The man was staring straight ahead of him and shivering like a dog that knew it was about to be beaten. 'Now this nice piece of paper,' O'Riley continued without pause, 'would also have a signature on it. One belonging to some big fat lazy judge. These . . . coppers . . . would show the paper to our host for the evening, Fishey Doolan there, and that would be that. No objections.'

Lowering his voice slightly, O'Riley continued in a conspiratorial stage whisper. 'Oh by the way, I wouldn't let Doolan there hear you call him Fishey. It refers not only to his bug eyes, but also to the fact that his mother – God rest her soul – never taught him any personal hygiene, which is why he smells like a fish gone off. For many years Old Fishey thought that hygiene referred to some tart spaced out on drugs,' he kept his face close to the young man's and shouted at the barman, '*Didn't ya Fishey?*' The young man jumped three inches in the air.

O'Riley slowly turned his head to stare at the barman, who stared back, rays of hatred flowing from his eyes. He didn't utter a word, merely clenched his fists more tightly as they rested on the bar top. One day, he promised himself for the umpteenth time, one day! O'Riley ignored the glaring eyes and turned back to the young man. Reaching out he grasped a handful of greasy hair. The other man flinched with the pain but did not try to struggle free.

'Now *I*, my good man, am a lazy bastard. Too much trouble to bother other lazy bastards – such as judges – for bits of paper.' Twisting with his hand he turned the other's head so that they were almost touching noses. 'Furthermore,' he continued, 'I don't *need* such bits of paper. Do I, Fishey?' There was no reply, and none had been expected. 'No my good man. I come in here any time I like, an-ee time. Know why? Well I'll tell you. I'm the rat catcher. Whenever I'm looking for rats I walk into places like this, poking here, poking there, I poke *everyfuckingwhere*. 'Cause I hate rats, hate them. I find them and I stomp all over them. I kick ass until the shit spurts out. You wouldn't like that to happen to you, Sonny, would you? Nah. I didn't think you would. You're new in town, don't know the rules yet, so I'll just leave you my calling card. Any time you think of something that might interest me, give me a call. You won't forget, because you'll have my card on you at all times.'

Averting his own body he smashed the young face down on to the bar top. Everyone present heard the crunch as the man's nose was crushed. Blood exploded from his face across the counter then poured down the front of his clothing as O'Riley pulled his head back. O'Riley once more twisted the head so that the smashed face was facing away from him this time, avoiding the blood. He leaned forward and spoke quietly into the other man's ear.

'My name, pigswill, is O'Riley – but you can call me sir. If I ever walk into a bar again and find you there, you keep your fuckin' mouth shut tighter than a duck's arse in a storm, unless I choose to speak to you. Get it?'

Tears mingled with the blood that flowed down the young man's face as his body shuddered with sobs. He had never been considered handsome, even by a long stretch of the imagination, but now he was marked for life. Coughing and spluttering he spat out several broken teeth, conscious that others were loose.

'Yes,' he managed to whisper between sobbing.

'Yes *what*, shit-face?'

'Yes sir,' he spluttered.

'See? Now we're on first name terms.' Twisting once more O'Riley pushed none too gently, knocking the man off the barstool and on to the floor. He lay there, knees drawn up in the foetal position protecting his groin, expecting to be kicked, his hands covering his broken face. But O'Riley ignored him and turned to face the other customers. 'Anybody else interested in seeing a search warrant?'

His eyes traversed the grubby room like lasers, boring into each man in turn. None dared to stare him out, eyes falling downward, pair by pair, until at last he faced Doolan. Doolan dared to stare back, his eyes almost glowing red with hatred as he held the soldier's gaze. O'Riley knew he would never survive a one-to-one with Doolan. Even if he shot him – which he would – he knew he'd have to keep shooting until Doolan went down for good. There would be no half measures when the day finally came.

'Good. I'll just borrow your office for a few moments Fishey, if you don't mind. I wish to have a few words with the gentleman who was so eager to leave on our arrival.' Without waiting for any kind of a reply he turned has back on the bar and led the way to the outside toilet at the back of the building.

A stranger, had he dared to remain, would never have needed to ask where the toilets were. All he had to do was follow his nose. Years of use and abuse had left a permanent stench that no amount of cleaning fluid could ever erase. The only addition ever made to the original outhouse was the mis-named stainless steel urinal trough. This was now encrusted with brown acid stains, the drainage hole caked over with cigarette ends and vomit. The doors to the two toilet cubicles hung from their hinges, making it impossible to close either for any degree of privacy. But just to make sure O'Riley kicked both doors to check for occupants. There were none. The two large silent men who had stood guard by the side exit of the pub had each grabbed an arm of the loner sitting at the table and frog-marched him to the toilet.

'Jamie. Eddie. Make sure we're not disturbed in any way, will you please?' Jamie, the larger of the two, nodded his head and he and his companion retreated out of earshot leaving their commandant alone with the other man.

O'Riley walked to the far wall, turned and leaned against it, staring at the other. Of medium build, dark haired and unshaven, the man stared back at the soldier. Digging out a packet of cigarettes O'Riley offered one. The man shrugged his shoulders, took a few paces forward and accepted it. O'Riley lit both cigarettes but remained silent. He could read uncertainty in the other man's eyes, but no fear. He understood this. The other man was unsure of what O'Riley knew.

'Somehow or other I think the smell out here is fresher than that in the bar, wouldn't you say?' It was O'Riley who broke the silence. Once again the other man shrugged his shoulders but remained silent while the eyeball-to-eyeball contest continued. 'I'm going to give you a choice,' O'Riley continued, blowing gently on the end of his cigarette making it glow fiercely.

'We'll stay here for thirty minutes and you need not say a word. After that I'll leave – and in twenty-four hours you'll be a dead man. Or, we'll talk, after which I'll have Jamie beat the shit out of you, and you'll survive another day. I would also like to point out that the shit-kicking you get from Jamie will be nothing compared to the treatment you'll get from your – what should I call them?

. . . associates? – before they put a bullet in the back of your head. You'll be praying for that bullet by the time it comes. I hear they own shares in Black and Decker they use their drills so often. Bit messy if you ask me, but there you have it. So what's it to be, sergeant? Talk, or die?'

'I don't know what the hell you're talking about,' the younger man replied, his voice giving no hint of the fear he felt. The accent was Irish – a little too pronounced O'Riley thought. Now it was O'Riley's turn to shrug his shoulders. He had a job to do. The methods he used didn't always please him, but the job had to be done, would be done, if not by him, then by somebody else. They continued to stare at each other in silence for several minutes. Finishing his cigarette O'Riley dropped it on the floor and it sizzled in the urine. He felt the sharp twinge in his gut from the ulcer and knew he shouldn't be smoking – but some things were harder to give up than others.

'Have it your way. I can see I'm wasting both our time hanging round here. You won't crack. I'll tell London not to expect you back home.' O'Riley started for the exit, stopping by the other man's shoulder. 'Anybody else you'd like me to give a message to? No? Well . . . so long then.' He started to leave once more and was almost by the door when the other spoke, almost with a sigh of relief.

'All right O'Riley. They warned me about you. What do you want to know?'

O'Riley turned back and once more took his position at the wall, facing the British undercover agent. 'Warned you about me did they?' he asked. 'What'd they say then?'

'That you were a right hard, ruthless bastard.'

O'Riley nodded agreement and smiled at this remark. 'I try my best, son, I try my best.' Taking the cigarette packet from his pocket once more he passed it to the other, offering him a light. He watched him greedily suck the nicotine-filled smoke deep into his lungs, then slowly exhale it.

'How did you know I'd be here?' he asked.

'I didn't,' O'Riley replied. 'I wasn't even looking for you.'

'So why blow me? We're both after the same thing O'Riley. After the same people.'

'I didn't blow you, dickhead. You gave yourself away. I'm saving your life. You should have just sat still and drunk your ale when I came in – then you wouldn't be in here now. If I hadn't brought you out here for a chat after your stupid action in the bar then you would have been dead before you got home to bed.

'You're new, so I'll tell you how I operate. I let some of your people slip in now and again. I don't mind, I really don't. You have your job to do and I have mine, and when and where possible I leave your people to get on with theirs while I get on with mine. But every so often I get pushed for one reason or the other, and when my own sources don't – or can't – come up with the goodies, then I have no qualms about getting what I want, how I want. Bob Geldof was asked by a rap band – when he was setting up Live Aid – why no rap band was picked to go on, yet he took the out-of-date Boomtown Rats on. His reply was "It's my ball and I'm the captain." Same applies here. You're on my patch. We might be on the same side, but I'm the captain.

'I'm truly sorry that you are about to get hurt – but we both know it's necessary if you're to get a chance at picking up your pension at forty. Right? So. Down to business. You know our dearly beloved Maura O'Grady got her brains spread all over her bedroom wall, along with hubby and beloved son. What I'm trying to find out is why, and by whom? Know anything about it? Like, can we look forward with pleasure to more of the same for other members of the Popular Front? Like is somebody trying to put in a takeover bid for control? Maybe Mr Flynn has his boogiemen in the Republic doing more than frightening the shit out of them? None of your friends are over on a flying visit are they?'

The other man shook his head. 'Nah, it wasn't any of ours. I'd have been warned – most likely pulled out in the knowledge that you'd go looking for us. I would not say that London has any regrets about the departed Maura – but they didn't sanction it. However, if you do find out who did it let us know. They'll probably be entitled to an OBE for their good work.

'All I know is that the shit has hit the fan where the Front is concerned. *They* are convinced – or at least those I spoke to – that an SAS team are here. Everybody's going to ground. Disappearing. Taking holidays. Nobody knows for sure why Maura was taken out, and McGuinness and his chief whip haven't been seen for weeks. Panic is setting in among the wolves. I haven't heard anything about an internal dispute. Maura was McGuinness's, one hundred per cent, so it wasn't him. And who'd want to mess with McQueedy – which is what you'd get if you went after McGuinness! Flynn's men are around all right – in fact you just beat the shit out of one of them down here on a bit of R&R. Not the usual kind of Flynn man I must admit. Maybe he'll learn, if he survives. So, Commandant, I'm in the same boat as you, knowing nothing, trying to find out everything. Or at least I was, until you turned up.'

'Bad timing, eh? Well I'm sorry about that – but like I said, you brought it on yourself.'

O'Riley digested the information with no change of facial expression. The agent was confirming what he suspected – that the British were not involved – but apart from that, what else was new? Nothing. Another brick wall. He was hearing exactly the same thing from agents throughout the country. Nothing. Big fat zero. Popular Front guys going to ground, nobody knew of any internal dispute, and Flynn had his men under control. 'Where's that last place you've heard McGuinness to be?' he asked.

'In the South somewhere. Spotted in a few places – here in Dublin about three weeks ago. I know a few places he visits – but I also know he has a couple of places he keeps well under wraps for his own protection. I've no idea where they are, and that's the honest truth, O'Riley.'

'I believe you, son. *Jamie*?' One of the silent men by the toilet exit came back in. 'I meant what I said earlier, son. Is there anybody you want me to get in touch with?'

The man shook his head. 'Nah. The wife's in Germany. She thinks I'm in Belize for six months. Just let London know I'm out of condition for a while. They'll do the rest. Somebody'll find out where I'm taken from here – the Mather hospital I suppose. I just don't want to have to drop out completely at this stage if I can avoid it. I'm getting in deeper.'

'Fine by me. I'll make sure London gets the info and I'll have a couple of my people keep an eye on you. If they hear any rumour about you being suspect I'll get you out.' He offered his hand to the agent. 'No hard feelings, eh?'

'Piss off O'Riley,' the other replied, ignoring the offered hand. 'I appreciate what you're going to do, but I'm fucked if I have to like it. Let's just do it.'

O'Riley let his hand drop. He took no offence at the rebuke. He raised his hand to the other's shoulder and gave it a squeeze, then slowly walked over to Jamie.

'Hurt him, Jamie, but make it look worse than it is, OK?'

Jamie looked at his boss and nodded. For just a brief moment O'Riley saw the resentment in Jamie's eyes at the order. But Jamie was one of the best. He could literally beat the shit out of a man – and had on several occasions, but he could also make it look like he had beaten the shit out of somebody, yet most of it would be superficial. There would be no internal injuries, no bones would be broken. He knew how to dislocate a joint so that to others it looked terrible, yet to put everything back in place would only take a hard, well-placed smack. There would be a lot of blood and snot – but no long-lasting after effects . . . when he was ordered to do it that way.

While O'Riley stood by the door to the toilets, his back to what was going on out of respect to the British agent, the air was rent with screams of pain. Every few seconds there was a ringing silence, followed by more screams. He finished yet another cigarette, then snapped his fingers. Jamie immediately ceased the beating, and was happy to do so. O'Riley took a backward glance at the bloodied heap on the floor. It looked good. All he could do now was hope it was good enough to keep the man alive.

As he marched back into the bar accompanied by Jamie and Eddie, his eyes staring straight ahead, nobody in the bar had moved, except for the young man with the broken nose. He had crawled across the floor under the watchful eyes of the other two soldiers by the main door, dragging himself up to sit at one of the tables. Doolan had thrown a damp and none too clean bar cloth to him, and this was now held to his nose in an attempt to stop the flow of blood. O'Riley could almost taste the hatred for him in the bar, and that pleased him. These men were vermin and he had no sympathy for them whatsoever. The man in the toilet would receive help after he had left. Yet, had he left him unharmed in the toilets, these same men would have tortured him with a power drill and bore – and would have laughed while they did it.

Slowly and deliberately he moved to the main exit, the other two close behind him. The others held the door open for their commandant and comrades, but O'Riley ushered the four men out in front of him, then turned back to face the sullen, silent men in the bar.

'Don't yez be drinkin' and drivin' now lads,' he forced his mouth into a smile and the effect was like a death mask. 'You know it makes sense, eh?' Again he turned to go, then, doing his Columbo impersonation, put his hand to his head and turned once more.

'Just one small item, Fishey. There's a pile of shite on the floor in the toilets. Get it cleaned up willya. Don't want the Health Inspectors paying you a visit now do we? You all enjoy the rest of your evening lads.' With that he was gone. There were other, similar, establishments to visit in the city. The night was still young. Whistling the tune to the Republican song 'Kevin Barry' he led the way to the unmarked car parked round the corner.

In other cities and towns throughout the Republic members of Irish Military Intelligence, both undercover agents and 'suits' like O'Riley, were making similar kinds of visits, all with the same aim. Find out what the hell was going on inside the Popular Front, and locate its leader, Thomas McGuinness.

Chapter Six

MONICA SAUNDERS WAS A VERY FRIGHTENED young woman. Ever since she had told Maura that she wanted out she had been scared every minute of every day. She had been scared to tell Maura of her decision and was even more scared when Maura reminded her of the 'golden rule'. It didn't matter which group you belonged to, they all had the same rule. Once in – never out. In for life. Ever since she had had words with Maura, Monica had been looking over her shoulder, her heart missing a beat every time anybody looked at her or walked in the same direction. And now Maura was dead. Killed without mercy while in the sanctuary of her own home, along with her husband and son. Now they weren't even safe in their beds. Monica's terror was overwhelming. If they could get to a woman as hard as Maura, a woman with two strong men in the house to help her, what chance did Monica stand on her own? There was nowhere she could go and no one she could turn to. She had no idea who her potential killers might be and no way of hiding from them. No door would keep them out, no disguise would fool them, she was a sitting target. All day long she had felt like screaming with pure terror at what fate lay in wait for her. The best she could do was to rent a room, a bolt-hole, and cower in it like a doomed rabbit. Three days previously she had seen a face in the street she vaguely recognized. She couldn't remember from where, but it was enough to set her running. She had moved quickly, taking several buses and two taxis before she was satisfied they were no longer following her. Arriving home safely she had not moved from the rented room since then, except to go to the bathroom. She dared not go back to her flat, she imagined they must already be there waiting for her.

At nineteen the fight had all seemed so glamorous, so exciting, to be a part of it all, helping to make Irish history. Along with her boyfriend, Frank, she had joined one of the active political groups at Dublin University. As Frank became more and more active, and loving him as she did, she followed his lead. When they transferred their allegiance to the Popular Front she was put to use as a courier. When she made those journeys to England, using a variety of disguises, she never questioned the contents of the packages she carried, preferring not to know, not really caring, just living for the thrill of the moment, her conscience easily appeased with simple rhetoric. She did not want to think about anything deeply because if she examined it too closely the fun might stop and her life would become as ordinary as everyone else's. But when Frank was killed, delivering a package which blew him up, she could no longer push the issue to the back of her mind. It was not a game any more and she realized that the work she was doing was bringing the same grief to other people as Frank's death had brought to her.

Forced to accept what she was involved in, she was also forced to look at the direct results of her deliveries. The Chelsea and Knightsbridge bombings. The King's Cross bombing. The hundreds of firebombs that went off throughout the country. She had been involved in them all in one way or another, but it was the car bomb at Notting Hill Gate that had sickened her most. The bomb had been intended for a retired British Army general who had at one time led his battalion in Northern Ireland. The device was fixed to be triggered by the movement of the car – which it did. Unfortunately it was not the general who was killed, but a group of children from a nearby nursery school out for a walk with their teachers. At the inquest a witness, living across the street from where the car was parked, told of seeing the children coming past in crocodile fashion, laughing and talking and play-acting while the teachers clucked around them. Two young boys, playfully punching each other, had bumped into the car and that had been enough to set the bomb off. One teacher and six of the children were killed. Some of them blown into so many pieces it was hard for the police to work out which limbs went with which bodies. All of the surviving children were injured, four of them seriously.

Watching the news coverage had turned Monica's life into a waking nightmare. If she closed her eyes she could still see the scenes as shown on every TV newscast. The quiet residential tree-lined street. The normality of it all. Then the crater where the car had been. A piece of twisted metal lying in the front garden of one of the houses. The ambulances, crew members carrying blanket-covered bodies on stretchers, with others holding aloft drip-feed bottles. Then there were the small bundles lying with sheets thrown over them. The news editors, all of them, had thought it too upsetting to show the state the bodies were in, especially after the great uproar from the King's Cross incident. On that occasion they had shown all the gory details, and all stations had received numerous telephone calls accusing them of voyeurism, of using real tragedy for commercial gain. The complainants had actually got it wrong – the attack had been so ferocious, so devastating, that each editor had independently taken the decision to try to shock the terrorists with their results.

Monica *had* been shocked by what she had seen. One scene in particular was indelibly imprinted on her mind. It was a shot of a body, burnt almost completely out of recognition as being human. It looked like it should have been taken from an oven at Belsen-Bergen. These charred remains, the newscaster informed the repulsed viewing public, had been a pregnant woman. Monica had been sick for a week but, having been assured that that particular kind of bomb would never ever be used again and that warnings would be given, she had made several more trips to the UK on behalf of the Popular Front. However, the Notting Hill Gate bomb ended it for her. She could not stomach any more guilt. She didn't need to see the state the small bodies were in to know what they looked like. Blackened and twisted, limbs missing – she could see it all. All she had to do was close her eyes and remember.

Ever since her childhood on a farm in County Sligo she could recall the stories that were told of 'the Struggle', stories of the men who had made Irish history, from Wolfe Tone to the present day. Young men like Dan Breen and Sean Tracy, the 'Butch Cassidy and the Sundance Kid' of the old IRA. If pop posters had been in vogue at the time, every young girl in the South would have had their pictures hanging on their bedroom walls. Young, dashing, brave, good looking, Breen and Tracy were gunmen heroes.

Then there were men like Michael Collins, military leader of the Irish Republican Army, a council member of the political wing, Sinn Fein, and also an executive member of the ultra-secret, almost masonic, Irish Republican Brotherhood. Collins had his own twelve apostles, men who carried out his orders unquestioningly, the same twelve who assassinated fourteen Irish-born British Intelligence Agents operating in Dublin one Sunday morning. This act was to lead to the infamous Black and Tan indiscriminate machinegunning of the crowd at Croke Park that same Sunday afternoon, killing twelve, while the All Ireland Gaelic Football Finals were being played. Sunday, 21 November 1920, was to go down in Irish history as the first Bloody Sunday. Michael Collins was led up the garden path by the political leader, Eamon De Valera, into signing the treaty with the British forces. Collins commented, while signing, 'Will anyone be satisfied at the bargin? Will anyone? I tell you this – early this morning I signed my own death warrant.' Six months later, as commander-in-chief of the Irish Free State forces, now in a civil war with their anti-treaty ex-comrades in arms, he died in an ambush at Béalnabláth, in his home county of Cork – an ambush that was never fully explained. In all the gunfire there was only one fatality – Michael Collins. So cherished was the man that, upon hearing of his death, a thousand IRA prisoners of the Free State forces held in Limerick Jail, fell to their knees to pray for the departed soul of their former leader. Even his enemies loved him.

They talked also of that other legendary gunman, Cathal Brugha, anti-British and anti-treaty. Surrounded in a Dublin hotel by Free State forces, whose commander tearfully pleaded with his friend and ex-comrade to surrender, Brugha emerged from the hotel with two handguns blazing to die in a hail of bullets in front of hundreds of weeping Dublin women who dipped their handkerchiefs in his blood, cleaning it from the streets. These were men who had fought the British, who had evaded the British and who could not be killed by the British. Irishmen, who were destined to die at the hands of other Irishmen. They were all men around whom legends were built, fighters to the end, but honourable men. These were the men the young Monica heard of in her childhood bedside stories. Her paternal grandfather had been 'one of the boys', on the run after the Civil War. The IRA were heroes to everybody in the community she lived in. Everybody, without exception, believed in the continued struggle for a totally independent united Ireland. She remembered the strangers who came, late at night, in the late sixties and early seventies. Never staying more than four days they would leave late at night to recross the border into Ulster. They came to rest from the constant state of alertness they lived under in the North, their guns never far from their hands. They were the heroes of her own generation. One day songs would be sung about them and she would be able to tell her grandchildren that she had met and known these men.

But she soon discovered that the Popular Front was not an organization that produced heroes for young girls to dream of. It was not hard targets – army patrols, barracks, police stations – they attacked. For them it was the soft option. The car bomb, restaurants, parcel bombs – anything they could attack without physical danger to themselves. It was only when their own devices blew up in their faces that they suffered any losses. There were no more heroes – only killers.

The realization of what she was involved in had destroyed everything she believed about herself and about her life. She had cried and cried and cried without knowing who she was crying for. Was it for the mangled, murdered children and their families – or for herself? To begin with it might have been for the children, but soon all she could think about was herself and what would happen to her.

She had to get out, had to stop her own involvement in the carnage of the Popular Front. Even before her change of heart she had begun to doubt the sincerity, the dedication, of McGuinness, who talked more of money than anything else, and everything about McQueedy terrified her. Whenever she was in McQ's presence she could feel the hairs on her arms and on the back of her neck rise, knowing that his greedy eyes were undressing her, and that he was imagining his hands on her body, not in any form of a caress but inflicting pain. She had heard so many stories about what he did to women. He knew the effect he had on her and enjoyed her fear, his leering smile promising 'One day, little girl, one day.'

She had tried to talk over her troubles with Maura, tried to explain to her, woman to woman, why she had to get out. Surely Maura, a mother herself, would understand the horror of killing babies. Surely she could understand the effect of losing the man you love. But Maura had just reminded her that she was in for life – and told her not to forget it. That had been three weeks ago. Now Maura was dead and Monica was even more alone.

The small room that had been her prison for the past three days contained a single wooden bed, a wardrobe, a small chest of drawers and a worn and faded carpet that did not entirely cover the linoleum floor. The large bay window looked out on to the front garden, enabling her to see the street and the passing traffic. It also enabled her to see anybody approaching the main door. Those few seconds' warning of approaching danger were her only defence, but it meant that she had to stay by the window all the time, ever alert, and that wasn't possible. Sometimes she would doze off for a few seconds or minutes, suddenly jerking awake, her stomach lurching with fear at who might have crept into the house while her eyes were closed.

Now she was thinking of food. She hadn't eaten in three days and the more she tried to ignore her hunger the more it made itself known by the rumblings in her stomach. She felt faint and sick and her head felt as if it were splitting. For the past hour she had been thinking of fish and chips. She could not get the image out of her mind. She could almost smell it, taste it. Sumptuous pieces of fresh cod, dipped in batter, and deep fried to a golden, crispy, brown; freshly cut chips – not the matchsticks you got in the burger bars but real chips, cut from real potatoes. The chips browning in the same fat as the cod, until they too were golden brown on the outside and fluffy on the inside. She thought of cod's roe with chips. To hell with it, she decided, she'd have both. Cod and cod's roe – and a double portion of chips. Her mouth watered at the thought and the bile rose from her stomach, burning at her chest and throat. And chocolate bars, Mars bars and Wispas, several of each, and some biscuits, and toffees. And something to drink. Some milk, or maybe a couple of bottles of Taylor Keith lemonade. If she didn't do something about it she was going to starve to death. The pains of hunger had finally become stronger than her fear of the world outside.

She had a choice of direction if she left the house. She could go towards the city centre to Doyle's Corner, where there was a chipper, a burger bar and a restaurant all within a block of each other, or she could go in the opposite direction, towards Cabra, and the chipper by the shopping mall. That was probably the best bet. If she went that way she could go to the late night minimarket and get in some supplies, so that she wouldn't have to go out again for a week or so. Some tinned foods like baked beans, and biscuits, they would last, and tea and sugar, things to keep her strength up as she waited.

She left it until 10 p.m., and in the last hour the weather grew colder. She buttoned her long overcoat right up to the chin, wrapping her old university scarf round her neck, pulling it over her mouth, partly to keep her warm, partly to hide behind. She stood by the window in the dark room, straining to see as far as possible in both directions. She saw nothing suspicious, nothing out of the ordinary. There was nothing to be afraid of, she told herself. They couldn't know where she was. All she had to do was open the front door, walk to the gate, open it and turn left. Just a few hundred yards to the junction and down Annamoe Terrace on to the Cabra road. The chipper was on the opposite side of the road. It was simple. What the hell had she got to be scared of? Nothing, that's what. Nothing. She took a number of deep breaths, pulling oxygen into her lungs and willing her body to stop trembling. Psyched up and determined now, she opened the door to her room, locked it behind her and went down the stairs to the front door. Despite the fact that it was several years since she had been to church she automatically made the sign of the cross, mumbling the words half out loud. 'In the name of the Father, and of the Son and of the Holy Ghost, Amen.' Taking a deep breath she opened the door and stepped out into the cold night.

Having spent the last seventy-two hours indoors the shock of the cold, moist night air took her breath away. Burying her face deeper into the woollen scarf she started up the Phibsborough road. Cars and buses passed her in both directions, but she ignored them. There was nothing out of the ordinary to be seen, and she began to feel foolish for having allowed her fears to make a prisoner of her for so long. She had, after all, no concrete evidence that anyone was after her, it was all in her imagination. She had whipped herself up into a frenzy of fear, and it was completely unfounded. All her concentration was now on getting something to eat. Did she have enough money with her, she worried. Yes, she assured herself, more than enough. Would the chipper still be open? Of course it would. They stay open until at least eleven, as did the minimarket. Didn't they? Just get down there, collect the food, do the shopping and hurry back to the room as quickly as possible.

She crossed the road near the traffic lights, looking up at the illuminated windows of the flats in the new development, where the old cattle market had once stood. They teased her with vignettes of the lives other people lived, normal, everyday people who went to work, came home again, ate, watched the telly, argued with their partners, shouted at the kids and went to bed to dream.

None of them shared the dreams she had. Of happy carefree children walking hand in hand, accompanied by their kindergarten teacher, then the horror of the first flash of the explosion followed seconds later by the noise of the blast, and everything in slow motion. Then, most horrible of all, the terrible silence that lasted for what seemed liked hours, before the screaming began. Tiny bodies torn apart, thrown into the air like a collection of rag dolls. For some, the lucky ones, there were no screams. They just lay silent and unmoving or were instantly blown apart. Other people would do their screaming for them, women opening front doors expecting the cheeky smile of their beloved children, only to face a policeman and policewoman, both with tears in their eyes. Husbands and fathers equally unable to comprehend it all. And the same question, over and over and over *Why*? Why her, why him, why us?

Those were Monica's dreams and she brought them on herself because she had hated having to live an ordinary life like all the people inside the flats. How arrogant youth is, to think that it deserves something better from life than everybody else, and how selfish in its pursuit of its thrills. But what a price to have to pay.

Turning down Annamoe Terrace at the traffic lights she was so deep in these thoughts she didn't even notice the car until it screeched to a halt beside her and she was grabbed from behind and thrown on to the rear seat – right into the arms of James Earl McQueedy. For a few seconds she thought it was another nightmare, but when he smiled at her and spoke and she smelt his breath on her face she knew it was for real. 'Howya been Monica? We've missed ya – but now we've got you all to ourselves. Eh lads?' The others joined in the laughter while Monica tried to struggle free of his grip to sit up. 'Hey, hey, hey. Take it easy. You're among friends, baby. *Boy*-friends, know what I mean? You're going to have such a good time, Monica. We're heading for a little party. You'll enjoy it, I promise. Bet you haven't had a fuck since that dickhead Frank blew himself up with his little parcel, eh? Well we're going to make up for that Monica. Aren't we lads?' More laughter greeted this remark. 'We're going to fuck you so hard, *you'll* think you've been blown apart by a bomb.' As he spoke through clenched teeth his grip on her arms tightened until she screamed with the pain, his fingers closing like a vice, cutting off the blood and crushing flesh and bone.

She thought she had known fear, sitting in her room,

watching the road from her window, but this was something wholly different and more hideous. Panic stricken she continued to try and struggle free, pushing and clawing to get away. She felt her elbow jab into his lap. He gave a shout of surprise and the blow she received on the side of her head brought stars to her eyes, taking her to the edge of unconsciousness for a few seconds.

'Okay you bitch, you want it the hard way, you'll get it the hard way.' Now he was angry as well as excited and he started to smack her about the face and head, all the time calling her names, each blow causing explosions of light in her brain. Donnelly, sitting in the front with the driver, turned to watch McQueedy softening her up for them, smiling at the expectation of what the night would bring.

'Stuck up little whore, aren't ya Monica? Too good for the likes of old McQ, eh?' His left hand held her hair in a twisted grip while his right continued to smack at her face. 'Oh yeah, your pussy is too good for the likes of me, isn't it, my pretty little girl? Well I got some news for you honey. Your little pussy is mine tonight, all mine. You ain't never been fucked until you've been fucked by little ol' me. Remember all those looks you used give me, looking at Jimmy like he was a piece of shit, just because he wanted to see what goodies you were hiding in your tight jeans? Well tonight's the night, baby. Tonight's the night Jimmy finds out what you've got to offer, and there ain't nothing you can do about it.'

She was limp now and sobbing, all the fight gone out of her, only the pain remaining. She felt his fingers at the belt of her jeans as he tugged it open. She couldn't make her arms move to try to stop him as his fingers roughly pulled at the zipper, dragging it open. Then his large calloused hand was inside, tearing at her cotton panties, searching for her opening. Finding it, he crudely and cruelly pushed a finger inside her vagina, his piggy eyes staring greedily down at her supine body illuminated in the passing street lights as it lay bruised and defenceless across his lap.

'What'd I tell you boys? She can't wait. Stupid bitch is soaking, soaking I tell you.' Using two fingers now he stabbed into her repeatedly making her whole body jerk and her head bang against the car door. 'Hmm, you like it honey, don't you? 'Course you do. I'll bet your tits are beggin' for a bit of action too, eh? Nipples all swollen, fit to burst, aren't they? Well let's have a looksee, shall we?' With his free hand he ripped the buttons from her coat, pushing her scarf out of the way. Forcing his fingers inside her blouse he tugged, ripping buttons and material and exposing her white bra. Pushing it up out of the way his fingers caught the tender flesh of her left breast, squeezing it like an orange to be turned into juice. He tugged at the nipple, pinching it tightly, pulling at it as though trying to rip it from her breast. Monica moaned in pain.

'Oh yeah, that's it. It's getting to ya, eh? Gettin' hotter little girlie, are we?' He took a breast in each hand and, lowering his head, his mouth captured the bruised nipple, drawing it inwards, gripping it with his sharp, broken teeth, chewing on it like a cigar butt.

Donnelly, wanting a piece of the action as well, leaned over the seat, his hand searching for the opening in the front of her jeans. Finding it he too pushed his fingers into her. Feeling the dampness he forced his hand in and out several times then withdrew it and placed it under the nose of the driver.

'Wanna smell me new girlfriend?' he asked, and burst out laughing.

'You stupid git,' the driver replied pushing his hand away, 'she's fuckin' pissed herself, you wanker.'

Bringing his finger to his own nose Donnelly sniffed at the urine coating. 'Ah who gives a shit anyway. Wet or dry we'll all get a good fuck tonight.'

Raising his head from her breast McQueedy snarled at the others. 'Keep your fuckin' eyes on the road, shithead. We don't want to be stopped by any gardai, do we? And keep the fuckin' speed down too. There's plenty on this little chicken for everyone . . . when I'm finished with her, that is.' With that his mouth returned to her bruised and bite-marked breasts and moved down over her heaving ribcage towards her hips tearing at her flesh like a starved dog. While one hand returned to her vagina the other one went under her buttocks, lifting them off the seat, the fingers roughly pulling them apart and ripping into her anus. It was at that point that Monica finally passed out and McQ continued to feast on her limp body.

Driving into the centre of the city, Cowboy's thoughts once more returned to the meeting he had had with Joan Blackmore. Did he really believe her? Really believe all this palaver about a spirit world and those who had died acting as spirit guides to the living, looking over them, protecting them, guiding them? But he knew what had happened with the milk bottle. He knew what had happened to him when he was a child. All of that he knew to be true. How did she know about the frame he had with the words of Crazy Horse? He had never spoken of it to anyone so far as he could recall. So how did she know? On the other hand, did believing in an all-knowing, all-seeing, all-wise benevolent god, with a heaven for the good guys and a hell for the baddies, make any more sense? In point of fact, he had to admitt to himself, he was more prepared to accept the idea of the spirit world than he was the idea of heaven and hell!

O'Connell Street loomed and put an end to his reflections. He parked the car close to what was still referred to by Dubliners as 'the Pillar'. Cowboy smiled, remembering the column that used to stand majestically on the site. It had been erected during the time the British ruled Ireland, and it was placed there in honour of Admiral Lord Nelson, a statue of whom stood on the top. Climbing the hundred-and-odd stone steps to the summit was a great tourist attraction, providing a panoramic view of the city. The area of O'Connell Street, in and around the Pillar, had been the traditional meeting place for young couples who lived on either side of the city. Now almost everybody had cars, but in those days most people travelled on the CIE buses, which even today still showed 'the Pillar' as a destination.

Admiral Lord Nelson 'disappeared' one night in 1966 with a mighty explosion, along with half of the column, leaving a large stump and thousands of pounds' worth of damage done to surrounding buildings and cars. It was something the 'old' IRA had been threatening for years, and finally did. The Dáil, embarrassed by the amputated stump, decided to finish the job once and for all and remove it totally. A military demolition team were sent in and, much to the delight of the Irish people – and Dubliners in particular – overdid it with the explosives, causing in excess of £30,000 worth of damage. One opposition TD couldn't resist commenting in the Dáil that it would have been cheaper had the government requested the IRA to complete the job. As well as being cheaper it would probably have been done more professionally.

Bits and pieces of the ruined column had been snapped up by locals and sold to gullible American tourists in sufficient quantity to rebuild the original ten times over, bringing in record amounts of foreign currency.

Cowboy set off for Madigans bar in North Earl Street. Going first to the lounge bar he descended the half dozen steps to the glass-fronted entrance and pushed open the door. It was 8.30 p.m. and the place was packed. Pushing his way into a corner at the bar he waited until he caught the eye of Declan, the head barman. Declan approached him, withdrawing a bottle of non-alcoholic beer and aiming the neck at Cowboy. Cowboy nodded and Declan uncapped the bottle bringing it and a glass with him.

'Evenin' Cowboy. The criminal classes keeping you off the beer are they?' He poured half the contents of the bottle into the glass and placed it on the bar top.

'Too bloody true, Declan. I could murder a right good pint of Guinness, but . . .'

'Doing the rounds are we?' Declan asked, knowing the other was going to be visiting as many pubs in the evening as he could. He would be taking a drink in most of them, but could not afford to get drunk. 'You're on the O'Grady one aren't you, Cowboy?'

'Got it in one. Anybody in who might be of interest to me?' Cowboy took a swallow of the cold beer.

'Well the funny thing is, Cowboy, it's not who's *in* tonight that might be of interest to you – it's who's *not* in. I'm down about six of my so-called regulars since the dearly beloved Maura went to the Happy Hunting Grounds, as you'd say. Seems like the rabbits got a sniff of the dog and have all gone to their little bolty holes.

Conspicuous by their absence, you might say. But if I hear anything I'll let you know.'

'What the fuck does a fellah have to do round here to get a fuckin' pint, eh? Gibber to the barman, or what?' Cowboy was squashed further into the corner by an irate customer who had been about to be served by Declan when he walked down the bar to speak with the detective.

Declan reached across the bar with one hand while sliding an illegal – but very effective – Garda truncheon from his trouser pocket with the other. Grasping the irate young man by the tie he pulled him halfway across the bar top.

'The first . . . fuckin' . . . thing a fellah has to do is wait his fuckin' turn. The second . . . fuckin' . . . thing a fellah has to do is ask fucking politely, using the fucking words "please" and "thank you". *Then* he might get fuckin' served. Is that clear to the little fuckin' fellah that's askin'?' Tapping the bar top with the truncheon Declan glared at the customer.

'Fuck me, I was only askin', wasn't I? No need to get so fuckin' stroppy about it all.'

Cowboy decided to leave in case Declan went into action. Leaving two one-pound coins on the bar he started to turn away. 'I'm off, Declan. I might be back later.' He winked as he edged away, a smile showing at the corner of his mouth.

'Aye, goodnight sir, and eh, thanks for your custom. Please come again.' Then turning to the now silent figure dangling from the end of his tie he growled, 'Now what the fuck do you want?'

'Could I have a pint of Guinness please . . . if you're not too busy, that is,' came the half-choked reply.

From Madigans, Cowboy walked along North Earl

Street visiting each pub on the way down and each on the opposite side on the way back up again, hearing the same story in each place. Certain individuals were conspicuous by their absence. Crossing O'Connell Street he walked down into Henry Street. Just as he turned the corner into Moore Street he collided with a man wearing a leather jacket. Cowboy caught him by the shoulders as he stumbled.

'Hey, sorry about that. You OK?'

The man looked at him, puzzled for a moment, then gave a half smile, nodded, and walked off towards O'Connell Street. Cowboy pushed the door to Flannigans open, feeling like he was getting nowhere. It had been the same thing last night and the night before, just different bars. Once again he ignored the main bar and mounted the wooden carpet-stripped stairs to the upstairs lounge. The crowd had thinned but the tang of ale and cigarette smoke was still thick in the air. He made his way easily to the bar and sat on a warm, vacant stool. Rubbing his eyes to clear them of the stale smoke they focused on a glass directly in front of him. The shape of the glass and the stained froth round the rim called to mind an Irish coffee. His tastebuds recalled the flavour. Just what he needed. One of them, then home to bed.

'Bring us an Irish coffee, Charlie,' he called along the bar to the bald-headed man pulling pints at the pumps. Idly Cowboy pushed the empty glass away from him – and found his fingers stuck to the glass. Once again the pain shot up his arm and into his brain. It was happening again. Once again he was the pigeon watching the flames trying to catch him as he sped out into space. Once again he heard the screams from those caught in the flames. Out into deep space, stopping, looking back at the earth, speeding towards it and at the same time changing into a hawk. With a great effort he tore his fingers away from the glass. Wiping sweat from his forehead he called to the barman. 'Charlie,' he shouted. 'Here. Now.' Cowboy quickly vacated the stool as Charlie approached, wondering what had upset the Cowboy. He wasn't one to push his weight around, demanding immediate service. 'Charlie, some bloke, sitting here before me. Drank from that glass. What was he like? How long's he been gone?'

Puzzled, but appreciating the urgency in Cowboy's tone, Charlie rested both hands on the bar, turned his head to one side, and tried to recall the customer concerned. 'Tall guy. On his Jack. Dark hair, wearing a leather jacket. Left just before you came in. You must have passed him on . . .'

Cowboy was already on his way out of the door. He'd bumped into the bastard and never knew it. 'Hey,' somebody called to him as he pushed through a group making their way up the stairs. 'Watch it.' But Cowboy was through the door and running down Henry Street. At the junction with O'Connell Street he came to a standstill. Breathing heavily he glanced in one direction, then the other and swore. The guy could have turned left or right – even crossed over the way Cowboy had come. Make a decision, he told himself. Don't just stand there. He turned left, half running, half walking, making his way through the strollers and revellers. He stopped opposite the Rotunda hospital. He'd come the wrong way and now . . . he turned and broke into a full run, back the way he came, every muscle straining and pumping, trying to recall the image of the man he had bumped into. Past the junction and on towards the bridge, passing the GPO. Nothing.

'Shit, shit, shite.' He bent down with his hands on his

knees, sucking in the cold night air. Blood pounded in his ears and his heart was going nineteen to the dozen. Then he remembered the glass. He pulled himself erect and ran all the way back to Flannigans. Tripping up the stairs he fell against the door and into the lounge bar.

'Charlie. The glass. The glass he was drinking from.' Charlie, towel over his left wrist, held up the glass. It was sparkling clean. 'Oh shit,' Cowboy mumbled and leaned back against the wall. 'Buggered, and then buggered again!'

He drove back to his apartment. After such a near miss he had no desire to go to any more pubs. There was no point in visiting any of the city's nightclubs. The people he was looking for did not frequent any of them. He debated going over to Marlane's, but decided against it. He knew she would have had a rough day. She had been scheduled for an early-morning shoot with Phil Stringer and Martyn Wright, the two photographers who had given her the break that started her on the road to success. She had left her warm bed at 5.30 that morning, mumbling and grumbling about certain people who could sleep in until at least 7.30. He smiled at the memory of her, feeling a warm glow inside as he recalled her small hand sneaking in under the warm duvet to arouse him. Then, having succeeded, she had kissed him quickly on the mouth, leaving him listening to her singsong 'by-ee' as she left. She would have been tired by the time she got in and was probably fast asleep. For his part he knew he could not sleep, not after that incident. Rather than wake her he headed for home.

Parking his car in the small underground car park of the converted Georgian building he walked up the stairs to his apartment and let himself in. He had bought the entire building shortly after his father's death, turning it into four apartments. His own was in the converted servants' quarters in the attic. Tossing his coat on to a chair he walked into the small kitchen, and set to work making himself some coffee. As he went back into the living-room, waiting for the water to filter through the coffee, his eye caught the frame beside his desk. 'And where were you when I needed you?' he asked out loud. His eyes fell on the block of A4-sized paper lying on his desk and the pens in the desk holder. The word 'draw' popped into his head. 'Okay, so maybe you are there.' He sat by the desk and reached for a pencil.

Art had never been one of his best subjects, but he attempted to sketch the face of the man he had collided with. He worked for fifteen minutes, drawing lines, erasing them, redrawing, altering the shape of the eyes, adding spectacles, and mouth, pencilling in a thin line on the upper lip, each time getting a bit closer to what he believed the man in the black leather jacket had looked like. He would use the auto-identity computer at the office in the morning, getting one of the experts to help him, but he wanted to jot down what he could while it was still fresh in his mind.

The aroma of fresh coffee brought him to a halt and he returned to the kitchen and filled a large mug. The mug was a present from Lane. It had a cartoon of a scantily clad female, with a black eye, standing in front of a cartoon man, peering from behind her shoulder. Across the bottom were the words NOBODY MESSES WITH MY MAN.

Before he returned to the drawing he went to his music collection and picked a cassette of Manhattan Transfer. Sipping the hot black coffee he pencilled in a narrative description of the man. Five eleven to six one, medium build, dark hair, a bit long by the ears and neck and slightly grey round the temples. And a moustache; a thin one, not fully covering the upper lip. Aged early to late thirties. Last seen wearing a dark leather jacket – most likely black – and dark pants. At the bottom of the page he added 'likes coffee – kills people'. At the side of the drawing he sketched in a swooping pigeon and a large question mark.

He stared at the drawing, willing it to give him more information. Who the hell was this man with whom he seemed to be linked? Why were they linked? He looked at the description he had noted. Same age group as himself, pretty much the same build and, he felt positive, shared the same nightmarish dream of a pigeon which turns into a hawk. Sipping his coffee the words from the stereo crept into his brain.

> I like coffee I like tea
> I like the Java jive and it likes me.
> Coffee and tea – the Java and me . . .

Across the bottom of the page he wrote the words in heavy hand, *The Java Man*.

He leaned back in the leather chair and swivelled round to face the rest of the room. His mind wandered, trying to catch something he might have forgotten, something that might be important. From wall to wall, on either side of the open fireplace, framed photographs of Geronimo and Sitting Bull gazed grimly down on him. On the mantelpiece itself rested a miniature totem pole of the Assiniboin nation from Canada, flanked by a genuine tomahawk and a collection of war arrowheads. The glass case at the other end of the room housed his collection of Indian dolls while on the other wall hung his collection of canvas prints by Remington and Charles Russell. His eyes fell on his favourite Russell print – *The War Party*. That's what this Java Man is on, he thought to himself. The fact that the 'settlers' were a bunch of arseholes who deserved all they got did not change the fact that he was part of the Seventh Cavalry supposed to save them.

His rambling thoughts were broken by the ringing of the phone. He reached for the receiver before the answering machine could cut in. It might be Lane calling him. He hoped it was. If she were awake he could drive over to her.

'Mr Johnson?' The voice was servile, not a quality he would associate with his girlfriend. It was also male.

'Who's asking?' he replied.

'It's me, Mr Johnson. Eddie. A little birdy tells me you are looking for somebody special.'

Eddie Gallagher. Small-time receiver of stolen goods, a harmless felon who was never caught with anything big, and who always refused to have anything to do with violence. He was also a man with radar ears. If he had anything to give he most certainly wanted something in return for it.

'Go on Eddie. I'm interested.'

'Well I just want you to know first of all that it's not something I'm certain of – but it could be useful to you.'

'Eddie, will you stop with the blathering. Just tell me what you have.'

'Eh, well, kinda like, eh, first of all, there's eh, a little bit of bother I'd like to talk ta ye about, hoping you might, like see yer way ta . . .'

'Eddie, you know how I operate. I never forget a favour,

so give, or I'll be round your place first thing in the morning turning your guts into garters. Now what have you heard?'

'Aye, OK Mr Johnson. You've never let me down yet. You know old Rafferty? The auld git over in the Coombe area.'

'Smelly old bugger? Always singing, usually drunk, tellin' tales about the good old days?'

'That's yer man. Well, I met him earlier on tonight and we gets to talkin' and he mentions your name, and about how good you were to him when you were in uniform. Bought him a fish 'n' chip supper many's a night according to him, not to mention the occasional odd whiskey and a pint, now and again.'

'Eddie. It's late. I'm in no mood for a trip down memory lane. Get to the point.'

'All right, all right, keep yer shirt on, I'm comin' to it. He gets ta tellin' me about an old way station for the boys – in the good old days that is – in Swords. Merrion Farm. He says he's heard it's back in operation again, and a certain fellah by the name of McQueedy is supposed to be there. And McQueedy's a very personal friend of . . .'

'McGuinness. Thanks Eddie, it's worth a checkout anyway. But how come old Rafferty didn't give me the information himself?'

'Well, you might say he owed me the odd favour, and he thought you might listen to me a bit better than him.'

'I doubt it Eddie. But I'll check it out like I said. If something comes of it, I'll see you right. Thanks for calling.'

'Er, hang on a minute Mr Johnson.' Eddie spoke quickly before Cowboy could hang up on him. 'There's that little problem of mine I mentioned earlier.'

'OK, Eddie, what is it?' Cowboy resigned himself to listening to a long story about how cruel the world was and how innocent Gallagher was.

'Ah sure Jezus Mr Johnson, it's just some misplaced silver. This auld woman comes into the shop with it, crying about how it's the last of her own wedding presents and she's having to sell it on account of hard times and all that shite. It's not worth more than a few pence, and I'm thinkin' I'm helpin' the auld biddy. Anyway, in comes yer man from the Coombe doin' a spot check and he has a look at the stuff. Doesn't it turn out to be nicked and the address the old bat gave me false, and lo and behold, I'm being done for receivin'! And them pieces the only nicked gear in me whole shop.'

Cowboy was smiling as he listened to the tale. 'What you're trying to tell me Eddie is that that good-for-nothing son-in-law of yours asked you to get rid of some stuff for him and you got your fingers burned. Don't try and flannel me Eddie. Who's got the case?'

'That nice Mr Murphy. A real gent he is and all, but not like yourself. There's not much give in that man, know what I mean? But I'm sure if yourself had a word with himself on my behalf, mentioning how helpful I've been in the past and all that. I'm sure you could persuade him to spend his time lookin' for the auld git that ripped me off, instead of going after meself – and me goin' straight now, and all.'

Cowboy couldn't help it, he laughed down the phone. 'Eddie, have you ever thought of going on the stage as a comedian? You going straight is like asking a corkscrew to become a six-inch nail. But for giving me a good laugh I'll speak to Murphy for you. But he had better tell me it *is* small. And if there was any violence at all attached to the gear, then you can say goodbye to the wife. You'll be off to the Mountjoy, and one of the fairies up there will most likely mount you.'

'Would I lie to you Mr Johnson? As God's me witness, I swear on my dear mother's grave – may the good Lord rest her soul – what I'm –'

'Goodnight Eddie.' Cowboy replaced the receiver. Going to his bookcase he withdrew an Ordnance Survey map from one of the folders. Spreading it open on the carpet he knelt down and with his finger traced the Swords area until he came to Merrion Farm. Well at least that part of the story checked out. But what about the source of the information, old Rafferty?

The first time he came across Rafferty the old man was lying face down in a side alley beside some bins. He had met him a few times after that and had been moved enough to buy him a fish supper now and again, along with an occasional pint. Rafferty was filled with stories of the early days of the fight for independence, talking nostalgically about men like Dan Breen and Sean Tracy, of Michael Collins and Eamon De Valera – whom the old man accused of starting the civil war that erupted just after the treaty. Rafferty spoke of these men as if he had personally known them, yet Cowboy doubted if he was old enough to have taken an active part. Rafferty never mentioned any actions of his own for that time – only theirs, and the price friends paid for the formation of the Irish Republic. Cowboy believed about fifty per cent of his stories. Still this information was worth checking out, it was after all the first sighting of either McQueedy or McGuinness in several weeks.

He looked at his watch. 11.15 p.m. He was still wide awake and knew he wouldn't sleep now, with this information to follow up. He looked out through the blinds. The street below glistened from the earlier rain, but it was fine now. He decided to go and take a look at the farm. He'd call in at the Castle and take a back-up with him and leave a message in Mooney's in-tray. Not for a moment did he have any fear or hesitation about making a late-night call on a suspect area. More than likely it was another dead end – but it had to be followed up. Although he was personally convinced that the killer was a loner, Mooney still wanted to 'speak to' McGuinness. Picking his coat up he switched the lights off in the apartment, resetting the alarm as he left.

Chapter Seven

AT AROUND THE SAME TIME that Cowboy had left to cruise the Dublin pubs seeking information, the man calling himself Joseph Gordon had left his small apartment to walk to O'Connell Street for a meal. He wore spectacles with ordinary glass in them and a pair of blue-tinted contact lenses to cover his brown eyes. The edges of his hair had been touched with some grey and a pencil-thin moustache was glued to his upper lip. It was not a great disguise, but enough to confuse at a quick glance.

He walked like a man who knew the city well, although it had been several years since he had last visited. Over the past few weeks he had taken many walks in the evenings, even in the rain, noticing the changes the years had brought. Burger bars – McDonald's and Burger King – now outnumbered the Italian families, the Fortes and Cafolas, who had once ruled the cafés and ice-cream parlours in the city centre streets. The latter were still in evidence, but fewer of them. The amusement arcades were still in business with their slot machines and electronic rifle ranges, but computer games seemed to attract bigger crowds. Some of the old places were long gone, like the Metropole Cinema and Ballroom which was now a British Home Stores. Video killed more than just the radio stars, he mused.

He chose to eat in a Chinese restaurant near O'Connell Bridge, upstairs above yet another burger bar. Once it had all been The Rainbow Café. Choosing one of the set meals he went over his plans for later that night as he ate. He had read all the newspaper reports on the O'Grady deaths, and how known members of the Popular Front seemed to have disappeared off the face of the earth. Tonight's mission would not be as easy as the first one. For a start these would be active members of the Front, which Maura O'Grady had not been. They would also be on their guard, expecting trouble, on edge and unpredictable.

Despite the assurance given by the British government through the media, that no SAS hit team was operating in the country, he guessed that that was who the Front members were expecting to come after them. No one ever believed the official lines doled out to the press. In the North the definition of an SAS soldier was a man who could speak six foreign languages fluently while disguised as a bottle of Guinness, and who knew more ways to kill than Attila the Hun. From what little he knew of them himself he didn't think the definition was too far off the mark!

So there would be some sort of security at Merrion Farm. It would not be a question of catching them sleeping. The question was what? A sentry? How many? Best to assume in the plural. Weapons? Most definitely – they would be much better armed than him, with his single revolver. Great care would have to be taken when he got there. His one, and probably only, chance of getting in and out alive was to take out the sentries and commandeer their weapons.

He looked at his watch as he finished his meal. It was 10.30 p.m. He had been out for almost three hours, but there was still plenty of time. The car was parked up at the back of the Rotunda hospital, well away from the apartment. He'd walk back to the apartment, maybe stop off for a drink on the way just to pass some more time, and wait until midnight, the killing as well as witching hour, before he set off. Paying for his meal he left the restaurant and headed back up O'Connell Street in the direction of the General Post Office.

He spent half an hour in Flannigans bar nursing an Irish coffee before returning to his apartment. Once more he oiled and checked the revolver before sliding it into the shoulder holster, settling the weapon beneath his left armpit. He took a handful of shells from the box and slid them into one of the zipper pockets on the leather jacket. Checking his black-clad image in the mirror to see if the gun bulged he was satisfied it did not. Switching off all the lights in the apartment he stood by the window, once more looking out across the city's rooftops. This time there was no dream to interfere, no vision to haunt him. Just his own thoughts. He stood immobile for ten minutes, staring at nothing, seeing nothing, then left by the unlit fire escape. Jamming a piece of folded newspaper between the door and the frame so that with one sharp pull it would open for him, he made his way silently down the stairs and let himself out of the yard by way of the small doorway cut into one of the tall gates. Locking the door behind him he set off towards his car.

He took the Monaghan road out of the city and this eventually brought him to the turning he wanted, just before Ashbourne. As he turned right off the main road, towards the layby where he intended to park, a Cortina, driving at great speed, shot across the intersection, heading inland. It was only thanks to his own driving skills that they did not meet head on. The other car continued on its way, but he pulled over and stopped. His hands were shaking at the near miss. He needed to wait, to relax, before he continued.

He sat for fifteen minutes where he was, the headlights switched off, his eyes growing accustomed to the darkness. Eventually he felt sufficiently in control to drive on, slowly and without the headlights, in the direction of the layby near the farm lane. Once parked he again sat and waited, watching and listening for any sign of movement. He felt all his senses heighten, like a nocturnal predator seeking its prey. Nothing moved or sounded that was strange to the night. The time was right. Half unzipping his leather jacket for easy access to his gun he opened the glovebox, taking out the black ski-mask and a three-foot length of nylon washing line with hand-loops at either end to enable him to grip better. In the centre of the line, about three inches apart, were two large, hard knots. Rolling the ski-mask down over his face he felt he was as ready as he ever would be. There was only the slightest click as he closed the door behind him. No interior light showed as he had taken out the bulb earlier.

The temperature had dropped and a cold wind sang through the trees and hedgerows lining the lane and road. It was like the quiet wailing of a woman, the legendary Banshee, roaming the darkened countryside, informing the living with her cry that one of them would be returning to the underworld with her that night. He felt it was a good sign. She had come to collect – his only hope was that it was not him she had come for. He shivered slightly with the cold, but felt it would keep him alert, and the wind would cover any small noise he might make on his way to the farmhouse.

Crossing the road he started in the direction of the lane, his rubber-soled shoes making no sound on the asphalt.

He entered the field on his side of the house, slipping through the bars of the gate. Using the hedgerow as cover he moved slowly towards the first tree in the lane, testing each step before putting his weight on it, just as he had done on the stairs in the O'Grady household. Only this time it was not a loose and noisy stair tread he was wary of stepping on, but a dry branch. Despite the wind a sharp 'crack' like that would travel. Every so often he stopped, dropping to one knee, listening for other movement. When he was crouched some twenty yards from the trees, listening, he heard a cough. It came from in front of him and to his right, by the edge of the lane. He remained motionless, listening, his heart beginning to beat faster as the adrenalin pumped through his body. Now he could hear the sounds of somebody leaning against one of the trees. And still he waited.

After several minutes the person by the tree took out a packet of cigarettes and lit one. He watched as the man's face was momentarily illuminated by the flame from the lighter, then all was black once again. Slowly and silently he moved forward on his hands and knees, his eyes never leaving the spot where he knew the other man to be. He crawled to within six feet of him before he stopped. He watched the end of the cigarette glow brighter as the man drew on it. It made him want a cigarette himself – but he knew better than the sentry. Easing himself up on to his feet he edged forward, keeping his eyes on the glowing red tip. It was pointed away from him. As long as it remained that way the sentry had no idea there was anyone close to him. His eyes still watching the cigarette he crouched down and his gloved hand searched the ground around him for something small to throw. It was the oldest trick in the book – but it worked every time. He found a small stone. Standing up straight again he took two paces forward until he was directly behind the tree, with the sentry on the other side. As he tossed the stone to his right he moved slightly to his left towards the front of the tree. The sentry turned in the direction of the noise, his back to Joseph Gordon. Crossing his arms over, Gordon slipped the nylon loop round the sentry's neck, pulling tightly on both ends. As the two knots gripped either side of the other's throat Gordon brought his right knee up into the man's back, pushing him away while pulling tighter on the rope.

No sound could escape from the sentry's throat. The cord bit deeply into his vocal cords and windpipe as he thrashed about in an eerie silence, his hands struggling in a futile attempt to get a grip on the cord. As unconsciousness hit him he slumped towards the ground. Gordon gave one last jerk on the cord, then let the lifeless body fall.

'You should have read the health warning on the packet, my friend,' Gordon whispered. 'Smoking can kill you.'

Before pushing the body into the hedgerow he checked it for weapons. A Stirling submachine gun, standard issue to the British Army, hung on a sling round the dead man's shoulders. Gordon knew the weapon well. Easing it off his shoulders he checked the magazine. From its weight he estimated it to be completely full, twenty-eight rounds of 9mm ammunition. Sliding his hands over the dead body he found a second magazine in the pants pocket. This too seemed to be full. Sliding the first magazine back on to the magazine housing of the weapon he slipped the second one into his jacket pocket. He arranged it so that part of the slightly curved magazine was exposed, jutting forward, ready for immediate access if it should be necessary. Slowly and carefully he moved out of the field and on down the lane in the direction of the farmhouse. Keeping close to the trees he stopped every so often to listen, but heard nothing out of the ordinary. At the edge of a small courtyard he stood in silence watching the house for several minutes. Moving round the perimeter of the house he searched for a second sentry. There was none. He moved in towards the buildings. He was surprised to find a Porsche inside a large barn at the back of the house, the engine still warm. So much for NORAID and its money, he thought as he slipped back outside.

He arrived at the back door of the farmhouse. Pressing down gently on the handle and pushing slightly with his shoulder he opened the unlocked door and found himself in a large kitchen. A door to his immediate right had a small heart-shaped window in it. The hall on the other side was empty with several doors leading off it. He listened at each door. Coarse, male laughter came from the first, but the rest were silent. He moved back to the first one. A single bulb lit the hallway and beside him, on the wall, was the switch. Very gently he eased back the bolt on the machine gun, cocking it. He flicked the switch and blended once more into the blackness. He waited while his eyes accustomed themselves to the dark, listening to the voices from behind the door. He heard what sounded like a smacking sound followed by a moan, but it was drowned in the laughter that followed. He reckoned there were at least three men in the room. Taking several deep breaths to steady his nerves he was ready. 'Here goes nothing,' he said as he turned the handle of the door and kicked it.

'*Freeze!*'

Dropping to one knee as he gave the order, the weapon held to his right shoulder, he scanned the room. The three men all stared at him, immobile for those few vital seconds he needed, staring at the apparition in black that had appeared from nowhere. Donnelly was the first to make a sound.

'Jesus, Mary and Joseph, don't shoot. Don't shoot. I've nothin' to do with these. I just own the farm. Don't shoot. Please don't shoot.'

One of the men reached for the revolver that lay on the table in front of him. From his kneeling position Gordon opened fire. The round caught the terrorist in the face, just above the eyes, blowing the top of his skull off. Donnelly was attempting to rise from his sitting position, his hands held high in the air, and caught the 9mm round in the stomach. He doubled over and fell backwards behind the table. The third man, still frozen in terror over what he was certain was an SAS raid, remained seated and took several rounds in his chest. Falling backwards his chair crashed to the ground and he lay in a bloody heap beside Donnelly.

Gordon now turned his attention to kicking in each of the other doors, the machine gun scanning the empty rooms. Silently he stood by the door to the kitchen, waiting in the darkness, just in case he *had* missed a second sentry. But there were no sounds of running footsteps either to or from the building, nor any shouts. After the noise of the gunfire the silence was almost deafening. He moved back to the room of death, pausing by the door, ensuring that none of them had had enough life left to reach for the revolver or any other weapon. All he heard was a series of moans from behind the door. Throwing himself into the room and onto the floor he turned his weapon in the direction of the sounds, ready to open fire. Just in time he saw the naked figure bound in the chair. 'Holy shit,' he muttered as he turned the weapon away. On the wall behind her hung a homemade Popular Front flag, spattered with her blood.

Her head was bowed and her long hair fell forward. With one gloved finger he gently raised Monica's battered face. Her eyes were swollen and more than half closed and blood trickled from her torn lips and nose. Her clothes hung off her in tatters and it seemed every inch of her exposed skin was covered in cuts and bruises. There was a pool of blood between her legs which had been smeared up over her naked thighs, leaving great, greedy handprints. He could smell urine and excrement.

'Please,' she whispered, 'please don't hit me any more. Please.' Tears oozed from her swollen eyelids mixing with the blood as they ran down her cheeks and dripped on to his glove. There was another moan, only this time from behind him. He released the girl's head and spun round, the gun aimed at the three bodies behind the table. Donnelly was moving. Gordon leapt across the room and dropped to his knee beside him. The man was crying from the pain of the gut-shot, calling for his mother.

'Mammy, oh Mammy, it hurts. Where are you, Mammy?' He coughed, and a thin line of blood trickled from the edge of his mouth.

Gordon reached out and gripped the man by the hair pulling his head back so he could look into his eyes. 'Where's McGuinness?' he hissed. The pain-filled eyes tried to focus on him and the mouth opened as if to speak, but no sound came. Instead blood erupted from his mouth running over his chin and down on to his chest. The eyes glazed over and he was dead.

'Shite,' Gordon exclaimed quietly as he rose to his feet. All of them dead. It was back to square one again. Or almost. He still had Maura's coded address book. There were others he could find, but this had been the address she had given him as the next link in the chain to McGuinness. This had been his best chance of finding him – and he had screwed it up by coming in like John Wayne and the Marines. Another moan reminded him of the girl's presence. What the hell was he going to do with her? Why was she here in the first place? Whoever she was she certainly wasn't a friend of the three dead men. He moved back to her and once more gently raised her head.

'Oh no,' she moaned, 'please, no more. Don't hit me, please.'

'Shush, it's OK, it's OK. Nobody's going to hit you any more. Can you hear me? It's OK. Nobody's going to hit you.'

She sobbed as he untied the ropes from her arms and legs. Once freed she instantly fell forward, and would have hit the ground had he not caught her. She cried out at the fresh pain which racked her body as the circulation came back into her limbs.

'Try to stand,' he ordered. She tried, but fell back, her legs unable to support her weight. 'Listen to me very carefully. You are going to have to fight the pain for a little bit longer. You are going to have to help me get you out of here, to my car. It's not far, and I know you can make it – but you've got to fight the pain. We have to get out of here, and fast. Do you understand me?' He shook her gently to make sure she was hearing. She nodded and tried to open her eyes a bit more. All she could see was a misty black shadow.

'Oh God help me,' she whimpered, 'I'm going blind.'

Needing to keep one arm free to shoot with he half carried, half dragged her back to the car. Pushing her on to the rear seat he ripped off the ski-mask and headed back to the city. It was 3 a.m. by the time he was closing the wooden gates to the yard and parking the car in the garage he had rented with the flat. He checked out the building as best he could, then the flat, before carrying the half-conscious girl up the stairs and in via the fire exit. Laying her down gently on the sofa he sat back in the armchair and looked at her.

'What in God's name am I doing?' he asked himself, watching her breathing. Why hadn't he left her at the farm? This could well be his first mistake, the one that could ruin everything. But the thought hadn't crossed his mind until now. Seeing her there, at the farm, bruised and beaten, had woken something in him, a kindred soul perhaps? All he knew was that those bastards had caused him a lot of pain – and this girl had also suffered at their hands. What was that quotation . . . 'The enemy of my enemy is my friend'? Something like that. The big question now was what the hell was he going to do with her? It was the smell that made the immediate decision for him. The clothes had to go, what was left of them, and she needed a shower, and some attention for her bruising. Then she needed to sleep. Maybe a solution would come to him in the morning. He leaned over the sofa, touching her hand softly.

'Listen to me carefully, girl. I have to get these clothes off you and get you washed,' her eyes flickered open as she tried to comprehend. 'Your clothes are in a hell of a state and you need new stuff. Do you think you can undress yourself?'

She tried to stand, but her legs gave way and he caught her as she toppled towards the floor. He laid her back on the sofa and undressed her, careful to avoid touching the cuts and bruises. She didn't struggle or object, accepting everything he did, too exhausted to care. He carried her naked body to the small bathroom and flicked the switch for the electric shower. Realizing he was going to have to hold her up in the shower he hurriedly undressed to his underpants and lifted her under the warm water with him, moving her around. It was like dancing with a slippery rag doll. He sat her on the floor of the cubicle while he washed her hair and gently soaped her body.

This was the first naked woman he had seen, never mind held, for several months, yet he felt nothing sexual, just an overwhelming compassion for her over what had happened and what had been intended for her. She looked like a badly beaten, half-drowned kitten he had pulled from a river. He could see, despite the bruising, that she was an attractive girl. She should have been out having fun, sharing a few drinks with friends, or lying safely in the arms of a lover. Instead she had been turned into an object, a piece of meat, trussed up, beaten, molested, and partially devoured. And now she was being washed clean by a murderer! The label did not worry him. He knew what he was, had accepted it, and was comfortable that he was justified in what he was doing. He was a killer, a murderer. So far he had killed seven people, including a woman and a boy – and all he felt was compassion for this unknown girl. He felt no guilt about the deaths he had caused and knew that, given the opportunity, there was at least one more to come . . . possibly more.

He turned the water off, sitting her back on the toilet seat and wrapping her in a large, warm bathtowel, with a handtowel round her damp hair. Carrying her back to the sofa, he left her for a few moments to fetch another towel to dry himself off in the bedroom, stripping off his soaking underpants and wrapping himself in his dressing-gown. Turning the bedclothes back he fetched her, laid her down gently, still wrapped in the towels, and tucked her in. She had been silent throughout it all and as he was about to leave her hand caught his arm for a moment. He looked down into her puffy eyes and saw tears welling from the swollen eyelids. She attempted to give him a smile, then surrendered to sleep.

He left her to make himself a pot of coffee. There were some extra blankets in the airing cupboard and he made a bed up for himself on the sofa. Lying there, sipping the coffee, his thoughts were of another girl, from another time, another place. His coffee finished, he was about to doze off when he heard her cry. Returning to the bedroom he found she was crying in her sleep, pleading not to be hurt any more, the tears running freely now down her bruised face. He sat on the edge of the bed, and stroked the back of her hand.

'Hush now, everything is going to be OK. Nobody will hurt you. You're safe. Try not to think about it. Just sleep. Sleep.'

His voice was low and soothing as he wiped the tears with the edge of the bedsheet, moving a patch of damp hair off her face. The towel on her head had loosened as she tossed her head about so he removed it, dropping it on the floor beside the bed, then returned to stroking her hand. He continued to make soothing noises to her until she fell silent once more and her breathing grew steady.

'You did *what*! You brought a *what* here? Are you off yer fuckin' rocker, Jimmy? Are you fuckin' *mad*?' McGuinness emphasized the word 'mad' by poking the side of his head with a finger. 'You brought a fuckin' copper *here*!' He hadn't believed it at first when McQueedy had turned up with the unconscious man. It was only when McQueedy threw the warrant card on to the kitchen table that he knew it was true – and that his friend had finally gone too far.

'Jesus, Jesus, Jee-sus Christ!' McGuinness paced the kitchen, his small hands bunched into fists, his arms rigid by the side of his body, his head tilted back to the ceiling as he screamed out his frustration. 'What a fucking moronic thing to do. What a stupid, idiotic, fucking thing to do. God, Jimmy, I'm beginning to think that you are the fucking loop a lot of people think you are. Why? I sent you to get us some money. To pick up that whore and get rid of her. And you bring me back an unconscious policeman! Why, Jimmy? Just tell me. Why?' His eyes were blazing with anger and a hint of contempt.

'Aw get off me back, willya Tommy. I thought I was doin' the right thing. You're always tellin' me to use me initiative. Well . . . ain't ya?' McQ was uncomfortable. He could see that he had made a mistake, but Tommy's contempt was almost more than he could stand. He had been rather proud of the way he had neutralized the copper, but now he felt humiliated, reminded of his reliance on his friend for his survival, of his own stupidity. The feeling made him angry, and he found the anger hard to control.

'Oh my, what big fuckin' words you use, Grandma. Having "thoughts" are you now? Using your "initiative"? Of all the fuckin' times you pick to use it, it had to be now, eh? Don't you realize, don't you understand, didn't it even *cross* your stupid fuckin' mind? They're going to go fucking *ape* looking for this guy. They – and by "they", Jimmy, I am referring to the members of the law – not fuckin' Flynn or anybody else – the fucking law. They don't give a shit how many of us cop it . . . but one of *them!* One of their *own!* They'll turn this fucking country upside down looking for him. And to make things worse, *we* don't even know what the fuck he was doing at the farm in the first place, do we? You hit him so hard he's still out for the count.'

McQueedy took a deep breath. If Tommy thought that was bad, he had worse for him. 'He wasn't the only one there, Tommy,' he said sheepishly.

McGuinness's eyes narrowed to slits, his voice quiet and now tinged with fear. 'What do you mean, he wasn't the only one there, Jimmy? Don't. Don't tell me. Please don't tell me that the rest of the lads are on their way back here with another one, eh? That's *not* what you are trying to tell me, is it. *Is it?*' He was screaming again.

McQueedy's eyes dropped to the floor. Tommy could remember that was how he used to look in their schooldays, when he had to face the Head. Any minute now he expected him to start shuffling his feet from side to side. 'No,' he eventually replied. 'The other one's dead.'

McGuinness looked at him, dumbfounded. 'This is a dream,' he whispered hoarsely. 'This is only a fucking dream. I want you to tell me it is only a dream. Somehow or other you are in my dream tormenting me with all this, right?' He sat in the chair and stared at his friend. McQueedy smiled stupidly back at him, unable to offer him any comfort. 'Tell me it's a fucking dream you moron!' he shrieked, jumping to his feet, knocking the chair backwards, and slamming his hands down hard on the table top, spittle spraying from his mouth.

McQueedy stood staring in silence, suppressing the trembling inside him. Half of him wanted to cry, to burst into tears like a small child. The other half wanted to hit Tommy, to silence him and stop the torrent of abuse. He had never seen McGuinness this angry before, never, and it overwhelmed him. Not once in all the years they had been together had it ever even crossed his mind to hit his friend but now he was having to struggle to control himself. Tommy wasn't being fair to him, was all he could think. After what seemed like an eternity McGuinness regained his self-control, turned, righted the fallen chair, and sat back down at the table.

'Sit down, Jimmy.' His voice had returned to its normal pitch. 'Sit down and tell me everything. Everything, you understand? Leave nothing out, from the moment you picked up the girl to you walking in here with that copper.'

McQueedy sat opposite, the trembling gradually fading, and told his tale. 'We had no problem at all pickin' the bird up. Doyle had spotted her in town about a week ago. He always fancied a bit there so he followed to see where she was going. She had moved. Was staying in a rented room on the North side of the city. As we were approaching the house she was leaving. We followed and just lifted her straight off the street and back to Donnelly's place.

'You said we could have a bit of fun with her first so I thought it would be fun to hold a court martial. Just like the one the Brits gave me, only with Monica as the accused. Doyle had one of those Front flags so we hung it on the living-room wall. Brought the table in from the kitchen and set it up with three chairs behind it. We tied her to a chair and slapped her round a little bit, softening her up, asking her questions, not giving a hoot what she answered.' He smiled at the memory, his anger now forgotten. 'It was so fuckin' good. She was shit scared. It gave me a hard-on just to look at her,' saliva bubbled at the corner of his mouth and his erection bulged uncomfortably back to life in his jeans. 'She's a fuckin' great bit of stuff, Tommy, great body. Tits you want to bite off and a pussy that just pleads to be fucked. I wish you could have been there. The slappin' around was just like a warm up until we got to the good bit. I was goin' to have her first, then the others, then we'd finish her off. I intended getting Donnelly to do that. He hates having to get his hands dirty and I wanted the bastard to have a witnessed kill under his belt. All this shit of his about him being more use to us *not* being involved in anything . . . load of crap. Anyway, there was Doyle, Fitzy, Donnelly and myself in the house with the girl, and McCann was outside on guard, down by the end of the lane. Suddenly we all heard a car drawing up the driveway.

'Doyle and I went out the back way leaving the others with the girl. I told Doyle to keep an eye out for anybody trying to come in the back way, and I'd take care of the front. We split up. This car pulls up. A Porsche! Whoever heard of coppers driving Porsches?'

'Never mind that Jimmy. This fucker did. Go on.'

'Two guys get out and I could hear one of them talking. Couldn't hear what was being said, just the sound of the voices, know what I mean? One moves towards the front door, in my direction, and as he passes me I hit the bastard in the ear with me fist. Drops like a stone. McCann had crept up behind the car, but I sent him back to watch the main road. I dragged my guy inside and Doyle brought his in. Trouble with the other one was that Doyle smashed his face against the wall. Flattened the guy's face and nose and I think that's what killed him. Maybe a bone splinter went into his brain – who the fuck knows, the guy was dead anyway. When we searched them we found the warrant cards.

'What I thought we . . . you . . . would want to know is . . . how did they know about the farm? Who told them? I told the others to finish off the bird and I'd bring this one back here. I figured you'd know how best to get the answers out of him. We pushed the Porsche into the old barn at the back of the building and dumped the other geezer in there as well. I told the others to clean the place up when they were finished with the bird and for them all, Donnelly included, to get back here when they were finished. Then I left. That's it. I didn't even stop to fuck her Tommy, I came straight back here to you. It seemed like the right thing to do.'

'OK, Jimmy. Now tell me it all again.' It was on the fourth telling that McQueedy first mentioned the car he had almost hit at the intersection. 'What fucking car, Jimmy? What car? What kind? How many were in it? Did they see you? Did they stop – what? You didn't mention this fuckin' car before.'

'I forgot. Sorry Tommy, it just slipped my mind.' McQ was now confused and panicky as he tried to make his slow brain take everything in and make sense of it.

'So start all over again and let's see if there's anything else that slipped your mind, eh? You got to Dublin, picked the others up and . . .'

McQueedy told the same story, with the same details another five times before McGuinness was satisfied he had heard everything. 'OK Jimmy, I believe you. Now go and see to that copper – and *don't* fuckin' hit him. See that he's all right. I need time to think. Just leave me alone with this for a while, right?' His friend nodded silently and left the kitchen.

Chapter Eight

'. . . WEATHER OF THIS MORNING should clear up by lunchtime. But now it's back to more requests and this one is for –' Mooney switched the ignition off and the radio went dead. Grabbing his briefcase from the rear seat he hurried through the drizzling rain to the main entrance of CIB headquarters at Dublin Castle. It was just after 8 a.m.

Arrangements had already been made for Bob O'Brien to fly to London. He would be meeting officers of the Anti-Terrorist Squad, asking for their help in tracing relatives of those killed or injured in bombing campaigns carried out by the Popular Front on the mainland. Mooney met the sergeant by the drinks vending machine in the hall, near their office. Bob fed in the money, pressed a series of buttons, gave the machine two whacks and a kick and his order appeared without any problem.

'How come you can get that bastard of a thing to obey you and I never get it to work for me? What's the secret?'

Bob tapped his nose and smiled. 'Some men have a way with women – like Cowboy. Some men have a way with men – like yourself, Boss. Me, I got a way with machines. What is it you want? Tea, with milk, and one sugar, right?' Mooney nodded. Bob looked up and down the corridor to make sure nobody was watching, tapped three times on the top of the machine, smacked it once, hard, pressed the required buttons, then kicked its base. Out came the cup, followed by the tea. He handed it to Mooney. 'Voilà!' he exclaimed, arms outstretched, making a theatrical bow.

'Am I going bloody barmy or what? I have a sergeant who can make love to a goddamn tea machine, a detective constable who thinks he's an Indian but gets called Cowboy, and insists on calling me Chief!' Tea in one hand, briefcase in the other he walked, grumbling all the way to the office followed by a smiling Bob. 'Am I the only bleedin' normal person round here?' Tossing the briefcase on the desk he sipped the tea while checking the messages in his in-tray. 'Jesus Bob, the tea even tastes better.' He continued to flick the small pieces of paper to one side; most of the messages he could ignore until he received a reminder. He picked up something in Johnson's handwriting, dated and timed late the previous night. He scanned the information and was about to speak when the door burst open and Commander Edwards entered.

'Frank, he's struck again. Four bodies this time.' Mooney looked up from the note. 'Some place in . . .' Edwards checked the piece of paper in his hand. '. . . Swords. Place called –'

'Merrion Farm,' Frank completed for him. Both the commander and Bob looked across at Frank, whose face had gone the colour of ivory. A uniformed garda arrived in the open doorway, just behind the commander.

'How the hell did you know that, Frank? The word's only just come in from the Gardai at Whitehall!'

Mooney held up the piece of paper in his hand. 'Note on my desk this morning. Johnson got a tip late last night. He picked up Russell and the pair of them were going to visit this Merrion Farm in Swords.'

'Excuse me a moment, sir.' It was the garda speaking directly to Mooney, 'they just found Cowboy's . . . I mean Detective Johnson's car at Merrion Farm.'

The stunned silence only lasted five seconds before Mooney moved towards the door. 'Let's go Bob.' Pausing at the door he spoke to the garda. 'I want a man named Eddie Gallagher brought in. He's a small-time fence on the south side. I want him here when I get back. Got it?'

'Keep me briefed Frank,' Commander Edwards called after their departing backs.

'Yes, sir,' Frank shouted without breaking his stride. At the front door of the building Mooney pointed a finger at another young garda. 'You. You're driving us.'

The young garda, excited at being caught up in some CIB work, ran to the collection of unmarked police cars, jumped into the driver's seat of Bob's 'personal' Jaguar and turned the ignition. The engine roared into life. Mooney opened the front passenger door and got in, Bob jumped into the back.

'What's your name, son?'

'Kirwan, sir.'

'OK, get this heap to Swords ten minutes ago, Kirwan – all systems go.' As he spoke, Mooney slammed the detachable blue strobe light on to the roof of the car and flicked on the siren. With headlights on full beam the car screamed out of the Castle in the direction of Merrion Farm.

The Jaguar screeched to a halt at the entrance to the farm lane. Several police cars were already parked in the immediate vicinity, there was an ambulance on the opposite side of the road, with two uniformed ambulancemen sitting smoking in the cab.

'Stay with the car, son,' Mooney instructed Garda Kirwan. 'Any calls for me you take, and get the message to me up at the house. Got that?'

'Yes, sir.'

The two detectives dipped under the white tape stretched across the lane and headed briskly for the house. A third of the way up the lane they stopped where the first body lay. It had a large plastic sheet thrown over it and a uniformed garda stood guard. Bob took a look at the swollen face of McCann, the sentry, which stared back with bulging eyes. He dropped the sheet again and shook his head at Mooney. It wasn't Johnson. As they approached the house the garda on duty stuck his head inside and shouted something. A uniformed inspector and sergeant came out to meet Mooney.

'Morning, gentlemen. Frank Mooney, and this is my sergeant, Bob O'Brien.' Mooney shook hands with the inspector.

'Good morning Frank. John Cahill, and this is Joe Lonnigan.' Hands were shaken all round and the four men moved into the house. Inspector Cahill led the way into the living room.

'It's a hell of a mess. Apart from the one in the lane, there are three in here, over behind the table. These were shot and I'd hazard a guess and say that that' – he indicated the machine gun lying near the chair – 'is the weapon.' Bob went behind the table to check the bodies. Looking over at Mooney he again shook his head. Now they had the four bodies, yet none of them was Detective Constable Johnson.

'Where's the Porsche?' Mooney asked.

'Round the back of the building, in the barn, along with the fifth body,' Sergeant Lonnigan answered.

'*Fifth* body!' Mooney asked.

'Yes, we found it when we started searching. By then the report of these four had already been sent to your lot. Can't tell offhand what killed him. Wasn't shot, from what we could see, and wasn't strangled like the other one. Probably beaten to death.'

'Has anything been touched by any of your men?'

'No, sir. The bodies are where they were found. Nothing's been moved.'

'Bob?' Without further instructions O'Brien left the group to check the barn. Turning to Sergeant Lonnigan Mooney continued. 'Tell me how the bodies were found.'

'Postman found them early this morning. Delivered some junk mail to the house and on the way back down the drive spotted a leg sticking out of the grass. When he discovered it was a dead body he returned to the house to get help and found this lot. He drove like a bat out of hell to the local and a couple of our boys came out to verify it all. They called in to Whitehall, and Inspector Cahill here and myself came out and then passed it all on to the Castle. We found the fifth body when checking out the barn. That's about it . . . except for this.' Lonnigan indicated the chair and Frank bent to his haunches to inspect it closer. The pieces of rope and the blood stains told their own story. Same MO as the Ballymun killings. Somebody had been tied to that chair – but why was the body moved? Just then Bob returned.

'It's his car all right Frank – but the body's Russell. From the looks of things he got his face smashed in good and proper.'

A look of excruciating pain flickered across Mooney's face, then disappeared, but Bob had worked with the man long enough to have recognized it, and knew how he felt.

'John, I want this place sealed tighter than a virgin's fanny. I'll have people out from the Castle as quick as possible, but we'll need all your men to comb this place, every inch of it. We're looking for a sixth body. That body in the barn is Detective Constable Russell of the CIB – and he was accompanied here by another detective – the third man in my team, Detective Constable Johnson. This case is personal, very fuckin' personal.'

'Oh shit – we've got us a cop killer,' Inspector Cahill replied. 'OK, Joe, you heard what the man said. Get on to the station and get as many men out here as can be spared. Get them to form up at the end of the lane to await orders from the inspector here.' The sergeant nodded and left, while Cahill turned back to Mooney. 'I'm sorry, Frank, about the two lads. Anything you want that we can provide – just ask.'

Back at Dublin Castle, having left the murder scene in the capable hands of the forensic team, Mooney and O'Brien reported to their commander. After briefing him on what they had found, Frank demanded that he be allowed to take the kid-gloves off in his handling of known terrorist sympathizers.

'I want to open this thing wide, Commander, and the only way to do that is to start hassling those shitheads. I want to crack down on those bastards. Personally, I don't give a shit if they bump each other off on a daily basis – but once they start killing coppers that's it. You know as well as I do that once they start that, anything is possible. They're just a bunch of gangsters anyway, and I want to go after them. Somebody out there *has* to know something. I want to take them in for jay-walking, for spitting on the pavement, for drinking after hours, speeding, farting in a public place. You name it, I want to book them for it, wring them out and hang them up to dry. If they get enough hassle, somebody'll talk.'

'Calm down Frank, calm down'. The Commander spoke sharply, as if delivering a verbal slap in the face to an hysteric. 'I know how you feel – especially about Russell and young Johnson. And you're right about the rule book going out the window on this now. I'm as mad as you are. Remember, Frank, *all* of you are my boys – and I don't want to be sending out teams to find more dead coppers. But either you calm down, get your brain in proper gear, or I'll take you off the case.'

'Try it. Just fuckin' try it.' With that Mooney stormed out of the commander's office, heading in the direction of his own.

Bob backed out slowly, making apologetic gestures to Edwards. 'Leave him to me, sir. I'll calm him down. Promise.' He closed the door gently behind him, let out his pent-up breath, and hurried after Mooney before either or both of them were called back in.

The door to the basement interrogation room crashed open, slamming against the wall. Eddie Gallagher jumped at the sound, spilling the cup of tea he had been nursing over his trousers. 'Right, Gallagher,' said Mooney without preamble. 'Where did you get the information about Merrion Farm that you passed on to Detective Johnson?'

'Mr Mooney, I've been telling the others since I was picked up – I don't know anything. I don't know what's going on, I don't even know why I'm here! Cowboy said everything would be OK.'

'When did you last talk to Cowboy?' Bob asked, his tone much milder than Mooney's. Gallagher barely managed to draw his eyes away from Mooney's glare. He was like a rabbit mesmerized in the glare of a car's headlights. Turning his gaze to the sergeant his eyes were desperate for someone to understand his lack of understanding.

'Friday night,' he replied. 'Late. About 10 p.m. Maybe a bit later, I can't remember exactly. Honest.'

'Why so late?' Frank demanded. Once more Gallagher's eyes snapped back to the inspector, not understanding his tone, only knowing that he was very angry – and it seemed to be all his fault! What the hell's going on, he wondered. For some reason, he seemed to be in really deep shit.

'I'd tried earlier Inspector, but I kept getting his answer machine. I . . . I can't talk to them bloody machines. I'd got some information I thought he'd be interested in. I'd heard the word was out he was interested in anything to do with the Popular Front – the thing over the murders in Ballymun. Mr Mooney, give us a break, willya? They're not a very nice bunch of people to get mixed up with. You could get me killed over this.'

Frank caught Gallagher by the lapels of his coat, and half dragged him across the table. His face inches from the other's, he spoke very slowly, very deliberately. 'You are in imminent danger of being the first prisoner to die of an unexplained accident in Dublin Castle since about 1916, unless you answer my questions. What the Popular Front will do to you is nothing in comparison to what I'll do if you don't give me some straight answers. I'll ask you once more. Who told you about Merrion Farm – and why?'

With that he hurled Gallagher back into his chair, causing him to rock violently backwards. Bob caught the chair just in time and settled the flustered Gallagher down.

'I should answer him if I were you,' he advised into the frightened man's ear, 'bcfore he really loses his temper.'

'OK, OK, OK. It was an old drunk by the name of Rafferty. The Cowboy has always been good to the auld fellah, and he wanted to return a favour. Trouble was, he didn't think the Cowboy would really believe him, thinking Rafferty was just lookin' for another handout. I know the auld geezer meself, and he knew I could pass on the message a bit more believably. The old git owed me a favour as well, so he was paying off the two of us in one go. Plus I'm having a bit of a problem myself with the boys at the Coombe . . . a silly little thing really, about some small bits and pieces of silver they found at my place and –'

'Gallagher . . .?' Mooney's voice cut into his ramblings like a machete and he realized that now was not the time to mention his own little problem.

'Oh ya, sure, Inspector, sure. I'm sorry. Getting a bit carried away I was. Sorry about that. Now where was I? Oh yes. Yes yes yes, I remember now. Rafferty told me and I eventually got through to the Cowboy. And that's all I know. Honest ta Jezus, I swear it Inspector. Cowboy will confirm it for me. Where is he by the way? He promised he'd help over my . . . my, er, little problem.' His voice trailed off as he realized that neither Mooney nor O'Brien was listening anymore. Mooney had turned to the garda who had been standing by the door.

'Mr Gallagher would like to stay here for a while – sort of protective custody you might say – until we find this Rafferty geezer. Wouldn't you, Mr Gallagher?'

Eddie nodded. There was no way he was going to argue or insist on his legal rights just now . . . assuming he had any that is. Screw Mooney, screw the Gardai, screw the Cowboy, but most of all, screw Rafferty, the bastard. Try to help somebody, and what happens? Banged up and frightened to death. And that bastard Murphy will be processing the friggin' paperwork over the stuff he'd bought from that other worthless piece of shit. Jezus, when would he ever learn!

Cowboy Johnson was woken from his troubled sleep by

several sharp smacks across the face. He opened his eyes and found himself lying on a bed in a strange room.

'Come on, come on, wake the fuck up. You've had enough sleep. You've been kippin' for the best part of a day and night. It's your early morning call.' The leering face of James Earl McQueedy stared down at him. Thinking swiftly before he spoke a word Cowboy ran his hand over his face and head, feeling stubble on his face and chin and bruising at the back of his neck, trying to recall what had happened. The late phone call from Eddie Gallagher, picking up Russell at the Castle, driving to the farm and . . . and what? The exploding pains in his head and the bruise on the back of his skull gave some indication as to what had happened. Seems like old Rafferty's tip was sound after all. Where was Russell, he wondered. The face of this ape was familiar – but from where? Mug shot most likely. He realized he had better say something, to avoid being hit again. 'Where am I?' he asked feebly.

'Never mind where the fuck you are, copper. Just get up. You're about to help us with our inquiries.' McQueedy laughed at his own joke and viciously kicked Cowboy's legs off the bed. 'So stand the fuck up when I tell you.' Cowboy was in no state to do anything but obey, he could see that this man was only waiting for an excuse to beat him, and wouldn't be too unhappy if he had to kill him. As he pulled himself to his feet his brain seemed to explode with pain and he wobbled towards McQ, who punched him hard in the stomach and shoved him towards the door.

'Don't try anything clever with me, you piece of shit, I just need one excuse to tear your fucking heart out.' He gave another push, sending him stumbling from the darkened room into the brightly lit passage outside. Cowboy looked quickly back into the room. The window, in the wall facing the bed, was covered with some sort of sheeting. He was going to need to keep his wits about him if he were to get out of this thing alive. As his eyes became accustomed to the light he got a better look at his tormentor. The man's shirt was rolled up to the elbow exposing a tattoo on his forearm of a winged dagger. His heart missed a beat and in his mind he heard the words of Joan Blackwell, and her warning.

'Move, arsehole,' the man pushed him hard, making him bounce off the walls as he desperately clung to his balance. 'A friend of mine wants to talk with you.'

McQueedy pushed and kicked him past a bathroom with the door open, and two other closed doors. Staggering more than was strictly necessary he fell down the stairs, grabbing the banister rail as he went, and landing heavily at the bottom. His cry of pain was no sham as he banged his head on the skirting board, but the blow seemed to clear his brain. Somebody else appeared in the hallway from one of the downstairs rooms, alerted by the noise.

'For fuck's sake, Jimmy, don't kill the bastard. Just get him in here.'

'I didn't touch him, Tommy, Stupid twat fell.'

'Well pick him up and get him in here. I'm nervous enough with him in the house.'

Cowboy offered no resistance or assistance as McQ stood him roughly on his feet again, one huge hand clamped around the back of his neck, the other painfully squeezing his arm. Half pushed and half carried, he was forced into the room after the other man. It was a kitchen, and he was shoved into a chair by a Formica-topped table, strewn with dirty plates, cups, saucers which had served as ashtrays, and cutlery. He looked across the table at the small, pasty man who faced him. Recognition came in an instant. Thomas McGuinness. So called chief-of-staff of the Popular Front for the Liberation of Ireland. That meant 'Jimmy' was James Earl McQueedy. No wonder his face looked familiar. Cowboy now realized he was in deep trouble and would have to be very careful if he was going to get out of this alive. He wanted to ask about Russell – but that would mean letting them know he remembered everything.

'Where am I?' he asked, bewildered, his voice low and weak.

'Never mind all that for the moment Detective Constable Johnson. Just answer my questions and no harm will come to you. You have my word on that.' Cowboy heard a sniggering sound from behind him. 'Why don't you do something useful Jimmy? Make us all a cup of tea. You'd like that, wouldn't you, Detective Constable Johnson? 'Course you would.' The tone was friendly and he smiled across the table at Cowboy. Behind his back McQueedy made a face but crossed the kitchen to fill the kettle.

'Now. Detective . . . by the way, what's your first name, eh?' Cowboy screwed his face up as if in deep concentration at a difficult question.

'Christopher,' he replied. 'Christy.'

'OK, Christy it is then. Just rest a sec and clear the old brainbox. That fuckin' tea ready yet Jimmy?'

'Yes *sir*, right away *sir*. Tea for three coming up, *sir*.'

McGuinness ignored McQueedy's sarcasm. It was *his* fucking fault the fucking copper was here in the first place. It was up to him, McGuinness, to make the best of a very bad situation. Three more cups were added to the disarray on the table. Without asking, McGuinness added two spoonfuls of sugar to one cup, poured in some milk, and pushed it in front of Cowboy.

'Here, drink this, it'll make you feel better.'

Cowboy reached for the cup with trembling hands, keeping up the pretence of being extremely weak. Lifting the cup to his lips with both hands he spilt some of the warm liquid, letting it dribble down his chin, on to his shirt front. He slurped the tea, relishing the sweet warm taste of it as it spread through his aching body. He would have preferred coffee but he didn't think now was the right time to complain. Finishing the tea in several gulps he replaced the empty cup on the saucer and mumbled 'Thanks'. McGuinness immediately pushed his own, untouched, cup across the table to him.

'Here. Have another one. It looks like you need it.' Steadying his hands a little, Cowboy drank from the second cup without spilling any. 'Now let's get down to business, Christy. Who, or what, brought you to the farm the night before last?'

'Farm? What farm?' Cowboy was genuinely surprised. It sounded as if they were no longer there. If they weren't at Merrion Farm, then where were they?

'Merrion Farm, Christy. The place you were, eh, picked up. What were you doing there? Who sent you? Who told you about it? Simple questions that require only simple answers. I want to know who's been talking to you.'

'I . . . I . . . can't remember.' Cowboy scratched the back of his head, wincing as he came in contact with the bruise, screwing his eyes up as if in deep thought. 'I remember being in my flat and . . . and the phone ringing.' He was silent for a few moments before he continued, 'The next thing I remember is waking up and yer man there pushin' and pullin' me about the place. Where am I and who are you? What's going on?'

McQueedy, who had been standing behind Cowboy, leaned over and placed one hand on his shoulder and the other on the table. 'Listen you bastard, *we* ask the questions, not you. If you want out of here in one piece you'd better fuckin' remember, and remember quickly. Who told you about that farm?'

'I've told you,' Cowboy protested, trying to turn his head to face McQueedy. 'I can't remember. All I can remember is –'

'Cut the fuckin' crap. Answer the question, or by Jesus I'll fuckin' beat it out of you. Who told you about Merrion Farm?'

Cowboy turned his head away from the ferocious onslaught. Speckles of foam appeared at the edge of McQueedy's mouth as he slammed his fist down on the table, making the crockery and cutlery jump.

'Jesus I can't remember. I don't know. I'm confused. You're confusing me. God I'm tired, so tired. My head hurts and I need to sleep. Please let me sleep.'

'I'll let you sleep all right. Permanently.'

'Hold off Jimmy, hold off.' McGuinness restrained his friend. 'Let him go back and have some more sleep. Let's face it Jimmy, you *did* whack him one hell of a blow. Killin' him ain't going to get us any answers. Take him back upstairs and let him sleep some more. We'll bring him down again later. Go on, Jimmy. Take him up.'

'Ah fuck it,' was the only answer McGuinness received. Lifting Cowboy by the scruff of the neck he brought him to his feet, and dragged him back up the stairs to the room he had taken him from, throwing him on the bed. 'You might fool him, copper, but you're not foolin' me. You had better remember everything when you wake up. You're pissing me about – and that's not a good idea healthwise, no matter what Tommy says. So sleep on that, bastard features.'

The door slammed shut behind him and the room was thrown into total darkness. Cowboy heard the key turn in the lock and wondered what his next move was going to be.

Later that same afternoon the threatened rain from the morning arrived. The wind, blowing in from the Irish Sea, pounded raindrops against the two men as they walked silently up the lane to the farmhouse. Mooney signed the garda's notebook as they entered, making straight for the living-room.

'What d'ya think, James?'

James O'Riley looked slowly round the room, noting the flag hanging on the wall, the position of the kitchen table with the chairs behind it, the bloodstains on the wall behind the chairs as well as on the furniture. He nodded his head. 'Doesn't seem any doubt about it Frank. A court martial was in progress. There would have been a revolver on the table there. Only one of two things happens at a thing like this. If the revolver points at you, you're dead. Points away from you, you walk away. That very seldom happens, I hear. Most of these terrorists live by the old Stalinist code that it's better ninety-nine innocent men die than one guilty man gets away.' He walked over to the chair Monica Saunders had sat in.

'You say this isn't Johnson's blood?'

'Nope. Wrong type.'

'Well, if I'm reading the signs right I'd say he interrupted the proceedings. Most likely the person in the chair was the one for the chop. The question is ... where's Johnson and the one in the chair? Sentry dead, the so-called judges killed, one of your lads killed round the back, Johnson and Mr X missing, and then there's the executioner himself! It was pretty crowded in here for a while last night, wasn't it?' Frank nodded, but didn't interrupt O'Riley's flow of thoughts. 'Leaves a few questions, doesn't it? Was the executioner a friend of the defendant? If not, where are they gone? Where's Johnson?

'The PIRA are not in the habit of kidnapping coppers – at least not here in the Republic. They know which side their bread is buttered. I'd be inclined to say that whoever snatched your man, along with whoever was in the chair, is not a member of any organization. That's just a guess mind you, but an educated one you might say. As the dearly departed are all known members of the Popular Front – with the exception of Donnelly – that lets them off the hook. Whoever's doing the killing is performing something of a service. There ain't too many members of the Front and it's getting less and less day by day.'

'You sure the PIRA wouldn't have taken Johnson, James?'

'As sure as one can be in this business without the actual facts. They ain't A-rabs Frank. They may deal with them, but they don't act like them. This ain't the Lebanon where they could take hostages in the hope of springing some of their own from jail. On this side of the border kidnapping is totally alien to them. What I can't understand is why one of your men is kidnapped, but the other is killed! Why? Why not kill both of them or take both of them? I suspect you may have two lots of killings mixed up here. Maybe the Popular Front killed your man Russell, then the Lone Ranger arrived on the scene, killed the sentry and the three in here, and scarpered with Johnson and Mr X from the chair!'

Mooney nodded his head slowly, taking in and weighing up all the various options. 'OK, James, but do this for me will you? I don't care how you do it and I don't want to know, but get a message through to Kevin Flynn. If the PIRA *do* have Johnson, I want him back – and he had better be in one piece. Politics ain't my game so I don't give a shit about the kid-glove treatment he and others get this side of the fence, but I want some action, and if I have to start it myself I will. I'll pick up every single one of those sons-of-bitches that I can find, on whatever pretext I can, and I won't care whose toes I tread on . . . am I making myself clear, James?'

The two men stared at each other. O'Riley read that his toes could be included in that threat. He was aware that Mooney could wreck a few operations and cause a lot of unnecessary problems before pressure could be brought to have him stopped. That he could eventually be restrained he had no doubt – but it was a question of how long it would take and the damage that could be done in the meantime. He nodded curtly. The message had been received loud and clear.

'One condition, Frank. Whatever I find out I'll let you know – but I'm in this until the end. I get to take anything I find that I want or can use, and it doesn't get written down in any garda's little black book. What you are asking of me is going to cost me favours – so it's got to cost you too. My work is not as clearly defined by rulebooks as yours. I deal in deals, favours, back scratching. You name it, clean or dirty, I use it. If I dip into my bank of favours I have to be able to replenish it wherever, whenever and however I can. Do we still understand each other?'

'We do,' Mooney answered immediately. 'Just find Johnson.' The two men shook on the deal.

Having found the sketch Cowboy drew and notified Mooney, Marlane did not know what to do. Sick with worry, her fertile imagination drew moving pictures of what was happening to Cowboy. Every ten minutes she wanted to phone Frank and ask if there was any news, but she knew it was pointless. If they knew anything she would be among the first to hear. It was early afternoon when she remembered the woman Cowboy had spoken of. At his desk she found his leather-bound address book and looked under 'B'. It was the last entry. Within minutes she was in her Golf GTi on her way to Joan Blackmore.

After explaining who she was, Marlane was ushered into the small sitting room by Joan, declining the offer of tea or coffee.

'I don't really know if you can help me or not, Mrs Blackmore, but I'm sick with worry and you are the only person I think might be able to help me.' She then went on to explain Cowboy's disappearance, the bodies found at Merrion Farm, the sketch she had found in his apartment, and what Cowboy had told her about his vision at the house in Ballymun.

Joan listened attentively to all the girl told her, feeling the fear and anguish the girl felt. Extremely sensitive to others she also picked up the deep feeling of love this girl had for the detective. Leaning across the small table she reached for Marlane's hand.

'Listen to me child, although Cowboy *is* in danger, he will be OK, I promise you. I know you won't – can't – believe me when I tell you, but he is being looked after by forces that are more powerful than you can imagine, and certainly much more powerful than those who hold him.'

'But what can *I* do?' Lane asked tearfully.

'Tell him you love him. Concentrate on him, and keep telling him you love him. That's all you can do at present. But believe me, he is not dead.'

'How do you know? How can you be so certain?'

'It would be too difficult to explain it all to you now, but believe me, I would know if he was. Would you like to stay with me for a while? Stay and have some tea. Stay overnight if you like. You are more than welcome.'

'Thank you, but no. I want to get back to Cowboy's flat. He, or somebody, might call. I want to be there, just in case. But thank you for the offer, I really appreciate it. You're very kind – just like he said you were.' Marlane rose to leave. 'Mrs Blackmore, I don't understand what this . . . this thing is; you know, the messages he – and I suppose, you – get. I don't understand it, and I'm a little afraid of it, but if you can help him in any way, then I'm thankful.'

'Don't worry, child. He will be back. I feel very certain about that.' As she spoke she felt impending danger. But not for herself, and not for Cowboy. But the feeling was strong, and once again she saw a winged dagger. She decided to say nothing about it to the girl. She was frightened enough as it was.

'Please call me if you should need me, Marlane. Don't hesitate. You have my number, just call. Promise?'

'Thank you, Mrs Blackmore. I promise.'

It was 9 p.m. when Mooney was told that Rafferty had been picked up and was in a holding cell. Mooney gave instructions for him to be brought to the office, and asked Bob to get them all some tea. Several minutes later Rafferty was escorted, under protest, into the office. The burly garda was trying to treat him gently, but every time he slackened his grip on the old man Rafferty tried to leave.

'Willya get yer great big paws offa me, ye feckin' big culshe,' referring to the Garda in Dublin slang for a country rustic.

'OK, Garda, you can let him go,' Mooney said, 'Mr Rafferty isn't going anywhere for a while. You can leave him with me.' He could smell the decay of the old man, urine mixed with unwashed body, and filthy clothing – but above all the stench of the dying. One day, soon, Rafferty was going to be found on the streets, in a heap. But for Rafferty the streets were home, it was where he would want to die, not in some hospice for the aged. Put him in one of those and he'd be dead in a week from boredom.

'Come in Mr Rafferty. Sorry about the mishandling you may have had, but it is very important that I speak to you. You may leave as soon as we've had a little chat.' Bob returned with the teas, wrinkling his nose at the smell. Placing the tea on the desk he drew up a chair for the old man, pushed one beaker across the table in front of Frank, then withdrew to the door, as far away from the smell as he could get.

'Come in, Mr Rafferty . . . Have a nice cosy little chat Mr Rafferty . . . Take a seat Mr Rafferty . . . Have a cup of tea Mr Rafferty . . . Why aren't you out doing some important policework . . . like nippin' a few kids for playing football on the street, or giving out parking tickets, eh? Instead of runnin' in auld men that haven't done nothin'.'

He looked down at his oversized overcoat, trying to fix yet another tear in it by fitting the pieces together. Mooney said nothing but led Rafferty gently but firmly to the chair and sat him down. Inwardly Frank was smiling at the old man's pantomine.

'Relax Mr Rafferty, relax. We are not going to hurt you, nor are you under arrest, I promise. Here, take a sip of your tea while it's hot.' Sitting down himself he reached into the drawer and withdrew the half-bottle of whiskey. 'Let me sweeten it a little for you.' The old man did not decline as Mooney topped up the beaker. 'Right, to business. The other night you asked a man named Eddie Gallagher to pass on a message to Detective Constable Johnson. It concerned a farm, Merrion Farm, in Swords. Yesterday morning the bodies of five men were found at that farm, and at least two other people are missing. One of the dead was a detective and one of the missing is Johnson. I want you to tell me everything, and I mean everything, you know about that place and the people who lived there.'

'Jay-zus, sure what would I know about farmin'? I'm city. I don't know what yer on about a-tall.'

Mooney's voice took on a hard edge, one that was known to many as 'Mooney's whisper'.

'Listen very carefully old man. I told you you could leave here when we've had our little chat, but *I* decide when the talkin's over, understand? I can think up any number of reasons to hold you here, for as long as I like – but you *will* tell me what I want to know eventually.'

Rafferty took another swallow of his tea. It was a long time since he had had any dealings with the police – other than being moved on from one place to another. Rafferty had no time for policemen of any kind – nor squealers or informers. But not all coppers were the same. There was one he considered different.

'What didya say your copper's names were?' he asked, looking Mooney straight in the eye.

'The dead one's name was Russell, and the one that's missing is Johnson. You'll know him as the Cowboy. And from what I hear, you know him well. He's the one who buys you meals now and then, and leaves drinks for you in pubs sometimes. You owe him, Rafferty. You owe him, and now is the time for paying your debts. He was at the farm, that much we know. He and Russell went there together. We found Russell with his head bashed in – but no sign of Johnson. As far as we know he's still alive – and that's how I want to find him. So give.'

The old man looked down into the empty cup and nodded his head. 'Yeah, I know the Cowboy. He's been good to me.' He looked up at Mooney. 'Can I have another cuppa?'

Bob left the office to get more teas while Frank poured another large shot of Paddy into Rafferty's cup, watching it disappear in an instant. 'I know they all laugh at me now, Inspector, but there was a time, a long time ago, when I was a lad – young and foolish – thinkin' I was doin' something right for this country. It was what we thought was best. "A Nation Once Again" and all that. Maybe we tried too hard – we found ourselves on the run from both the Free State government *and* the Brits. Maybe we should have waited, done it differently, with less bloodshed. But . . . we were young and full of foolish dreams – and very impatient!' Bob returned with fresh tea and once more Mooney added a sweetener to it. Rafferty took another swallow and continued. 'Merrion Farm was owned by a man named Donnelly. Norman Donnelly. In those days he ran what we called a way station. Donnelly was never known to be involved in the Movement, and he took great pains that nobody should think he was. He was a good man and nobody ever grassed on him, and the Free Staters never got a whiff of what he was up to.

'If you were on the run – and most of us were at one time or another – then Donnelly was the man to see. There used be a room under the dirt floor in the barn and we'd hole up there until arrangements could be made for us to go west. Much safer over there despite the number of Free State soldiers that used to operate in the area. Failing going west we'd be got out of the country – mostly to America.

'You only got to know about Donnelly if it was absolutely necessary for you to know. Sometimes men were brought there blindfolded so they wouldn't know where they were. And if you had used his hospitality, then you made sure the secret was kept. I spent a few days there myself, Inspector, in that room. Nobody, to the best of my knowledge, ever talked about him or that room.'

He accepted the cigarette Mooney offered with a 'thanks' while Bob, who was back in his corner downwind of Rafferty, looked on in amazement. Frank had actually bought a packet of fags! Maybe his own wouldn't disappear so quickly now, but his joy was short lived as he watched Mooney push the packet across the table, and saw it disappear into one of the deep pockets in the old man's torn overcoat. Rafferty inhaled deeply on the burning ash, coughed, then blew the smoke out with relish. He was more used to fag-ends from dustbins, ashtrays in pubs, or the pavement.

'I'm not always drunk Inspector – but most people assume I am. I'm a nobody. I'm there, but I don't exist.

People talk about me when they are standing right beside me, as if I'm blind, deaf and dumb. Or, like your friend there in the corner, they move away.' The old man smiled at Mooney while Mooney looked across at Bob, who had the decency to blush. 'Not many baths in alleyways these days I'm afraid, and they've closed the Public Baths. If you go to any of the churches they either turn their noses up at you, or expect you to join in with rendering a chorus of Hail Marys, Our Fathers, or what have you. Who needs that shit to get a bath? Ya get used to the smell after a while – or at least I did – and sometimes you hear things that under normal circumstances you wouldn't. Like I say, people talk about me and around me as if I didn't exist.

'Couple of days ago I overheard a couple of young shites talkin' in a pub over on the south side. I'd seen 'em before and I knew who they were involved with. They were on about this farm where, as they put it, you'd be all right if things went wrong.

'Old man Donnelly died a few years back, but he had a son. Jimmy I think he was called. I had heard before that this young fellah was "involved". It wasn't hard, even for an auld bastard like me, to put two and two together to at least suspect that the old way station was in operation again. When I heard the Cowboy was lookin' for information I thought he might be interested. I didn't think he'd listen to me, what with the drink and all that, so I told Eddie. I owed him a favour or two also. He's not a bad lad himself Inspector. He was in a bit of bother with that bast –, with Mr Murphy, at the Coombe, so I knew Cowboy would probably help him if the info was any good. Obviously it was too bleedin' good. I never thought any harm would come to Cowboy, and that's the honest truth

Inspector. He has always been good to me. I'm not a squealer by nature – but I don't like the things these bastards are doing – especially the so-called Popular Front for the Liberation of Ireland. Popular with whom? And the only liberation they are interested in is money from other people's pockets. Personally I hope you don't catch whoever is doin' the killings if it's them he's killin' – but I'll help you hang him if he harms the young fellah. That's it Inspector. That's the honest truth.'

'I believe you, Mr Rafferty. Now what about these lads you overheard. You said you knew them, had seen them before, and knew they were involved. Got any names for them? Places they might hang out?'

'No, no names Inspector, but I'd know them again. Haven't seen them for a few days, but I know a few pubs they tend to frequent, as the old song goes. I'll keep me eyes skinned for them and if I see them, I'll get in touch. You have my word on that Inspector.'

'OK, Mr Rafferty, I'd appreciate it very much, and the sooner the better. But be careful. There have been enough deaths recently. I don't want your name on the list.'

'I'll be careful, but sure you've got to go some time haven't ya, and I've long thought that my time was years ago – I just missed the call.'

'Thanks again, and here, take this for your trouble.' Mooney offered the old man a twenty-punt note.

'I don't need your money Inspector. And as you so rightly said, I owe the lad.'

'Take it anyway. If you're going to do the rounds you'll be better off with a bit of folding stuff in yer pocket. Here. Take it.' Mooney came round the desk and shoved the note into the same pocket that the packet of cigarettes had disappeared into. Rafferty let it stay. 'Bob, take Mr Rafferty down to the canteen and give him a slap-up meal, on the house. Can we have you driven anywhere after that?'

'Aw, sure I'd only get used to havin' a chauffeur. But thanks for the meal, that'll be grand. I don't suppose there's any chance of usin' a bath while I'm around, is there?'

'Oh, I think Sergeant O'Brien here will be only too pleased to arrange that for you Mr Rafferty, won't you Bob?'

Bob gave his boss a dirty look, but on reflection decided that the bath might be the best thing for the auld fellah *before* taking him to the canteen. The other two shared a laugh at Bob's discomfort as they shook hands.

'Oh, and by the way Inspector . . . you make a grand cuppa!' He gave Mooney a wink, then followed after Bob.

Commandant James O'Riley was dozing in his chair at the desk. It was 2 a.m. and he was waiting for a call. The phone was in a locked drawer of his all-metal desk and the line did not go through the barracks' military exchange. On the desk lay the last two sandwiches from a plateful he had brought from the officers' mess earlier in the evening. Beside it a plastic flask, a mug with a half-inch of cold tea in it, and a half-bottle of whiskey. The instant the phone rang he woke and unlocked the drawer, taking the receiver from its cradle.

'Speak.'

'Commandant James O'Riley?' the voice at the other end of the line inquired.

'The same,' he replied.

'You're very abrupt with old comrades.' The voice was friendlier and spoke in Gaelic.

'Hello Liam,' O'Riley replied in the same language. 'It's been a long time. How have you been?'

'Oh, surviving, surviving. I won't talk too long, you'll understand I'm sure. But I got your message and the man you wish to speak with has agreed to meet with you – and *only* you, James. Do you still have the card?'

He was referring to a griddle card, a mixture of letters and numbers which enabled map grid references to be given in code, providing the users were using identically coded cards. When the cards were changed periodically O'Riley would receive a phone call and a short message prefixed by a recognized PIRA codeword.

'Yes Liam. What's the reference?' He wrote six characters on a jotter.

'I won't be there myself to meet you James, but you'll be brought to me first. You'll be watched all the way from the border, so please be careful. *I* know you'll come alone and without making contact with the Brits – but you'll understand that not all of my friends have the same trust in you. If you're stopped by a patrol for any reason, the meeting is cancelled. I'll call again to arrange another meeting if that happens. If everything goes okay you'll be met at that grid reference at 0300 hours the day after tomorrow.

'Be careful old friend. There are a lot of new personnel around me, and you'll be on the wrong side of the border, illegally. They won't hesitate to eliminate you if they think you are up to any tricks. No wires, no tracker on the car and no weapon. You have to come in cold. I've given my word that you will. Don't let me down.'

'I won't Liam. I want to trade. I understand the conditions, don't worry. I'll be seeing you. And thanks for calling. I appreciate it.'

'Take care James. See you soon.' The connection was broken.

While O'Riley was receiving his phone call, the man calling himself Joseph Gordon lay tossing and turning on the sofa. His dream had returned to haunt him. Once again he was the pigeon watching the woman, *his* woman, walking towards the luggage locker. He didn't want to see what he knew was coming. He began to murmur in his sleep. Softly at first, but as the scene in his head continued his murmuring turned to cries of anguish, begging the events to stop, for the dream to go away.

In the small bedroom Monica Saunders woke to his cries. For three days now this man had been looking after her. He had bought her a couple of pairs of blue jeans, a sweater, some T-shirts, underwear and trainers. He had bought brassières two sizes, not being sure of her measurements. She had smiled at this, considering that he had held her naked in the shower, washing her like a baby. He had put ointment on her bruises, fed her soup and eggs and yesterday, a large steak. Apart from her name she had told him nothing and he hadn't asked any questions. All she knew of him was his name, Joseph, or Joe. He had been there when she had woken, crying not to be hurt. He had dried her tears and stayed with her until sleep had once more claimed her. Now it was she who woke to his cries. Moving her bruised body slowly she eased out of bed, pulled on a pair of jeans and a T-shirt and tiptoed into the living-room.

He lay on the sofa only partially covered by a blanket, sweat running down his face and bare chest. As he moaned his head tossed from side to side. She went to the kitchen and ran a clean tea-towel under the cold water, squeezing the excess water from it. Returning to the living room she knelt by his side, just as he jerked upright, eyes wide open but unseeing, his mouth open in a scream. What frightened her most was his silence. His mouth was stretched open, she felt the air rushing from his lungs against her cheek, but not a sound escaped his lips. She gave a cry, quickly stifling it with her hand, and moved back from the sofa. It was her cry that woke him.

He looked about him, bewildered and frightened, like a child coming out of a nightmare. At first, when he looked at her, she saw what she thought was relief in his eyes, even happiness. Then total recognition appeared and he lowered his head into his hands, covering his face. No longer afraid she moved closer to him, placing the damp cloth on his shoulders and neck, massaging the coolness into his feverish skin.

'Lie back,' she instructed. 'Lie back. I'll freshen the towel. You've been dreaming, but it's all right now, you're safe. It's over. Just lie back.'

He did as she told him, staring silently at the ceiling. She returned from the kitchen with the same bowl he had used to clean her. First she wiped him with the cold damp cloth, then, dipping it into the hot water in the bowl, repeated the process. After several applications of the hot towel he sat up. Taking the cloth from her hands he wiped his face and neck roughly with it.

'You OK now?' she asked. 'Can I get you something?'

'A cup of coffee would go down just great.'

When she returned with his coffee he had pulled on his jeans and was sitting on the sofa with the blanket wrapped round his bare shoulders. He took the mug from her hands and swallowed several mouthfuls before speaking again.

'God, that felt great. Thank you.' Looking at her he tried to smile. 'Did I say anything? Did I speak?'

'Just mumbling, sort of . . . just noises. Know what I mean? But then you sat up and, well, screamed but didn't scream. You frightened the life out of me.' She grinned at him now, making a joke of her own terror, covering up her own embarrassment.

This time he did smile as he looked at her. It was only the second time she had seen him smile, and his whole face changed. She could see that it had once been a happy face – but something had happened to change him from that smiling man into the expressionless killer she knew him to be. But she had no fear of him at all. Quite the reverse in fact. She felt totally safe with him.

'I'm sorry. I didn't mean to scare you.'

'That's OK,' she smiled back. 'Do you . . . do you want to talk about it?'

He shook his head. 'No. Not yet. Think you could rustle up some breakfast for the pair of us? Are you up to it?'

She got to her feet. 'Sure. What would you like – or shall I just see what's there and make a surprise?'

'Make a surprise. We could both do with it.'

Chapter Nine

BOB EMERGED FROM HIS HOUSE in Drumcondra just as Mooney's car drew up outside. It was 7.30 and Bob was catching the 9 a.m. shuttle to London from Dublin International Airport. Later in the day he would be meeting with representatives of the British Anti-Terrorist Squad, trying to see if there was any connection between the murders of the Popular Front members and the relatives of those killed by Popular Front bombs. Frank had offered to pick him up so they could have a last quick discussion on the journey.

'Go for the most obvious one first, Bob. Time is the enemy and I'm pissed off with staring at this brick wall. We need something, anything, that will take us a step further. Phone me each evening and then fax through each day's reports, just the basics to keep me going. If anything looks really promising, phone me immediately. Got it?'

'Yes Daddy,' Bob replied with a smile. 'And I'll remember to brush my teeth each evening, OK? Stop worrying, Frank. I'll do my job and you'll hear from me every day because I'll want to know how *you're* getting on. I'm sure that whoever is holding Cowboy, once they realize he's a copper, will get rid of him – and I don't mean kill him. They'll dump him somewhere for us to find. He's too hot. They've stirred up a hornets' nest – one they'll wish they hadn't. Every garda in the country is looking for Cowboy. He'll be fine.'

'You're assuming, Bob, that he's in the hands of the Popular Front. They've already killed one copper. What's another to them? What if it's this geezer – this Java Man geezer that has him. *He's* wiped out enough people to have earned himself a special place in the annals of Irish crime!'

'Whoever he is his war is with the terrorists, not with the police. If he has Cowboy, then it's a mistake, and as soon as he realizes that, then he'll let him go. Trust me Frank, Cowboy is going to be all right.' Despite his brave words Bob hadn't even convinced himself. He knew Frank was worried on a personal level about Cowboy, like a father about a son. He was worried that Frank's judgement was clouded by that affection. If that was so then Edwards would take him off the case – and as far as Bob was concerned Frank was the best chance Cowboy had.

'You're about the only one I do trust, Bob. There's too much politics in this for me. O'Riley only gives me what he knows I already know – or thinks I know. Getting information out of him is like extracting your dick from your pants' zipper. Not exactly impossible – but very painful. As for Edwards, our illustrious leader! He's getting flak from above. The shit is piling high Bob. And you know what they say about shit – it rolls downhill. Give me an honest-to-God fucking villain any day. At least we can understand their motives.'

He flashed his lights and tooted the horn as he overtook a more than cautious driver, who gave him a two-fingered salute as he passed.

'Where do you reckon Cowboy managed to get a glimpse of this character?'

'You tell me Bob – but I'm sure it *is* him. I've had a suspicion that Cowboy was holding something close to his chest. He knew I knew, and I think he was going to tell me what it was – then this. But that sketch is our man all right.'

The sketch had been found by Marlane. Before the story had broken in the newspapers Frank had visited her to tell her personally what had happened, and to try and reassure her that everything was being done to find Cowboy. After he had left Marlane had gone to Cowboy's apartment, to feel close to him, to smell his cologne, touch his clothes, feel his presence. On finding the sketch she had immediately called Mooney.

Frank drew up outside the main entrance to the airport, flashing his warrant card at the approaching airport security guard. He stayed in the car while Bob collected his suitcase from the back seat, and proffered his boss some advice.

'Give the newspaper and TV people a good crack at this. Get everything out on *Garda Patrol.* Somebody will have seen something, wait and see. And in the meantime, let the bad guys know it's open season on them. The papers in particular will love the name Java Man. It has a ring to it. Let 'em use it. Anyway, Frank. Take care. I'll call you tonight.'

Frank nodded his head slowly. They shook hands through the open window and before Bob was through the automatic glass doors Frank was already moving off, heading for the office.

He went home early that evening to try and think in peace. He had had meetings with Commander Edwards, given interviews to the press and TV and called other CIB offices throughout the country. He had arranged for the immediate printing of thousands of copies of the Java Man sketch and for their despatch all over the country. Now he was sitting viewing the edited version of his press conference from his armchair, wishing he had taken the advice of the television make-up girl. Marjorie voiced his own thoughts when she remarked that he looked totally washed out on the screen – 'like you had a night on the town'.

'I hate these bloody things,' he replied watching himself responding to questions from the invisible reporters.

'Is there a connection between the two sets of killings Inspector?'

'We are currently working on that theory. Maura O'Grady was the spokeswoman of the Popular Front, and the others were all members of the same organization.'

'Seems somebody has it in for the Popular Front, Inspector.'

'So it would seem. I wouldn't particularly like to be a member of that organization at present. Next question?'

'What about the death of Detective Russell, and the kidnapping of Detective Johnson? Hasn't the killer overstepped the line there?'

'Listen, this killer overstepped the line when he committed the first murder. Murder should not be condoned, no matter who the victim or victims are. But to answer your question, we are not too sure that the killer of the terrorists, this . . . Java Man, . . . is the same killer of Detective Russell or the kidnapper of Detective Johnson.'

'Are you saying that there is more than one killer involved, Inspector? That we have two, separate, killers at the same scene?'

'I said we were not sure. You'll be the first to know for definite once I *am* sure. You can read it in the papers.'

This remark brought the only chuckle at the conference.

'Have you eliminated for definite the possibility of an SAS team operating –'

At this point Commander Edwards interrupted. 'We have the full and unequivocal assurance of the British government that there are no members of their special forces operating in the Irish Republic. I think that's about all we have for you at present gentlemen. You have all been issued with a sketch of the man we are interested in questioning. If you require more copies, please ask. Thank you gentlemen, and good morning.'

'Where did the description of this man come from for the sketch, Commander?'

But both Mooney and Edwards chose to ignore the question and walked away from the reporters without looking back.

Frank was thinking of turning in for an early night when the phone rang. It was Bob, in London.

'What sort of reception did you get, Bob?'

'The best, Frank. They are doing everything they can to help. I've been at the Yard most of the day with an Inspector Dunlop. We went through the lists and we came up with a highly possible. A guy named Kane. Dunlop remembered him in particular. He's a soldier. His wife was killed in the King's Cross bombing. There is one other thing that puts this guy as a top nominee – he's Irish! Dublin born and bred.'

'Sounds good. Any idea where he is now?'

'I'm not sure yet, but at the time of the attack he was stationed in Scotland. I'm flying up there tomorrow to visit his unit and hopefully him. But at least I'll find out *where* he is, if he's not there. I'll have better information tomorrow.'

'OK Bob. At least we have something to start on. Good work.'

'How'd the press conference go? Any news on Cowboy?'

'Nothing I'm afraid. His photo, along with that of his

Java Man, are plastered all over the evening papers and on the box. Might bring in something – although that also means that we'll have five thousand sightings of each of them to follow up which will be a total waste of time. But . . . better than sitting on our arses, eh?'

'Don't give up Frank. He'll be OK. Listen, I'll call you tomorrow night after I've found out about this Kane character. Talk to you then. 'Night Frank.'

'Yeah, OK. 'Night Bob.' He replaced the receiver gently. Maybe the break they were looking for had happened at last.

Joseph Gordon had also seen the press conference and read the evening editions of the papers including a profile of Cowboy Johnson, accompanied by a photograph of him and of his girlfriend, Marlane Davis. Something about the photograph of the policeman bothered him, it was as if the eyes in the picture were staring at him. But it was more than that. He knew for certain what the Gardai did not, that Detective Constable Johnson *was* in the hands of the Popular Front. He was also convinced that the car he had almost collided with that night was the one that Johnson had been taken away in. He hoped the policeman hadn't come to any harm. As far as Gordon was concerned Johnson was an innocent bystander, even if he was a member of the team that was hunting him. For some strange reason he felt . . . what? An affinity? . . . with the man. It was as if they were in some way linked to each other. He was certain of one thing. If he could help Johnson when the time came then he would.

The name they had given him amused him – the Java Man! What did they think he was? Some sort of Neanderthal? He understood why they had done it. The label had given him an identity, an image which people could fasten their minds on to. He was no longer an invisible force. He had a name, he could be referred to, talked about, psychoanalysed, imagined. Although he would not be considered a serial killer in the same way as the Son of Sam or Ted Bundy, that is what he was. They would try to build up an identity profile on him, seeking a weakness, or a pattern, something they could use to catch him. They would be trying to work out what sort of man could do what he was doing. What started him? What was his aim? Where would he strike next?

He understood the process perfectly well. He had read of Son of Sam, of Bundy, of the Boston Strangler, of some of the tactics used by police forces to apprehend such killers. It usually worked in the end – but there was one flaw in his particular case. These other serial killers had been psychopathic and the system worked because of the assumption that they would carry on their indiscriminate killing until caught. Usually they *wanted* subconsciously to be stopped, to be caught. But he was different. He had an aim – McGuinness. Once he had him, then it was over . . . wasn't it? He certainly had no desire to be caught. He wanted to complete the job he had set himself, then go away somewhere and try to start a normal life again.

Only two people knew exactly who he was, and only one of them knew why he was doing what he was doing. The girl, Monica, was one – but she owed him her life. She knew precisely what would have happened to her if he had not arrived when he did. But neither of them had spoken of their reasons for being at the farmhouse that night. Maybe it was time they had a talk.

Commandant James O'Riley was preparing for his journey

north of the border. The action he was about to take was not within the boundaries of his official duties, but was one he had undertaken several times in the past. Sometimes it was unofficial meetings with members of the British security forces, sometimes contacts with the PIRA. They were not recorded in writing anywhere, although he always made sure that all the orders that came to him were. He knew that he could not afford the professional risk of committing everything to paper himself. He made these journeys personally in order to get the information at first hand and so that he wouldn't have to share it with anyone else.

Although most of his meetings across the border had been with the British, over the years he had built up a series of contacts with members of the terrorist groups operating in the North, considering himself to be something of a broker. An exchange-of-information broker. You traded one against the other, always striving for the best deal, the one that brought you out on top, leaving the other side still owing you. It didn't always work out that way – but often enough. It was risky, and there were times when his life was on the line, like it would be tonight, but it was the risks that kept him 'alive'. Despite the ulcer and broken marriage which his addiction to his job had caused he still loved the wheeling and dealing.

For the third and final time that evening he checked every item of his clothing, plus the contents of his wallet, to make sure he carried nothing that would associate him with the Irish Army. If he were stopped by a British patrol, then he would try to bluff his way out. Failing that, he had a name and a telephone number imprinted in his memory that he could use, but that would cost him dear in bargaining power. At the moment he held the upper hand with this particular contact. To have to use their name for a favour would lose him more trading power than he could afford. Tonight he could not afford to get stopped. If he did his first meeting with Kevin Flynn would be cancelled and he had a lot to gain from talking face to face with the mysterious chief-of-staff of the PIRA.

Back in his office safe was a sealed enveloped addressed to Sergeant Kelly. The front of the envelope authorized Kelly to open it only if O'Riley had made no contact with the office for a full forty-eight hour period, starting at midnight tonight. Enclosed in the envelope were instructions to the deputy head of intelligence who would act on them immediately. He was playing this one close to his chest because he didn't want to fail. There was something about McGuinness, something he could only describe as evil, and he was determined to neutralize him one way or the other.

Flynn was a different kind of man. If the choice was up to him he would as soon hand McGuinness over to Flynn as to the security forces. The end result would probably be the same – McGuinness would simply disappear. His picture would remain on the list of the ten most wanted terrorists – but the word would be put about among the security forces not to bother looking any more. No questions would be asked as to why. Flynn might make a better example of McGuinness – but the Brits would be willing to pay more for him.

It was approaching midnight when he left the city heading north on Route 1, towards Drogheda and Dundalk. He drove carefully, taking his time, not wanting to draw attention to himself. At Dundalk he joined Route 22 taking him across country to the Monaghan road. At Cullaville, with the lights of the car switched off, he crossed the border on a small dirt road. His ulcer gave a rumble as he stepped out of the car on to Ulster soil. He stood stationary for a few moments, waiting to hear the fatal 'clicks' of weapons being cocked and searchlights being switched on. But nothing moved and the only noise he heard was his own heart beating.

From the boot of his car he withdrew two metal ramps – the kind a DIY mechanic would keep in his garage at home for small repairs to his car. Driving very slowly he got out every so often and placed the ramps over the spikes set deep into the road. This was the worst part of the journey. If he got stopped at this point he would have found it hard to explain and he would be in very deep shit indeed. But Lady Luck continued to sit on his shoulder as he navigated the series of road-spikes without interruption. Once in the clear the ramps were returned to the boot and he continued his journey, heading for Crossmaglen.

Crossmaglen. The name carved deep into the conscious and subconscious minds of every British soldier stationed in Northern Ireland. This was bandit country. Like the old days in the Wild West, when the Cavalry protected themselves against Indian attacks in their wooden forts, the British protected their 'cavalry' in iron forts, with wire mesh stretched across most of the tops to deter mortar attacks. Except for the heavily armed patrols the only way in and out of the forts was by helicopter. Even the drinking water was brought in that way.

At Crossmaglen he turned left, heading for the village of Cullyanna. A mile along the road he came to an old milestone set in the hedgerow. He stopped the car, switched the lights and the engine off, and waited.

An hour passed, and another. He sat sipping hot tea from a flask, occasionally stretching his limbs. He knew that his movements would have been monitored from the moment he had crossed the border on the dirt track. Even though he expected to be contacted, the tap on the window gave him a start. In the surrounding darkness a darker shape had appeared.

'Out and hit the deck, arms and legs spread. Before you open the door, unscrew the interior lightbulb.'

The voice was young but experienced and confident. O'Riley did as he was instructed and lay face down on the road. He heard feet clad in soft-soled trainers approaching down the road. Rough hands searched his body and he heard whispered instructions followed by the sounds of the car doors being opened. The vehicle was being as thoroughly searched as he was.

'Your name?' It was the same young voice.

'O'Riley,' he replied, his mouth feeling dry. These were the youth of the PIRA and reasonably expendable. No senior member of the organization would have risked coming to meet him, in case it was a trap. Being young made them prone to mistakes – and any mistake on his part would lead to his death.

'You'd better be, for your own sake. Stand up and put your hands behind your back.'

Once again he did as ordered, moving slowly and carefully. His hands were roughly bound behind his back and a blindfold pulled over his eyes. Then he was bundled into the back seat of his car, cracking his head on the edge of the door frame. The journey took about ten minutes. As he was taken from the car he banged his head again and swore under his breath. There was a smell of manure, a cowshed he assumed. He heard a whispered conversation, then he was half led, half dragged into another building and the blindfold removed.

He was in a small, bare, whitewashed kitchen along with four others, three of whom were masked. All were dressed in black, reminding O'Riley of a shadow puppet group. The windows of the kitchen had been covered over and the light nearly blinded him after the darkness of the blindfold. Blinking his eyes he looked round him.

Behind him stood the first of the black-clad members of the PIRA, the slight swelling of breasts the only indication of her gender. In her arms she held an Armalite, pointed directly at him. His eyes flickered to hers, barely visible through the mask. She showed no nervousness. She had the gun, and knew how to use it. Either side of her stood two similarly clad male figures, also armed with Armalites. The man in front of him was unmasked and smiling as O'Riley turned his attention to him.

'Welcome to Occupied Ulster, James. As they say, "long time no see". The voice was warm and friendly, like his smile. He turned to the others and gave an order. 'Untie him. This is Commandant O'Riley.'

The nylon cord around his wrists was cut and he stretched out a hand to clasp that of Liam Daley, ex-Lieutenant of the Irish Army.

'Hello Liam, how are you. Not taking any chances these days, are you? Whatever happened to the trust there once was?' The question was asked with an ironic smile on O'Riley's face.

'Times change, James. Yesterday's friends are today's enemies. Maybe tomorrow we'll all be friends again. Who knows? Take a seat, we'll be here for a short time yet. When the time is right you'll be taken to another location not far from here to meet with our Numero Uno, eh?' The friendly smile was still on his face, both men genuinely pleased to see each other despite their differences.

O'Riley rubbed his head where he had hit it twice on the car.

'Headache?'

'Nah, let's just say that your friends here were not too careful how they bundled me into the car.'

Daley laughed. It was warm and infectious and O'Riley couldn't help but smile.

'Sure now isn't everybody saying that we're a bunch of headbangers anyway? Never mind, James. Would you like a drink? We have tea, coffee . . . or would you prefer something a bit stronger? Fight the cold damp air.'

'Any of your da's Potheen about?'

''Fraid not. We do have some, but not his. Got a bit too old for makin' it he did. Too damp in the hills for his old bones. Stuff we have is not too bad – but not in the same class as Da's. It's barley instead of potatoes. Good vintage though – this summer.' He walked to one of the kitchen cabinets to get the bottle of clear white liquid with a slightly vinegary smell. Using teacups in place of glasses he poured both of them a drink, ignoring the other three. Handing one cup to O'Riley he raised his own.

'Sláinte,' he toasted.

'Sláinte leat,' O'Riley replied. Both men took a small sip, neither following the custom of draining the first glass straight off. Although the memories of a once-close friendship had been rekindled in both of them, both intended keeping their wits about them. Conscious they were not alone O'Riley looked round at the others, staring in particular at the young masked girl. Daley noticed the attention she got.

'Women's lib I suppose Liam, and from the looks of it, quite young.' He did not add that she also looked quite dangerous. Who was it that said the female of the species was more deadly than the male? It didn't matter, but she certainly looked the most deadly of the trio.

'Oh aye, she's a cracker that one. Got more balls than half the guys. Hard as nails – and like you say, quite young. Impatient too. All the youngsters are like that. Want it all over quickly. Like next week, or next month, but at least by Christmas. The Brits just packin' everything up after all this time, marching down to Belfast docks and sailin' off to their motherland. All the lads and lassies comin' out of hiding, marching through the streets to the sound of the bagpipes and the cheering crowds, and into the empty barracks. Just like our granddas did James, all those years ago.

'No thought of course of the odd million or so Protestants who might make an objection to the entire thing ending like that. Nah, it'll be just like in all the good stories. The happy ending to hundreds of years of strife.'

O'Riley smiled a sad smile at the picture Daley had painted. The impossible dream that took place once – but this was not 1920 – and even then the northern Protestants had made sure that they retained their control over Ulster, no matter what the southerners wanted. No thought of the civil war that would immediately follow the British withdrawal from Ulster – just as it had preceded the 1920 treaty with Britain. Thousands of armed Protestants against the hundreds of Catholics. The pressure on the Irish government to send in Irish troops would be impossible to resist – to be immediately followed by the return of the British troops to defend the Protestants. Neither the British nor the Irish government would want to do it – but would have to.

'It's hard for them to understand,' Daley continued. 'Hard to accept what we older ones have accepted, that it won't be over by Christmas. Not this one, not the next one, nor the one after that. I sometimes wonder what they'd do if it *were* over by next Christmas.'

'You talk too much Daley,' interrupted one of the other two men.

'That's today's youth for you James,' Daley apologized for the rudeness, his voice still soft and friendly. 'No consideration at all for their elders. I blame it on the schools myself. They should never have given up the strap. Never did us any harm, did it James? And those Christian Brothers knew how to lay it on. No, a couple of good hidings as a nipper and these surly buggers wouldn't be so lippy, especially with guests.'

'Ah fuck off, Daley,' the young man replied, irritation in his voice at being put down in front of what he considered to be one of the enemy. Daley turned and faced him.

'No, sonny boy, *you* fuck off, and fuck off out of my sight *now*.' The friendly smiling tone had gone, replaced with a voice so icy cold that the atmosphere in the room seemed to drop below zero. For a few moments the two men glared at each other, then the younger left without saying a word.

'Another drink, James?' The friendly tone was back, the bottle held over O'Riley's cup. O'Riley shook his head.

'No thanks Liam. I've a drive back later – don't want to get stopped for drunk drivin' now do I?' and both of them laughed.

'Go after him girl,' Daley ordered the masked woman. 'Keep an eye on the Masked Saviour and make sure he doesn't do himself any damage with that rifle. Commandant O'Riley won't be getting up to any tricks or going anywhere, now will you James?'

O'Riley looked at the girl and shook his head. As she

left the room Daley changed the subject to the days they had shared at the Curragh Officer Cadet Training School. The remaining gunman stayed silently by the door, apparently paying neither of the two friends any attention, but all the while watching Commandant James O'Riley.

An hour passed before the conversation was interrupted by the muted ringing of a telephone in another part of the house. Daley excused himself to go and answer it and on his return picked up the blindfold that lay on the table.

'Time to go, James. I'm sure you don't mind the blindfold. What you don't see you can't report, can you? It's just a short journey. No need for your hands to be tied.'

Blindfolded once again O'Riley was led back to the car. This time Daley told him to duck his head to avoid banging it. He estimated they drove for about fifteen minutes before they stopped. Unknown to him they had returned to the same farmhouse, this time parking at the front. Again Daley assisted him and led him into the house, taking him to the front room, where the blindfold was removed.

Yet another small room, with heavy black drapes covering the windows. The only light in the room came from an architect's lamp clamped to the edge of the desk in the corner, tilted so that the light was directed towards the floor. In front of the desk was an empty chair. The figure seated behind the desk was just a black shape.

'Sit down Commandant O'Riley.' The voice was cultured and not too old – possibly early to mid-thirties O'Riley guessed. The northern lilt was evident in the accent, but not the harshness of Belfast. Definitely male. The darker shadow of an arm crossed the table indicating the seat. The black leather-gloved hand was not being offered as a handshake, and O'Riley did not presume it to be so. This then, he knew, was the legendary Kevin Flynn, chief-of-staff of the Provisional Irish Republican Army. Everything he had on file about him – which was little enough – was evident in the caution showed by this man in front of him. He was unaware that this was the same masked man, the third 'guard', who had listened in silence to him and Daley reminisce about their youth. Flynn had wanted to know a little more than he already knew about O'Riley – which was considerably more than O'Riley knew about him – before he was prepared to trade with him. He had wanted to observe him, without O'Riley's knowledge. Know thine enemy was Flynn's first commandment.

O'Riley sat in the proffered seat. 'I take it I am talking to Kevin Flynn?'

'I'm afraid that you are going to have to take my word for that, Commandant. Yes, I am Kevin Flynn. But it's not who I am, but what I am, that matters to you. Right?'

'Right.' O'Riley knew full well why there was so much secrecy surrounding Flynn. As the man had just said, it wasn't who he was that was important, but what he was – the undisputed leader of the PIRA.

In the late sixties and well into the seventies, when the current problems came to the fore, the chiefs-of-staff all became known to the security forces, and, once known, a large part of their power was broken. Followed everywhere, photographed relentlessly from all angles, they could not take a crap without being handed a piece of toilet paper by a member of the forces. Profiles were made on them, background information gathered, friends, relatives and even the guy they had a pint with in the pub the night before were watched.

Three years earlier the inner command of the PIRA

had held a meeting. The current chief-of-staff was sacked there and then and told to leave the meeting. The three remaining members then voted in their new Chief – before he even knew it himself! They required a new leadership, with new ideas and one with the determination to carry them out. The man they picked, Kevin Flynn, was even more determined than they knew. Within a short space of time the three men were all dead and the legend around Flynn began. Nobody knew for certain who he was or where he came from – but his orders were obeyed to the letter. A bloodbath followed his election and at the time the security forces were quite pleased with it. Men they knew but could not prove in open court were active members of the PIRA turned up as slabs of meat in the mortuaries throughout the province. Too late it dawned on them that their replacements were unknown to them and they were now facing a totally anonymous enemy force.

After sorting out the PIRA, Flynn then turned his attention to PIRA offshoots. Smaller, independent groups of terrorists were given the choice: either put themselves under his command or leave the country. If they chose to remain, they wound up dead. The only group still outside his control was the Popular Front, under the leadership of McGuinness. McGuinness had no choice now, because Flynn wanted him dead anyway – but as long as he remained in the Republic he would not be touched. Flynn's orders on that score were clear. No action whatsoever was to be carried out by members of the PIRA in the Irish Republic.

He had also ceased the attacks on what had been considered prime targets by previous leaders of the PIRA – the 'soft' targets. His orders were that he was commanding the Provisional Republican *Army* – and that was how they would behave – as an army. The police and the British Army were all targets, both in Ulster and throughout the world – but there would be no more civilian bombings. Undercover agents, 'spies', would be executed without mercy, but they were the only 'civilians' he took action against. At first the security forces and Royal Ulster Constabulary disbelieved him, but within six months he had proved that he meant what he said. Ten members of the PIRA had disobeyed his orders, planting car bombs in civilian areas, and their bodies were dumped near RUC barracks with notes explaining their 'crimes' and the sentences carried out on them.

But Flynn had created more than a disciplined group of men under his autocratic command. By making sure that his particulars remained a mystery, should he himself be shot or captured by the security forces, then another figure would step out of the shadows as 'Kevin Flynn' and the command structure would remain intact, and after him another, and another. O'Riley was reminded of his favourite comic-book hero – the Phantom. The ghost who walks. He who never dies. O'Riley smiled at the simplistic idea that worked such a treat.

'I might need a favour in the future Commandant, and I am led to believe that you are a man with a good memory who pays his debts. How can I help you?'

'The missing policeman, Johnson,' O'Riley came straight to the point. 'Plus the killings in Ballymun and Swords. I don't suppose it will do me any harm to ask if all or any of them were carried out on your orders?'

From behind the mask came a sound which O'Riley took to be a chuckle.

'Commandant, I am a man who knows which side his bread is buttered. I have given *very* strict instructions about actions taken in the Republic – none! Despite the Anglo-Irish Agreement there are still people in power in the South who are, shall we say, sympathetic to our cause. As long as we keep our noses clean down there, we don't have too much trouble. The Brits put in their extradition warrants, but usually there is something "wrong" with them. They arrive too late, the comma is in the wrong place, the name is misspelt . . . whatever. So I make sure that noses are kept clean down there.

'I can assure you – as I suspect you already know – that the PIRA had nothing to do with any of these incidents.' He paused before continuing. 'So what is it you really want to know, Commandant?'

O'Riley smiled and nodded. He was virtually certain that the PIRA were not behind the murders or kidnapping – but it didn't hurt to ask. 'What about McGuinness?' he asked in reply to Flynn's question. 'Any ideas where I can find him?'

'And what will happen if you do get your hands on him?'

'If we apprehend him, and can tie him in with any of them, then he'll stand trial of course.'

This time it was more than a chuckle that came from behind the mask. It was derisory laughter.

'Please don't take me for a fool, Commandant. If *you* get your hands on McGuinness you have already promised him as a birthday present to certain people in British Intelligence. You'll hand him over the border immediately, no paper work, no fuss. One second he's in the Republic, next he's in the North. If this Inspector Mooney gets him he *might* stand trial – and he might also walk free afterwards! Thomas McGuinness has tried to keep himself Teflon-coated, but let's assume I could find him for you. If – and that's a big if – if I find him I'll tell you on one condition. You hand him over to *me* to deal with.'

O'Riley knew why Flynn wanted McGuinness. He had already been tried and sentenced for stealing funds designated for the PIRA. He also led the only group outside Flynn's control. Kill McGuinness and the Popular Front died. O'Riley had little doubt that Flynn knew exactly where in the South McGuinness was hiding, but as long as he remained in the South, Flynn would not touch him – even by remote control. McGuinness knew this – but now he was being hunted in the South by an unknown force. He had nowhere to run – and like a cornered rat this made him extremely dangerous. O'Riley sighed, but he knew they were going to trade.

'I can't agree to that and you know it. I can't even hand him over to the British any more. It was different when he had a clean nose down there – but the death of one garda and the kidnapping of another changes the rules of the game even for me. This Inspector Mooney wants his balls on a plate. But let's assume – just assume, mind you – that I could hand him over to the British. They would either shoot him out of hand, or put him on trial – and he wouldn't walk free up there. So what would he get? Life. And where would he spend it? In the H Blocks. And who controls the H Blocks? You do. So we'd both get what we wanted. Don't worry about him walking free in the South. If the CIB get him he'll go down, don't worry about that. And where will they put him? Top security in Portlaoise, or Mountjoy. Both places you control. You still get him.'

'So why should I help you Commandant? According to you I get him whatever you do.'

Now it was O'Riley's turn to smile. 'Because I'll owe you a favour.'

This remark was followed by silence for a few moments while Flynn digested it, then he started to laugh. At first it was a chuckle, then it built up. Daley too began to laugh and soon all three men were laughing.

'I think we have a live one here, Liam. Oh yes, you're a cagey bastard all right Commandant – and no offence intended. If you are willing to owe me a favour – then somebody somewhere must be willing to owe you an even bigger one. Is that it? Is that the trade-off?'

'Got it in one, Flynn. You get your favour, whenever, and I get mine from the CIB as soon as we get McGuinness and the missing garda – unless of course this so-called Java Man gets there first. Either way McGuinness gets caught by the bollocks by all three of us. What'ya say? Do we trade?'

'What of this Java character? Who is he? Where the hell did he come from?'

'I don't know,' O'Riley replied. 'He's not one of mine, he's not one of yours, and he's not from the Brits. He could be somebody inside the Front – but I've heard nothing of any problems of that nature.'

'Me neither. With McQueedy as his right-hand man McGuinness manages to keep a firm grip on things. So where does that leave us?'

'A joker in the pack. A wild card. A civilian if you like, with one hell of a grudge against the Front. Let's face it, there's more than enough out there with that kind of grudge.'

'Some civilian! I wish I had a few more like him with me. Whoever he is he's doing both of us a favour. Is he expendable – or do you want him as well?'

'I've no interest in him other than curiosity. All I want is McGuinness and the cop.'

'OK, Commandant, we have a deal. If I find McGuinness's location, he's yours. If we find this Java Man as well, we'll throw him in for good measure. Call it a promotional gift. No extra charge . . . that I can think of at the moment.' The chuckle returned and this time the gloved hand stretched across the desk was for him to shake. O'Riley leaned forward and grasped it. The handshake from both men was strong and firm, each knowing what was expected.

'OK, Liam, take the Commandant back to his car and make sure he has no trouble getting to the border road. I suggest you leave the ramps, Commandant, and go home across a recognized border crossing. We don't want you getting stopped on the way back, do we?' Flynn stood up from behind the desk, confirming to O'Riley the height of the man noted in his files. Six feet. 'Take good care of yourself now. I have an investment in you, so drive carefully.'

Once more O'Riley was blindfolded, led to his car, and brought back to the original pick-up point. There he and Daley took their leave of each other, two friends who travelled separate paths, each hoping they would never have to face each other with weapons drawn. Both knew how they would react. Both had made lasting decisions years previously.

His return journey was uneventful, crossing back into the Republic with merely a cursory check at the border.

It was just after 8 p.m. when Bob's phone call came to Mooney's office.

'So how'd it go with this Kane character, Bob? Anything definite on him?'

'I've got a bit more on him – but I think it's a dead end. Pity really, because he made a beautiful class A prime suspect. He certainly had the motive – wife and unborn child killed in the King's Cross bombing. He's had the army training to do the job – although he's not yer Gung Ho type of soldier. He was a finance clerk in the Royal Army Pay Corps – basically an office type, but they all do the normal military training. The system in the British Army is that you are a soldier first, and whatever kind of tradesman second.'

'He sounds like an odds-on favourite,' Mooney commented hopefully.

'Yeah, but there's a little snag. He couldn't have done the O'Grady job. He was in Hong Kong at the time. He's in Taipei at the moment. He left the Army a few months back and decided to get away from it all. Booked a six-week tour of the Orient. Been sending cards to the office now and again. His ex-CO – the last one, at Army HQ – confirms it's his handwriting.'

'What about friends there. Any relatives in the UK?'

'The only relatives over here are his parents-in-law. He has a few friends in the area – civilian as well as military – and his best friend is stationed here.'

'Who gave you all the background information on him? His mate?'

'No, he's away on holiday at present. Somewhere in France, touring. There's a few cards for him from Kane, waiting for his return. I got all this from his CO. 'S funny, but I also got an impression that there was something he *wasn't* telling me. Like the death of his wife wasn't the only thing in the story. But you know what military types are like. They keep everything close to their chests.'

'Tell me about it! What about the parents-in-law?'

'They live in Salisbury. I haven't spoken with them though. The local bobbies did a discreet check for me. The mother-in-law had a serious heart attack after her daughter was killed. She's on the mend, but is not the same woman. There was no friction between them and Kane. Quite the reverse in fact. Thought of him as the son they had always wanted. They only had the one child, and apparently still consider him as their own.'

'What about over here?' Mooney asked.

'Sure. A sister, funnily enough living in Glasnevin. Parents are dead and she was on his documents as his next-of-kin. This guy was so good I knew there had to be something wrong with it all. Motive, background military training, possible desire to see some kind of vigilante justice carried out. I'll fax you my report in the morning, including the name and address of the sister. I'm off to Birmingham tomorrow to check on another geezer down there. His brother and sister-in-law were killed in the restaurant bombing. I'll phone you from there tomorrow night round the same time.'

'OK, Bob, keep digging. Something is bound to turn up . . . he says hopefully! These people make mistakes, no matter how good they are. Like Cowboy finding those prints on the milk bottle. I'm getting more and more convinced that Cowboy is right. And O'Riley for that matter. We have a loner going amok among the Popular Front, and the answer lies somewhere in that list of names you have. I think Cowboy must have walked in on something entirely different. McGuinness has him. It's a two-in-one situation, both of them mixed together.'

'You could be right, Frank. Anyway. I'll call tomorrow. Take care and hey . . . find the Cowboy.'

'I will, Bob. Goodnight.'

For more than an hour Mooney sat in his desk chair thinking about Bob's report, and wondering if Johnson was still alive. He was finding it difficult to think straight. Logic and personal feelings were getting confused. His logic told him that this Kane guy was too good to drop. But he couldn't be in two places at once. Mooney was convinced that the same killer was involved at Ballymun and Merrion Farm – but if Kane was in Hong Kong for the O'Grady job . . . Even the area the guy originated from was a coincidence. Glasnevin, a middle-class suburb, was not a stone's throw away from Ballymun.

But while his logic grappled with the problem of how somebody could possibly be in two places at once, his heart was worrying over Cowboy. Almost from the day they met there was a bond between them. Marjorie was the one who put her finger on it, the night they had all gone for a meal – him and Marj, Bob and a girlfriend, and Cowboy and Marlane. They had always wanted a child, but had never been blessed that way. 'You know, Frank, if we'd had a son of our own I would have liked him to turn out like that young man.' Yes, he was personally involved in this one – and that could be dangerous. Dangerous for Cowboy.

Chapter Ten

'I HAVE TO HAND IT to you, Jimmy. When you do something, you really do it.' McGuinness was reading the newspaper article on the career of the man held prisoner in the upstairs room, his lips curling sarcastically. 'Oh yes, Jimmy. Not for you any two-a-penny copper. Oh no. You had to pick the most well known, lover-boy, rich bastard, with an equally rich and famous girlfriend. Here. Read all about it.' He slung the paper across to his silent, glowering friend. When his eyes fell on the two photographs it was the one of Marlane Davis that immediately caught McQueedy's attention. His heart missed a beat and he felt small prickles of sweat break out on his forehead. His crotch swelled uncomfortably in his jeans and he shifted in his seat to try to ease it. He ran an ugly tongue over his thick, dry lips and remembered the scene of Monica tied and helpless, naked and accessible. His heart beat increased, and an angry frustration rose inside him. He imagined Monica's place being taken by Marlane, and the picture made him short of breath and flooded his mouth with saliva. He stared closely at the picture, drinking in every detail. He had never in his life seen a more beautiful woman. His whole body quivered with anticipation, he had seen something he wanted very badly indeed.

McQueedy's parents were both drunks who abused him in their different ways. Everything he wanted or needed he had had to fight for or steal. He had vague memories of his childhood, of crying alone, tired, hungry, wearing soiled clothing and listening to his parents screaming abuse at each other. He had learned early on not even to try to stop them. When he had tried they had combined their spite and malice against him, beating him viciously, first to punish him and then to make him stop crying. He had frequently watched his father beat and rape his mother and believed that was the way all men were expected to treat their women. His parents stayed together, having nowhere else to go, and on rare occasions showed each other, and him, small signs of affection which he interpreted as love. In McQueedy's slow, dim brain some sort of logic began to form and he drew conclusions which set his behaviour patterns for life. If Daddy beat Mummy, and Daddy and Mummy loved each other, then that must mean you always beat the one you love. At fourteen he broke both his father's arms and threw him down the stairs, telling him never to return. On release from hospital the old man was not seen again, but his mother now lived in fear of her son and did everything he told her until the night she choked in her own vomit after a drinking binge.

When he was fifteen the local council decided to have no more to do with him and banished him from school. He was on his own. His most pleasurable memory from that era was of waiting one evening, near his old school gates, for Brother Williams, or 'Waddle' as he was known owing to his obese figure which made him waddle like a duck. By the time McQueedy was finished with him he never walked again.

Sex to him was all about give and take. The woman gave and he took. He lost his virginity at the age of twelve to one of his mother's drunken friends and from then on, when the urge took him, he went hunting. He was legally guilty of at least forty individual acts of rape – but who had the courage to go to the police about him? He had never felt any pang of tenderness or love in his life but his lusts sometimes drove him close to the brink of clinical madness. He stared long and hard at Marlane's picture and saliva bubbled from the corners of his mouth.

'Jimmy, bring that bastard down here again – gently.' McGuinness interrupted his thoughts, 'Let's see if he can remember anything by now. It's been two fucking days for Crissake. When will you ever learn your own strength?'

Upstairs Cowboy was still trying to prise the inch-thick chipboard off the window of his cell. He realized he could not keep up his pretence of amnesia for much longer. Three times now he had been taken to the kitchen to be questioned over who had informed the Gardai about Merrion Farm. He knew that both McQueedy and McGuinness were making plans to leave their present location within a day and he firmly believed that taking him along was not on either of their agendas. Hearing the footsteps on the stairs he lay back down on the bed. The key turned in the lock and the door opened.

'On yer feet. It's time to have another little talkies.' Sexual frustration was ticking inside McQ's head like a time bomb as he pushed and hustled the policeman downstairs. Once again Cowboy was pushed into a chair at the kitchen table, facing McGuinness.

'Thought you might be interested in reading this, Christy – or should I say Cowboy?' McGuinness passed the newspaper across, open at the article about him. Johnson attempted a puzzled look while studying the photographs. He had to hide his surprise at seeing the sketch he had drawn of the Java Man.

'Seems like your friends aren't exactly sure where you are, Cowboy, sharing our company or with this other gentleman. Says here that you drew the sketch. So you've met him. Who and where is this bastard and why is he on the rampage? Who told you about Merrion Farm – and more importantly, who told this fucker about the farm? My patience is wearing thin Cowboy. I want straight answers or I'm afraid that my Indian friend here is liable to lift your fuckin' scalp.' McGuinness rose from the table and walked round towards Cowboy. For a split second he turned to McQueedy, who stood with arms folded, by the sink, telling him to put the kettle on 'so we can have a nice cup of tea'. In that brief moment Cowboy slipped one of the stainless steel dinner knives that lay on an unwashed plate up his sleeve. McGuinness leaned over his shoulder.

'So what have you got to tell me, Cowboy? Who is this geezer?' His finger pointed to the sketch of the Java Man, his knuckles turning white with the pressure.

'I . . . I don't know. I can't remember even drawing this picture, let alone know where I met him. Do you have any aspirin? My headache is back, I'm sorry.'

McGuinness's fists clenched as he swung away from Cowboy, his eyes flashing with anger. He wanted to smash somebody's head on to the table top. He wasn't sure which of the two he wanted to do it to, Cowboy or Jimmy.

'Let me sort him out, Tommy. He's lying. He's fucking lying. You know he's lying, I know he's lying, and *he* fucking knows he lying.' McQueedy moved towards Cowboy, but McGuinness stopped him.

'Leave him, Jimmy. I have a better idea. One I think you'll like even better than kickin' the shit out of him. Take him back upstairs and I'll tell you all about it. This way we'll find out for definite if he's lying. Oh yes, Mr Christopher Cowboy Johnson, we'll soon know if you're lying or not.'

Cowboy lay on the bed in the darkened room for a long while before he made any move. Shaking the knife from his sleeve he slid the blade between the window frame and the chipboard covering, gently but firmly applying pressure on either side of the nails that held it in place. While the chipboard was new the window frame was old and weatherbeaten, and in parts rotten. Slowly but surely the nails moved under the pressure and a gap appeared large enough for him to get a firm grip on the sheeting with his fingers. Dusk was falling outside so he decided to wait until it got much darker before attempting his escape. He had one, and only the one, chance of getting out. If they caught him they would know for certain that there was nothing wrong with his memory. He didn't think that even if he told them the truth – that his information came from a snitch looking for a favour – that they would believe him now. He remembered the case of the undercover SAS officer captured by the PIRA several years back. He had been tortured to death. The newspapers had not given the full details of it but Cowboy had seen a copy of the RUC report on the state of the man's body; there had been hardly a piece of it which hadn't been broken, torn or burnt. Whatever the PIRA could do, he felt sure McQueedy could come up with something better.

He sat on the edge of the bed waiting for the stillness of night. He heard voices below and the slamming of the front door on several occasions, but was unsure of the exact number of Front members in the house. Positive he would not be left in the house alone, he sat and waited until he felt his chances were best for making a move.

His thoughts dwelt on ways of beating the shit out of McQueedy. He wanted to smash the man's legs, to immobilize him, then to dance around the stricken monster with a hurley stick, breaking his arms one at a time, then a boot in the ribs, several kicks to the kidneys, followed by a swift mouthful of shoe leather. He amazed himself with the depth of his hatred.

Feeling slightly sickened by his own dreams of violence he purposely turned his thoughts to Marlane, reliving some of their moments together, like the night of their first meeting. He remembered the feeling he got the moment he saw her. His breath had caught in his chest as he stared across the crowded theatre foyer at her. She had felt his stare, despite the distance between them, and had turned in his direction. She was used to men staring at her, occasionally with admiration but usually with desire or lust in their eyes. Women also stared, some with envy, some with admiration and some with hatred, and even on occasions with the same lust as the men. This time, she later explained to him, she felt a tingling down her own spine and the tiny hairs on her arms stood to attention, giving her goose pimples.

He had locked into her unblinking blue eyes as he was sucked deeper and deeper into a whirlpool of emotions. They gazed at each other for what seemed an eternity, then she recovered her composure and smiled. It was such a teasing, knowing smile that he had almost laughed out loud with joy. The twinkle in her eyes said it all. 'So, you think you could tame me? Others have tried and failed. But maybe you can, only I won't be as easy for you as others have been.' The smile was still on her face as she turned her back on him and walked into the theatre with her group, some of whom he knew, such as Phil Stringer, a photographer friend. At the supper party afterwards he had looked for her. Spotting Phil he asked who she was.

Phil smiled and told him, then added that she had also asked about him.

'What'd she say?'

'"So that's the famous Cowboy is it? Humph! I suppose he thinks I'll be a pushover like all the others."' Phil laughed, adding that she too had laughed as she said it.

It was to be several weeks before they were officially introduced. This time her smile was shy, almost schoolgirlish. She played him like an expert angler, reeling him in slowly, apparently confident he was not going to get away – and he loved it. He loved the game they both played, because each of them, deep down inside, knew what the end result would be. All it took was patience.

Other memories went through his mind as he sat in the darkness. The night she had asked him to stay with her, explaining in the same breath, almost as if he would be frightened off, that she was a virgin and wanted to stay that way until she felt ready. Despite the erotic postures of her photographs, despite the knowledge that thousands, hundreds of thousands maybe, had seen photos of her in swimwear and scanty underwear, she blushed as he undressed her that night. She had been afraid of him for the first and only time when he got into bed beside her. But the fear melted when he took her in his arms, laid her head on his chest, and told her to sleep.

She told him later that she had pretended to sleep, listening to his heartbeat, knowing he was excited and wanted her, until she felt his heart slow down, and he slept. Then she had eased herself out of his arms to look at him. She had seen plenty of photographs of naked men, and had worked with scantily clad male models – but he was the first naked male she had seen so close. He had slept like a log throughout her inspection. 'What did you think, what was your impression?' he had asked when she told him much later, beginning to feel embarrassed himself. She put her arms around his neck and brought her mouth close to his ear. 'I thought you were beautiful,' she whispered. Then, to bring him down to earth again, added 'but I thought your little willie was funny, all curled up and asleep.' Then she giggled, once more the little girl. In retaliation he had pinned her to the bed and very gently entered her. 'Still think he's little and asleep?' he had asked, smiling down at her. Her eyes had darkened as her body reacted to his movements. She had pulled him down to her so she could feel his weight on her. 'Oh no,' she had whimpered in delight, 'he's not small, and he most certainly is not asleep.' Was it any wonder, he asked himself, that he felt this woman was so special?

The house had been quiet for a long time. He decided to make his move. Returning to the window he pulled on the chipboard, feeling it move further and further away from the window frame. One of the nails made a screeching noise and he froze. It was then that he felt the chill warning of danger. At first he thought he might have been heard. He made his way to the locked door, pinning his ear close to the edge. Nothing. Silence. But the feeling wouldn't go away. The small hairs on the back of his neck and on his arms were raised. Something was wrong – but what? 'Sit,' the voice in his head told him. 'Sit and open your mind, my friend.'

Without feeling silly in any way he did as instructed. Remembering how he had seen Mrs Blackmore act, now he too began to relax, to breathe in deep. Deeper and deeper he drew air into his lungs, allowing his chest to expand and contract. 'Open your mind,' the same voice instructed. 'Open and see.' For just a moment he caught a glimpse of a man's face. Deeply tanned with coal black eyes, the hair – same colour as his eyes, hanging on either side of his face in plaits. He knew instantly that this was the face of the voice, the face of his spirit guide. This was Blue Water. The face disappeared and in its place a fog began to form. Like a swirling mist it grew thicker and thicker – then began to disperse. Through the fog he could see a flight of stairs. There was something familiar about them and as the fog thinned he recognized them. They led from the street to Marlane's front door. He felt himself slowly walking up the stairs, approaching the door, which also began to materialize from the mist. But there was something wrong. The cold grip of fear tightened as he got nearer to the door. He saw the broken frame where the security chain had been attached. As he slowly entered the apartment he could smell James Earl McQueedy. If Marlane wasn't already a captive of the Popular Front, she very soon would be. Rage and anger replaced the fear he had felt for her. He knew why she was being taken. McGuinness wanted whatever information he had – not knowing that he had very little anyway – and was going to use Marlane to force Cowboy to talk, and then they would both die. He had to move fast. The rage he felt blanked the image from his mind and once more he was back in the locked room.

He pulled again on the chipboard and it came away from the window. Moonlight streamed in as he carried the sheet of wood across to the door and laid it on the floor, the nails sticking upward. Pushing as hard but as quietly as he could he jammed it as close to the door as possible. It wouldn't stop anybody from getting into the room for long, but it would give him a few, perhaps vital, seconds. He returned to the window.

It was an up-and-down sashcord type, with the catch in the middle. Sliding the catch to one side he gripped the painted-over brass handles on the lower frame and tugged. It wouldn't budge. 'Shit,' he whispered in frustration. Sweat broke out on his forehead as he gripped the handles again and strained. His arm muscles bulged, the sweat dripped down his face and his ribs began to ache, but still it wouldn't move. Taking a break he wiped the sweat from his eyes and ran his fingers around the frame, eventually detecting the tiny tell-tale bumps near the base. 'Shite, shite, shite.' The window had been nailed shut, and not recently. He was about to give up when he realized he hadn't tried the top half. Using his fingers he pressed on the bottom half of the top frame, on either side of the catch. It moved. 'You moron, Johnson,' he castigated himself for not trying it sooner. Able now to get his fingers on the top of the frame he pulled downwards. The window was stiff, but moved. Slowly but carefully he pushed downwards on either side of the frame and it jerked and ground, inch by inch, further and further until the top part of the frame was almost level with the catch.

He stood inhaling the cold, moist night air for a moment. Clouds glided across the moon, occasionally obliterating it. He'd have to be very careful – but quick. The ledge was bound to be damp and he couldn't afford to slip at this point. Marlane kept popping into his mind, and he had to fight to keep her out. He needed all his concentration to get away from here, to find a phone, and get help for her. But if he slipped, then they were both dead. He crossed the room once more to listen for signs of movement within the house. There was none. It was silent. Time to go.

Easing one leg out of the window he bent at the waist

and slid out on to the narrow ledge, drawing his other leg after him. In the darkness below he made out a rectangular shape sticking out of the side of the house to his right. It was some sort of roof. An outhouse or a porch, he wasn't sure, but it was his only way down. He hoped it would hold his weight. Digging into his trouser pocket he found a handkerchief. Going down on one knee, holding the window frame with one hand, he dried the ledge as best he could and began his descent.

Left hand still holding on to the frame above his head, praying it wouldn't fall apart, he eased his body off the ledge, gripping it with his right hand, letting go with his left. His right hand bore the full weight of his body for the split second before his left hand made contact with the ledge. He almost fell as pain shot up his right arm to his shoulder, the breath knocked out of him by the sharp drop. His ribs throbbed painfully and he knew he could not hold his own weight much longer. Swinging his body from left to right a couple of times he let go on the rightward swing and dropped to the roof below. It creaked loudly but held. He froze for several seconds, but there was no sign of movement. Working quickly now, he slid off the roof and dropped to the ground.

Gravel crunched beneath his feet as he tried to get his bearings. He was in front of a detached house. No lights showed and he moved cautiously along the short driveway towards the road. Looking backwards he felt relief as the house remained in darkness. His feet were now on a tarmac road. But which way to go? Right or left? He chose the right as the road seemed to steepen to his left. Why walk up when he could walk down? He passed several houses on his right, all in darkness, but he dared not wake any resident, it would involve too much noise and it was unlikely they would help him. Sensible families did not let bruised and dirty looking strangers into their homes in the middle of the night, and he had no means of identification on him. A hedgerow to his left seemed solid; he guessed that fields must lie behind it.

Several hundred yards from the house he came to a crossroads. Instinct led him to take the left arm, the road once again going downhill. Two minutes later he was in a small village with the street lights out. So what did that make the time? 2 a.m.? 3 a.m.? He found a phone kiosk and swore out loud when he discovered it had been vandalized. Looking round he realised he was standing outside a sub-post office. Taking his shoe off he put it over his hand and punched through the window. Immediately the quiet country night was rent by alarm bells. Grabbing a large sweet jar through the broken glass he prayed the Gardai would get here soon. He had to get help for Marlane before McQ got to her. As he ate the sweets, regaining strength from the sugar, all he could do was mentally call her name and beg her to be careful. He tried to imagine her, asleep in her bed. Leaving the jar of sweets to one side he again tried to concentrate all his energy in his mind, to send her a warning. 'Wake up,' he pleaded. 'Please please please. Wake up, darling. Get up and get out of the flat. Quickly.' He then sent a plea to his spirit friend. 'Please, Blue Water. Please help her.' But he received no reply, no indication that his words had been heard by either. He tried one last time, this time screaming the words out loud into the cold night, venting his rage at the darkness. '*Marlane. Don't open the door!*'

While Cowboy had been planning his escape, McQueedy

and his sidekick Deegan had left in a Ford Transit van to pick up Marlane. Deegan noticed immediately that McQueedy was in an unusual mood. He was pensive, pent up, and silent for the best part of the journey. Deegan was more than happy to leave things that way. McQueedy was the last man on earth he wished to put into a bad mood.

It was shortly after 1 a.m., while Cowboy was struggling to get the chipboard sheet off the window frame, that the van drew up outside the shop beneath Marlane's apartment.

'Got the chloroform?' McQueedy asked, breaking the silence that had lasted for the past hour. Deegan leaned over and opened the glovebox, producing a bottle of the knockout liquid and a bag of cotton wool.

'Give it here,' McQueedy ordered, taking both and getting out of the van. Deegan noticed that his hands were shaking. The streets were damp and silent. McQueedy pressed the buzzer on the intercom, keeping his finger on it until he heard a click as the handset was lifted in the flat above.

'Yes?' a sleepy, female voice asked.

'Miss Davis, it's Detective Sergeant O'Donnel from CIB. Can we come up please. It's regarding Detective Constable Johnson.'

Marlane's heart skipped a beat. About Cowboy. Why wasn't it Cowboy himself? Had he been found? Was he injured? Or was he . . . She refused to even think of him being dead. Oh God, please let him be all right.

'May we please come up?' the voice on the intercom asked once again.

'Ah, oh yes, sorry. Just push the door.' She pressed the lock release button on the intercom panel and heard the buzzing sound as the electronic lock was released and then men's footsteps on the stairs. It was only then that she realized something was wrong. If Cowboy hadn't come – couldn't come – why hadn't Mooney come to tell her whatever it was she had to be told? Vaguely, at the back of her mind, she heard a tiny voice – it almost sounded like Cowboy whispering to her to be careful, warning her of danger. There was something else that bothered her. Something the man on the intercom said . . . Her thoughts were interrupted by the doorbell. The security chain was still engaged as she opened the door and saw the two men through the narrow gap. One of them was holding a warrant card in his hand. She gave a sigh of relief.

'Just a moment, Sergeant,' she said, going to push the door closed again to unlatch the chain. At that moment she heard Cowboy's voice screaming in her inner ear '*Don't open the door!*' and she realized what it was she thought strange about what the Sergeant had said. It wasn't *what* he said – it was the way he said it. His accent. It was Northern. Alarm bells started ringing in her mind and she tried to slam the door shut. It was pulled from her hand and then came back at her. The chain and socket were torn out of the wood and the door slammed into her, knocking her backwards onto the floor. She attempted to scream but something was placed over her mouth and she started to choke.

It took the two uniformed gardai almost fifteen minutes to arrive in answer to the post office alarm. Cowboy informed them who he was and demanded to use their car radio to be patched through to CIB Headquarters at Dublin Castle. After a brief argument one of the gardai recognized him from the newspapers and he got his message through to send a car immediately to Marlane's flat, and passed another message through to Inspector Mooney that he was safe and well.

The senior of the two gardai then spoke to his superiors and asked for armed backup for a raid on the house where Cowboy had been held, and an ambulance for Cowboy, despite his insistence that he did not need one. Cowboy instructed the garda to tell the cars to arrive with no sirens or blue lights. Ten minutes later the two cars arrived under the command of a uniformed Inspector Brown. His men were armed with automatic pistols and machine guns, and wore lightweight body armour. Further cars were on the way. Cowboy briefed the inspector on what he knew of the layout of the house and his estimate of those inside. Despite only having seen and spoken to McGuinness and McQueedy he had heard other people moving about in the house. He had heard departures earlier on – what he now estimated to be around midnight – but wasn't sure who, or how many, remained there. Cowboy feared that the sounds of the first gardai cars might have alerted them, despite the house being some distance away.

'Believe me,' he warned the Inspector, 'this is not going to be easy, especially if they expect a raid. These are hard men, and they are cornered. I can personally vouch for the kind of man McQueedy in particular is.'

'Thank you for the advice, Detective Johnson, but we'll take it from here.'

'I'm going in with you Inspector,' Cowboy insisted.

'No, you are not. You're injured – how badly you don't know. You stay out of it.' Even as he spoke the ambulance arrived, siren blaring its distinctive 'doo-dah doo-dah' sound. A garda ran towards it, arms indicating for silence, and the sound slowly died away.

'Get in the ambulance, Detective, and stay out of this.

And that's an order.' With that Inspector Brown walked away to brief his men.

The vehicles drove at walking pace up the hill with sidelights only, the armed gardai using them as cover. At the driveway to the house Inspector Brown ordered the first patrol car to block the road heading up the hill, away from the village, and the second to block the slope leading down to the village. Two of his men were instructed to make their way round the side of the house, towards the rear, and to let him know on their personal radios the moment they were in position. Another was posted behind a bush in the front garden and the fourth at the edge of the house, with a clear view of the front door. Nobody was to open fire until he gave the order. He was waiting for the reinforcements before he made any move to arrest those inside.

The ambulance carrying Cowboy to hospital met the reinforcements heading in the opposite direction with blue lights flashing and sirens blaring. The three patrol cars roared past, like the Seventh Cavalry with the bugler blowing the charge, heading for the village.

'Fucking, fucking morons,' he said quietly. He hoped that Inspector Brown's men had good body armour. They were going to need it. Any surprise Brown intended was certainly blown now – just as loudly as the patrol cars blew their sirens.

Chapter Eleven

DINNER WAS OVER, one bottle of wine was finished and the second only half full. Pushing the plate away from him Gordon topped their glasses up. As he did so he found himself smiling.

'What's so funny?' Monica asked, unable to suppress a grin herself.

He continued to smile for a moment, then replied. 'Don't you find it amusing, in a way? Here we are, just finished a nice meal, sharing a couple of bottles of nice wine. We should be planning to go out somewhere, to a pub or the cinema, something like that. Instead we will spend the evening watching the television, wondering about each other. What were you doing at the farm? Who am I? Why were they beating you? Why was I there?'

The smile disappeared from both their faces as he reminded them of the reality of their situation. With the help of the wine Monica had temporarily forgotten the violence of that night, and the memory made her shiver. She now knew he was not a violent man. There was a kindness and gentleness to his nature that had made him bring her back here when he could just as easily have left her where she was, badly beaten and tied to that chair until found by the police. But he had brought her back, washed her, rubbed ointment on her bruises, bought her new clothes and spoon-fed her when she couldn't feed herself. All of these things – and no questions asked. He had helped her to laugh once more, like last night, watching the television. Something he said about one of the programmes they had been watching had made her laugh. That had hurt and he had shown concern – but that seemed funny to her as well and she laughed more, setting him off. Each time they looked at each other they started again and it really was beginning to hurt her.

He had gone to the kitchen to make coffee, but even there she could still hear him laughing. Then a wall of silence had built up between them. There they were, like millions of other couples having a warm drink before bed – but that wasn't the reality of it. And when they had decided to go to bed there was a strangeness between them that had not been there before. He had seen her naked body several times, had washed her, massaged her, and had not seemed to think anything of it. Now it was like two people going to bed together for the first time, each so shy that neither of them could look at the other. She had wanted him to sleep with her that night. Not because of any feeling of love or from any physical desire. She had just wanted to feel his warm body beside her. To have been able to turn to him when she woke in the night, which she knew she would, and be reassured by his presence beside her. She had seen a similar longing in his eyes too, she was sure of that. It was like a cry from the wild, two animals wanting each other for comfort, nothing else. Yet they had gone their separate ways. She to his bed and he to the broken sofa.

He rose from the table to take the dishes to the kitchen, but she stopped him. 'Let me do those.'

He started to protest, but realized she wanted a few moments to herself, away from him. She wanted to collect her thoughts, to get them into order, so she could tell him who she was and why she had been at that farm. He sat back down without a word and let her take the dishes away.

While she was in the kitchen he put away the small drop-leaf table and stacked the two chairs in the corner. Darkness had fallen while they had been eating and now he drew the curtains across the windows and switched on the large, old-fashioned standard lamp by the sofa. He heard the coffee machine make spluttering sounds.

She came back to the sofa, handing him a mug as she sat down. Perching right on the edge of the seat, coffee mug held in both hands, she seemed to withdraw into herself, making herself even smaller than she actually was, trying to disappear. He didn't speak, other than a murmured thank you. She would talk when she was ready and he was prepared to wait. He lit a cigarette and she held her hand out to him, still silent. He passed it to her and lit another for himself. He had only seen her smoke two or three in the days she had been in the flat. She drew deeply, coughing slightly, trying to steady her coffee mug.

Eventually she began to speak, softly at first, her words hesitant and slow, but as she went on her confidence increased and her voice grew in strength. She told him everything without once looking at him. Her background, where she came from, how she got involved in the PIRA, then the Popular Front, and her eventual realization of what McGuinness was really after, what he really wanted from all of this, and her attempt to break away. It took the best part of an hour for her to tell her tale, during which time he sat quietly, listening, smoking several cigarettes. At last she brought him up to date on why she had been at the farm.

'Now you know the full story. I owe you my life – if you haven't already realized that. There was only one kind of verdict that so-called court martial would have given me. Death. And it would have been McQueedy's kind of death. There would have been no merciful bullet in the back of the neck or anything like that. Oh no. McQueedy and the others had different plans for me. They would each have had their fun with me, and if I hadn't died during their assaults on me they would have killed me immediately afterwards. By the time they were through with me I'd have been looking forward to dying. And then you arrived.'

Her coffee had gone with the telling. He took her mug, plus his own empty one, and went to make refills. When he returned she was still sitting in the same position, eyes staring in front of her, at a spot on the threadbare carpet. In her hand she held another of his cigarettes. He put the coffee mug on the floor beside her.

'It's over, Monica. You *are* out, just as you wanted, and alive. I can help you further, if you want. Help you get totally away, away from Ireland, away from the past. There's enough money here in the flat to arrange all that for you. Don't talk any more tonight. Just finish your coffee, then go to bed. Try to sleep. Tomorrow will be a better day for you. It's all off your chest now, you've spat it out, and you'll begin to get a better look at life in the morning.'

She turned and smiled at him, a sad smile that did not quite reach her tear-filled eyes. She wanted to accept everything he said – but didn't quite believe it was all as simple as he made it out to be. They sat in silence and finished their coffees. Once more he took the empty mugs and told her to go to bed. She called to him as he was about to enter the kitchen and he turned to look at her. She was standing just outside the light from the lamp. For a brief moment she reminded him of somebody else. They stood in silence, looking at each other.

'Thank you,' she whispered, then turned and went into the bedroom.

She woke with a shock of fear, not knowing where she was. As realization crept in, her fear lessened. Then she heard the noise again, coming from the front room. Slipping out of bed she walked to the door in the darkness. She recognized the sound. He was crying.

He was tossing and turning on the sofa, the blankets thrown to one side, sweat covering his face and chest and his damp hair plastered to his head. He was mumbling and sobbing, tears mingling with the sweat. Slipping off the T-shirt she used as a nightgown she knelt by the sofa and started to dry him, patting his face and chest with the soft cotton. Among the incoherent words he muttered she made out a name – Annabelle.

'Shush,' she whispered. 'Shush now. It's OK, I'm here.' Dabbing at his face she wiped his tears.

'Annabelle? Annabelle? Oh, Annabelle, I'm sorry, I'm so sorry.' More tears welled up behind the closed eyelids and trickled down his cheeks. She continued making soothing sounds, her hands now caressing his face and damp hair. Whoever this Annabelle was, he needed her, desperately. She decided he should have her.

The sofa was quite wide. Lifting the sheet and blankets off the remainder of his body she lay down beside him, wearing only the panties he had bought for her, all the time making soothing sounds to him. She placed her arm round his neck and drew his head to her naked breast. 'It's OK, my darling, it's OK. I'm here now. I'm here.'

He sighed as the tension left his body. His arms went round her, his head resting on her breast. His tears quietened as she held him. She once again stroked his face, starting with her cool fingers on his forehead, over the damp salty skin of his cheeks and chin, down his neck and eventually on to the top half of his chest. She felt him shiver, but not from the cold. She moved her body slightly until the nipple of her right breast was close to his mouth.

'Open your mouth, my darling. Open.' As he did so she pressed the nipple into his mouth and drew his head closer to her.

'There now, there now, there now. Don't cry. Please don't cry any more. I'm here with you, my man, my prince. It's OK. It's all over. We're together again.'

He nursed her breast like a small child, gently drawing a small portion of it further into his mouth. She felt her nipple grow hard as he suckled, drawing strength from her, easing his troubled mind. He was still asleep, still in his dream, but the horror was disappearing. She could feel his body reacting to her closeness. With her left hand she started to scrape gently with her nails, on his chest, feeling the goose pimples rise on the aureole of his nipples, his chest hair rising with his excitement. Her hand moved up his chest and on to his shoulder, the nails continuing to scrape gently on his skin, down his back and along his arm. His right arm moved across her body to hold her, but she laid it back by his side. He did not object, his mouth still sucking at her breast. Down his right arm to his wrist, over the back of his hand, and on to his lower stomach, her scraping fingers continued their journey. Moving in small circles her fingers moving lower and lower all the time. His body began to shiver in anticipation as her hand moved to his thigh as far as she could reach, then worked back up to the swelling at the front of his underpants. He was hard, his cock restrained by the elastic, pointing towards his stomach. Her fingers moved to cup his testicles, squeezing ever so gently on them. Releasing them she allowed her nails to scrape round their shape, then up and down the length of his hard penis. She eased her nipple from his mouth.

'Don't move,' she whispered. 'Keep your eyes closed tight, and don't move. Let me do it all, darling. Just relax and enjoy it.'

She moved her body until she lay across him. Her hands cupped his face, kissing his forehead, his ears, his cheeks, and round the edges of his mouth. She licked his lip with her wet tongue, feeling the dryness of his mouth. His breathing pattern had changed and he was slowly panting, drawing in the air she breathed towards his mouth. His tongue licked at his dry lips and she immediately drew it into her mouth, sucking slowly and gently on it. She covered his mouth with hers, her tongue licking at his teeth and gums, breathing gently into him, her saliva a nectar to his parched mouth.

Leaving his mouth she kissed her way down his throat on to his chest, her teeth nipping his skin gently. She could feel the pounding of his heart as she bit his left nipple, worrying at it like a small terrier with a bone. Now his hands moved, enfolding her, caressing her back, filtering through her hair, holding her head. He moaned as she bit harder on his nipple, then her mouth was on the move again, her hands scratching at his ribcage, until at last her lips were at the elasticated rim of his underpants.

Sitting up for a moment she caught the rim and drew his pants downward, easing the front part over his blood–engorged penis. He automatically raised his hips to allow her to slide the cotton pants down his legs. Kissing the tip of his penis she moved so that she could remove his pants totally.

The excitement swelled in her also. What had started as

an act of kindness had become personal. She could feel the dampness in herself. Without knowing anything about him she had realized that his Annabelle would not be returning, and she wanted to give him a gift in return for her life. But her seduction of him had aroused the excitement in herself. Her own damp panties joined his discarded underpants on the floor. Once again she knelt by the side of the sofa.

While her right hand made caressing circles on his chest, her left hand captured his swollen cock, squeezing it gently in her hand. His hips pushed automatically against her fingers, forcing it deeper into her hand. Switching hands she now cupped his swollen, tight testicles, straightened his cock and lowered her mouth over it.

His hand gripped her hair tightly as he exhaled all the air from his body, sucking in fresh through clenched teeth. She moved his foreskin backwards and forwards slowly, her mouth sucking on him, while her wet tongue gently licked the head. She felt a great pleasure building up inside herself as she squeezed his balls. Pleasure for him in how he was feeling through her ministration, pleasure for herself in the knowledge that she was pleasing him, and sexual delight in what she was doing. She licked the juice that seeped from him, her tongue searching for more. Her right hand, stroking his cock, moved faster, then slowed, then faster again, bringing him nearer and nearer to the point of no return, then refusing him the relief he craved. Her own excitement was building up also and she could feel her own lubricating juices trickle down her naked thighs. Giving his cock one last flick of her tongue she released it and got to her feet.

Still in his dream world he moaned in dismay at her sudden absence. But in an instant she had climbed over him on the sofa, guided him to her opening, then eased herself down on to him. Now it was her turn to moan as shivers of pleasure shot through her body. His hands were outstretched in front of him, searching for her. As he felt her sink down on to him he threw his head back in ecstasy, straining the tendons in his neck. His eyes were screwed tight and he sucked in air once again through clenched teeth.

She began to move, slowly at first, riding up and down, taking him to the very tip of her opening, then swallowing him again deep inside as far as he could go. Her juices were in full flow, flooding him with each movement. Leaning forward she gripped his shoulders as he began to move to her rhythm. His left arm went to her neck drawing her closer to him, while his right hand clasped her small, hard bottom, ensuring she couldn't escape, even if she wanted to. Faster and faster they moved, each approaching their climax. She was now sucking air as desperately as he, inhaling through her open mouth, hanging on tightly as he pumped into her. Both of them were moaning, demanding of each other the satisfaction their bodies craved. At last he came, his hips thrust forward off the sofa, burying himself inside her as deeply as he could. Head arched back he screamed his release as her internal muscles milked him, drawing every drop of his seed deep inside her. As she felt him come she too shuddered to her climax, her body shaking as if in an epileptic fit. Each burst of his sperm gave her another climax, and another, until her body was a nervous wreck, every single muscle seeming to go into spasm at the same time.

His head relaxed, his face relaxed and finally his body sank back on to the sofa. She watched his face and felt a glow of happiness spread throughout her entire body, like an aftershock. Sweat poured off both of them from the heat of their lovemaking. She lowered her head and rested it on his chest, listening to the pounding of his heart decrease as he grew smaller inside her. With automatic reflex motions his hands were about her body, stroking slowly and softly across her shoulders and down her back. She knew the demon inside him had gone, and he fell into a peaceful sleep. His physical body had reacted to her every move, while his injured spirit had allowed him to sleep through it all, keeping alive his thoughts of his Annabelle. Wiping his face and chest once more with her T-shirt she covered him with the sheet and blankets, then returned to her bed.

She woke to the feeling of a hand gently brushing the hair from her face. She opened her eyes to find him sitting on the edge of the bed, mug of coffee in hand. There was a strange look on his face, one she had not seen before. It was such a gentle look she almost didn't recognize him. He smiled.

'Hi,' she whispered, not knowing if he realized what had occurred between them in the night. Would he be pleased if he knew, or angry?

'I don't know why you did it . . . but thank you. I know she's dead and won't come back. I've missed her so much, so very much. But . . . as much as I loved her, you deserve better than being loved in the place of a dead woman.'

'You're not angry?' she whispered back, her eyes watching him, like a frightened animal.

Once more he smiled at her and his entire face seem to light up. 'Of course not. If what I can remember from my "dream" really happened . . . how could I possibly be angry with you?'

'How do you know it *wasn't* a dream?' she coyly smiled in return.

This time he laughed out loud. 'I don't think I'm capable of taking my underpants off in a dream – or of sneaking in here and taking your T-shirt off, and then sneaking back to the sofa. Do you?' He smiled as he watched her blush.

'No, I don't suppose you are.'

'Sit up. I have some coffee for you.'

'Can I have my shirt back first?' Now she felt embarrassed for him to see her breasts. They were still bruised from the treatment she had received from McQueedy. But it wasn't just that which embarrassed her, she knew. It was the shyness of waking up naked, before the man she had made love with for the first time the previous night. He started to laugh again. She had expertly seduced him, and now she wanted to hide her body from his eyes. She realized how foolish she was being and when he returned from the living room with her T-shirt she was sitting up in bed, bare breasted, drinking her coffee.

'Just throw it over in the corner,' she told him, then they both collapsed into convulsions of laughter. She screamed as she spilt hot coffee on her bare breast, which caused him to laugh more. Taking the mug from her hand he gently wiped her with the shirt, then had to sit on the floor for laughing. She threw herself back on to the pillows, their laughter filling the room, and the more they looked at each other, the more they laughed.

Chapter Twelve

'ANNABELLE WAS MY WIFE.'

It was early afternoon on the same day. After their bout of laughter each had taken a shower, but separately. Both now felt a little unsure of themselves and of how they should behave together. After his shower he had left the flat to get some newspapers and groceries. Deciding to do a little thinking about what his next move should be, he went for a walk. He was beginning now to feel he was two people. One was a cold-blooded killer who seemed to have the capacity – or sheer luck – to carry out his mission. The other, that part he had thought dead until this morning, was a lonely man. A man who had loved and been loved in return. An ordinary man who used to get up each morning, take a shower, kiss his wife goodbye, and go to work. A man who enjoyed his day's work, who then returned to the home he shared with the woman he loved. A man who worried about the normal, mundane, problems of life – paying the bills, getting the car to start on a winter's morning, doing the garden, repairs to the home. He had been a lucky man. A normal, healthy, everyday man-in-the-street, until another man, one he had never met, never knew, never hurt, blew that normal mundane world to pieces. He missed that life, yet he knew he could never return to it and be the same man again.

Crossing O'Connell Street he found himself outside Bewley's Café, in Westmoreland Street. The smell of freshly roasted coffee brought back even more memories.

He walked through the confectionery department to the restaurant at the back and ordered a pot of coffee.

He remembered the very first cup of coffee he had ever tasted. On his tenth birthday his eldest sister had taken him to the cinema, then to this very restaurant for a meal. He couldn't remember anything about the movie he saw that day, nor what they had to eat, but he never forgot the taste of his first sip of 'grown up' coffee. He was hooked and from that day onwards coffee became the only beverage he would drink.

He had brought Abel here, the first time she came to meet his family, telling her the story of how he got hooked on the bean. As they left through the confectionery department he had bought her a box of Bewley's fudge – and it had been her turn to get hooked. From then on, whenever they came to Dublin, they visited Bewley's for coffee and fudge the day after their arrival.

He had made no contact with his family. He couldn't. They assumed he was travelling in the Far East, trying to get over the death of Abel. So . . . where did he go from here? What was his next step? How did he find the next link in the chain to McGuinness? Did he want to continue now, after last night? What about the debt he owed, he argued with himself. To Annabelle, his Abel? To her parents? To himself? It had all been so clear yesterday, but last night seemed to have changed it all. Abel was dead and buried, along with the kind of life he had lived with her. But he had his own life left, plans to make for the future. She would always be there, in his mind, with him wherever he went . . . but the killings had to stop. He had to look beyond his desire for revenge. He had been lucky so far. Damn lucky. How long before he made a stupid mistake? *Had* he already made a stupid mistake?

One the police knew about, but of which he knew nothing?

He had enough money to make a good life for himself wherever he chose to go. The endowment mortgage he and Abel had on their home had been paid on her death and the debt on the house cleared. He had immediately sold it and all its contents. He could never have lived there again, nor used any of the items of furniture they had bought and renovated together. The money he had taken from the house in Ballymun, money meant for the coffers of the Popular Front, was now in several bank accounts. He had everything he needed to make a fresh start.

Last night the girl had freed him. A simple act of lovemaking had taken the great pressure from his mind and awoken something within him he had thought was dead for ever. He didn't love her, and he was equally sure she didn't love him, but a bond had been formed between them. He now felt something for another human being, for her. He also wanted her to get away from the life she had led, away from her past, to start a new life, in a new country. They would not be together, but he would not forget her and what she had done for him.

Anyway, he reasoned with himself, the line to McGuinness was cold. He still had the address he took from Maura O'Grady, but it would mean even more killings to find a new lead. If he could have found McGuinness there and then he could still kill him – but how many more would have to die first? As he finished his coffee he made his decision.

It was over, finished. He would tell Monica the reason why he had done what he did, tell her it was now over, give her enough money to make a new start in life, then they would go their separate ways and he could become human once again. As he walked past the confectionery counter he hesitated, looking at the trays of fudge. Without buying any he walked out and headed back for the flat.

'She was my wife,' he repeated, standing by the window, looking out at the boarded-up building opposite. 'I loved her more than life itself and always felt loved like that in return. Sure we had our ups and downs – every couple does – but we were happy. Very very happy.

'There was only one thing missing in our lives as far as we were concerned. A child. We tried – oh, believe me we tried. We even went to a specialist to see if either of us had any problem in that department. We didn't. He reckoned we were just trying too hard. He told us to relax more.' He smiled a little as he remembered those good times. 'She used to do really daft things to try and get pregnant. Somebody told her that they had got pregnant after eating garlic. We were on garlic for a month – no one else would speak to us. Another time, after we'd made love, she turned round in the bed and put her feet up along the wall, to keep the sperm inside. But it didn't work. Nothing did – or at least so I thought. But something did work.

'She was one of the victims at the King's Cross bombing. She was so badly burned that if it hadn't been for her belongings that were scattered about, along with a gold heart and chain I had given her, nobody would have known who she was. She was pregnant when she died – and I didn't even know it at the time. So you see, I not only lost the woman I loved, but our unborn child as well.

'My real name is Christopher Kane. I had made a bit of a play with words on the engraving I had done on the heart. It was inscribed "To Abel from Kane". The chain had broken and was in her case when she died.

Most of her belongings survived, including my letters to her – but she didn't. That bastard McGuinness had used some kind of petroleum jelly in the bomb. It was the first of its kind used in a terrorist attack and was as deadly as napalm. Tiny bits of paper with words on them, clothing and other personal belongings . . . they all survived, but not her.'

Monica was sitting on the sofa as he told his story. His back was to her, so he didn't see the startled look on her face, nor the small jerky movement her body made. She remembered that particular bombing incident, and the two that followed. She remembered them only too well. Up until King's Cross all she had been asked to do by the Popular Front had been to take the explosives to England. But for that one Frank had asked her to help him deliver it.

It was partly the ferocity of those attacks at King's Cross, Chelsea and Notting Hill Gate – deliberately designed to inflict casualties as well as property damage – that had caused her to question not only her own motives but those of the Popular Front. Now, for the very first time, she was listening to a relative describe the full horror of what had happened. How could she tell him of the revulsion she had felt? How could she tell him how sorry she was, how she wished she had seen earlier, known earlier, what the Popular Front and McGuinness really wanted, really stood for? She couldn't. He lit another cigarette, and continued.

'I was a soldier. A British soldier. Nothing really special about that, there are thousands of Irishmen, North and South, who serve in the British Army. I was reared here in Dublin. I was never much into politics. To me, joining the British Army was a way to see the world and nothing else.

I wasn't even a soldier in the real sense. I was a clerk in the Royal Army Pay Corps.

'I was on a pay and documentation course at our HQ near Winchester. A bunch of us went to Salisbury one night, did the rounds of the pubs, and ended up in some disco. I was drunk – but not so drunk that I didn't fall in love with her the moment I saw her.' He laughed quietly, remembering the night. 'Do you believe in love at first sight?' He turned to look at her as he asked the question.

'Yes,' she answered quietly, seeing the pain in his eyes. He turned his back to her once more and gazed out of the window at nothing.

'She was an only child. Her parents were . . . are . . . the greatest people in the world. It took Pop a while to accept that his lovely little girl had grown up and fallen in love with another man – and a soldier to boot! But in the end he accepted me like the son he had always wanted, and became a second father to me. Both my own parents were dead.'

He went to take a swig of coffee and found the mug in his hand empty. 'Is there any more coffee in the pot?' he asked of her.

'No,' she replied, getting off the sofa, 'but I'll make some. I could do with some myself. Don't stop talking. I want to hear it all.' He followed her to the small kitchen and leaned against the door frame, continuing his story.

'My last posting was to Scotland, to Edinburgh. As a member of the pay team I joined a Scottish regiment who were about to be posted to Northern Ireland on a four-month emergency tour. And that's where my problems started – and of course Annabelle was affected too.

'I didn't want to go to Ireland – any part of it – in the uniform of a foreign army. I felt that if I went, there would come a time when I would have to ask myself the question: was I an Irishman first and British soldier second – or vice versa? Whichever choice I made I would be wrong. Damned if I did and damned if I didn't.

'I've met a lot of Irishmen in the Army, from both North and South, and for the most part we never had any problems about where we came from or what our religion was. We were soldiers, comrades. But all the guys from the North said the same thing. It's different when you are there. Then you *have* to choose, like it or not. I didn't want to be put in that position.'

She turned from the coffee machine and handed him his mug, filled with the fresh brew. She followed after him as he returned to the living-room, once more taking up his position by the window, staring outwards.

'I won't bore you with all the details but my commanding officer at that time was a complete shithead. I asked for permission to remain on the mainland with the rear party, as I was quite entitled to do. He wanted a reason so I told him the truth – inner conflict. He sat on it for several days, then word filtered down to me that I was staying behind.

'Around about the time the rest of the boys came back from Belfast I was due to be promoted to sergeant. There was no reason why I shouldn't get my promotion as I had put in the time, passed all my exams; all that was needed was the CO's signature on the promotion order. He refused, saying that I had refused to serve in Northern Ireland. He had effectively thrown my career in his waste bin. Commanding officers of line regiments have a lot of power with their command. I was to remain a corporal as long as he was my CO.'

'In the end I was promised my sergeant's stripes, but it

had all put a terrible strain our my marriage. Abel went to stay with her parents for a while. From the moment she left I missed her. Then she was back again, and a week or so later I got my promotion. To celebrate we went and bought our first – our only – home.

'Last Christmas, as usual, we went to Salisbury to spend it with her parents. On New Year's Day her mother had a heart attack; not a major one, but serious enough. Annabelle stayed on to be with her mum and look after Pop. She was on her way back to me when she was killed.

'I had done everything I possibly could to keep out of it all. I put my career on the line, almost put my marriage on the line as well because of those bastards and others like them. I didn't want to be involved . . . and ended up being as personally involved as any man could possibly be. They killed my woman.

'When I went to London and found that the body they had tagged as Annabelle Kane was pregnant I was actually delighted. I was sorry for whoever it was, but it certainly wasn't my Annabelle. She wasn't pregnant. But of course she was. She had told her parents a day or so before she was due back. She had said on the phone before she started back that there was something she wanted to tell me as soon as she returned. Not only did I lose the woman I loved, but the child we had both wanted so very badly.

'The police were very sympathetic, promised to do everything in their power to get the bombers, bring them to trial. But I didn't *want* them brought to trial.' She noticed the change in the tone of his voice now. It was harder, cruel even, as he continued. 'I wanted the bastards *dead*. But in particular I wanted the man who had sent the bombers in. I wanted McGuinness. I wanted his balls on a plate and his face at the end of a gun. I wanted to look into his eyes. I wanted him to know he was going to die. I wanted to see terror in his eyes. I wanted him pleading for his life, crying, saying how sorry he was, how it was all a mistake, how he'd never do it again – then I wanted to blow him to kingdom come.'

He was silent again while he drank some coffee, lit another cigarette and let the rage in him die down a little. 'The worst part of it all for me is that I have seen – and keep seeing – Abel die. I watch it all happen, time after time after time. Dreams – nightmares – always the same one. I'm a pigeon, sitting on a ledge at King's Cross station. I watch her arrive, carrying her suitcase, getting her bearings. As she moves across the station I fly just above her, following. She heads for the big arrivals and departures indicator. There's an hour yet before the Edinburgh train leaves. She looks around again, speaks to a porter, and heads for the left luggage lockers. She puts the case in one of the larger lockers, searches in her purse for a coin, drops it in the slot and locks the door.

'That's when I begin to feel afraid; really, really afraid. She has to move. Quickly. As fast as she can, away from those lockers. I try to scream a warning to her, but of course all that comes out is the coo of a pigeon, not words. She looks up at me, straight into my eyes, surprised, as if she actually recognizes me and can't understand what the hell I'm doing there as a pigeon. She smiles at me – then the doors of hell itself burst open with a mighty roar, and flames spew out all round her, engulfing her. She disappears right in front of my eyes.

'All round me there is screaming and crying – and in the midst of it all I hear her calling me, using her pet name for me. "Help me, Bear," she screams. "Help me, help me, help me." And I can't. The flames are after me too and I turn my back on her and fly; fly, away from that terrible place, up into the dark night sky, heading for outer space.

'I've had that dream almost every night since she died in one form or another. There was only one way I was sure I could stop it. Kill McGuinness. Then Annabelle and I could both sleep in peace. So . . . I made my plans, and here I am.'

The coffee was cold again, but he drained the mug anyway, moving forward and placing it on the coffee table.

'But won't the police eventually come looking for you?' she asked. 'You've seen the sketch in the newspapers. It's not a very good likeness of you, but they have ruled out all the other ideas they had about possible internal disputes, PIRA hitmen, even the SAS. So they must be thinking about relatives of those killed in the bombings, looking for a suspect. Your name will crop up eventually, and that will be that.' Now she was worried he might get caught. He would not last long in prison. He would be killed there, one way or the other, even if he was given solitary confinement. They'd get to him. He lit cigarettes for both of them, passed her one, then answered.

'Maybe, maybe not. I've done what I can to avoid it, with the help of the best friend any man could ever ask for. I've always felt I could trust this man with my life, and I suppose, in effect, I have. You see, if the police go looking for him, Christopher Kane is in the Far East.' He gave her a weary smile, blowing smoke out through his nostrils.

'But how?' she asked, not understanding.

'As I said, with the help of a good friend – and the help of a couple of soldiers who died in Northern Ireland. Part of my Army job was processing the papers of those killed in Ireland. I found a couple who had never had a passport. I put in applications, using their names, but with my photograph, requesting the passport be sent to the Army Pay and Documentation Office, Edinburgh – where I opened and processed the mail. I also took their driving licences.

'I got the first one back no problem, but Olly – Oliver James, the other sergeant in the office, and my best mate – he opened the second one. He passed the envelope across to me without a word. He knew I was up to something, so I told him everything. In the end, it was he who came to me, with the other idea.

'I was actually entitled to *two* passports. An Irish one, issued here as a born citizen of the Republic, and a British one, as a member of the armed forces. I had my British one, but I'd never applied for my Irish one. By now I had three passports, all British, and three driving licences. Olly applied for my Irish passport, in my name, using my birth certificate, but with his photograph. He became me.

'I eventually got a compassionate discharge and secretly went on a package tour of the Far East, taking in Bangkok, Hong Kong, Taipei and Singapore. On my travels I bought loads of postcards, filling them all in with news about what I was doing, what I was seeing, etc. I addressed them all – but never posted them. I then started to gather all the information I could on the Popular Front and in particular on Maura O'Grady. She was the main link to McGuinness, being the political spokesperson for the organization.

'When I was ready to make my move I notified Olly. I gave myself a time limit of one month; I didn't think I could keep the pressure on the Front successfully for longer than that. They'd scatter and disappear for a while – or I'd get myself killed in that time. So Olly put in for his leave, telling everybody that he had always wanted to go touring round Europe, and set off to retrace my steps in the Far East, staying in the same hotels I'd stayed in, seeing the same sights I'd seen, eating at the same restaurants. Of course he also had all the postcards I had written, and this time he was posting them back to various people at different times on the trip. My alibi was set up. I was in the Far East.

'Everything was going according to plan until I turned up at the farm, and ended up killing them all before I could get any information as to the whereabouts of McGuinness. I had hoped either to find him there or to get the info I needed. But now they're all dead and the trail has gone cold . . .' His voice trailed off.

Monica sat in silence digesting what he had said. All she wanted to do was to get away from McGuinness and McQueedy, away from all of it. But could she, with both of them still alive? Would the same thing not happen again one day? She would be walking along a street, a car would pull up, and she would disappear inside to be welcomed by that sadistic bastard McQueedy. She shuddered, remembering how it felt as his hands searched the intimate parts of her body. As well as that the bombing would continue. More and more innocent lives would be blown to pieces by the Popular Front on the orders of McGuinness. There was only one way to stop it all – finish the Popular Front. And the only way to do that was to kill McGuinness. She was sitting with a man who had every reason to want him dead, who wanted to do the killing himself. How many had he already killed trying to get to him? Six? Seven?

'You didn't lose the trail at the farm,' she told him, her voice low and shaky.

'What do you mean?' he asked, turning to look directly at her.

'I know where McGuinness is. I can take you to him.'

He stared at her, his eyes open in disbelief. A tiny voice in his head reminded him that he had intended to stop the killings. 'Leave it,' the voice continued. Then another voice came to him, a terrified Annabelle, crying for his help. 'Help me, Bear, help me, help me, help me.' His eyes narrowed to slits as he continued to stare at her.

'Tell me,' he demanded.

Chapter Thirteen

AS THE VAN APPROACHED the village the Gardai activity was obvious, the darkness broken by the flashing lights of squad cars and ambulances.

'What the hell's happened, McQ?' the driver asked, his voice cracking with fear.

Laying the Browning pistol on the floor beside him McQueedy checked the pump action shotgun and broke open a box of shells. 'I don't know. Just keep driving nice and easy like. Don't speed up. If you get waved down, just slow down as if you re going to stop. I'll take care of the rest, OK?'

'Jesus, McQ, I'm not too sure about all this. If we get –'

'I'm not askin' if you're sure or not, Deegan. Just do as I tell you.' Something in McQ's voice told Deegan that he would be in more danger from inside the van than from outside if he messed this up.

'How in God's name could they know so quickly about the tart? And the house? We drove straight back, so how did they get here before us?' He couldn't stop himself jabbering on.

'They don't know about her you dickhead. Do they, darling?' He diverted his attention for a moment to the bound and gagged girl lying beside him in the back of the van. He gripped her knee, squeezing painfully. She jerked her leg away in revulsion.

All she could remember after the door smashing in was a hulk of a man rushing at her, forcing something over her face, and then nothing. When she woke she was bound and gagged and this same man was sitting opposite, staring at her. Her waking caught him unawares and before he could look away she had seen the look in his eyes. It was the look of a half-starved man gazing at a royal banquet. He couldn't believe the beauty and richness of what was spread before him. McQ had never been this close to someone so perfectly beautiful. The closest he had got were pin-up magazines, tabloid newspapers and pornographic videos. Every day for years he would look at the magazines or Page 3 girls, then watch a porn video, masturbating several times during the film. The more perverted and cruel the video, the more he masturbated, sometimes working himself up into a frenzy which he would take out on the first woman that became available to him. Now he actually had the real thing laid out before him, and he could do whatever he wanted with her.

Marlane had no idea who McQ was, but it was obvious to her that he was not only repellent to look at and to smell, he was also a savagely dangerous animal. Her mind was racing as she tried to work out the best way to handle him. She was practised at rebuffing men who came on too strong, without upsetting them, but this man was not like anyone she had had to deal with before. She had to find a way to make him her friend, and quickly, if she wasn't going to be torn apart before dawn.

The important thing was to keep calm. As long as she remained calm she still had some degree of control. She stared up at him, watching his nervous movements as they drove on past the flashing lights and activity, determined to show no fear in her eyes. She had felt the strength of his fingers and knew they could crush the life out of her.

Deegan made a slight detour which took them away from the centre of the village, away from all the police activity. 'Jesus, what do we do now McQ?' The temptation for him to push the accelerator to the floor was almost as strong as his fear of what McQueedy would do to him if he did, but not quite. At that moment Deegan would have given anything to be somewhere else.

'Just keep driving nice and carefully. Don't do anything that will give cause for those fuckers to come after us.'

McQueedy was asking himself the same question Deegan had just asked. He was not a man used to thinking on his feet, being more prone to making physical reactions – usually violent ones. But this time he tried to think hard to find a solution. Somehow or other the Gardai had found the safe house and it was odds on that O'Sullivan – the only other one he knew that was left in the house – was either dead or arrested, and that bastard Cowboy Johnson freed. But what of Tommy? Had he too been caught, or had he not yet returned from his meeting with that sand nigger from Libya, Abu Nabi? What of this girl? If they had lost Johnson, Tommy would say that she was excess baggage now. She was of no use to them. Tommy would tell him to dump her and to move fast which would mean killing her before he had time for anything else. But he wasn't prepared to accept that. For the first time in his life McQ felt an urge which was stronger than his urge to please Tommy. He knew that he would never again get a chance at having his way with a woman like this. It was a once-in-a-lifetime opportunity, and he wouldn't give it up for anybody. And he didn't mean the usual quick shag and then pass her on to the others. He wanted to have every bit of her, to take his revenge for all the lonely hours he had spent in his life pulling his dick and staring at videos of good-looking women being screwed by other men. He wanted to taste and touch every part of her perfect face and body, he wanted to maul her and lick her and suck her and bite her from her perfect nose to her perfect toes, he wanted to consume every part of her, fill every orifice with his tongue and his cock, explore her inside and out and find out what all these girls whose pert tits and pouting smiles had teased him from pictures would have tasted like, smelt like and felt like. His hunger consumed him. He wanted her, and if he had to go against Tommy to keep her, well so be it.

Never before had he disagreed with his friend's decision, always accepting that Tommy's brain would work for both of them. But things had gone wrong recently, hadn't they? This fucking Java Man had started the whole thing, going round wiping everybody off the face of the earth. Who the hell was he? Then those two coppers turning up at the farm that night. Who sent them? And what about that bitch Monica? Not a word about her in any of the newspapers or on the telly. Had the cops got her? It would appear that way, what with the raid. She knew about this place. But why had it taken them so long to arrive? Why hadn't she told them earlier? Jesus, why wasn't Tommy around when he was really needed? His head began to hurt trying to think of a safe solution, one that would allow him to keep the girl, not antagonize Tommy, and get them out of the country.

'Head for Waterford,' he ordered Deegan. 'Then we'll start to cut across towards Clonmel, Tipperary and Limerick. There's one place they won't know about yet.'

'Where?' Deegan asked.

'Never mind, I'll tell you how to get there – you just

concentrate on the driving and make sure we don't get stopped.'

Cowboy sat on the edge of the sofa staring at the brass framed photograph of Marlane. He had taken it from beside his bed and placed it in the middle of the large, solid oak, coffee table. In his hands he held a mug of coffee, his fourth since returning home. Mooney had ordered him home, and told him to take an enforced period of sick leave – or be officially removed from the case. Mooney had suggested it politely at first, but when Cowboy balked at the idea, he gave him the ultimatum. Take a few days off – or off the case completely.

'You'd do it too, wouldn't you?' he glared back at his superior and friend, his voice seething with repressed anger.

'Don't push me, son. I mean it. You're in no condition to go gallivanting round looking for Marlane. You've had a rough time and you need to rest. I'm as concerned as you are – and you know that full well. I'll move heaven and earth to find her and get her back in one piece, and as quickly as possible. At the present moment you'd be a hindrance to me. I'd be worrying about you too much. If you want to help, then go home for a few days' rest. I swear to you that you'll be in on the ending. As soon as we know where she is and who's with her, I'll get you. You have my solemn word on it.'

'We *know* who's with her, for God's sake Frank. That's what worries me to death. You have no idea what that . . . that friggin' *animal* McQueedy is like. The other one, McGuinness, is a weedy little shit – but that bugger? I want him, Frank. I want a hurley stick and ten minutes alone with him.'

'In the state you're in you could have half an hour with him, with his arms broken, and he'd still kill you. Go home and rest, and let me get on with finding them. Don't make me do it officially.' Mooney's eyes showed pain as Cowboy looked at him. He knew the pain was for him and Marlane and that Mooney was just as worried about her as he was. One of them had to think clearly, unclouded by emotions, and Frank was accepting that part, knowing Cowboy was incapable of it. Seeing no alternative Cowboy allowed himself to be driven home from the hospital. Lying in an almost boiling herbal bath he considered all the cock-ups that had occurred, starting with his own – going to the farmhouse without proper backup. Had it been his vanity that got to him, wanting to be the hero – the single-handed hero who found the killer? Or was it that he hadn't entirely believed the story Eddie Gallagher had told him, especially as it had come from an old drunk? Who really believed what drunks said?

He also blamed himself for not realizing what McGuinness had up his sleeve to get Cowboy to talk. He should have sussed it out. McGuinness must have realized that he would never beat the information out of the detective, even if the amnesia was a farce as he and McQueedy suspected. He realized that with Cowboy he would have to find another way, and if Cowboy had been thinking clearly and had analysed what was was most likely to make him crack, he would have seen this coming sooner.

Then there was the débâcle of the uniformed branch turning up with lights and sirens blasting. Having already warned the inspector in charge, the warning to the reinforcements had gone unheeded. The lone terrorist who had remained in the house had opened fire and the gun battle had lasted for ten minutes. According to Mooney the ten armed gardai had used enough ammunition in those ten minutes to have equipped a small army. When found, the body of the terrorist had forty-three bullet holes in it – or what was left of it. McQueedy wasn't spotted at all and it was only later that a motorcycle garda, stationed on the outskirts of the village, mentioned the Catholic priest he had stopped in a car, warning him of the events going on in the village. Shown a photograph of the two wanted men he pointed to the one of McGuinness as being the priest. Mooney had turned up at the Mather hospital casualty department, where Cowboy had been taken, to tell him what had happened. He also had the bad news about Marlane. A patrol car had been sent to her flat after his message – but it had been too late. They found the door forced and Marlane gone.

Cowboy had been unable to tell Mooney the truth about how he had known she was in danger. He told him he had overheard the instructions being given to kidnap her before he could effect his escape. It had seemed logical and had been accepted, but he himself knew that it had been a message. A message from beyond the grave.

Lying in the bath he had tried to make contact with those in the spirit world who were helping him, trying to find where she was. He also tried to send a telepathic message to Lane, telling her to hold on, that somehow he would find a way to get to her. Pulling himself out of the bath with slight difficulty he re-applied the chest bandage the hospital had put on to protect his ribs.

For an hour he paced his apartment like a caged animal, not knowing what to do. He prepared some food in the microwave – then couldn't eat it. He poured a glass of whiskey – but couldn't drink it. Coffee was all he could tolerate. Then it came to him. Where – who – could help him. Locking the flat behind him he made his way to his car and drove to the estate where Joan Blackmore lived. As he parked the Porsche outside her house several youngsters crowded round it, all excited to see such a car on their estate. He turned to the biggest of them, a gangling, short-haired boy of about twelve sitting astride a battered BMX bike.

'If anything is touched on that car, anything broken or damaged, I'll find you. I'll find you, and I'll break your fuckin' legs. Do I make myself clear?'

Sensing that he would do as threatened, the boy nodded his head, while the other children watched in silence. There was something about the manner of this adult that they understood. Cowboy walked briskly away from them and started up the garden path. Half way up he paused, turned round, and came back to the boy. Drawing a five-punt note from his wallet he handed it over. 'I still mean what I said about breaking your legs. Understand?' The note disappeared inside the chest pocket of his torn trainer top. 'Yer motor will be all right when you come back, mister. I'll see to it. Are ya goin'ta see the witch?'

'Yeah. And if you don't keep an eye on the car, not only will I break your legs, but I'll shove her witch's broom up yer arse.' With that he resumed his journey to Joan Blackmore's door.

She answered his knock almost immediately, delighted to see him. 'I've read about your lucky escape. I'm so pleased you are not badly injured. Come in, come in. Go straight in to the sitting-room. I'll just pop the kettle on.'

'I'm fine, Mrs Blackmore, honest. Don't bother about me. I just need to talk to you.'

'Nonsense. You go in, I'll only be a minute. And what did I tell you? It's Joan. Right?'

'Thank you, Joan.'

As he entered the book-cluttered room, he once again felt himself relax. What was it about this room, this house, this woman, that could make him feel like this? In his own apartment his nerves had been stretched like a piece of elastic that was close to breaking point, yet now he felt as if every muscle in his body were relaxing. Once again Joan came in bearing a tray with a mug of tea, one of coffee, and a plate of chocolate biscuits. Placing the tray on the small table she took the mug of tea, sat in her chair, and leaned back. 'Now Cowboy. How can I help?'

Very quickly he explained to her what had happened in the room where he had been held. The vision he had had of Lane's apartment and of smelling McQueedy – and then finding that it had all happened. Now he had to find her. He did not mention what he felt was going to happen to Lane in McQueedy's hands. He didn't want to think about it himself.

'Well, for a start, we both know that you are psychic, so that can explain the vision you saw. Secondly, love – that wonderful, beautiful feeling – is a very powerful element. It is what draws human beings together. You love Lane, physically as well as emotionally, therefore your psychic connection with her is very strong. It is even possible that she can send a message to you, although, like with most things, if she doesn't believe it, the link would be very, very weak. But yours is strong, you can send messages to her.

'Love is the key to the universe. I know it sounds trite, but it's true. It's what makes the bond between us and those who have gone on before us. I am not talking about the love of a man for a woman, or a woman for a man – though that is a very strong bond. I'm talking *love*.

'Have you ever told a man that you love him, Cowboy? Your father, an uncle, someone like that? What about a good friend?' She smiled a warm smile at him, not teasing him in any way with her question.

He shook his head. 'I'm sure I must have told my father I loved him, when I was a child. But I can't remember doing it as an adult. I can remember thinking it, as he lay in his coffin, wishing I had told him when he was alive. There are one or two men whom I love dearly, but I've never told them so.'

'But I'll bet you've insulted them, called them names, never meaning a word you said – quite the reverse in fact. Am I right?'

He smiled, thinking of the names he sometimes called his Uncle Ron, or how he teased Frank Mooney, calling him Chief, knowing it annoyed him. He smiled and nodded.

'It's not the words that are important Cowboy, it's the feeling. Anybody can say "I love you" and not mean it. Remember that. It's the feeling that's important.'

He was sitting hunched forward on the sofa, drinking the coffee, his overcoat lying beside him. He found himself thinking of his father, the games they had played together, mostly Cowboys and Indians, on the living-room floor, each armed with a toy pistol, his mother complaining of the smell of the burnt caps in the room. This usually resulted in both he and his father turning their guns on her and firing as many caps as they could at her, screaming with laughter. She would storm out of the room complaining to her husband 'you're worse than him'. He could smell his father's cologne.

'I can smell it too, Cowboy. That's another sign of spirit presence. It's your father, isn't it? What's the smell? His aftershave?'

'Yes. Old Spice. My mother used to buy it for me to give to him each Christmas and on his birthday.'

'I think it's time you two met again. Finish your coffee and ease yourself back into the sofa. I'll just draw the curtains over. It helps if you are not distracted by the light. I want you to imagine a walled garden,' she instructed him. 'This garden has only one gate, and you hold the key to it. I want you to open the gate, enter the garden, and lock the gate behind you. Nobody can come into your garden unless you want them to. You are in complete control of it, and everything in the garden is as you wish it.'

Lying back into the sofa Cowboy closed his eyes and did as she instructed. The walled garden he imagined was the garden at his parents' home, only now it had a ten-foot wall all round it. Inside he could see and smell the flowers and the grass, the mint plants, the strawberries and raspberries that his mother grew. Over in one corner were the apple and pear trees, and in the vegetable plot potatoes, cabbages, parsnips, carrots and Brussels sprouts. He sat in his favourite corner, his dog, Blackie, dead since Cowboy was twelve, came and sat beside him, licking the back of his hand. Birds were singing in the trees, insects were buzzing round, and the sun was shinning in a clear blue sky.

'Open up your mind, Cowboy, and listen with your heart.' He heard Joan's voice, as though coming from a distance.

His father appeared, smiling at him. He was so real and so close Cowboy felt he could reach out and touch him. 'Cowboy,' even his father had used his nickname, when he was young. 'Someone is here with me who can help you much more than I. He will explain things to you, and you will know what to do. Just remember I am always around you, near you.' As his father walked away, smiling and waving at him, another figure appeared. He knew, instantly, who this man was. Tall, broad shouldered and deeply tanned, he wore a pair of soft buckskin leggings held at the waist by a thong. His long black hair blew freely in the wind and the arrogant, cruel features of his face were softened by a broad smile. This then was his main guide, Blue Water, a spirit who had once been the war chief Crazy Horse.

'Come with me, friend, and I will show you something of how you once lived.' The voice was deep and as friendly as his smile. Cowboy rose and walked towards his guide. As they came together, the secret garden disappeared. In its place was a vast openness of wild grass.

'This was a time that was yours as well as mine. Although I am your guide now, you and I once lived a life in the body, sharing the same time, though different nations. Look, and see part of your previous experience on the earth plane.'

Distant, faint memories of another time and place came back to Cowboy as he looked out over this vast wilderness. This, he knew, was the Comanchería, the name given by the Mexicans to the land of the People, which was what they called themselves. To everybody else they were Comanche, the enemies of the Mexicans, North Americanos, and all the other tribes of the Indian nations. Pushed south by the advance of the white settlers to the east and north, they had arrived here, on the vast buffalo plains of Texas, a hundred years before. They traded with anybody, even their enemies – or they killed them and took what they wanted. From the Spanish they got the horse, and it changed their destiny. Their ponies became an extension of their bodies. In later years they would be known as one of the finest regiments of light cavalry ever. It was the Comanchero, that mixed band of white and Mexican badmen, roaming the areas of Mexico, Texas and New Mexico, who first brought the guns.

Cowboy Johnson looked down into the vast area known as Palo Duro canyon. It was more than one hundred miles long and was where the People lived. Few white men ever dared to enter it. The encampment he looked at was a mixture of tepee designs, picked up on the Comanche's way south. Once their home had been in the rugged Rocky Mountains, but as they were pushed south by the advance of the white man they collected customs and ideas from others on their way. Some of the tepees were similar to those of the Cheyenne, others were Ute, although most were of a small, compact design, taken from the Pawnee. From one of these he saw a white man step out into the bright sunlight. This man was his brother, his blood brother, and had shared his lodge for several summers.

The man, the Comanche, that Cowboy had once been, had been out hunting, seeking the vast herds of buffalo, when his horse had been frightened by a rattlesnake. Falling badly he had broken his leg. After three days of crawling he was found by the white man. Weak from lack of food and water he had expected to die, but the white man had straightened his broken limb, fed him sips of precious water from his canteen, and eventually brought him back to the lodges. They were enemies who became friends, men who became brothers by joining their blood. When he could ride again he had gone hunting for deer. Not for the meat, but for the skin. This he had given to his mother and unmarried sister and ordered them to make a jacket for his brother and to decorate it with the finest design and colours. The white man wore this buckskin jacket and, although faded, Cowboy could see the design on the back of it. A white bird – almost like a pigeon! Realization came to Cowboy in an instant, even before he heard the whispered words of Blue Water. 'This man was your brother, and will be again.' Everything began to fade and Cowboy found himself sitting on the sofa once more.

'Have you found something you were looking for, Cowboy?' Joan asked him.

'Partly. Some understanding of the message you gave me earlier. Remember? About the pigeon and the winged dagger? The winged dagger was a tattoo on the arm of James Earl McQueedy. The pigeon . . . I think I'm beginning to understand that too.' He did not want to tell her that this pigeon was the man responsible for the recent bout of deaths that had been reported in the papers. It was as if he wanted to protect him.

'Call this pigeon, Cowboy. Call him – I'm sure it's a man – call him and ask for his help.'

Later that same evening he was sitting on his own sofa, coffee mug in hand, staring at his favourite photograph of Marlane, trying once more to send her a message.

'Marlane. Marlane. Listen to me darling. Listen, and hear me. I'm home. I'm home, safe and sound. Please hang on. Hold on. We'll find you, don't worry. I love you, I love you, I love you. If you can hear me, then try and let me know. Call to me in your mind. I'll hear you, I promise. Just concentrate on me, and call.'

He sat staring at the photograph, repeatedly calling her name for over an hour before he went to bed. His head felt groggy and his body ached. Taking the framed photograph with him he returned it to its place beside his bed and climbed in. The moment his head hit the pillow he was asleep.

Sitting on the ledge he looked downward. People of all sizes and shapes, of different nationalities and colours moved to and fro. Some hurrying, some strolling, some standing in a long, winding queue. He noticed one young man picking pockets, while several others worked the queue standing by the Casey Jones hamburger bar, begging for change. W.H. Smith was closed, as was the Journey's Friend, tobacconist and sweet shop. He was about to move when he spotted her. Of medium height, with short, jet-black hair, she was struggling with a large suitcase, stopping every few moments to rest and switch hands. She had come up out of the Underground and after a slight hesitation headed for the large indicator board.

Launching from his perch he flew in her direction, gliding in the last few yards, landing close to her feet. She looked down at him, ignored him, then turned her eyes back upwards to the indicator. He flew up above her, landing on the top of the board, looking down at her. While her eyes were screwed up in concentration he could still see that she had a pretty face, bordering on beautiful. Her clothing, whilst not new, was modern and well cared for, even if a little on the conservative side. Having made a decision she started to move away. He followed with his eyes until she was beginning to get caught up in the winding queue that curved its way round the concourse, then launched himself once again into the air and followed.

Still struggling with the suitcase she walked down the

side of the last platform, passing the restaurant, the coffee and sandwich shops and the pub. She ignored the stares she got from the few men who sat just outside the pub. She paused at the left luggage counter, but it was closed. She spoke briefly to a porter then carried on walking towards the twenty-four-hour left luggage lockers. He began to feel uneasy. Something was wrong, but he didn't know what. Landing on top of the lockers, to her right, he looked about. Everything seemed to be as it should, but the feeling of foreboding would not leave him. Flying up to one of the high girders in the glass roof for a better view, he looked about him again. Everything was still the same. Nothing out of the ordinary, but the feeling within remained. While he sat there she fumbled with her handbag, searching then for the coin she needed for the locker. Finding the correct one she lifted the heavy case into one of the larger, ground level, lockers. An alarm bell sounded in his head as she closed the door. The bell in his mind clamoured *Danger, Danger, Danger!* Whatever it was, he had to warn her. As he dived in her direction she started to move away. He screamed at her and she looked up. She seemed to recognize him and smiled – such a wonderful smile. What was wrong with her? Didn't she hear him? Didn't she understand? He circled round her, away from her, intent on making another swooping pass at her when the lockers exploded.

Like a giant hand-grenade, thousands of pieces of hot metal hurled in all directions. Close behind the explosion, heading for both of them, was a wall of liquid flame. He banked to his left and started to climb, climb, climb. He was flying for his life. His last image of her, just as his tail feathers started to singe, was of the wall of flame sucking her into its gaping mouth, then she was no more.

Cowboy sat up in the bed, drenched in sweat. He winced as he leaned forward, both hands covering his face. Bunching the cotton-covered duvet he wiped his face, chest and armpits with it, then threw it aside and sat on the edge of the bed breathing slowly and deeply. He glanced at the bedside clock. Through the darkness the illuminated digital numbers glowed back at him. 04:20. What time had he got to bed? About 5 p.m. He had been asleep for eleven hours.

He rose to his feet, wrapped his towelling bathrobe around him and padded barefoot to the kitchen. Flicking the light switch he was about to reach for the kettle to make coffee when he noticed one of his cassettes on the edge of the draining board: Manhattan Transfer – the one he had been listening to the night he set off to Merrion Farm. The one that contained 'The Java Jive'. How did it get there? He hadn't used the tape deck when he got back, and he certainly wouldn't have left it in the kitchen. He was always very careful with his music. Puzzled, he reached out to check how much water the kettle held and cried out with pain. The kettle had boiled only moments before – but he had been asleep! He turned back to stare at the tape, the sudden movement of his head giving him a sharp pain. His hand went to the bruise at the base of his skull and as he did so he distinctly heard a voice.

'Go with your heart' the voice ordered him. 'You were brothers once, and can be again.'

He didn't need to ask who his 'brother' was. All of that had been explained to him that lunchtime. 'How do I find him?' he asked out loud. But the voice inside his head was disappearing, fading away as though in a tunnel. 'Believe,' the faint voice advised him. 'Believe in your past and in yourself. Believe . . . believe . . . believe . . .' Then it was gone.

He made instant coffee from the near-boiling water in the kettle, then took the mug into the living-room. On the leather sofa he tried to recall every detail of his dream. The woman's face haunted him. He had seen her before. But where? That the incident had occurred in a train station was obvious, but which one? It wasn't a CIE one. It wasn't anywhere in Ireland, of that he was sure. British then. He tried to recall the destinations shown on the indicator board. Edinburgh came instantly to mind. But where was the train leaving from? The station was large, so could it be London? Where did trains to Edinburgh leave from in London? Euston? No, that was the one the Irish boat-train left from. Victoria? No, that fed trains to the South. King's Cross? Then it came to him. The bomb attack, back in February at King's Cross. The fire the bomb had caused, and the deaths. Definitely King's Cross. But who was the woman? Where had he seen her before? In a flash it came to him. She was the same woman he had 'seen' in Marlane's bed. And now he knew who she was. She was the wife of this Java Man, killed at King's Cross. He remembered the depth of love he had felt for this strange woman – and also knew that what he was feeling was another man's love of this woman.

He knew how to find the Java Man. Bob was in England, Frank had told him, working through a list of relatives of those killed by the Popular Front. On that list was this man's name. He lived in Scotland and his wife was travelling north on the day she died. It shouldn't take long to find him. When Frank had filled him in on those investigated in the UK he had mentioned the prime suspect, Kane, but added that he had been discounted. But Cowboy knew they must be wrong – or they had missed somebody off the list.

'But do I *want* this man found?' he asked himself. 'Look at what the Popular Front has done, the numbers of deaths they have been responsible for. Look what they did to me. And now they have Marlane.' Had he not already told Mooney that he'd kill the bastards if he had the chance? Mooney and the entire police force had not been able to find him while he was imprisoned, or this Java Man. Would they be any more successful at finding Marlane? No. There was only one man who could help him do that. The newspaper Mooney had given him, showing the sketch he had drawn of the Java Man, lay on the coffee table in front of him. Mooney had wanted to know how he had drawn it, where he had met or seen the killer. Cowboy had put on an act for him, claiming that he couldn't remember, because of the blow to his head. Mooney knew he was lying, and he knew that Mooney knew that. But he had let it pass, for the moment. How long could he put off telling his chief the truth? And how would Mooney react to that truth when he heard it?

He stared at the sketch. The room seemed to dim and disappear and all he could see was the other man's eyes. Deeper and deeper he felt drawn into those eyes, as though hypnotized. He didn't resist the pull, believing that it was leading him somewhere important. He felt a bonding with the man, a closeness of a kind he had never experienced before – or had he? How many times had he wondered to himself what it would take to drive an honest, law-abiding citizen to kill? Now he knew. He understood this man's desire for revenge. It was not a prison sentence this man wanted, but the biblical eye for an eye. Cowboy was trying desperately hard not to imagine what could be happening to Lane in the hands of a psychopath like McQueedy, but images forced their way in. He wanted the same thing this man wanted. He did not want to arrest McQueedy or McGuinness. He did not want to see them sentenced to a prison term of any sort. He wanted them dead, gone, out of this world to wherever. The more he stared at the sketch the more everything else disappeared from his vision, until he felt that all he had to do was reach out, and he could touch this man.

In his flat in the centre of the city Christopher Kane was once more visited by his nightmare. Again he was the pigeon witnessing Annabelle's death. Up and up he flew, his feathers pushed back tight to his frail body by the wind as he sped higher and higher, upwards towards space. Eventually he slowed, turned, and looked down. The earth below him was a blue and white ball. Then the dream changed. Another speck seemed to burst upwards from the world below, heading in his direction. It flew faster than a bullet, aiming towards him, but he knew instinctively that he had no need to fear. As he hovered in the calmness of deep space he watched the speck draw closer and closer. It flew past, turned, then came back and hovered beside him. It was another pigeon. They hung there, looking at each other. Then their shapes changed from pigeons to hawks. Talons appeared, razor sharp, and their beaks took on the curved pointed shape of birds of prey. Their eyes were piercing and their ability to see was increased a hundredfold. They were hunters.

They stared at the change in each other then moved together, wings flush with their bodies, legs curled, eyes trimmed to mere slits, and they dived. The blue and white ball grew in size. They could see the shapes of continents forming, the ball expanding all the time. They were baptized together as they entered the earth's atmosphere, the flames burning their minds, but not their feathers. They were a team.

He woke with a start remembering every element of the dream. What did it mean? Two hawks in place of one? Why? He knew he was one hawk – but who was the other? Gently, so as not to wake Monica, he eased himself out of the bed. He looked at the clock: 5.30. Grabbing his dressing-gown he went into the shabby living-room. He felt uneasy, as if he were being watched. They had drawn the heavy curtains back before going to bed the night before. Outside there was a kind of second twilight before the dawn and light filtered in through the net curtains. He crossed to the window and stood beside it, peering down onto the street below. There were no watchers, not even a parked car that could have contained anybody keeping the flat under surveillance.

Quietly he moved to the sofa and pulled his briefcase out from underneath. Holding the spring clip so as not to make a snapping noise as it opened, he released each catch separately. He felt inside for the revolver and took it out. Holding it in his right hand, uncocked, he checked the small kitchen and bathroom, feeling rather ridiculous as he did so. But the sense of watching eyes persisted. He had every reason to be careful with both the Gardai and the terrorists hunting him. He checked the fire exit door. It was still firmly secured with the crash-bar that could only be opened from the inside. He went back to the living-room, picked up the pack of cigarettes lying on the small coffee table and lit one. Once more he checked the street below. Still deserted, not a car in sight. Drawing the curtains he turned on the standard lamp and sat on the sofa. His gaze fell on the newspaper. Beside the sketch purporting to be of him were the twin photographs of the girl Marlane Davis and the policeman, Cowboy Johnson. The article gave the story of Cowboy's escape from the terrorists and the kidnapping of his girlfriend. His eyes were drawn to the photograph of the man. Once again he had the strangest feeling that he knew him. But from where? Was it from childhood? Had they gone to school together? He tried to think if a rich kid had attended school, sure that if there had been one it would have been the talk of the school. None came to mind, so where could he have known him from?

Then it all came to him in a rush. The feeling he had had of being watched was from the eyes in the photograph, and they were the same eyes as the other hawk, and the reason was obvious. He was killing terrorists because of his dead wife – this man s girlfriend was now in their hands. As he lit another cigarette the eyes of Cowboy Johnson beckoned to him and he felt compelled to stare at the photograph. Everything else seemed to disappear and all that remained were the piercing eyes of the second hawk. Then he heard the voice. It was a whisper at first, in the deepest recess of his mind, but as he welcomed it it grew stronger.

'Listen with your heart,' the voice said. 'You were brothers once, and will be again.' The voice trailed off and was replaced by another and he knew he was listening to the man in the photograph.

'Listen to me. Listen. The voice you are hearing is inside your head, but please listen to it.' It was fading in and out, like bad reception on a radio or telephone. 'Listen to my voice and concentrate on it.'

Not knowing if he was going mad, he continued to stare at the eyes, concentrating on the voice, and as he did so it grew stronger, more pronounced, the static disappearing.

'I know about the pigeon,' it continued. 'I have seen what the pigeon has seen. I have *been* the pigeon. I have seen the dark-haired woman. She died, and the pigeon saw it all.'

He listened, with a mixture of disbelief, bewilderment and amazement as the message was repeated several times. Then, seemingly confident that he could receive what was being transmitted, the voice continued.

'My woman is missing. Held by the same people you are hunting. I need your help. I can help you. Trust me. I am acting alone. Same . . .' The static returned, breaking up the message, as the link began to fade, the connection broken into a thousand fragments. 'Trust . . . call . . . together . . .' These words were little more than distant whispers, then nothing. The voice in his head was silenced.

Back in his living-room Cowboy was once more bathed in sweat. His head ached and he felt terribly weak, drained of energy. Had it worked? Had he got through? He felt a degree of certainty that he *had*, that the man his message was meant for had received it. But how would he react to such a strange communication? Would he, *could* he, comprehend what was going on, that they were both in some way linked to each other through time immemorial? What was it the voice had told him? *You were brothers once, you can be again*.

He staggered to the kitchen, his hand pressed against his head. From the fridge he took a bottle of plain mineral water. He was parched. Unscrewing the top he drank straight from the bottle, the coolness of the liquid soothing his dry throat. From one of the cabinets he withdrew a small plastic container of paracetamol. He popped two of the tablets into his into his mouth and filled it with water. Taking the bottle of water with him he returned to his bed. All he could do now was to wait and hope that the Java Man would contact him.

Chapter Fourteen

THE TWO MEN FACED each other across yet another grimy kitchen table, arguing over the fate of Marlane Davis.

'For fuck's sake Jimmy, can't you see? She's a hindrance. In the way. Bad luck. Ever since that fuck-up – a fuck-up of your making – in bringing that friggin' copper back, we've had nothing but bad luck. We've got Flynn chasing our arses, the bloody Brits chasing our arses, and the only safe haven we ever had – the South – has gone, because of a stupid mistake. We *still* don't know how those coppers got on to Merrion Farm, *still* don't know who, what or why some bastard is trying to kill us. We lose a safe house and a good man because that copper escaped. Now we're here, with our backs against the wall, nowhere to go but out of this motherfuckin' country – and what do you go and do? Fall in love with a stupid tart. Jesus Mother in Heaven, can't you see we have to get rid of her?'

'I'm not "in love",' McQ protested, afraid even to say the words in a normal tone of voice – but the protest was only half-hearted. He certainly did feel strange about the woman, otherwise why had he not screwed the shit out of her yet? She had completely thrown him with her reactions towards him. When he had finally taken the gag off her she hadn't screamed or called him names as he had expected. She had sort-of smiled at him and simply said 'Thank you, it's good to be able to breathe again.' She hadn't shown the remotest sign of fear towards him, in fact she had talked to him as an equal. He had never had that happen before, not even from Tommy, and most especially not from the women he had had. He was used to people being frightened of him, or hating him, and now he was completely off balance. He couldn't take his eyes off her when they were in the same room, watching every move of her lips, the way her breasts pressed against the T-shirt because her hands were pulled tightly behind her back, her jeans clinging to her legs, hips and crotch. He was mesmerized, almost frantic with lust, yet he was unsure of how to proceed.

'And now it's all *my* fault, is it?' he turned his frustrations on to Tommy. 'Who got himself fooled by that "stupid" copper? Who wouldn't let me beat the information out of him like I wanted to? Who sent me after the girl? Who's so clever that he can't even get assistance from the fuckin' sand nigger to get us out of the country? Who gets told "It's too hot at the moment" and to go paddle his own canoe – yet it's still all my fault?'

McGuinness sighed. He knew it would happen one day. They were coming to the parting of the ways, Jimmy and he. Time to start thinking just of Mary Thomas McGuinness and nobody else. But he needed to keep Jimmy sweet for the moment, right up until the very end, because Jimmy was dangerous – no one knew that better than Tommy, and when he discovered that his best friend was ditching him he would be likely to kill everyone in sight.

'There's truth in what you say, Jimmy,' he tried to calm the situation. 'Yes I was fooled by the detective. I admit that. But you and I have been through a lot together over the years, so let's not start fighting over who did what. The time has come for both of us to retire, to enjoy what we've got, get a little pleasure from life. There's all that money I've been investing on our behalf for this day, plus we have those two lovely bundles of lolly over there.' He indicated the imitation Welsh dresser by the far wall. 'We can disappear off the face of the earth – as far as anybody in authority is concerned, that is. We're set for life. It doesn't matter that that sand nigger, as you call him, in Dublin won't help. The Colonel will look after us all right once we get there. Libya's quite nice this time of year, I hear.' He smiled across the table at McQueedy, trying to pacify him. 'I managed to get word to Patrick Mullarkey. He'll come and get us. He should be able to land that small plane of his somewhere along the coast near here. Then it's Belgium, a visit to the bank to sort out the rest of the pension fund, then a scheduled flight to Libya, and Bob's yer uncle. You can lie on the beach all day long if you want Jimmy. I hear there's lots of sand.'

'Har-fucking-har.' McQueedy didn't appreciate his friend's attempt at humour. But he knew it was true, they had to get out, and get out fast. There were too many people looking for them now, and it was getting way too hot for them. But . . . he wanted the girl. He wanted everything, but most especially, her.

'Only joking, Jimmy. I'm sorry. But for God's sake will you please listen to me.' The smile and the banter in his voice disappeared. 'The girl is trouble. She'll be the death of both of us. I know you want her – so go and have her. Shag her until the cows come home – but just do it, get it out of your system, and then let's get rid of her.'

McQ didn't answer, just sat staring straight at McGuinness, the cogs in his brain slowly clicking into place. He wanted this woman more than anything in the world, the very thought of it made him break out in a sweat and his stomach turn cartwheels. But he didn't want to kill her. He wanted to screw her and be able to go on screwing her for the rest of his life. The thought of losing such a wonderful woman as soon as he found her was unbearable. But he knew it would be impossible to take her with them, they would never be able to get away with her in tow. So if he didn't do as Tommy suggested and take her now, he might miss the opportunity for ever and have to spend the rest of his life wondering what she might have felt like and tasted like, how she would have moaned when he touched her.

'OK, Tommy,' he nodded eventually, 'you're right, as always.'

And with that he turned and walked out of the room, leaving McGuinness sitting at the table, wondering if he really had got through. He didn't really care, as long as the girl was disposed of before she could do anything to hinder his escape. The tart had been here too long. Two days too long. He'd had enough. This was it, the break in the chain. He'd give Jimmy the details of the plane he had arranged, but the date would be out by a day or two. All he had to do now was think of a way of either getting Jimmy out of the house so he could move the money, or move it without Jimmy suspecting what he was planning.

It was after 2 a.m. when the persistent ringing woke him. His arm reached out to pick up the bedside phone.

'Hello,' he mumbled, trying to shake the sleep from his brain.

'Detective Johnson?' a female voice inquired. Immediately he was fully awake.

'Speaking.'

'Detective Johnson, you don't know who I am, but I was at Merrion Farm the night you were taken by McGuinness.'

'Who is this?' he demanded to know.

'It doesn't matter. You won't have known, but your timely arrival that night saved my life. They were about to kill me. I've read about you in the newspapers and about the kidnapping of your girlfriend. I can help you find her.'

'How?' He wished he had a cigarette.

'I know where she will have been taken.'

Cowboy's heart missed a beat. His hand tightened on the receiver, squeezing it as though trying to wring the information from the unknown caller.

'Tell me where she is. Please. If I saved your life, please help me to save hers.'

'I don't want the police involved. I know you are a policeman, but I'm giving this information to you personally. I'm prepared to meet you – but only you. And it has to be tonight.'

'How do I know I can trust you?'

'You don't. You'll just have to take my word for it. I swear to you you won't be harmed, and I do have the information you want. I don't think you have any choice. I'll be by the Half-Penny Bridge at three-thirty. I want you to come alone. Walk to the middle of the bridge and just wait. I'll watch until I'm sure you are alone, then I'll come and meet you. If you're not there by a quarter to four I'll leave.'

'Wait. How will I know –' But the caller had replaced the phone at her end.

Built in the late 1800s the Half-Penny pedestrian bridge, named from the toll imposed at the time for using it, was just down the river Liffey from O'Connell Bridge. At that hour a lone person standing in the middle of the bridge could be watched from either side of the river. Cowboy looked at his watch: 2.50. He had forty minutes to get there. He dressed hurriedly in jeans, polo shirt, black sneakers and dark brown leather zip-up. Collecting his car keys, locking the main door to the flat behind him, he took the stairs to the small underground garage. He pressed the timer switch for the lights, but the garage remained in darkness. Cursing the inconvenience he groped his way to the car. He was just about to put the key in the lock when he heard the click of a gun being cocked.

'Please don't make any sudden moves, Detective Johnson. I have no desire to hurt you. Please place your hands on the roof of the car and, as they say in the movies, assume the position.' There was a slight trace of humour in the voice, but Cowboy could tell that the man was serious. He had no need to ask who he was. It was the killer he himself had named the Java Man. Spreading his legs he leaned forward, gripping the roof of his car. In the darkness he saw no movement and shuddered slightly as hands ran over his back and chest, paying particular attention under his arms and at the base of his spine, up and down both his legs, going right to his crotch, searching for a weapon. The man was thorough before he was satisfied.

'I'm sorry about this, but I'm sure you'll appreciate that I have to be careful. Please stay as you are while I explain. I am responsible for the deaths of Maura O'Grady and her family, plus those at Merrion Farm – and I'd do the same all over again. I have no regrets about any of them. When I arrived at Merrion Farm I was almost hit by a speeding car – Mr McQueedy and yourself I presume, driving away to wherever it was you were taken. Inside the farmhouse I killed three terrorists. What is it the Yanks like to say? – "Terminated with extreme prejudice!" I also found a woman bound and gagged and tortured by Mr McQueedy and his friends. I took her away with me and helped her to recover. That was the woman who spoke with you earlier and arranged to meet you at the Half-Penny Bridge. As you have probably surmised, she is not there. I wanted you out of the flat so I could meet you. I know where McGuinness and your lady are, and I am prepared to help you get her back. You and I have a common cause, and we share a similar grievance as regards these bastards.'

'I know,' Cowboy replied. 'They killed your wife in a bomb attack on King's Cross station.'

Silence followed this remark for a few moments, then Kane spoke again. 'Then the police know who I am?'

'No,' Cowboy replied. 'Only I know – and even I don't know your name, although it would be easy to find . . . should I choose to look. Do you mind if I turn round? I'm unarmed as you know, and I have no intention of harming you. I am not interested in who or how many people you have killed. I am in the same boat as you. Neither the Gardai nor the CIB will get to Marlane quick enough as far as I am concerned. I want your help, and I am prepared to help you . . . if you'll let me.'

'You can turn round.'

Slowly Cowboy straightened himself and turned to face Kane's silhouette in the darkness; their eyes stared through the darkness at each other.

'Let me fix the lights,' Kane said. He turned the light strip, remaking the electrical contact and pressed the light switch. The light blinked for a moment then came on. Kane looked across to where Cowboy was still standing by his car. He drew the ski-mask off his face, sliding the gun back into its holster under his jacket.

The two men stood staring at each other for a few moments. Cowboy was the first to react as he offered his hand to the other with a slight smile. 'The Java Man, I presume?'

Kane returned the smile and clasped the extended hand. Both men felt the tingle of electricity run up their arms. Expecting something like this, Cowboy grasped Kane's hand tighter to stop him withdrawing it.

Time itself seemed frozen. The garage and everything in it disappeared and was replaced by wide open space. In the far distance were hills, and all around was open prairie land. The sun was high in a cloudless sky. The man whose hand he held wore buckskin pants tucked into knee-high riding boots, a faded checked cotton shirt, the sleeves rolled to the elbows, and a multicoloured bandanna round his throat. His face and arms were deeply tanned and on his head he wore an old, wide-brimmed, sweat-stained hat with a snakeskin band round it. Round his waist hung a leather gunbelt, with the single holster tied low on his hip, a strip of rawhide round the cocking lever. Just behind him, where a car had been, stood a shaggy-haired pony, its head lowered to nibble at the sharp prairie grass.

Cowboy was wearing a soft buckskin loincloth and leggings. His bare chest had a deep red tan and his hair hung down either side of his head in pony tails. In a belt on his waist hung a leather scabbard containing a hunting knife and in his left hand he held a Sharps repeating rifle. His own shaggy-haired pony stood behind him. He recognized the scene. It was the same camping ground that he had been shown by his spirit guide. Now he understood the significance of the pigeon emblem from spirit. It was the decoration that Cowboy – in another life – had ordered to be put on the buckskin jacket he gave as a thank-you present to the white man who had saved his life. The same jacket that now lay across the haunches of his pony.

While Cowboy understood his past life, this man, this Java Man, did not know his. They had been blood brothers once – and now they would be again. In his vision the two men were taking their final farewell of each other. For the last four years the man in the check shirt had shared his lodge as his brother, hunting buffalo together, fishing and capturing wild ponies. But now it was over. In the morning the lodges would come down and the People, the Comanche nation, would move further west, following the buffalo. The call of his own people was taking the man in the check shirt east. He had explained that the Americanos were going to war with each other. The call of his own was strong, and he was returning to fight for the new Confederation of States against those who would try to stop it. They both knew that they would not meet again. But now they had. Just as swiftly as it had all appeared, the vision disappeared and the dimly lit garage returned.

'Have we met before?' Kane asked as the handshake was broken.

'The night you went to the farm – outside a pub on the corner of Henry Street. I bumped into you.'

'That's it?' Kane asked, 'That's the only time we've met? I get the feeling that we actually knew one another, but I can't for the life of me figure out from where.' Baffled, he changed his line of questioning. 'How come you know so much about me and about my . . . about Annabelle?'

'I'm not sure I can explain it – any more than you can explain why you are taking such a great risk in contacting me. I'm a policeman. My job was to catch you – yet here we are, partners I suppose you might call us. I have seen your wife's death in a dream – nightmare really, I suppose. She was killed in a bomb attack on King's Cross station in London, wasn't she?'

'Yes.'

'In the dream I was a pigeon, watching her walking across the concourse, looking at the departures board. I watched this petite, dark-haired woman turn towards the left luggage lockers – and then all hell broke loose. I know you'll find it difficult to accept but it's the truth.'

'Oh I believe you all right. I've been having the same dream, night after night after night. But tonight it was different. Tonight there was another pigeon with me – and I knew it was you.'

'Let's go up to my flat. I'll make us some Java.' Without waiting for an answer Cowboy started towards the stair door.

'Some what?' Kane asked, following after.

'Coffee. Where do you think you got your name from? You drank a cup of coffee at the O'Grady household, didn't you?'

'How did you know that?' Kane asked, then remembered taking his gloves off to make the coffee. 'I washed everything I used and put it all back where I found it.'

'Yeah, but you forgot the milk bottle in the fridge.'

'Shit,' was all Kane could answer as he followed Cowboy.

Inside the flat Cowboy prepared some coffee, while Kane viewed his collection of Western memorabilia. He paused by the collection of 54mm hand painted models of Indians and cowboys, his gaze resting on one of a Comanche warrior encased in a glass dome. Beside it stood another, a cowboy wearing a light yellow buckskin jacket. Idly turning the model round with his fingers he noticed the motif on the back of the jacket. Like a white dove, or pigeon. He had a sneaking suspicion he had seen both figures before – or something like them – but couldn't remember where.

'How do you take your coffee?' Cowboy called from the kitchen.

'NATO standard issue' he replied automatically, giving the British soldier' s reply.

'And what, may I ask, is that?' Cowboy asked, turning as the other man came to the kitchen door.

'Sorry. Old habit. White with two sugars thanks. I can see why they call you Cowboy,' he continued. 'That's quite a collection you have in there. Valuable?'

'Some of it. Never play Cowboys and Indians as a kid?'

'Of course, who didn't?'

'That's where my interest started. I always wanted to be the Indian though. I seem to have an affinity with Indians. Maybe I lived as one once,' he added, testing to see if the other man made any connection.

'Do you believe in that sort of stuff then? Reincarnation, life after death, and all that?'

'I believe in something; what, I'm not sure. But yes, I think I once led a life as a North American Indian.'

Kane took the mug of coffee he was offered and moved out of the way as Cowboy came back into the living-room. 'As a kid I once thought I was a cowboy, a real one. The idea of living that kind of life appealed to me but . . . I grew out of it.'

'So, where do we go from here?' Cowboy asked.

'We wait for a while, then we have to pick up the girl. She wants in on it too. Mr McQueedy had a very special end in mind for her and she wants to make sure the bugger is dead once and for all. She deserves the chance.' He paused, scrutinizing Cowboy carefully. 'Ever kill anybody in your line of work?'

'No. But I've met both Mr McQueedy and Mr McGuinness and I can't think of a better pair to start with.'

'Killing is not something that comes easy, Cowboy. Yes I've killed, with good reason. The dark-haired woman you saw in your dream *was* my wife. My pregnant wife. To begin with I wanted to tear McGuinness to pieces with my bare hands – but first I had to find him. It's easy to kill in a rage, or if somebody is trying to kill you. But as time passes the rage dies down, and that's when you start to question whether you can kill or not.' He reached into his leather jacket and produced a pack of cigarettes. He offered them to Cowboy who hesitated for a moment, then took one. Kane lit both of them before continuing.

'Tracking Maura O'Grady was easy. Newspapers give a lot of detail and anyway, it was my home town. I grew up on the north side. Glasnevin. Not far from Ballymun, though for many years Ballymun meant the countryside to me, few houses and lots of fields. Different now of course. A multistory, inner-city garbage dump. I planned everything very carefully. Bought these clothes in different shops in England. My weapon was a fisherman's gutting knife. I broke in, managed to tie them all up, then had to get out of the room before I fainted. Went to the kitchen for some coffee. I'm always drinking the stuff. I needed one to steady my nerves. All I wanted from Maura was information; I didn't intend to kill her or the others. But the rage built up inside me again.

'I found her little office with a box of money and the gun. The ammo was with it – dum-dums. I'd seen the effect they have on people, men I knew . . . not friends as such, but men I saw on a day-to-day basis. Being shot is one thing, being hit with one of those things is something else. A shot in the shoulder will take your arm and half your body away with it, plus sending splinters showering into other parts of your body. A shot in the chest and you can forget it – even if it doesn't kill you there and then, you re a dead man breathing.

'I found Maura's little black book and her diary. The entries in the book were in code and I needed the key. She wouldn't give it. The bitch thought I had come to rape her. Jesus, you'd be sick to have wanted to rape her, the way she looked, her nightgown soaked with piss where she'd wet herself thinking about it. She was responsible for the deaths of I don't know how many – and she's pissing herself thinking about getting raped!

'I don't know what it was, but some time between me tying them all up, leaving them to have the coffee, going through the small room and returning to them, she had got the spit back in her eye. She seemed confident that I wasn't going to harm her. The rage was building back up inside me. I was that close,' he held finger and thumb up, slightly separated, 'that close to McGuinness, and this woman was holding out on me. I told her who I was and why I wanted McGuinness. Know what she said?' He looked Cowboy straight in the eye. Engrossed in the story Cowboy merely shook his head. 'That I deserved everything I got. I was an Irishman in the uniform of the enemy. Me and mine were legitimate targets! I was worse than the Brits because I was a turncoat.' His voice was changing as he recalled the scene. The rage was controlled now but still evident. His eyes narrowed and his nostrils flared slightly.

'Me and mine were legitimate targets! My wife, who never hurt a fly in her life, was a legitimate target. My unborn child, who hadn't even taken his first breath of polluted air, was a legitimate target! Whatever can be said of me, it was untrue of them. They were innocent. That's when the rage really returned. I walked across to where her husband was, tied on the bed. If me and mine were legitimate targets, then so were she and hers. I folded a pillow, placed it at the back of his neck, and shot him with Maura's pistol. Now she knew what it was like. Walk a mile in my shoes? She was standing in them, feeling the pain and suffering I had gone through. The terror she had helped to inflict on others had come home to roost.'

He was silent for a few moments, the knuckles on his hands white as he gripped the coffee mug, his mind back inside the bedroom, looking down on the destruction he had caused. Cowboy remained silent, watching the man struggle with his devils, bringing himself back under control.

'I remember reading,' he continued, 'of an incident during the Vietnam War. The Americans had picked up four Viet Cong and were flying them back to base in a helicopter, questioning them on the way. All four refused to even give their names, never mind any other information. They were flying at 800 feet and a war photographer in another chopper got a picture of two of these guys being thrown out, back into the jungle. When questioned, the intelligence officer who did it said that after he had thrown two out, he couldn't shut the other two up! Got information on nineteen hidden ammo dumps and found something like thirty other Viet Cong in Saigon. How many Americans were saved by finding those ammo dumps and the Viet Cong living amongst them? And what was the price? Two guys who would have done worse to any American they could have got their hands on.

'Maura was like that. After she got over the shock of her old man being shot, she started blabbing away. I got the code out of her, checked it, and found it worked. But the rage was still inside me from those words; me and mine as legitimate targets. Who was she? Trash. So I repeated the procedure with her and her son. She took mine . . . I took hers.

'It was when I got back to my flat that the realization of what I had done set in. I puked and puked and puked until I thought my arse was going to come out of my mouth. I shivered and sweated. I needed two hands to hold my mug, they shook so much. But I'll tell you something – I got my first good night's sleep for ages after that.' He drained the rest of the coffee and put the mug down on the table.

'You have your job to do, Detective Cowboy Johnson – but those people don't care a hoot for law and order, until such time as they are captured. Then they know every law in the book about how they have to be treated. But when they are out planting their bombs, killing innocent people, they don't give a shit for any law other than the law of the jungle. That's why they hate having the SAS on their trail. When they go in to take them out, they do just that. No prisoners. It's the only thing they understand.

'When I went to Merrion Farm it was to kill. I was becoming just like them. Killing is addictive, Cowboy, like a blood lust. There is a power inside you, the power of life and death – and believe me, you don't want to know about it if you can possibly avoid it.'

'Let me ask you something about the O'Grady one. Why did you leave that fifty-pound note in the cash box?'

'I dunno really,' Kane replied. 'I think I was trying to leave a message that it was not a robbery gone wrong – just in case the police thought that's what it was. Maybe I was trying to justify it all to myself. I just don't know. Now let me ask you a question. How did you find out about me, about the dream, the pigeon, all of that?'

Cowboy smiled. 'Can I have another cigarette before I begin?' Lighting the cigarette Cowboy started to explain, as best he could, the psychic events which had eventually led to the two of them meeting.

'I'm not saying I don't believe you,' Kane spoke as the other finished, 'but are you sure we don't know one another from years back? Kids somewhere? I knew, instinctively, when I had the dream of the two hawks that I could trust you.' He laughed slightly. 'Took a bit to convince Monica to call you, she was very very reluctant. She thought that it would end in me going to prison the moment we met.'

'That's the girl, is it? Monica?'

'Yeah. A misguided kid who eventually saw the light and wanted out – only to be told that the only way out was by being dead. Mr McQueedy was going to take care of that after he'd had a bit of fun with her first.'

This brought the images of McQueedy having his way with Marlane flooding back into Cowboy's mind, making him feel nauseous and explosive at the same time. This, he knew, was the rage which the Java Man had described to him. He tried to force the pictures of McQueedy's mouth and hands on Marlane's skin out of his mind.

'Don't we have some work to do, Java? . . . or what do I call you?'

Kane told him who he was, then added. 'Remember what I said about killing, Cowboy. Don't expect to walk away unscathed. If you're coming with us, then you do as I tell you, when I tell you. I don't want to have to worry about you and Monica. She understands what is expected of her and I want you to understand the same. I'm not saying I'm an expert, but, well, I've done it before and I believe there is a better chance that we might all come out of this alive if you agree to do as I say. Do we have a deal?'

Cowboy nodded. He was willing to accept this man's authority. 'I too want us all to come out alive, so . . . you're the chief.'

'What happens when it's over? Assuming, that is, that we all make it out alive. You'll still be a policeman, I'll still be a murderer.'

'When it's over, I'll be in it as deeply as you. As far as I'm concerned you can go on your way. It will be finished – but I can't say the same for Mooney. He's no idiot. His sergeant is in the UK going through the list of relatives of victims. Your name has cropped up, and you were the prime suspect, although for the moment you seem to be off the list But Frank Mooney can be like a terrier with a bone at times, just won't let go. If that happens, then we're both in the shit. I'll be an accessory to the murd –' he hesitated over the word, then continued, 'the killings up to now. But I'll be a participant in any future ones. I'll be going down with you.'

'Well, we'll just have to hope that your Inspector Mooney or the sergeant accepts what they have on face value. But that's life, eh?'

'One of them anyway,' Cowboy said. 'Let's do it'.

'Why not,' Kane replied and they both stood up.

Chapter Fifteen

IT WAS STILL RAINING as Kane drove down on to the quays along the Liffey, heading for the N4, the main route to the west of Ireland. All three occupants of the car were engrossed in their own thoughts. Monica was still suspicious about Cowboy. He appreciated her concern and did his best to rid her of it. Outwardly she accepted him, but inwardly she had decided that if he made any attempt to contact his police colleagues she would kill him. While Kane had the only gun between them she had slipped a kitchen knife into the inside pocket of her jacket just before they had left the flat. The same knife Kane had used the night he broke into the O'Gradys.

Fiddling with the car radio Kane found some music. Leixlip, Maynooth and Enfield were soon behind them as they headed for Kinnegad and the N6 for Athlone. As the rented dark blue Mercedes ate the miles, Kane asked Cowboy to explain more to him about his psychic ability. In the back seat Monica listened as Cowboy explained in more detail how he had always had the gift, but had suppressed it for years. When he got to the part where he had found the milk bottle he heard Kane murmur an almost silent 'Shit'.

'What's the problem?' he asked.

'I'd forgotten about those damn fingerprints. I thought I'd been so careful, even to taking the piece of glass from the back door away with me.'

'I wondered about that. What did you do with it?'

'Threw it in the Tolka. But . . . now my prints are on file, right?'

Cowboy nodded his head. 'Yes – but that's only a problem if we get caught . . . or you get arrested for something else.'

'Well if we get out of this alive I won't be back. I don't know where I'll head for – Far East, maybe – but I'll be gone from Ireland for good. I don't suppose I'll ever be the same man I once was – but staying in either Ireland or Britain would only help to keep the memory alive. I'll try to build my life elsewhere. The Popular Front supporters have very kindly made a hefty contribution to my pension fund.' He smiled across at Cowboy, remembering the amounts that had been destined to buy arms and explosives for the terrorists that now lay in his various bank accounts.

'Do I get to know where we're going yet?' Cowboy asked.

'All in good time,' Kane replied. 'Just sit back and enjoy the ride. Captain Kane and his crew will take you on a magical mystery tour!'

As Kane drove at a steady pace he was thinking of their destination, a place he knew well but had not visited for – how long was it, he wondered? He had been a young boy of nine when he had first visited the place, on a month's summer vacation. Now he was returning as a killer.

Sixteen miles to the west of Galway city, on the coast road, lay the village of Spiddal. The village Kane remembered and loved was tiny, its one main street forming part of the coastal road. While the road in the centre of the village was quite wide it narrowed both entering and leaving it, especially on the western side where it crossed over a small stone bridge. The centre of the village recalled days of portable paddocks, erected to contain the animals brought in on market days. Horses, pigs, sheep, cattle, geese and chickens would clamour to be heard above each other, while offers and counter-offers were made in the pubs on either side of the main street.

As a boy, Kane had had no interest in the pubs. His interest had lain in the selection of sweetshops and the post office. The post office was where he cashed the postal orders his mother sent as pocket money and the sweetshops were the recipients of the cash. Each shop had its own speciality for Kane, either in their sweet assortment, or their ice-creams.

Everything in and around the area was in Gaelic, the language which the Sassenach – the English – could never beat out of the Irish, no matter how hard they tried. Throughout the centuries of occupation, first by the Normans, then by the English, the people held fast to their language and their religion. English was a foreign language spoken only by foreigners – and anybody from outside Connemara was a foreigner, most especially the Dublin city slickers – the 'Jackeen'.

The men and women of the west were a different breed from those from the east. They worked a cruel land, their smallholdings – never more than a few acres – had more granite rock than soil. In this farming community everything was done by hand. The land was ploughed by hand. Where needed it was fertilized with seaweed, and then seeded by hand. Finally the harvest was brought in by hand. Modern farming implements were useless – a tractor that could plough rock had yet to be invented. This was the land to where the English Lord Protector, the puritanical dictator Oliver Cromwell, had sent the Catholics of the Northern Province of Ulster to, with the cry of 'To Hell or to Connaght' still ringing in their ears. And Connemara was the roughest and toughest part of Connaght. The men, and women, of the west could take it all, and still come out on top.

As Kane drove with his silent thoughts, Cowboy tried to engage Monica in conversation. He had agreed with Kane, before meeting her, not to ask questions relating to her background, or how she came to be at Merrion Farm that night. But his attempts at light conversation with the girl only elicited monosyllabic replies, so he gave up and the journey continued once more in silence.

Kane had learned from Monica of the new houses that now dotted the shoreline to the west of Spiddal. One of these new houses had been turned into the final bolthole of McGuinness. She was sure that this was where he would go, as it was the last haven he had. It had only been by accident that she had learned of its existence, and she had kept the knowledge to herself, until now. She was sure, she had told Kane, that her knowledge of this place was the reason McGuinness had decided to have her killed. Knowing him, she felt sure that not only would McQueedy be there, but several other hardened terrorists, and that they would be heavily armed. Those remaining there would have kept themselves well away from the locals and a few well-placed words here and there would be all that was needed to ensure their privacy, and forestall any questions.

Kane had asked about the Gardai station he remembered as a boy, in the centre of the village. Long gone, she had explained, with Gardai assistance for the area now localized in Galway city. In any case McGuinness would have been considered 'one of the boys', and providing he kept his nose clean in and around the area, he would have been left alone. When he had asked her if the kidnapping of one of their own – Cowboy – would have made any difference to that attitude, she had replied 'I wouldn't bet on it. He's a Jackeen.'

It was late afternoon and the rain had stopped when they crossed into County Galway at Ballinasloe. The Mercedes made good progress and it wasn't long before they entered Galway city itself. Kane ignored the ring road and drove towards the city centre. He wanted to see it one more time. He knew that whatever the outcome of that night's work, he would never return again. This city, and the surrounding countryside, were infused with his childhood memories. Neither passenger queried his decision.

Driving up by the side of Kennedy Park he glanced at the statue of Padraig O'Conaire, the Story Teller, who sat on his plinth looking out at Eyre Square. Kane remembered the annual summer funfair that pitched its tents, dodgems, merry-go-rounds and other assorted amusements in the park. Turning left on to Williamsgate Street he drove along Shop Street and High Street, crossing the river Corrib via the Wolfe Tone Bridge.

They passed by the old fishing village of the Claddagh, now a suburb of the city. It was this village that gave its name to the famous rings. These rings were cast like a pair of hands holding a heart surmounted by a crown. The ring symbolized 'I give you my heart, crowned with my love'. Kane knew all about these famous Claddagh rings, he wore one on the wedding finger of his left hand. Cast in heavy gold it bore the inscription of the date of his wedding to Annabelle.

At Salthill, on the western outskirts of the city, he parked the car on the seafront. He wanted to stretch his legs, but he also wanted to talk to Monica before they commenced the last lap of the journey. In asking her to walk with him he indicated to Cowboy that he should not join them. Cowboy picked up on the hint and remained in the car while the others strolled along the windswept promenade with their jackets zipped up to the neck, their collars turned up against the sea wind and their hands deep in their pockets. For a while neither spoke.

Monica broke the silence. 'My father used to tell me stories about this place.' They entered a breeze shelter and sat on the wooden bench, watching the waves pound the shore. The spray, caught by the wind, fell on them like salty rain. They stared out towards America, thousands of miles away. 'Apparently my great-great-grandfather's brothers and sisters all sailed from here at the time of the great famine. Can you imagine what it must have been like at that time? People dying by the sides of the road from malnutrition, and ships, laden with beef and grain, sailing daily from Dublin, for the English markets. All they left for the Irish were the potatoes – and when they rotted and died in the ground, we began to die in our thousands – hundreds of thousands. Apparently it was only when the emigrants started to send back food ships that Whitehall took any notice.

'We are a strange race of people, aren't we Chris?' She linked her arm through his and rested her head on his shoulder, looking up into his wet face. 'Blessed with a beautiful country, and cursed with a memory that goes back centuries, like those things only happened last week.'

Kane nodded. As a young man, barely more than a boy, he couldn't wait to get out of the country to see the world. Yet wherever he went, when asked about Ireland, he talked of the beauty of his native land, and especially the wild beauty of Connemara. He had heard it described as a terrible beauty, which he had never understood. Now he did. A beauty ruined by the deeds committed in its name, first by the English against the Irish, then by the Irish against the Irish in the civil war of the 1920s, and now by the Irish against the English and the Loyalists in the North. Very little of it all had touched the South – until he had returned, he grimly reminded himself. But it all left a sour taste in the mouth, reading of the kneecapping, torture, extortion, blackmail, death and destruction. And there was some more on the way. It was what he had come here to do.

'I want you to stay here, Monica,' he said, breaking his own silence. 'Better still, go back to Dublin. Go to the flat and take the money I showed you. Get out. Get away. Take the chance while you can. Please?' He turned and looked at her as she pulled her head from his shoulder and moved a few inches away from him.

'No, Chris. Don't you understand that I *have* to be here? I have to finish it, or be finished – the same as you. I have my own contribution to pay. You have never asked me about myself, never intruded, and I appreciate that. There is much for me to be ashamed of, much to pay for, and this is the only way I know how. Don't you also think I have a right to be here, to help rid us all of the likes of McGuinness and McQueedy? If I don't see the pair of them dead I shall never be able to sleep without fear again, always wondering if they are coming after me. Before I can start afresh I have to wipe out the past as best I can – and they are my past. I need to be there.'

Kane slowly nodded his head, fully understanding her reasons and, he assumed, her right to be in at the end. Only a short time ago he had decided to call it a day, but had realized he could not walk away, not when he knew where McGuinness was. He too was committed to finishing what he had started. He wiped the spray from her face and gave her a half smile. 'Let's go get the Cowboy and go after the bad guys'. She too smiled with her lips, but her eyes reflected the sadness he felt deep inside himself. Cowboy remained silent as they both got into the car again. Without a word Kane drove off, heading west.

McQueedy balanced the tray on his left hand and unlocked the door with his right, pushing it open with his shoulder. Marlane's head swivelled as she heard the key turn in the lock and watched. She forced herself to stop trembling and to hide the fear and hatred in her eyes as he came in.

She was gagged and tied again, her arms and legs spread-eagled on the bed. He placed the tray on the chair, then came and sat on the edge of the bed. Her body stiffened and she willed it to relax. She knew that he was puzzled and thrown off balance by her lack of fear. She mustn't lose that advantage. She gritted her teeth behind the gag, and attempted to smile at him with her eyes.

'Promise you won't scream,' he whispered into her ear as he leaned over her. When she nodded her head, he released the gag and sat on the bed, his hands resting on her thighs, the fingers kneading her flesh absent-mindedly as he gazed down at her mouth. She licked her lips and smiled, with only the smallest tremor.

'Thanks. I need to go to the bathroom desperately,' she whispered, her voice dry and cracked. He nodded. 'Great. Thanks. After that we'll talk, yes? Get to know each other better.' He slowly undid the ropes, savouring the feel of her fragile wrists and ankles in the palms of his hands. 'What should I call you?'

'Jimmy,' he didn't look at her face, unable to take his eyes off her body, 'you can call me Jimmy. We are going to have such a good time, you and me.' Now he looked her full in the face, and smiled, revealing his yellowed, jagged teeth. He took her face in his hand and squeezed the cheeks together until she felt her jaw would snap. 'I'm going to show you what it's like to be screwed by a real man.'

'OK, Jimmy. But I gotta get to the bathroom,' she reminded him.

'OK.'

He helped her to her feet. She almost fell, her legs were so weak, but he caught her, pressing her body against his as he led her along the passage to the bathroom.

'Don't lock the door,' he ordered, 'or I'll break it down. Now hurry up.'

Closing the door behind her she immediately relieved her aching bladder, her eyes scanning the room, terrified that if she took a moment too long he would burst in. The half window, set high in the wall, was frosted. She could neither see out, nor be seen. The lock on the door was a tiny flimsy bolt; one push from McQueedy and it would fall off.

'Oh God, Cowboy. Where are you darling?' Tears held back for so long now streamed down her face as she sat on the toilet, her thoughts going out into the ether. 'Please come for me. I'm so scared. Please.' Blowing her nose on some toilet paper and dabbing at her eyes she went to the basin and rinsed her face with cold water. She longed for a bath or shower, but dared not, knowing that would be tempting providence too far. She knew what a dangerous line she was treading by encouraging McQ like this, but it seemed her only chance. If she could convince him that she intended to have sex with him later on it would at least buy her some time. Since she guessed that he intended to rape her anyway, she had nothing much to lose. The question was, how long could she keep stringing him along? It had been two days now and still he hadn't done more than touch her. Yesterday she had hardly seen him at all, but she guessed that today was going to be the day. She also guessed that once he had had his way he would probably have to kill her. She had met McGuinness and heard the raised voices between them, and guessed it was about herself. McGuinness wanted her dead. If only she could find some way of goading McQueedy into defying his friend, perhaps set them against one another, that might save her life, at least for a little longer, giving Cowboy more time to find her. She believed, without a shadow of doubt, that he would come.

'You finished in there yet?' he called from the other side of the door. Unwilling to use the towel – which looked like it had been there for weeks, she grabbed another handful of toilet paper to dry her face. Opening the door she allowed him to lead her by the hand back to the room.

He had made breakfast for her, with a pot of tea and a plate of toast. There was also some butter and marmalade beside the milk and sugar bowls. It looked as if he had gone to some trouble. Sitting on the bed she forced some toast down her dry throat, and relished the warm tea.

'I'll cook you a proper meal later on. Some steak and potatoes and some veg. You're too thin. You need a bit of fattening up.' He was smiling as he spoke, and gave her waist a painful squeeze.

'That would be great,' she laughed, 'I'm surprised a big guy like you knows how to cook.' Yesterday's only meal had come from a tin.

'Oh sure,' he grinned proudly, 'a little, I cook for Tommy sometimes.'

'He should be kinder to you then,' she said mischievously, 'he's lucky to have a friend like you.'

'Jimmy, where the fuck are you!' Tommy's voice came along the passageway. 'Don't take all fucking day about it.'

She saw how he changed at the sound of Tommy's angry voice, almost jumping to attention, and then appearing angry at his own reaction. She was unable to control her fear completely and let out a small cry as he knocked the cup from her hand, sending it smashing against the far wall. Throwing her back down on to the bed he snatched up the ropes and roughly tied her hands and feet to the bedposts, so that her legs were splayed out again, and he could see her ribcage heaving fearfully beneath her T-shirt.

'Jimmy, please, you re hurting me!' she cried.

'Shut up,' he snarled, forcing the gag back into her mouth.

McQueedy believed if you wanted a woman, you took her. Against a wall, in the back of a car, on the floor, in a bed, it made no difference. Giving no thought to the woman's pleasure he would fuck her, just like a bull servicing a cow, until he exploded his sperm, then it was over, until he wanted it again. Why should this bitch be any different, just because she was better looking? He would sort Tommy out and then he would come back and give her one.

Arriving at Spiddal, Kane slowed as they drove through the village. The 'new' Spiddal looked entirely different. The sleepy country village had thrived in the years since he had been there. The layout was the same. The shops he remembered were still there, but the hand-painted signs above the doors were now up-to-date fluorescent, though still in the Gaelic tongue. The ponies and traps he remembered standing outside the pubs and shops were long gone, replaced by every kind of modern car. The days of walking miles, or going by pony and trap from one place to the other were over. Ireland's entry into Europe had brought the country forward in leaps and bounds. But it had gone too far too fast and the sudden halt to the good life was starting to take effect.

As they drove through the centre of the village Cowboy suddenly brought both his hands to his head, pressing tightly against his temples. 'We're close,' he whispered, 'she's here, close by. I can feel it. I can hear her. It can't be far away.'

Both Monica and Kane were impressed as Cowboy had not been told where they were going. Only they knew that their final destination lay just over the hill, beyond the village.

Dusk had fallen and, with dipped headlights on, they crossed the new, wide bridge which had replaced the old hump-backed one Kane remembered on the western end of the main street. This bridge traversed the outlet to the sea for Boliksa Lake, to the north, which flowed through the estate of Lord Killannan on their right. A few yards beyond the bridge, on the seaward side, was a small narrow road leading down to the fishing jetty of Spiddal harbour. Topping the rise the road led straight on towards Inveran.

'Keep your eyes on the houses built on our left, backing on to the sea,' Monica instructed.

They were a mixture of bungalows and two-storied houses, each one detached from the next by quite a distance, all standing in their own grounds fifty to a hundred yards from the main road. It was Cowboy who spoke first.

'That one,' he pointed, indicating the fourth house along from the harbour turnoff. 'I can feel her presence. Am I right?'

'Yes,' Monica whispered, newly amazed. She hadn't even told Kane which house it was. Holding back that last bit of information had been her insurance that he would not leave her behind. She felt a cold shiver of fear as she realized how close they were to McQueedy.

The bungalow was built of natural Connemara granite. A cattle grid was sunk into the ground where a metal, five-barred gate blocked entrance to the driveway. The driveway itself was in the same state of untidiness as the rest of the grounds, hard, flattened earth, and tufts of coarse grass. The entire garden was dotted with boulders, some large and standing alone, others in small clusters. The house itself had four large windows facing the front, with the main door set at the side, designed to escape the winds that blew down from the inland wilderness of bog towards the sea and back. To the rear and side of the building was a double garage, built of the same granite as the house. No lights shone from the front windows, but as they drove past they could see lights to the rear. The Atlantic Ocean was three or four hundred yards further back from the garage. Even before he had seen it, Kane had decided that the way in was from the seaward side.

About a mile further on they passed a small cluster of houses on both sides of the road, with a single minimarket indicated by a neon sign. Kane gave a casual glance inland. Just out of sight was the home of his long-lost boyhood love, Nancy Keedy. Where was she now, he wondered? Did she still have laughing eyes and a soft smiling mouth? Did she remember that Jackeen boy she had once loved? A little further on they passed another boreen – little more than a dirt track – that led to the house where he had spent four happy summers. What had happened to the couple who had treated him like a son? Probably both dead, he thought.

His memories were of sunshine and laughter, sandy beaches and the wildness of Connemara, where time seemed to stand still. Home made breads and treacle cake, freshly dug boiled potatoes, chickens roasted in a large black pot that hung over an open turf fire, a fire that hadn't been allowed to die out for over three hundred years. Fried mackerel for dinner, caught by the farmer that same morning from a reed-made, canvas-tarred currach that bobbed on the ocean waves not a quarter of a mile away, the same currach he lay under with Nancy. Wonderful memories that had brought him pleasure over the years. He had always promised Annabelle that one day he would bring her here for a holiday, but had never got round to it. Now it was too late. They had not only killed his wife and unborn child, they had killed his happy boyhood memories as well.

Sitting beside him in the passenger seat Cowboy picked up on some of the memories that flashed through Kane's mind. It was like looking through somebody else's photograph album. He watched the man as he drove silently through the now darkening evening, wondering to himself what would have become of Kane had the events at King's Cross not happened. He also wondered what would become of him after this night was over.

Kane, unaware that the other man was receiving some of his thoughts, drove on in silence to Mann Cross, near the foot of the Mamturk Mountains. The rain had returned accompanied by sea spray, chilling everything in its path. I ever there was a night for the Banshee to be abroad, this was such a night. All three of them heard the soft howling wind above the quietness of the Mercedes engine. All three of them thought of the legend and hoped that she was coming for McGuinness and McQueedy and not for them.

At yet another small village, little more than a pub with a filling station and a grocery store, they stopped to fill up with petrol, then all three went into the pub for coffee. While the other two sat at the table furthest from the bar, Kane collected three cups of instant coffee. The publican asked where they came from and where they were heading. In what he hoped would pass as an American accent, Kane replied that they were heading for 'a small town called West Port', and asked how far it was. The publican told them that they still had a fair bit to go, but that the roads would get better when they reached Route 71 at Leenane. Quickly drinking their coffee the trio set off again with the publican's best wishes for a safe journey ringing in their ears. Kane went north for a further ten miles, in the direction of West Port, before he turned the car round, heading back the way they had come, driving slowly and carefully.

Between Inveran and Dooletter he stopped the car and got out. The darkness was cut by a great flash of light followed seconds later by a thundering roar. Looking up into the sky, through the now pouring rain, he watched the moon glide slowly behind the dark clouds, as if hiding from the night's forthcoming events. From the boot he brought a small suitcase back into the car. In the warmth he peeled off the light blue, V-necked jumper he had been wearing and pulled on a black polo-necked sweater from the case. Over this he strapped on the shoulder holster, laying the revolver on his knees.

Despite having oiled and cleaned the weapon every day since he took it from the house in Ballymun, he checked it once more. Reaching into the case again he took out a small cardboard box. Opening it he withdrew a single round and offered it to Cowboy.

'Run your finger over the point. Can you feel the unevenness of it?'

Taking it in his hands Cowboy did as instructed. He reached up to turn on the interior light, but Kane's hand grasped his wrist.

'No lights. Just feel it.'

As Cowboy ran his finger over the head of the projectile, Kane unscrewed the bulb from the overhead light and dropped it into the case.

'It's not exactly smooth like I'd expect it to be,' Cowboy replied.

'Right. One of Maura O'Grady's little specials. Head bored and filled with mercury, then refilled.'

'Yeah, I know. Forensic found traces of mercury in the bodies in Ballymun. We thought you'd done it.'

'No. I just wanted you to know the kind of person Maura was. You don't go to all the trouble of making such a bullet unless you intend to use it, and in using it you know the kind of effect it is going to have when it hits somebody.' Kane turned his body so as to include Monica in what he was about to say. 'I want both of you to listen to me very carefully. I want it understood that from here on in both of you do exactly as I tell you. With a bit of luck I'll get us in – and hopefully get us out again, along with your girlfriend, Cowboy. But it is vital that I know where each of you is at all times. We will all have fears, and the adrenalin will be pumping. It will act like a drug, giving you a high that will enable you to keep going. One of two things will happen. Either your senses will be more alert, or you will freeze, in which case you die. I don't want to die just yet, and I don't suppose either of you two do – so do what I tell you, when I tell you. Is that understood?'

'Yes,' Cowboy replied.

'Monica?' he turned to face her across the back seat.

She nodded her head in the darkness. 'Yes,' she whispered.

'Good. I lead, then Cowboy, and you last Monica. Make sure to keep in that order, then I'll know where each of you is.'

From the case Kane took a small plastic bag containing surgical gloves. Handing a pair to each of the others he pulled on a pair himself. Taking a small clean rag from the case he now cleaned every part of the gun, including each round of ammunition. Satisfied, he returned the pistol to the holster, and drew on a pair of tight-fitting black leather gloves. The last item he put on was the black ski-mask, leaving it rolled at his forehead. Closing the suitcase he passed it over to Monica, who laid it on the seat beside her. Without another word he put the car in gear and drove off, back towards Spiddal.

The road they travelled was flat and straight. If there were any guards by the house they would have seen his headlights long before he got near. With that in mind he continued on past the house, down the hill into the village and carried on in the direction of Galway city. Five miles beyond the village, on an empty stretch, he turned back once more. It was now almost 11 p.m. and the main street was empty, though lights were still to be seen in a couple of the pubs. Crossing the bridge Kane turned off the car's lights, reducing their speed to a crawl. At the top of the hill, his eyes now accustomed to the darkness, he turned left, down to the jetty. The gentle purring of the motor would be drowned by the noise of the rain and the wind. If McGuinness had guards outside – and Kane was betting that he would have – they would have seen and heard nothing out of the ordinary.

In front of him, in the darkness, was a black shape. The car was travelling very slowly now and Kane used the handbrake to avoid the brake lights which would inform of their arrival. Handbrake on, car in neutral, Kane got out and checked the black shape. It was an old weather-beaten hut, smelling of fish. Returning to the car he allowed it to roll forward into the darker shadow of the hut. All three got out and stood in the darkness.

'This is it, folks. We go in from the sea. It's the area they'll least expect anybody to come from.' He turned to Cowboy and offered him his hand. 'Good luck, Cowboy. I'd like to have known you under different circumstances but . . .' His voice trailed off.

Cowboy returned the firm grip. 'Good luck to you too, Chris. I appreciate the help.' He turned to Monica. 'Thank you too, for your help.' She took his hand and gave it a squeeze. Kane led her to one side.

'You can still stay out of it, Monica. Just wait with the car until we get back – or get the hell out of here if –'

'No,' she interrupted him. 'I'm going in too.' In the darkness she reached up to his face with both hands and drew his mouth down to hers. The kiss was gentle.

'Chris, I . . .' she struggled for the right words.

'I know,' he whispered. 'I know what you want to say, and I feel the same.' His gloved hand stroked her face.

'Remember what Dave Allen always says: "May your God go with you". I hope luck is on our side tonight and against McGuinness. You're a nice girl, Monica Saunders, despite what you feel about yourself. Remember that, and tell yourself now and again, OK?'

'I will Chris. And I can say the same thing about you. I'm sorry for what happened to your wife and child, please believe that. It's important to me. I'm sorry what the whole thing has done to you. Your wife was a very lucky woman to have been able to love you – even for a short time – and to have been loved by you. It may sound strange, but I do hope that God *will* look over you tonight and keep you safe. That way it will all be over for you. You will be able to sleep in peace again, and get on with the rest of your life. I'm glad I met you and was able to say these things to you. Maybe one day you'll understand why. Now let's go.'

While the other two talked quietly to each other Cowboy stood by the car. Blanking everything from his mind as best he could, he tried to talk to her with his mind. 'Lane, I'm here. Close by. We've come for you, kitten. Don't give up hope. We are here, we are here, we are here. I love you.'

As the others rejoined him Kane had the ski-mask down over his face, and Cowboy recognized the image he had seen in the mirror, during that first psychic experience. The pigeon, Christopher Kane, had become the hawk, the Java Man, the Angel of Death. He had become a part of the darkness that surrounded them. Cowboy shivered as he watched the transformation. He was extremely glad this man was on his side, and not coming after him.

In the back bedroom of the house several hundred yards

from where they stood Marlane woke suddenly from a restless sleep. Her arms ached from the cramp and she moaned gently with the pain, her wrists and ankles sore from rope burns. She could still feel where McQueedy's hands had hurt her before he had gone off to do Tommy's bidding, promising to return before the night was over and show her what a stud he could be. It was Cowboy's voice that had woken her. She had heard it as clearly as if he had been standing beside her. He was coming, as she always believed he would. Tears of relief began to flow, unchecked, down her cheeks. 'I'm waiting, darling,' she mumbled into the gag. 'Please please please, be very careful.'

Chapter Sixteen

THE DAY HAD BEEN a long one for Frank Mooney. Everything from the house where Johnson had been held had been brought to the Castle and scrutinized for any clue as to where they might have taken Marlane, but they still had nothing. True to his word he had contacted O'Riley, apologized about the way the raid had been handled by the uniformed branch, and offered complete access to the house and its contents once the formalities were completed. A small quantity of Semtex plastic explosive had been found, along with six Kalashnikov rifles, a Winchester pump action shotgun – with most of the barrel sawn off – a mixture of handguns, one Ingram submachine gun, and enough ammunition for each weapon to start a revolution. The bullet-ridden body of the single terrorist shot by the gardai had been taken to the morgue. Fingerprints had confirmed that both McGuinness and McQueedy had been there, along with Johnson. While both had already been suspects for Cowboy's kidnapping an APB had now been sent all over the country naming both of them as wanted men. Their days of covering their tracks, ducking and diving in the mish-mash of Irish politics and laws were over. They were now nothing but common criminals.

O'Riley had the serial numbers of the weapons and was now using his own sources to trace them, although he was already sure that they had come in from Libya. The Gardai had begun an inventory, on Mooney's orders, of everything the house contained and until that was completed O'Riley got nothing more. He was frustrated, only half believing Mooney when he explained that, because it was the uniformed branch that had carried out the raid, the situation was out of his hands. O'Riley could only accept.

Mooney was also frustrated because there was nothing that led him any further. Several times he had reached for the phone to call Cowboy, and each time he had changed his mind. Why call him with nothing new to report?

He stayed late at the office to catch up on the backlog of paperwork that never seemed to get any smaller, and to await Bob's call from England. Would he have anything new on the search for this bloody Java Man? What a twisted world it was at times, he mused. The CIB were not only hunting the hunter, but the hunted also. This Java character had started the ball rolling by killing members of the Popular Front, who had now managed to kill one detective and kidnap another, plus kidnapping a civilian. Not only was he under orders to get McGuinness for the murder of Russell and the two kidnappings, but he also had to get the other guy who was hell bent on killing McGuinness! Jesus, he thought, why not let the Java Man finish the job – he was certainly having more luck than they were. He might be a murderous bastard, but he was making a very nice job of it. Leave him to it and he'd have the whole Popular Front wiped out by the end of the week.

Bob's call from England brought no new leads. The trail had gone totally cold. Everybody on the list was accounted for, even Kane seemed to be in the clear. Frank had been to visit Kane's sister, and she had shown him postcards she had received from her brother, confirming that they were in his handwriting. Mooney had noted the franked date stamps and had spoken to a friend in Aer

Lingus, to see if it was possible for Kane to have got in and out of the country to do the killings. It wasn't.

He had asked the sister for an example of Kane's handwriting other than the postcards. She had given him a letter written to her several weeks before the killings started, explaining that he was going to the Far East to 'try and find himself again', as he put it, after Annabelle's death. Even before he got the result from forensic Frank knew that the handwriting was the same. The postcards were not forgeries. Dead ends, dead ends, dead ends. Certain things did not tie up, did not fit into any pattern, and they should. This Java character was certainly not a psychopathic serial killer, motivated by voices in his head, but what *was* his motivation?

The break-in at the O'Gradys was a professional job. Neat entry, neat exit – and even the piece of glass the guy had licked had gone, preventing any DNA testing. The gun, the rounds used and the manner of the killings all smacked of a pro hitman. Yet no professional hitman would make himself a cup of coffee and leave some nice prints behind him – but this guy did! Why? What was the meaning of the fifty-pound note in the box on the desk? And no professional would have taken the gun from the scene. It would have been a 'clean' weapon, never used before. One hit, drop the weapon, and walk away. To have been stopped for any reason, with the gun in his possession . . . that would have been the end.

The murders at the farm were also different. To be as good with a machine gun as this guy must mean military training – which pointed to this man Kane. But Kane couldn't have done it! He had told Bob to wrap everything up in the UK and come home in the morning. Frank had contacted the Hong Kong authorities about Kane, in the hope that it might provide that one little thing they needed to solve the jig-saw puzzle, but he didn't expect any joy.

'Goddamn it,' he said out loud to his empty office. 'I need a drink, then I'm going home.' Locking his office door behind him he was halfway down the corridor when his phone rang. He didn't hear it.

Commandant James O'Riley was also having a late night at the office. Around seven he had gone for a meal to a small commercial hotel near the barracks owned by a former military police sergeant with whom he had served in the United Nations forces in the Lebanon. Since the breakup of his marriage O'Riley ate at the hotel on a regular basis, and had a private arrangement with the owner over costs. Having finished his meal he had decided to return to his office to put in a few more hours' work before retiring for the night to his flat. His operatives throughout the Republic had all been on the lookout for McGuinness, and although several sightings had been reported, none had borne any fruit. It was almost nine when his hot line rang. Unlocking the desk drawer that housed the phone he pressed the 'record' button on the small tape machine and lifted the receiver.

'Speak,' he ordered into the phone. Few people had the number and they all knew that only he answered it.

'Evening, Commandant. I have a message from a mutual friend.' O'Riley recognized the voice of Liam Daley.

'I'm listening,' he replied.

'There is a very interesting piece of property on the West Coast. Just outside the village of Spiddal, Galway. The property backs on to the sea and is fourth on your left as you come out of the village. It would seem that the regular occupants received some visitors recently – presumed to be the absent owner and his managing director. They also brought along a reluctant secretary. Others are also looking for this secretary. We're not too sure of her present condition, but I would suggest that fingers be extracted from anuses. Are you with me so far, Commandant?'

'Oh I'm with you all right.'

'Now I've given you this information on trust, you understand, but our mutual friend has a request to make. One that would pay off some, I repeat *some*, of the debt your company owes . . . are you still with me?'

'All the way. Go on.' O'Riley had expected that whatever would be asked of him immediately would only be considered by Flynn to be a down payment for the information he was passing on.

'The owner of the property used to work for our company,' Daley continued. 'When he left, rather hurriedly as you know, he took some negotiable samples with him, in order to start up his own company. We would like these negotiable items returned, if at all possible. We'll pick them up ourselves if you like, or collect from any third party who may get them first. I'm sure some of them are in a secure place, maybe even a numbered secure place. Not much to ask, is it?'

As far as O'Riley was concerned it was. It was known that McGuinness had depleted the coffers of the Provos by quite a few thousand pounds, and had since been adding to that total. O'Riley's department could well do with a substantial windfall that would be untraceable, and unaccountable to any government department.

'I personally don't see any problem with such a request,' he lied. 'I have an agreement with the other party involved with me on this one. If I come up with an address, then I get first choice at any papers or documents found. I'll see what I can do. You have my word on it.'

'As an officer and a gentleman?' came the soft, laughing retort.

'No, more as a businessman who may want to do further deals with your good self and the managing director of your company. Is that good enough?'

'More acceptable than the officer and gentleman bit I can tell you.'

'Good. I'll be in touch. In any case, please tell your MD that I appreciate the call. I'll remember it.'

'Oh I'm sure you will, James, I'm sure you will. You'll play it back several times on the tape, just to make sure you haven't missed anything – just like I'll play mine back. And just in case you *did* happen to forget . . . sure we'll remind you. Oh, I almost forgot to tell you. We have withdrawn all our regular sales staff from the area of the property I mentioned – just in case anything should go wrong. We'd hate for any of our staff – on holiday in the area – to get caught up in any liquidation of our competitor's firm. Good night to you James, and sláin leath.' With that the line went dead. O'Riley pressed the 'stop' button on the recorder and leaned back in his chair.

He could well understand Flynn's desire to get his hands on any funds McGuinness had with him. Times were hard for everybody these days, what with high inflation and less interest from countries that had, in the past, provided 'goodies' for free. There was only one real supplier left, now that Eastern Europe was coming in from the cold. The Libyan Colonel was still supplying more than deep-fried chicken, but he'd go bankrupt if he kept supplying freebies – especially as he was having to send four shipments to ensure one got through! Locking the direct phone away he reached for the desk phone and dialled Mooney's office number.

Frank Mooney was sitting with a large Irish, swirling the amber liquid round and round in the glass, watching it, yet not seeing it.

'No need to wash the glass, Frank, we do that as a matter of course once a week.' Brendon, the barman, leaned across the bar, attempting conversation.

'I know, Bren,' Mooney replied, half smiling. 'It's just one of those days. A bit pissed off with everybody and everything.'

Brendon nodded his head in agreement. He would have nodded his head in agreement if the statement had been something else. Being barman to the CIB did have certain compensations – like never being raided for after-hours drinking – but, then again, the offenders were mostly CIB officers anyway. To keep everybody sweet, Bren, as everybody called him, agreed with all the comments made to him by his customers. On one memorable occasion Frank and some of the others had set Bren up. One complained about the 'fuckin' lousy weather', while another commented that 'it was lovely to get some rain for a change'. Bren had agreed with both of them, which led both to complain that Bren was takin' the piss out of them, and the two CIB men squared up for a punch-up, declaring that the winner was going to kick the shit out of Bren for starting the fight. Poor Bren hadn't known what to do. He could hardly call for the Gardai to sort out some of their own. He tried appealing to others in the bar, but they all said it had nothing to do with them, and turned their backs on him. Just as he was at his wits' end, and before the two had started to trade blows, the entire bar had erupted in laughter.

'No news on the Cowboy's girl, Frank?'

'Nope. And that's what's pissin' me off most.' Mooney drained the glass, replacing it on the counter top. 'I'm off home to the better half. For a start off she's better lookin' than you.'

'Oh yeah? But does she always agree with you, like me?'

'Goodnight, Bren,' Mooney called from the door, and waved.

As he stepped through his own front door he heard his wife's voice, speaking on the phone.

'Just a sec. I think that's him now. Frank? It's for you. Says it's urgent.' She handed him the phone while he kissed her cheek.

'What d'ya mean "I think it's him"? Who were you expecting, the milkman?'

'No,' she replied, smiling, 'he left an hour ago.' Receiving a pat on the bottom she left him with the phone and headed for the kitchen to put his dinner in the microwave.

'Mooney speaking' he barked down the phone. He did not like taking calls at home.

'Inspector Mooney? It's Rafferty. Sorry to bother you at home, but I thought you'd want this information as quickly as possible. I think I know where a very popular gentleman is.'

'Hang on a second and let me get a pencil and some paper.' He opened the drawer in the telephone stand and withdrew a notebook and pen. 'OK. Shoot, Mr Rafferty.'

'It's on the west coast, beyond Galway city. A village called Spiddal. I have a rough idea of the area Inspector. You go straight through the village and just beyond are some houses that back on to the sea. Take a few good men with you, men you can trust, and expect some fireworks. I heard a rumour that a certain Mr Flynn from the North was lookin' for the same person as yerself, and I've still got a little standing with some of his people. I think it's a winner, Mr Mooney. It's certainly worth a look over.'

'Thanks, Mr Rafferty. It's the first bit of news we've had that we can act on. I appreciate the help. Let's just hope it turns out all right. In any case, I owe you one.'

'I'm doing this for the Cowboy, Inspector. It is I who owes him.'

'I'll make a point of telling him that it was you who passed on the information.'

'No need, Inspector – but if you're makin' the tay the next time I'm passin' yer office, sure I'll just pop in. You make a grand cuppa, so you do.'

Mooney laughed. 'You're on, Mr Rafferty. Any time. And thanks again. Goodnight.'

Mooney stood looking down at the silent telephone debating if he should call Johnson. He decided to leave Cowboy out of it, and face his wrath later. He turned in the direction of the kitchen.

'I'm sorry, darling, but I have to go out straight away. Don't expect me back until you see me.' He heard the timer on the microwave go 'ping' as he spoke, informing him his dinner was ready, but he wasn't hungry. His wife came towards him with her hands behind her back. As he kissed her once more he saw the package she held in her hands, what she called the emergency pack, a small plastic container which he knew would hold four sandwiches, two chocolate bars and a miniature bottle of whiskey.

'What would I do without you?' he smiled as he put the packet in his overcoat pocket. It was only then that he realized he hadn't even had time to take his coat off.

'Probably starve,' she replied, smiling. 'Is it about Marlane?'

'Yes. And the information comes from a very good source, one who is also very fond of Cowboy.'

'Go and bring her home, Frank.'

'I'll do my best.'

She stretched up and kissed him on the mouth. 'And make sure *you* come home too.' She worried about him when he went off like this, but she knew better than to show it. He needed all his wits about him, to be able to concentrate fully on the job. But, like all policemen's wives, she lived in fear of a knock at the door when her man was on a case.

He nodded and stroked her cheek. Opening the front door he came face to face with James O'Riley, his finger just about to press the bell.

'That's bloody quick. I hadn't even rung yet. I've got something for us, and it's 24-carat.'

'Me too, James. Let's talk on the way to the Castle. I have to get Edwards in on this. We'll take my car. I can arrange for him to be brought in, by radio, while we move.'

They conferred on the way and both men were convinced that, coming from two separate sources, the information had to be genuine. At the Castle they sipped whiskey-laced tea while they waited for Commander Edwards to arrive. Eventually they heard his footsteps coming along the corridor and went out to meet him.

'This had better be good, Frank,' were the Commander's first words as he passed them. 'I'm getting too long in the tooth for these late night calls.' They followed him into his office. 'Close the door and grab a seat,' he barked, walking behind his desk and sitting down. The other two drew up chairs and sat in front of the desk.

'It is good, Boss. Both the Commandant and myself have had tips from two good sources. I think we have McGuinness.'

'About bloody time too. Right, what do you need? Weapons and backup, and I suppose the locals will have to be in on this.'

'That's one of the points I wanted to talk to you about, sir. My call came through on my home number, and James got his on an unlisted number. We are the only three who know.'

'Meaning?' Edwards asked, knowing full well what Mooney meant, but wanting to hear it said.

'Meaning that that's the way we'd like to keep it. We know McGuinness has the girl. While James here wants him, I'm more interested in getting the girl out alive. If we bring locals in on it we can't be certain that word won't get out, and the birds will have flown the coop – and it's odds on that Marlane Davis will be dead before we get there. I don't want to take that chance.'

Each man knew exactly what Mooney was saying; that the IRA and the Provos had many friends, not only in high places, but also within the Gardai and the armed forces. Had the information been passed to either man on an open line, it would have been picked up by others and quite possibly passed on. At this point they knew the information was secure. Commander Edwards was well aware that neither man had told him where they were going. He was quite happy to have it that way. He trusted Mooney and knew Mooney trusted him, but if things *did* go wrong, at least Mooney could still be certain that Edwards had nothing to do with it.

'OK, Frank. What do you want?'

'A small backup. Gibbons, Matty Hennigan and Frankie

Kennedy. That's enough for us to do the job I think. Small, but each man trusted and tried.'

Edwards leaned over the desk and pressed a button on the console. The sergeant at the main desk answered immediately. 'Find Sergeants Gibbons and Kennedy and Detective Hennigan. I don't care what they are doing – or who, for that matter – I want them here, in my office, by . . .' he looked at his watch, '. . . midnight at the latest. Send out cars to bring them in. Got that?'

'Yes, sir. Gibbons, Kennedy and Hennigan – by midnight.'

'What about Johnson?' he asked of Mooney. 'Want him in on this? Is he well enough for it?'

'I've thought about it Boss and decided against it. He's too personally involved. It's his girlfriend they have. And . . .' he hesitated for a moment, taking a deep breath, 'just in case anything should go wrong, and we're . . . too late, I think it might be better for everybody if Johnson knows nothing about this until it's all over.'

'Agreed.'

Edwards unlocked the safe in the corner of his office, and withdrew a pad of firearms authorization forms, quickly signing a blank one. He handed it to Frank.

'Take what you need and make sure you all come back.'

'Thanks, Boss.'

From the Commander's office Frank led the way to the basement armoury, manned twenty-four hours a day by a uniformed sergeant and one garda. Picking his weapons, Mooney placed them on the desk so the sergeant could log each weapon by its serial number.

'Four Browning automatic pistols, two Carl Gustaf sub-machine guns, two Winchester pump action shotguns and ammo for each. Having a private party, Frank, or can anybody come? What the hell do you have in mind? World War Three?'

'We're going pigeon shooting, and expect the little buggers to fire back.' He turned to O'Riley. 'I almost forgot, James. Care for anything?'

The soldier opened his suit jacket to reveal a shoulder holster containing a .44 Colt Magnum. 'Make my day, sucker.' He grinned at Frank. 'I thought we might be going on holiday, so I packed my own toothbrush.'

'Holy shit, who'd believe it. Dirty Harry, alive and well, living in Dublin.' Mooney was impressed.

'We'll be back later for this lot, Harry. We're waiting for the rest of the team to arrive. Just make sure nobody snatches them.'

'*Two* World War Threes in the one evening! I doubt it, Frank. They'll be here when you want them.'

In the motor pool, Frank picked an Opel Kadett Estate. It was spacious enough for the men and weapons and had a souped-up engine. By 11.30 the three other men had arrived and were fully briefed. Mooney trusted each one, and they him. There would be no leaks. Shortly after midnight the armed detectives were on their way to the West Coast. It had started to rain again.

Eddie Carlisle cursed his luck. Sitting all day in the house, nice and dry, and now he was having to do a tour of guard duty in the piggin' pouring rain! And where was the great lord and master? Inside drinking whiskey, in a nice, snug, warm kitchen. Not that he was going to complain, mind you. Oh no. While McGuinness would listen to complaints – always saying that if you had a problem to come and see him – he also had the habit of having that big ape, McQ, answer for him. No thanks. Better to be out in the rain getting your balls wet, than inside complaining and quite possibly getting them turned into mincemeat by McQueedy. Eddie had made the mistake earlier of commenting on Marlane's body, telling McQ he wouldn't mind a bit of it, after he had finished, of course. For a moment he had thought he was dead. McQueedy had got him by the throat, lifting him several inches off the floor, pinning him to the wall. 'You keep your fucking dick zipped, Eddie,' McQ's spittle had sprayed his face as he spoke, 'or I'll cut it off for you. This one is just for me.'

No one had ever heard McQ get possessive about a woman, he was always happy to pass his scraps on. Something was definitely wrong. Furthermore, there was something funny going on between the two Macs. There had been a lot of huddled conversations which seemed to dry up whenever anybody else came into the room, and then the pair of them shouting – well it was McQ who was doing the shouting, about who was clever and who was stupid.

Life had been nice and peaceful for the past few months, nothing to do but a bit of fishing along the beach, drink a few pints – not in the locals, mind you, they were out of bounds. But it had been easy. Then, out of the blue, McGuinness arrives, followed shortly after by McQueedy and the girl. The flap was on. He knew it would be, the moment he heard about the copper being taken – and then getting away! For Christ's sake why hadn't they just finished the bugger off and dumped him somewhere? And not only does the big prick turn up with a girl, but she happens to be the *copper*'s girl! Jesus! What a mess this was all turning into. Life had been fine until this Mad Max character, the Java Man, had appeared. Now the organization was running around like a flock of headless chickens. Things were getting just that little bit too hot for Ma Carlisle's boy. Deegan had had the right idea. He'd gone shopping for supplies and hadn't come back. Mind you he'd caused a bit of a stir until they found the car in the car park at the train station in Galway. Maybe the time was coming when he should be thinking of doing the same thing. The problem was – go where? There wasn't a safe house left in the friggin' country. *Everybody* was doing a disappearing trick!

Then there was the question of money. He didn't have any. He knew there was money in the house, a lot of money. He even knew where it was – but getting it was another matter. It was more than his life was worth to go and help himself. Everybody was extremely edgy. McQueedy was as close to being in love as he was ever likely to be, and McGuinness was convinced that this Java character was coming after him personally. He was certainly taking his time about it if he was, and a lot of other people's lives along the way. First the O'Gradys – never liked that hard-faced bitch anyway – then it was Fitzwilliam, Doyle, McCann and Donnelly. Eddie Carlisle shivered, and not entirely from the cold.

He stomped his feet to get a bit of circulation going. What with the cold and the damp he could hardly feel them. And the bloody rain certainly didn't help. Even in a British Army surplus poncho the friggin' stuff got in everywhere. Fuckin' cold, fuckin' rain. Why the hell did McGuinness have to pick this godforsaken part of the country? He needed a fag. Even that was against orders now! 'No smoking on guard duty.' Shit, yer man'll be doing inspections on them soon, before they go on duty. Well bollocks to it all, he was having a fag. Bugger orders, bugger McGuinness, bugger McQueedy, bugger everything.

He moved back in the direction of the stone-built double garage. Five minutes behind it for a quick drag, and nobody would be any the wiser. At least he could have a shifty smoke. Poor old Rooney didn't have it so good. He was round the front of the house, where there was no shelter at all.

Imagine putting a guard at the back of the house. What for? What did McGuinness expect? A British submarine surfacing in Galway Bay, just to get him? Carlisle chuckled to himself at the idea of a sub, with a rubber dinghy coming up on to the beach and a team of crack commandos pouring up to the house just to get their hands on –

The nylon cord bit into his throat, cutting off all chance of his making a sound. The Kalashnikov fell from his fingers, only failing to hit the ground because of the strap across his shoulders. His last thought before dying was 'Holy shit, they *did* send a sub!'

Kane eased the body to the wet ground. Looking back towards the pile of rocks he waved his hand sideways in a wide arc. Cowboy and Monica moved slowly, bent forward at the waist. By the time they reached Kane he had taken Eddie's poncho and was pulling it over his own head. He had laid the Kalashnikov on the ground and he was running his hands over the dead sentry. He found a second magazine for the rifle and a scabbard containing a fishing knife – just like the one he had bought before he had paid his visit to the O'Gradys. Cowboy knelt beside him. Putting his hand close to Cowboy's ear he whispered. 'Do you know how to use one of these?' He picked up the assault rifle. Cowboy shook his head.

Kane reached in under the poncho and withdrew his

pistol, handing it to the policeman. Cowboy took it and nodded. He knew handguns. Hitching the rifle over his shoulders Kane took the knife from its scabbard.

'I'm going round the front,' he whispered, 'if there's one back here, then there's one in the front. If you hear firing, then it's all gone wrong. It will be up to you to decide what to do then – go on, or go back. Understand?' Cowboy nodded.

Monica moved up beside the two men. She looked at Kane, but was unable to see even his eyes. He was just a shadow. Before he moved off he whispered once more in Cowboy's ear. 'Look after the girl if you can. Good luck.' Slapping Cowboy's shoulder he headed for the front of the house.

Moving cautiously he stopped at the gable end, listening, his eyes trying to penetrate the darkness ahead. The ski-mask over his face was now soaking and water was trickling down the back of his neck. Standing motionless he scanned the piles of rock that made up the front garden. He was positive there would be another man here somewhere. It was the most obvious place to watch the main road. The problem was distinguishing a man from the rocks. A muted cry of pain and a mumbled 'Shit' drew Kane's attention to the largest pile on the right. The man had stumbled forward from his crouched position, banging his knee. Kane bent into the wind and rain and moved across in the other man's direction.

'Where the fuck are you?' he croaked loudly.

'Over here, Eddie. For God's sake keep your voice down. We don't want them in the house to hear us. Got a fag on ya?'

By now Kane was up close to him. 'No,' he replied, 'but I've got a Fisherman's Friend.' He lunged forward with his right hand. The tip of the knife cut the man's body like soft butter, just above and to the left of the waistline. Kane stepped forward and hugged the man to him, his left arm round the body, pushing up with the knife.

A faint 'Oh my God' escaped the dying man's lips as his blood gushed out on to Kane's poncho. Kane waited as the man died in his arms, then lowered him to the ground. Beneath the man's now torn poncho was yet another Kalashnikov, plus another magazine. Taking both, leaving the body where it lay, he made his way back to Monica and Cowboy. Monica was relieved to see him and wanted to touch him, but he shook her arm away.

'Later,' he barked. 'Do *you* know how to work one of these?' He held up the second weapon.

'Yes,' she whispered, chastised by his rebuke.

'Here's a second magazine. Know how to load and unload?'

'Yes.' She had learned all about this weapon in the mountains near her parents' home. Then it had been exciting. Now, knowing she might well have to use it for real, she felt only fear. Firing at old tin cans, trees and rabbits was one thing – firing at people was, she knew, quite different. She hoped she wouldn't freeze when the time came. As they huddled together in the rain Kane gave them their final orders.

'We're going in. I go first, then you, Cowboy, then you, Monica. Watch my hands. If I point in a direction, then that's where I want you to go, and where I'll expect you to be.' He stripped the poncho off and threw it to one side. 'Monica, you stay with me when we get in. Where I go, you follow. Stay about ten feet behind me, and try and keep your body in line with mine. Whatever you do, don't move into my arc of fire. Got that?' She nodded.

'Cowboy, your job is to find your girl. Find her, then get her and yourself out and back to the car as quickly as possible. I don't want you hanging around. I'll do whatever has to be done with anybody else in there.'

Cowboy made as if to argue the point, not wanting to leave them without his support, but Kane stopped him.

'Don't argue, Cowboy. It's too late for that now. Just do as I tell you, and you and your girl might get out alive. Do you understand?'

Reluctantly the other man nodded, knowing that what Kane said was the best advice if he was to get Marlane out.

'That's it then,' Kane said. 'Let's do it.'

I don't believe this,' Mooney roared. 'I just do not *believe* it!' He kicked the car. The two sergeants were busy changing a wheel. Five minutes earlier they had had a blowout, and had it not been for the experience of the driver, they could all have been lying in a tangled pile of metal.

'Calm down, Frank. We'll be on the road again in a few minutes.' O'Riley tried to stifle a chuckle, unsuccessfully.

'What's so fucking funny?' Mooney demanded.

'Aw come on, Frank. Look at us. Five heavily armed men, driving like the clappers across country to rescue a damsel in distress and take out the bad guys – and what happens? We get a blowout. Wouldn't the British press love to get hold of this? Well? Wouldn't they? It's straight out of an Irish joke book.'

'If any of you,' Frank turned on his team, '*any* of you, ever breathe a word about this to anybody, I'll fuckin' . . . Aw, shite!' He too was unable to suppress a chuckle. It *was* funny – or it would be, were it not for the seriousness of what they were doing and where they were going.

One of the men changing the wheel called out to him. 'Almost finished, Boss. We'll be on the way in five minutes.'

'It could have been worse, Frank,' O'Riley said, still smiling.

'How?' asked Mooney.

'There might not have been a spare . . . or we might get another blowout.' O'Riley was enjoying Mooney's embarrassment

'Jesus, James, don't mock providence, for Christ's sake. Please?'

Chapter Seventeen

JAMES EARL MCQUEEDY did not know what was happening to his life. He was not used to making decisions, and it was confusing him. In the British Army he had allowed his superiors to make all his choices for him – except the one he made to kick the shit out of that stupid Jock platoon sergeant. With Tommy again he had always been quite content to let him decide everything, until now.

He had left the house around 9 p.m. and walked the quarter of a mile or so into Spiddal. Sitting in the lounge bar of Rory O'Conner's small hotel he had consumed several large whiskeys and four pints of Guinness. Nobody approached him as he sat by himself in a corner. He did not look like a man who wanted any company. Later, even more confused from too much drink and thinking, he had taken a six-pack of Guinness and a small bottle of Bushmills down by the side of the church, past the village school, and on to the deserted beach. He ignored the rain and the wind, seating himself on the wet, grassy sand, his back resting against an upturned currach.

The only friend he had ever had in the world was Tommy McGuinness and now that was over. He knew he wasn't very clever but neither was he totally stupid. Tommy was going to do a runner on him. He knew it. In a funny way he couldn't blame Tommy, but it still wasn't fair. They had looked after each other for years – and now it was all falling apart.

Deep down he knew that Tommy was right, he would never be able to keep the girl, and he would probably have to kill her before morning, but for the first time in his life the prospect of killing someone saddened him. Not only was he going to lose Tommy, he was going to lose the woman too. Once he had finished the whiskey he would go back and screw her. It would be the best fuck of his life, and hers. He was pretty sure that the copper wouldn't know how to give a woman what she wanted, but he knew how. He had been giving it to them all his adult life. They liked a man to be the boss. They liked to be taken. They liked to suffer some pain. They liked to feel his hot, hard cock ripping into them. Just thinking about it made him spill whiskey down his chin.

He drained the bottle and wiped his mouth with the back of his hand. He had arrived at his decision. He would deal with the girl first, and then he would worry about McGuinness. He had better get back before one of the others decided to take advantage of his absence to dip their wicks. He had already had to tell Eddie off once and Deegan had made a remark about her too, until his nuts had been gripped in the vice of McQ's fist. McQueedy had squeezed until tears had appeared in the other man's eyes, politely asking Deegan if he would care to repeat his remark. He hadn't – and the following day he had done a runner. He had wasted the best part of yesterday trying to find the little shit, eventually finding the car parked at the train station in Galway city. Leaving the car where it was he had returned to tell Tommy the bad news – more bad news, as Tommy put it. They had argued again, about everything, but especially the girl. He had wanted to go and shaft her there and then, but that wasn't the way he had wanted – planned – it to be. Instead he had got blind drunk. But enough was enough. Tonight she was going to get the fuck of her life. Her best fuck – and her last.

Once the girl was out of the way he would confront Tommy. He began to feel sentimental about his old friend again – it must be the whiskey getting through to him. They were a pair – no girl could come between them. He was sure of that. He would *make* it work. Tommy had all the money, knew where it was all stashed. He had to make Tommy see sense and take him with him.

Standing up, he stretched. He was soaked through to the skin. Throwing the empty bottle towards the sea, he kicked the only remaining can of beer to one side, and made his way back up to the road. As he walked his anger grew and he wanted to smash something – preferably flesh – and he wanted Marlane. His stride quickened at the thought of her, tied down on the bed, just waiting for him. Sex and violence, a heady combination for McQ.

As he neared the house he knew who would provide that flesh for smashing – Rooney. He'd be sulking somewhere, trying to keep out of this rain. Well he'd teach him a lesson. Guard duty *meant* guard duty. He was probably round the back of the house with Carlisle, the pair of them sitting in the garage, havin' a fag. Wouldn't they get a nice surprise when he paid them a visit. He was smiling as he left the main road, entering the property of the house adjoining theirs.

The dividing walls between the houses were made from rocks and stones cleared from the fields over the years and placed on top of each other in a haphazard way. Openings of any size could easily be made and rebuilt in a matter of minutes. He moved noiselessly through the garden like the trained paratrooper he was, crouching low for the last fifty yards to the boundary wall. Peering over the top he searched for Rooney, and froze. His animal survival instinct told him something wasn't right. It wasn't that he couldn't see Rooney – he hadn't really expected to – but he smelt danger.

Keeping low, he rolled himself over the wall, silently catching a stone which his foot had dislodged. He knelt behind a large rock pile. Placing each hand and knee gently on the ground to avoid any sharp edges, he made his way on all fours round the rock, and came upon Rooney's feet. He knew immediately that the man was dead. He found the knife still in the body and the entrails lying in a pile beside him. McQueedy removed the knife and searched round for Rooney's weapon. It was gone.

In the kitchen McGuinness made himself a pot of tea and sat by the table, pondering what to do with both the girl and McQueedy. Mullarkey had made contact. In two days his plane would land on a tiny airstrip just outside Galway city. He would wait no longer than thirty minutes before taking off again. Either they made it on time, or he would be gone and they would be stranded.

There had never been any intention of taking Carlisle, Rooney, Holden or Deegan. Deegan was gone, and the other three would just have to take care of themselves. He had only ever planned for himself and Jimmy to leave – but that was changed now. He could see that he wouldn't need Jimmy where he was going. From now on he was in retirement, which meant he didn't need protection any more, and he suddenly felt no wish to share his bank balance with his old colleague. On his own he was invisible. He could disappear and reappear anywhere he wanted, melting into the local scene. But Jimmy was someone who stuck out. The further they got from Ireland the more Jimmy would be noticed. How could he hope to build a new life for himself with such a millstone round his neck? On top of that Jimmy made too many mistakes. Not killing this bloody girl, for instance, showed just how far Jimmy's touch was slipping. He had thought of killing her himself while Jimmy was out of the house, but the thought of what Jimmy might do – would certainly do – on his return dissuaded him.

What the hell did he want her for? With all the money they had he could buy ten exactly like her, if that's what he wanted. Black, White, Chinese, Arab, Asian – for God's sake the choice was endless. A pussy was only a small hole, but that little hole was sucking McQueedy in like a vortex – and he hadn't even stuck it to her yet for cryin' out loud! The fact was that McQueedy could no longer be relied upon. His total loyalty to McGuinness had been called into question. This had to be the end of the road. He'd tell Jimmy that Mullarkey was arriving a week tomorrow, that he had to go to Galway to sort out a few last bank details, then he would disappear for good. Jimmy could go fuck . . . He heard a noise, a quiet squeak, just outside the door.

'Jimmy?' he called quietly. Automatically his hand moved to the kitchen table drawer, where he kept a Chinese-made Mauser automatic pistol. His hand froze as the door opened inwards and a black-clad figure appeared, aiming a Kalashnikov directly at his head.

McGuinness felt faint. His bowels and bladder evacuated into his trousers. First his hands began to shake, then his entire body.

'Put both hands on the table in front of you where I can see them,' Kane ordered. McGuinness was quick to obey.

'What the hell . . .' he began, his voice raised an octave. He stopped, made a dry swallow, and tried again. 'What . . .'

'Shut up. Don't say a word and don't make any move

whatsoever. Nod if you understand.' The voice was soft-spoken, clear and calm. McGuinness nodded.

Outside the kitchen Monica covered Cowboy as he made his way quietly along the corridor, trying each door in turn. The first, to the left, was a living-room. Empty. He crossed the hallway to a door on the right. Some sort of parlour. It too was empty. He moved to the next one on the right and eased it open. The curtains were drawn back and he could see it was a bedroom. Empty. He moved to the next one. Same thing. At the next he found a key in the lock. She was here. He knew it, felt it, almost smelt it. His heart started to beat faster. He turned back to look at Monica. He gave her the thumbs up pointing to the door. She saw the smile on his face. He had found his woman.

Outside, McQueedy had moved round to the back of the house and found the body of Carlisle and the discarded poncho. Once again the weapon was missing. Like a predator, his eyes searched constantly for more signs of danger in the darkness. The house was quiet – deadly quiet. Were the others dead already? Who had done it, and how many of them were there? Were they waiting for him inside?

Knife in hand he went back to the front of the house. The gable end room was where Holden and Carlisle slept. Was Holden also down? The silence was almost deafening as he approached the window, his body pressed flat against the stone wall. All his senses were now on an acute level as the adrenalin surged through him. He knew that this was the one where he either got them first or perished. This was not a police raid, nor a visit from Flynn. This was the Java Man and one of them had to die. Well, he thought to himself with a grin, let's see which of us walks away.

Kneeling close beneath the window, he heard snoring. Holden was alive. Asleep, but alive. He pushed gently on the window, praying it wouldn't make a noise. There was a slight resistance, and a sudden creak, then it moved noiselessly upwards.

Easing himself up on to the ledge he flicked back the curtains. Darkness and snoring. He slipped his head in through the gap, followed by the rest of his body. There was a smell of unwashed clothing and stale male sweat. He dropped to the floor and crawled across to the bed. His hand landed on Holden's mouth and squeezed tightly. Holden woke with a start, his eyes almost popping from his head at the vice-like grip on his jaw. McQueedy turned the man's face in his direction and lowered his mouth to his ear.

'Don't make a sound, Harry,' he whispered. 'Rooney and Carlisle are both dead, and we've visitors in the house. Nod your head if you understand what I'm saying.'

Harry moved his head up and down furiously. McQueedy released his grip.

'Get up, Harry, and let's see what the fuck is going on.'

Reaching under the bed McQueedy withdrew the shotgun he knew Holden kept there. From under the pillow Harry withdrew a Second World War Browning automatic pistol. Slipping it under the blankets he cocked it quietly, then nodded to McQueedy. He was ready. McQueedy moved to the door and reached for the handle, turning it quietly.

Seeing Cowboy move into the locked room Monica stepped into the kitchen behind Kane. An alarm bell went off in Kane's head as he registered her presence. McGuinness also saw her.

'Jesus, Monica, am I ever glad to see you. I've been worried sick over you.' He tried to smile, but all that appeared on his face was an upturn to his lips, turning his face into a sort of grotesque mask. 'I sent Jimmy to pick you up and bring you here, where you'd be safe from this . . .' He hesitated to use the word 'killer', his eyes darting nervously towards Kane, then back to Monica. 'Where you'd be safe,' he repeated. 'When I heard what Jimmy had done I was livid. I gave him shit for misunderstanding But you know what he's like. Not much in the brain department, has he, eh?' He made a sound like a chuckle.

'Shut up,' Kane ordered. 'Just sit there, keep your hands where I can see them, and your mouth shut tight Monica, get back out there and cover Cowboy.'

She blushed slightly at his rebuke, while McGuinness went even whiter in the face hearing Cowboy's name. She re-entered the corridor just in time to see McQueedy come out of the room opposite the one where Cowboy and Marlane were. In his hands, pointed into the room Cowbo had entered, was a shotgun.

'*Cowboy!*' she screamed.

McQueedy had opened the door noiselessly, just a crack and peered out. He immediately saw the open door opposite. The room where Marlane was. Anger, tasting lik bile, rose within him, and it felt as if his brain was abou to explode. Nobody, no-fucking-body, was taking his gi from him. Opening the door more he saw a man crouche by the bed, undoing the ropes that bound her. He seeme to pause for a moment and take something off his hand then went back to the ropes.

McQueedy's eyes darted along the corridor. Empty. H had a clear shot at the kneeling man and was about to fi when he realized that at this range he would not only ki the intruder, but Marlane as well. No, he decided, he' take this bastard Java Man alive. Then he'd take hi outside, stick the barrels down the fucker's throat or u his arse, and blow him to smithereens. As he moved across the corridor he saw Marlane sit up, rubbing her wrists, then turn her head in his direction. She pushed at the kneeling man's head, knocking him off balance, and just as she screamed, he heard another woman scream Cowboy's name.

McQueedy froze for a second, caught between the two sounds, then swung to see where the second scream had come from. Without further hesitation he turned the shotgun along the corridor and pulled the trigger, immediately pumping the reload action, and firing a second time.

The first blast caught Monica full in the chest. Forgetting all about McGuinness, Kane watched as, almost in slow motion, her body was lifted off the ground and thrown backwards, being hit by the second blast while still in midair, then she crashed into the door they had entered by.

Back in the bedroom Cowboy, knocked off balance by Marlane's push, grabbed the pistol he had laid on the floor while he untied her. Lying flat out he gripped the handle with both hands, his arms outstretched in front of him, and fired off three rapid shots.

The first mercury-tipped round hit McQueedy in the shoulder, blowing his arm completely away from his body, causing the shotgun to fall to the floor. He screamed and fell sideways. The second shot caught the motionless and terrified Holden in the chest and, as he fell to his knees, the third round caught him in the head, blowing his brains back into the room he had been sleeping in.

Kane threw himself out into the corridor landing flat on his stomach, the assault rifle aimed at McQueedy. As Cowboy's shot hit McQueedy and he fell Kane fired a burst of five rounds, each one hitting the fallen terrorist.

One tore his bent kneecap off and carried on into his stomach, the next four hit him in the chest.

'Cowboy?' he shouted. 'You OK?'

'We're okay here,' came the reply. 'We got two.'

For the first few moments of the shooting match McGuinness froze, rooted to the spot. When Kane threw himself out into the corridor he scrambled with shaking hands to get the weapon out of the table drawer. In his nervousness he pulled too hard and the entire drawer came out of its casing. The unexpected weight forced his hand downwards and the contents of the drawer, including the pistol, fell to the floor. In a blind panic he bent to retrieve it when a burst of fire splintered the wooden table top. With a frightened scream McGuinness fell back on to the floor.

'Kane?' Cowboy called from the other bedroom, moving on hands and knees to the doorway, pistol in hand.

'I'm OK, Cowboy. Get the girl. I'm OK.'

Walking slowly back into the kitchen, Kane ordered the terrified McGuinness to get up.

'Don't shoot. For God's sake don't shoot. Please.' Quivering, he managed to get to his feet, eyes wide with terror staring, pleading with the man in black. 'For God's sake listen to me mister. I don't know who you are or what you want – but I've got money here. Lots of it.' He pointed to the kitchen cabinet where the bags lay. 'Take it. It's yours. All of it. Just take it. But for God's sake, please don't shoot.' He was babbling now, almost incoherent.

'How much?' Kane asked sarcastically, smiling slightly behind the mask.

'Jesus, there's thousands. A hundred thousand at least. Maybe more, I . . . I . . . I . . . can't remember exactly how much.' He forced a smile, his confidence returning. Wh cared about that piddling amount? He had hundreds of thousands stashed away in accounts all over the continent. 'There's enough there to set you up for life – a comfortable life. None of it traceable, I swear. Take it. It's yours. All yours.'

One hundred thousand pounds, thought Kane. That is his price for Annabelle. Slowly he raised the rifle to his shoulder and took careful aim at the now smiling man in front of him. He watched the smile disappear as quickly – quicker – than it had appeared.

'FOR FUCK'S SAKE WHO ARE YOU? WHAT DID I EVER DO TO YOU? TELL ME. FOR GOD'S SAKE TELL ME.'

Kane gently squeezed the trigger and watched as the rounds tore into McGuinness's chest, knocking him backwards. He was dead before his body hit the floor.

Kane ran to where Monica lay, crumpled in a heap. Vaguely he saw Cowboy approaching along the hallway, his arm supporting a sobbing girl. He fell to his knees beside the ragged, bleeding doll that had once been a warm, gentle human being. He ripped his ski-mask off.

'Monica?' he called gently to her. She turned her head, lying at an angle, to face him, her glazed eyes peering through the mist in front of her, trying to focus on him. Her tongue flickered at her lips.

'You made it?' Her voice was a whisper.

'We made it, thanks to you. Now don't talk. Try and lie still.' He wiped a strand of hair from her face.

'You've forgotten . . . our agreement. You . . . have to leave. There's nothing . . . you . . . can do.' Her speech was laboured and she struggled to draw air into her lungs. Kane heard the gurgling and knew she was drowning in her own blood.

'Don't talk stupid girl. I'm not leaving.'

'You . . . have to.' Her voice was fading. Her arm came up and weakly caught the sleeve of his leather jacket. She tried to hold on, but her strength was going. Her hand slid down his arm, banged off his thigh, and fell to the floor. 'Neighbours . . . police . . . got to go. But I want . . . want to tell you . . .'

'Will you shut up girl. Save your strength.'

Cowboy and Marlane stood just behind the kneeling Kane. Marlane had taken one look at the bloodied form, with the gaping hole where her chest should have been, and turned her face into Cowboy's shoulder. He held her tightly to him, listening to the dying woman.

'Listen . . . please, it's important. The bomb . . . King's Cross . . . your wife . . . it was me . . . me. Didn't know I swear . . . thought warning given . . .' Tears ran down her face and she coughed. A small rivulet of blood appeared at the edge of her mouth and trickled down her chin. 'Supposed to be warning . . . they left it too late. Please forgive . . . please forgive . . . plea –' Her eyes glazed over completely and she died.

For just a moment Kane remained kneeling beside the body, sorting out his thoughts over what she had said.

'Chris?' Cowboy laid a hand on his shoulder. 'Chris. She's dead. We've got to get out of here.'

Kane shook his head, as if clearing his mind, and rose to his feet.

'You're right. Is Marlane okay?'

'We're both fine,' he replied.

Marlane turned and for the first time looked up into the face of the man who had come to rescue her. His hair was wet and his face sweat-streaked from the mask. She gave him a brief smile, confirming Cowboy's words as best she could.

'Listen. You two stay here. I'm going for the car. Take this, Cowboy.' Kane changed the magazine on the Kalashnikov, cocked it, and handed it to Cowboy, taking the pistol in return. 'All you have to do is pull the trigger. Anybody who comes within the next few minutes will not be friendly, believe me. Can you manage while I get the car?'

'We'll be all right,' Cowboy replied, the rifle in his right hand.

Kane left the house and ran back the way they had come, down to the beach and along the shoreline. The car was where he had left it. He put his hand under the offside mudguard and found the ignition key resting on top of the tyre.

With only reversing lights on he roared backwards up to the main road, turned, and sped along to the house, stopping just beyond the metal gate. Reversing gently he bumped the gates open and backed down to the house. As he got out he opened the back door of the Mercedes and called to Cowboy. He noticed lights being switched on in the neighbouring houses.

Cowboy emerged, still supporting Marlane. He dropped the rifle by the door and helped her into the back seat. Kane re-entered the house and went to the kitchen. Going straight to the cabinet that McGuinness had indicated he kicked both doors open. Lying casually inside were two holdalls, both packed tight, the zips straining to keep them closed. Taking both grips he returned to the car and threw them into the boot. Seconds later the car was out on the main road and entering the village. In the centre of the village Kane took a left turn, up by the old post office. Only as they passed out of the village did he turn the main lights on.

They were heading north, in the direction of Moycullen. He intended joining Route 71 on the way, turning back in the direction of Galway city and the main road to Dublin. It was only a small diversion, but if the car had been spotted the report would say it was heading north – and 'north' to most meant Ulster. Any search for them would, he hoped, commence in that direction, while they hurried back to Dublin. In Galway city they joined Route 4 going east. At Athenry they passed a speeding Opel Kadett with five men in it, heading west. Strangers passing in the night.

All were silent on the journey home. Marlane fell into a troubled sleep in Cowboy's arms and Kane relived the words Monica had spoken just before she died. He had never known who had actually planted the bomb that had killed Annabelle. He remembered the report made by a British Rail porter of a young couple he had seen shortly before the explosion. The young man had been carrying a suitcase very carefully, ensuring not to knock into anything or anybody, and the girl had kept looking round nervously. The porter had seen them heading in the direction of the left luggage area, but had not actually seen them place the suitcase in a locker. At the time it had crossed his mind that they were a pair of runaway lovers, nervous that they were being followed. After the explosion the media had appealed to the young couple to come forward, guaranteeing them anonymity – but nobody had taken up the offer. Had they been Monica and her boyfriend? Or had she lied to him, doing one more service for him before she died – giving him total peace of mind? Despite the death of McGuinness – the man who had ordered the bombing – might it not have picked at his mind that the actual bomber had never been caught? Monica had, in her dying words, confessed to a crime she knew he desperately needed to know had been totally punished. Maybe now he could hang up his gun belt, as Cowboy might put it.

'I'm sorry about the girl, Chris.' It was Cowboy, breaking into his thoughts. 'Was she special?'

Kane remained silent for a few moments before replying. 'Yes, she was. But not exactly in the way you mean it – not like you and Marlane. But she was special, and I had hoped she could have been with us now.'

'Me too,' Cowboy responded. 'I know for certain she saved my life at the expense of her own. What I can't understand is why McQueedy didn't fire when he had the chance. I had my back to him.'

'It was because of me, I think,' Lane butted in. I think . . . I think he . . . sort of fell in love with me.'

'Jesus,' Cowboy exclaimed. 'Who would believe it? The beast tamed by the lamb! Who can predict the power of love?'

All three fell silent once again as the car ate the miles on the way to Dublin. With few exceptions the road was deserted, but Kane kept within the speed limit. It would do nobody any good to be stopped by the Gardai for speeding.

'What happens now, Chris? We can't just turn up with Lane, can we?'

'I've been thinking pretty much the same thing myself, Cowboy. Most importantly of all, how to keep you out of it. I've been in it since the start – but nobody knows anything about your involvement. As far as I'm concerned, it's over. I've done what I came to do. Now, if possible, I want to make a new start – providing you'll let me.'

'Chris, I don't know what it is that bonds us together, but somehow I think we've been through something similar in . . . yeah, well, in a different life. You don't have to believe that – but it's the only thing that makes sense to me. And if you think I'm turning back into a policeman like Cinderella at midnight you're wrong. I have somebody very special to me back again, safe and sound, because of you. Without you, it might have turned out differently. So . . . I'm listening for any idea you might have that can help us clear all of this up.'

'What about you, Marlane?' Kane asked, peering in the rear-view mirror, trying to see her through the darkness.

'I don't know who you are, or why you were after those people, but to me you are both knights on white horses coming to rescue me. I only know whatever it is you want me to know. Nothing else.'

'Thank you, both of you,' Kane replied. 'So we have to get Marlane back, and we have to manage it without involving you, Cowboy.'

Silence fell once more as all three of them tried to think of some way out of their predicament. Eventually it was Marlane who came up with an idea.

'Look, the police already know that I was there, and will also assume that the killings were done by the Java Man and the girl. They don't know that Cowboy was there. There's no reason for them even to suspect that. Just drop me off here and I'll stop a car and ask for the police. I can say that you rescued me – which you did, and I shall always be grateful to you for that, Chris. I can . . .'

'No,' Cowboy interrupted. 'I want you checked out in a hospital. You're in no fit state to be dropped in the middle of nowhere, hoping that a car will come along. No. It's too risky. Forget that idea, Lane.' There was no way he would even consider leaving her stranded on the lonely road in the hope that a passing motorist would stop for her. No way. Even if, please God, she had not been raped, she was still in need of urgent medical treatment.

'But –' she began.

'No, Lane. It's too risky. I'm not taking any chances on your safety, ever again. We'll have to think of something else.'

'OK, how about this?' countered Lane. 'Take me to a hospital in Dublin, but don't take me in. Leave me outside and you get back to your flat, Cowboy. If I wait half an hour before going into casualty that should be enough time, shouldn't it?'

'Why the wait, Marlane?' Kane asked.

'What would be more natural for me to do than have them call the police and my boyfriend? By which time you'll be home to take the call, Cowboy. Then you come to the hospital and act all surprised and relieved that I'm free and being looked after. I tell everybody about the masked man and the girl who rescued me, how the girl got killed, and the masked man took me with him back to Dublin and dropped me at the hospital. I don't know who he is, and I never saw his face. How does that sound?'

'I think it'll work,' said Kane. What about you, Cowboy? Agree?'

'I think I'm in love with a very clever girl, that's what I think, Chris. I think it's a brilliant idea.' He squeezed her very gently, afraid he might hurt her.

Epilogue

A WEEK LATER, the two men were sitting in the coffee shop at Dublin International Airport.

'Lane says to say thank you and to wish you all the best for the future, wherever it is you're going.' Cowboy played with the empty coffee cup, turning the saucer round and round.

'Thank her for me. Is she going to be OK?'

'Oh I think so. She's a tough cookie that one. She looks like peaches and cream – and she is, most of the time. But inside, there's solid iron. She'll be fine.'

'You're a lucky man, Cowboy.'

'Tell me about it,' he replied, smiling broadly. 'Did you do as I told you?' he continued, his tone changing and his voice lowering. 'Did you get rid of the revolver?'

'Yeah. I took it to pieces and fed it to the Liffey, bit by bit. Ammo too.'

'Good man. Remember what I told you. If you ever decide to come back to Ireland, then let me know first. For God's sake keep your nose clean from now on. Those prints of yours are on file still. As far as everybody is concerned the case is over, what with McGuinness and McQueedy dead, but the file is still open. We don't want you picked up for something that would cause you to be printed, do we?'

'Don't worry, Cowboy. The job's done and I have no desire to do anything that might interest your colleagues. I doubt if I'll be back. Too many nasty memories here for me now. I'm not particularly proud of what I did. I believe it had to be done, but I'm not proud of it. Plus, there's the memories of Annabelle, and then there's Monica. I read that at least she was going home for a decent burial. It was nice of Marlane to put in some good words on her behalf. I'll find a place, somewhere far away, and settle down. I'll drop you a card and let you know where I am. Maybe you and Marlane will come on a visit one day. Who knows?'

'Yeah. Who knows? What's the immediate plan when you get off the plane at the other end?'

'Look up an old Army mate. Best mate in the world. We have a few things to sort out, he and I.'

The conversation was interrupted by the metallic voice calling Kane's flight number.

'Well, Cowboy, that's for me.' He got to his feet, picking up the weekend case and the briefcase. The rest of his luggage had already been checked through. 'Time to go. You get smart and marry that lady of yours pretty damn quick. She's too good to let slip through the net.'

'The thought has crossed my mind,' Cowboy smiled, offering his hand. Kane grasped it and squeezed hard, once, then let go. 'Take care, Chris, and like they say, may you be dead an hour before the Devil knows it.'

'I'll bear it in mind, Cowboy,' Kane replied, smiling. They walked in silence to the security check. Kane sent the two small cases through the X-ray machine, then stepped through the archway, picking the cases up on the other side. He turned back once, just before he rounded the corner. Cowboy was still standing by the security checkpoint, watching. Kane gave him a military salute, smiled, then disappeared from view.

Cowboy walked out on to the terrace to watch the plane take off. He pondered over what he and Kane had done, and about how he had rejected his profession as a policeman and allowed a wanted killer to walk free. It was something that had bothered him over the past couple of days. Had he done the right thing? Not according to the law. But, he argued with himself, was the law always right? Laws were made to help men to live in civilized harmony with each other. They were the guidelines to live by. Without them the world would be filled by men like McGuinness and McQueedy and there were already more than enough of them in positions of power around the world. Without laws men like them would be in power in *his* country too. Kane had helped to rid not only Ireland, but also the world, of people it could well do without. They had been responsible for the deaths of many innocent people. He had almost died at their hands himself, and so had Marlane. No, he finally decided, he hadn't made a mistake. There was room in a civilized society for people like the Java Man.

As he stood on the terrace waiting for the plane to move down the runway he felt somebody come and stand beside him. He wasn't totally surprised to find it was Frank Mooney.

'I take it it's all over, and he won't be coming back?'

Cowboy nodded. 'Yes, it's finished. It ended with McGuinness. His job is done, and he won't be back. How long have you known? How did you find out?' He turned to look at the older man.

Frank leaned forward, resting his hands on the metal railings, looking out over the runways. The weather had cleared and although there was a cold wind, the sun still shone.

'About you, or about him?' he asked, turning to look at the young detective, a half smile on his face.

'Well, both I suppose,' Cowboy replied.

'Until Spiddal, we were only looking for one man – but there were three involved in Spiddal, despite what the sweet Marlane would have us believe. She said there were two. The hooded man, and the girl, Monica Saunders. The firefight involved two weapons, one Kalashnikov and the dum-dum firing revolver. They were not fired by the same person, and the Kalashnikov by the side of the dead girl hadn't been fired – so who was the third man? We found a pair of surgical gloves on the floor, near the bed where Marlane had been kept. We also found a set of fingerprints on the metal leg of the bed.'

Cowboy's heart sank as he remembered taking the gloves off to work the ropes that bound Marlane. When she pushed him over he had grabbed the leg of the bed to try and stop himself from falling. It had been purely a reflex action on his part. The gun would also have held his prints – but that was now in the Liffey – and he vaguely remembered seeing Kane clean the rifle he had held.

'Like I told you previously, Bob came up with a prime suspect in England. The soldier, Christopher Kane – but he was in the Far East when the killings began. Postcards – in his own handwriting, and franked on dates that put him there – were arriving at different locations. The guy was Irish, his wife had been murdered by the Popular Front, he came from Dublin, he had the training, he had the motive. But he was in the Far East – or was he? He was too good to let go, so I chased it myself, on the quiet. Contacted Hong Kong and asked if they could assist. They take photocopies of all passports on the way in. They sent me a copy.'

He put his hand inside his jacket pocket and withdrew a piece of paper, handing it to Cowboy. Cowboy opened it and looked at the passport details of Christopher Kane – but the photograph was not of Kane.

'Who's this?' he asked.

'I'm not too sure, but I think it's a photograph of Sergeant Oliver James, Royal Army Pay Corps, currently serving at the British Army HQ in Scotland. He also happens to be the best friend of one Christopher Kane. Case solved.'

'So what happens now?' Cowboy asked.

'Well, somehow or other the fingerprints taken at Spiddal have got lost. Can't find the damn things anywhere. I was sure I had them. Checked the print file myself and got a positive ID on a certain stupid, dickhead policeman who let himself get carried away. I can't prove anything any more, so the statement of Miss Davis, that there were only two people involved, will have to stand. I don't think she'd budge on the issue, even if I put pressure on her. Do you?' He turned to look Cowboy straight in the eye.

Cowboy held the gaze for a few moments, then lowered his eyes. 'No, I don't suppose she would.'

The scream of the jet speeding down the runway made both men turn to watch. It soared into the air, on its way to Heathrow. They watched it become smaller and smaller until it disappeared into the skies. Cowboy looked down at the piece of paper in his hand.

'So what happens now, Frank?'

'About what? Certain miserable scum are no longer in existence, scum that killed one of my fellow detectives and kidnapped one of my best, if highly irregular, ones – and would most likely have killed him too. The same scum that would have killed a young lady I happen to be very fond of. I can't go after one gunman without going after the other, can I?'

'I suppose not, Frank. But what about the Commander. And Bob?'

'To hell with Edwards. You win some, you lose some. I'm entitled to make a few mistakes. As for Bob, he knows nothing about what I've just told you. It's between you and me. Marlane's home, safe and sound. McGuinness and McQueedy – and the others – got what they deserved. O'Riley got what he wanted – though he was a bit disappointed to find there was no money in the house. He expected to find Front funds. Know anything about that?'

'No,' Cowboy replied, remembering the two bags that Kane had taken from the house and thrown into the boot of the car.

'Well, never mind. O'Riley got enough out of it, including me owing him a favour. Shit doesn't always roll downhill as far as I'm concerned, Cowboy – but favours do. You owe me, sonny boy.'

'Right, Chief.'

'And will you *stop* calling me "Chief".'

Cowboy smiled. 'Yes sir, anything you say, sir.'

'Right then. Let's go and have a cup of Java. I suddenly feel like one.'

'What about this?' Cowboy asked, holding up the photocopy.

'What about it?' Frank replied, turning and walking back towards the door from the terrace.

Cowboy smiled and tore the paper into little pieces, then opened his hand. Like confetti, the wind took the small white shreds and scattered them out over the runways.

'I'll get the coffees,' he called after Frank.

'Too true you will, sunshine. Too bloody true.'